What Reviewers
Barbara Ann Wright's

"[A] healthy dose of a very creative, yet believable, world into which the reader will step to find enjoyment and heart-thumping action. It's a fiendishly delightful tale."—*Lambda Literary*

"Barbara Ann Wright is a master when it comes to crafting a solid and entertaining fantasy novel…The world of lesbian literature has a small handful of high-quality fantasy authors, and Barbara Ann Wright is well on her way to joining the likes of Jane Fletcher, Cate Culpepper, and Andi Marquette…Lovers of the fantasy and futuristic genre will likely adore this novel, and adventurous romance fans should find plenty to sink their teeth into."—*The Rainbow Reader*

"*The Pyramid Waltz* has had me smiling for three days…I also haven't actually read a world that is entirely unfazed by homosexuality or female power before. I think I love it. I'm just delighted this book exists…If you enjoyed *The Pyramid Waltz*, *For Want of a Fiend* is the perfect next step…you'd be embarking on a joyous, funny, sweet and madcap ride around very dark things lovingly told, with characters who will stay with you for months after."—*The Lesbrary*

"This book will keep you turning the page to find out the answers… Fans of the fantasy genre will really enjoy this installment of the story. We can't wait for the next book."—*Curve Magazine*

Thrall: Beyond Gold and Glory

"[I]ncidents and betrayals run rampant in this world, and Wright's style successfully kept me on my toes, navigating the shifting alliances…[*Thrall*] is a story of finding one's path where you would least expect it. It is full of bloodthirsty battles and witty repartee… which gave it a nice balanced focus…This was the first Barbara Ann Wright novel I've read, and I doubt it will be the last. Her dialogue was concise and natural, and she built a fantastical world that I easily imagined from one scene to the next. Lovers of Vikings, monsters and magic won't be disappointed by this one."—*Curve Magazine*

By the Author

The Pyradisté Adventures

The Pyramid Waltz

For Want of a Fiend

A Kingdom Lost

The Fiend Queen

Thrall: Beyond Gold and Glory

Paladins of the Storm Lord

Visit us at www.boldstrokesbooks.com

PALADINS OF THE STORM LORD

by

Barbara Ann Wright

2016

PALADINS OF THE STORM LORD

Credits
Editor: Cindy Cresap
Production Design: Stacia Seaman
Cover Design by Sheri (graphicartist2020@hotmail.com)

Acknowledgments

This book was a long time in the making, and so there are lots of people to thank.

Ross encouraged me to write sci-fi. I got as close as I could. :)

My mom encouraged me to write whatever I wanted. This is it.

Robbie and Jennifer listened to me ramble at many a Mardi Gras. This is a long way from that, but better, imo.

Sarah, Joelie, Jana, Sara, Nish, Janet, Nia, and Trakena read my early drafts. Thanks for the love.

Erin, Natsu, Matt, Angela, and Deb read my later drafts. Now I know that not everything has to be a mystery.

And in 2004, a short story with aspects of this world took 1st Runner Up in the Isaac Asimov Award for Undergraduate Excellence in Science Fiction and Fantasy Writing. Thank you for the confidence.

And thank you, reader. I hope you enjoy reading about these people as much as I enjoy writing them.

To Robbie and Jennifer,
who slogged through many a swamp with me.

PROLOGUE

Everything started and ended with the alarm: all of Dillon's memories, the whole of time and space. It yowled through his ears and straight into his brain, going from soft, almost gentle shrieking to an ear-splitting whistle, like a steam train from an old vid. He remembered Sunday afternoons, trawling the TVLib with his old man. His father would have been, what, eighty this year? Eighty-five? God, he couldn't think with the fucking alarm!

But alarms only happened when events went severely sideways. Dillon's eyes cracked open, gummy with something, and he saw a swath of gray fabric secured under the black spider-leg bands of a safety harness. His chin was on his chest, his upside-down name staring at him from where it was stitched across his uniform. The emergency lights coated him in red, yellow, red, yellow, red.

God, he was going to throw up if that didn't stop soon, reminding him of one of his first missions as a colonel, commandeering fishing boats on some backwater piece of shit and pounding back nausea meds so he wouldn't blow chunks down the side of the boat.

No, not a boat. He was on a ship, and something was fucked. The *Atlas*, colonist babysitting. He'd been on a bridge rotation. Dillon forced his head up. With the flashing lights, the twisted shards of metal seemed more like the mouth of a cave than the nerve center of a starship. All the holo displays were out, making his console just another hunk of black plastic. He rubbed his forehead, wincing at the burn of a cut, but the blood was almost tacky. How long had he been out?

"The fuck happened?" he said, faint and slurry.

Someone tottered into view, dressed in the blue jumpsuit of ship personnel. The cute one, pert little bum. Her name was...something.

He couldn't get that far, needed to get up first. She reached for someone who was still slumped over. And she was walking, not floating. That was important. Not floating meant they were spinning, and they weren't supposed to start spinning until they got where they were going.

"Nichols?" She shook the slumped man's shoulder, disbelief in her voice. What the hell was her name? He couldn't think with the—

The alarm died as she fiddled with something. Dillon breathed deep as the flashing lights settled into a dull glow. The woman looked up, small face bathed in amber, eyes wide. *Lessan*, her jumpsuit read. Right, the navigator. All it took was a little peace and quiet, and things just fell into place. Dillon retracted his safety harness, freeing himself.

"Colonel?" Lessan asked.

"I'm fine." He took a deep breath, no ribs broken, just a headache the size of a mule.

"Nichols, the pilot." She looked to him again, and Dillon didn't know if her disbelief was because of some injury, or if this was her first starship accident, or maybe just her first dead body.

Dillon skirted a pile of twisted metal and bent to look at Nichols's face, the lower half of which was gone. Dead was right. Double-dead. Triple.

"Is he dead?"

He thought about saying, "Ya think?" but she was so *young*. What, twenty-eight, thirty on the outside? God save him from kids in space. "Nothing you can do for him now."

Two more people in ship blue were shuffling around the other side of the bridge, calling out the stations of the dead, including the nightshift captain, the XO.

Lessan wet her lips. "Nichols, the pilot, he's dead, too."

The new pair stepped into the light. They had lieutenants' bars, but he couldn't remember their names, either. He usually didn't bother to meet anyone who was just giving him a ride. He took a second look at the woman of the pair, a brunette with *Marlowe* stitched on her suit. She looked a bit older than Lessan, more serious but still sensual. The other, an unremarkable blond man, was labeled *Christian*.

"Lessan, find out what happened," Marlowe said. She and Christian started sorting through debris again.

Lessan stared after them, rubbing her arms, as lost as anyone could be.

"Hop to, navigator!" Dillon barked.

She nearly leapt in the air, staring at him.

"You're alive. You want to stay that way?"

"Sir!" she yelped.

He pointed in the direction she'd staggered from. "Hustle to that console and do as the lieutenant says!"

"Sir!" She hustled, fumbling with her controls until the displays winked sluggishly back to life. "We hit something." She bit her lip. "There's been a hull breach. Some of the Chrysalis pods have ruptured." Her hands picked up speed. "One fifty scrapped, no life signs. Some were spaced when we hit. Ten have broken open behind the emergency doors. Their occupants are still alive."

Marlowe bent over another console. "I'm giving them some air."

"What the hell did we hit?" Christian said. "An asteroid?"

Could have been a fucking fork for all they knew. Skipping space was dangerous enough, but their path should have been clear. It was Pross Co.'s job to clear it so their transports wouldn't be adrift in space with one hundred and fifty dead colonists.

Dillon spotted a boot sticking out of the debris, and what he could see of the uniform looked green, colony personnel. And the only colony personnel assigned to the bridge were medical staff, just what they needed. He knelt and gave the leg a tug.

"I'm alive! Don't you dare say I'm not!"

Dillon had to laugh, remembering this guy. Small, dark blond, nervous, weasel face, glasses. Who wore glasses anymore? "Can you get up?"

A sheet of plastic shifted, and Dillon helped him up, but his glasses were God knew where. Blood trickled along his hairline and ran across his temple. "What happened?"

"That's what we're trying to find out, Doctor…" He looked down for the name. "Lazlo?"

"Uh, Simon Lazlo, right. Everyone calls me Lazlo, ever since college, or Dr. Lazlo, but usually Lazlo since—"

Dillon held up a hand, not knowing if the babbling was his usual nerves or a concussion. "Do you remember where the med kit is?"

Lazlo just stared at the bars on his uniform. "You're a captain?"

"Colonel. Dillon Tracey." When Lazlo just stared, Dillon slowly said, "I'm Dillon. You're Lazlo. Where is your med kit?"

He felt his head, stared at his bloody fingers, but the trickle had already stopped. "I don't think this is deep." He peered at Dillon. "Your forehead is bloody."

Dillon rolled his lips under, resisting the urge to bark obscenities. "We're all a little banged up."

But the longer Lazlo stared, the better Dillon felt, as if his headache was soothed by concern more than anything. It sounded like something a crystal-carrying weirdo would say.

"Yours must not be that deep, either," Lazlo said.

"Deeper than you think," a woman's voice replied.

Dillon turned but saw no one. The words seemed to echo around his skull.

Lazlo knelt next to a pile of detritus and felt around as if seeking a way in. "That's the copilot. Ms. Dué? I'm sorry. I can never remember who has what rank. Are you stuck?"

The rubble shifted, and Dué stood gracefully, debris falling from her like rain. She stepped into the amber glow, her left eye fixed on the front of the bridge as if she could see through the hull; her right was nothing but a smear of gore down her cheek and neck. She swayed as if caught in the grip of beautiful music.

"God Almighty," Lazlo whispered. He scrambled to his feet. "Someone help her!"

Dillon shook his shoulder. "You're the doctor."

"I'm a botanist, a biologist. I was only supposed to assist the doctor in emergencies."

"Looks like an emergency to me!"

The lieutenants came closer, stares fixed on Dué. "The doctor is dead," they said together.

Lazlo spun to face them. "Then wake another from Chrysalis. I'm a...a...glorified lifeguard!"

"No one wakes until we reach the target," Dillon said.

"This isn't your command," the lieutenants said in sync.

God, he wished they'd stop doing that. Just how long had they been serving together? "The civvies are under my orders."

They looked at one another as if wondering how far they could push him. He cracked his knuckles.

"Ms. Dué, would you like a bandage?" Lazlo asked, and he sounded two steps away from full-blown hysteria.

Lessan stepped toward them, hands clasped together like a supplicant. "We're light-years off course. I don't know how many. We took fifteen skips instead of five, and I don't know why. And I don't know how long we've been going, or how long we were all unconscious."

The lieutenants sagged against a chair. "No one's ever skipped that long."

Dué swayed. "It called to me."

With a grimace, Lazlo peered up at her face. "The eye's been destroyed, but she's not bleeding anymore. The cavity appears to have sealed."

Dillon tried to look and saw nothing but ichor. "How can you tell?"

"I have no idea."

Lessan took another step. "The dayshift captain is still alive inside Chrysalis."

Dillon gave her a long look. "We shouldn't wake anyone else until—"

"This mission is screwed!" She raised her arms, dropped them, fingers curled into claws. "We're lost. We're hurt. We could be suffering some kind of mental thing from having skipped so long!"

Dillon reached for her. "Calm down!"

"I'll do it myself." She shrugged out of his grasp and stalked toward the door.

Dillon grabbed her arm, twisting her around. Kid or not, if she wouldn't listen, he'd strap her to a chair. She jerked, and he held tighter, thinking she meant to pull away, but she shuddered as if she'd stepped on a live wire, teeth clicking together. Her eyes rolled back to the capillaries, and the scent of burnt meat wafted off of her.

"Colonel, let her go!" the lieutenants called.

Lessan dropped like a stone and twitched, smoke drifting from her open mouth. Dillon stared at his hand, at the deck, but everything else was fine.

The lieutenants backed up, the debris moving out of their way as if pulled by invisible magnets. "Medic," they said, faces pale.

"She's already dead," Lazlo said.

A tingle passed over Dillon's scalp. In his mind's eye, he saw a spinning green sphere hanging against unfamiliar stars.

"Home." Dué's voice but still in his head.

A dull, grinding sound filled the ship, distant booms and the shriek of metal on metal. "Satellite transformation initiated," the ship announced, its voice cracking through twisted speakers. "All personnel stand clear of satellite joists."

"No!" the lieutenants said. "We haven't reached the target planet!" Dillon looked to Dué. "Who the hell keyed it in?"

She grinned through the gory mess of her face and didn't answer.

Lazlo knelt in front of Dué and dabbed her face with an alcohol swab. He'd managed to find a med kit in the wreckage, but cleaning her up was all he could do. He supposed the swabs were for sterilization, but when he'd found them, he couldn't help but compare them to wet wipes, as if the inventors had been prepared for a barbeque emergency.

Dué snorted a laugh as if he'd spoken aloud.

"Just hold still." He tried not to look at the goo as he cleaned her. Since he'd helped Dillon shift Lessan's body to the corner, he'd tried hard not to look at anyone. He hadn't even looked at Lessan, except to lace her hands across her stomach. It hadn't made her look any less dead.

Lieutenants Marlowe and Christian stood near the captain's console, not speaking to anyone, though they nodded or gestured, acting as if lost in their own mental conversation. And Lazlo could *feel* them standing there, could hear their heartbeats in his ears, and he could sense something around them like a holographic overlay, an invisible umbilical between them.

As Marlowe gestured over her shoulder, a piece of debris shifted, and Lazlo sensed a spike in her brain, as clear as when she'd flexed her arm. Christian had a discernible heat that hadn't been there before, like a proverbial fire in his belly.

Dué brushed Lazlo's leg, and he jumped. "I'm sorry, Ms. Dué." He tried a nervous chuckle but cut it off quickly. "I'm guess I'm a little preoccupied."

"That's how he'll get you."

"What?"

The door to the hallway slid open, and Dillon walked in, rubbing his hands together nervously, just as he had ever since Lessan died. He glanced at her, gaze lingering and becoming a worried, almost lost, look. Damn. Lazlo had never been able to resist the wounded ones. "Are you sure you're all right, Mr. Tracey?"

"Dillon. I'm fine."

Lazlo felt a blush, and by Dillon's wry smile, Lazlo was certain he'd noticed, but God, he was handsome. A little older than Lazlo preferred, but the gray at his temples and the lines near his eyes gave him gravitas. Double damn.

Lazlo couldn't help staring as Dillon put his hands on his hips. They were strong hands, lean and certain, just like the rest of him. Triple damn.

"Breachies are safe," Dillon said.

Marlowe and Christian ignored him. "Breachies?" Lazlo asked.

He jerked a thumb over his shoulder. "The people whose Chrysalis pods breached, the ones who lived." The ten breachies stumbled through the door, blinking away the fatigue that lasted for hours after stasis. They huddled in a corner. "The intact Chrysalis pods are fine, ready for the colony whenever the hell we get there." He nodded at Dué. "She any better?"

Lazlo shrugged. Besides the promise of coiled power, Lazlo sensed something else in Dillon, an imperfection: the cut on his forehead that had stopped bleeding but was still open. "I can fix that," he muttered. All it took was a little concentration.

Dillon rubbed his forehead, but Lazlo knew he'd find no cut, no pain. Shivers ran up and down Lazlo's spine, mingling with disbelief. Oh God, all the things he could do.

Dué, her eye. He turned, ready to help her, but her palms cupped his cheeks, and her empty socket seemed to flash blue. She leaned forward as if to kiss him, and he tried to pull away, but her grip was as unarguable as stone. She tilted her head, breath tickling his ear.

"Touch me with that power, Simon Lazlo, and I will pluck your brain from your skull."

He could feel the strength in her, layer upon layer. It tingled over his body. He'd had several conversations with her before the journey, finding her a friendly, if distant, woman. When she pulled away now, he realized he'd never met this woman, this great force. No one could ever claim to *know* someone so vast.

Lazlo stood and cleared his throat. "Are we ever going to talk about this?" Even Marlowe and Christian turned to look at him. "The elephant in the room, hmm? Hearing one another's thoughts, moving things without touching them, and..." He glanced at Lessan's body.

"We can't afford to lose focus," Dillon said. "We have to get the ship right."

Marlowe and Christian nodded. Avoidance. Fantastic. It was holidays with the family all over again. On the floor at his feet, Dué threw her head back and laughed.

One of the breachies shuffled forward, pulling an emergency blanket tighter around her shoulders. "We need water."

Dillon waved her back. "The waiter will be around in a moment."

Lazlo tried to smile for her. "We'll get you something as soon as we unearth it, Ms..."

"I'm the requisitions officer," she said through clenched teeth.

Dillon gave her a wide smile. "Then fill out the correct forms in triplicate, and we'll get back to you in seven to ten days."

Before she could retort, alarms blared through the bridge again, bathing them all in another wash of amber.

"What now?" Lazlo yelled.

Marlowe and Christian bent over a console, working in tandem. "Copilot Dué's codes have launched Chrysalis."

Dillon pointed to her. "She's sitting on the floor staring into space."

"The colonists are headed for the planet?" Lazlo asked.

"With no way to recall them," Marlowe and Christian said.

Lazlo looked to their display, where the bright flare of the pods hurtled toward the green planet, the same one Dué had shown him before.

How could the day get any worse?

Marlowe and Christian both looked at him, looked through him. "It couldn't."

"Is that planet even habitable?" Lazlo asked.

"We will care for them," Dué said, "and they will live." She stutter-stepped to the display and ran one finger beside it as if caressing the planet's curve. "We shall be as gods over men."

CHAPTER ONE

Two Hundred Fifty Years after Planet-fall

Cordelia slid her gloved hand along the grip of her blade. She didn't blink, and the boggin's chubby eyestalks were fixed on her steadily. Standing just over three feet tall on two legs, it held a crude wooden spear in its clawed hands. The weapon hung low in front of its bloated belly, and the creature didn't even glance at the bodies of its comrades floating in the dark, shallow water.

A shaft of sunlight pierced the rustling branches overhead. Any deeper into the swamp and the canopy would have been too far overhead to admit direct light, but if the boggins had stayed deeper in the swamps, they wouldn't be having this little dance. Cordelia shifted, waiting for the boggin to throw itself at her as its fellows had done, but this one seemed more cautious. It took a little step to the side and back. Cordelia followed. It could bolt, she supposed, but by the Storm Lord, she hoped it wouldn't. It retreated again, the shadows making patterns across its oily green hide. Its wide, full lips pulled back in a snarl.

Cordelia took another step, and the boggin just backed up. Its eyestalks bobbed downward as if looking at her feet, and she wondered if it was calculating how fast she might be in her armor, but boggins didn't think like that, didn't think at all, really. Even with the spears, they were little more than animals. It moved a bit more to its left and then hopped back. If she kept forcing it to retreat, it would run into a tree, and then she'd have it.

Her right foot came down on nothing, sliding into a sinkhole. With a grunt, she fought to keep her balance. The boggin leapt, and she brought her blade up to catch its spear. Her left leg had sunk almost to the thigh, her right leg bent too far for good leverage. The boggin's sticky toes clung to her armor, and it bounced, trying to drive its spear into her face, but she forced herself to look past the length of wood to four rows of sharp teeth. If it knocked her over in the water, it'd have the upper hand.

But that might be the only way to shake it loose. She grinned into its snarl and tensed, ready to throw herself backward and launch it over her head. A crack of displaced air came from her left, and the boggin's head jerked to the side. It stood for one moment, its face gone slack, before it toppled backward, one foot stuck in her belt. Cordelia forced herself to breathe again. As she clambered out of the hole, the boggin hung from her hip like a trophy.

Liam stood in the shadows of the nearby trees, his armor gleaming in the sun, making him look like a knight from some old story. He winked, the bastard, green eyes sparkling as he holstered his sidearm.

"A waste of power," Cordelia said. "And you stole that fucking kill from me."

"Stole a kill, saved your life, what's the difference?"

"I had that covered." She waved at the bodies. "I got the rest of them."

"Whatever you say, Delia." He pointed at her belt. "You going to wear that all the way home?"

She shook her hips back and forth, making the dead boggin swing, its long arms trailing through the water. "Jealous?"

"Not for me. Looks good on you, though."

She shook the boggin loose, then dug the slug out of its skull, grimacing at the grisly work. "How many did you find?"

"Six, though none as frisky as yours."

"Mine led me toward a sinkhole, so it either knew the hole was there, or it made one." Terrifying if she thought too hard on it, but exhilarating on the surface. "I'd expect tactics like that from a drushka but a boggin?"

"You've never fought a drushka."

"I bet they'd be more of a challenge."

"Come on, back to town before more of them appear."

She looked to the trees. "Think there might be more?"

He dragged on her arm. "Yes, a host of boggins riding an

enormous pack of progs and a group of drushka lobbing angry turtles with hangnails."

She let him lead her out of the soup and onto a narrow dirt path. "Boggins using tactics. What do you think that could mean?"

"They use spears. They hunt in packs."

"They use sharp sticks that they probably find, and most of them don't use anything at all. And pack hunting is different from preparing a battlefield."

"Let Captain Mom figure it out."

"Mama's boy." When he gave her a look, she laughed. "Wait, who has the hangnails, the turtles or the drushka?"

"You decide, and I'll back up your story to my mother."

Cordelia snorted, and they fell into an easy silence as they walked, following the road until the large trees that stood between civilization and the giants of the swamp thinned almost completely. Within an hour, they reached the outskirts of Squall, though how a cluster of wooden houses and a few acres of crops rated a name, Cordelia had no idea.

Squall's mayor waited for them in his tiny, unadorned office inside the largest house, wiping his neck with a handkerchief. "Did you get them?"

"We're fine, thank you," Liam said under his breath.

Cordelia held in a laugh. "Fourteen accounted for and dispatched. If you see any more, you might want to move your people closer to Gale."

"The Storm Lord knows I've thought about it often enough, but we've made a home here." He nodded, still wiping, eyes shifting back and forth between them. Cordelia waited for more; some gratitude, maybe.

He looked from one of them to the other again. "Is there something—"

Liam cleared his throat. "We'll be on our way." He waited until they were outside to say, "The nod means, 'You can go now.'"

"What an asshole."

"I'll assume you mean the mayor."

"They could have built their farms north of Gale, anywhere but closer to the fucking swamp." She pointed farther southwest, toward where the first human settlement used to be. "Did they not see the ruins? Everyone's at least heard of them."

"Well, the drushka wiped out Community. Maybe they think it's only fitting to let the boggins take out Squall."

"Like I said, assholes."

An hour's hike brought them in sight of Gale, where the trees of the swamp had thinned away but still provided some shade, and before the plains began in earnest. The wooden palisade surrounded the city, with the Paladin Keep rising like a spear over the eastern side. The Yafanai Temple guarded the southwestern side, but unlike the keep, its wooden gaps were filled with brick and stone quarried from the mountains to the north. The keep's sides flashed with metal scavenged from the first settlers' pods.

Cordelia looked on all of it with pride. Two hundred and fifty years of scraping and clawing at the dirt, of trying to coax reluctant metals out of the mountains. Humanity had accomplished so much in the face of hardship, but they never could have done it alone. Before she and Liam passed through the gate, she took one look upward, to the unblinking star, the Storm Lord who watched over them, bringing sweet rain when they needed it and sunshine when they didn't.

He'd never build on the swamp's fucking doorstep; that was certain.

The leathers on guard duty saluted. Cordelia and Liam returned the gesture, and Cordelia gave them a grin. She'd been in their shoes not long ago, sweating and itching in that damned boiled hide. A promotion to lieutenant would earn them the metal and polycarbonates that made up her armor; still heavy, but damn, it moved so much better. If they still had the means to power it, the paladins would be unstoppable.

At midday, the crowds around the gates were thick with people moving to and from the market at the city center. The wealthy, their clothing covered in embroidery, rode in rickshaws with servants hollering at people to clear a path. Everyone else clogged the street, moving aside after a glance at paladin armor, but it was still slow going, and the noise and clutter surrounded them like a childhood blanket. Cordelia wasn't even angry when they had to step around a broken-down rickshaw that took up half the street. It gave her an opportunity to study the rickshaw runner, a curvy woman with dark brown hair. When she straightened, adjusting her money belt, she kicked the rickshaw's broken wheel and cursed like a sergeant. She had pretty, dark eyes, and the anger in her face gave her cheeks a nice glow. But as the woman's gaze passed over them, she lingered on Liam and batted her lashes.

Cordelia nudged him. "That's your cue, hero."

"I'll meet you at the pub." He slowed and turned to the rickshaw runner. "May I be of assistance, madam?"

Cordelia chuckled and continued through the crowd to where the street split, one avenue leading to the keep and another toward her favorite bar. Her shift wasn't over yet, but she could turn her armor in early. Nah, she liked making Brown wait for it. Made her appreciate it more.

Cordelia smiled at the thought and stepped quick to the Pickled Prog. Walls lined with mesh-covered windows let in the light and kept out most of the dust, leaving fresh air along with the sweet smell of dried flowers that Edwina used to scent the place.

"It's our favorite pally," Edwina called from behind the bar. "Mead? Or hanaberry juice for those still on duty?"

"Mead. I'm off-duty enough." Cordelia took off her helmet and gloves, laid them on the wooden bar, and smoothed her short, sweaty hair away from her face. Edwina served the few other customers who were scattered around the tables, chitchatting with everyone. Cordelia eased onto a stool, waiting. Edwina would serve her last, like always, ever since their brief fling. It was her subtle reminder, a way to say, "You could have been served first if you'd stuck around."

"How's that mead coming?" Cordelia asked as Edwina came around the bar again.

"It'll be there when it gets there." She didn't look up, but Cordelia could see the starch in her shoulders, the irritation in the way her hips twitched beneath her skirt.

When Cordelia took a slow look around the room, though, her grin dropped away. A pair sat at a table, wearing light-colored robes and hoods. She couldn't see their faces, but the golden sunburst embroidered on one's robe and the blue and silver moon on the other's told her all she needed to know.

"Serving heathens now, Ed?" Cordelia asked.

The robed figures looked to her, pushing back their hoods and revealing a man and a woman, but she'd known they would be. The Sun-Moons always came in such pairs.

"Don't mind them," Edwina said. "They've come to trade."

"Please to forgive us, madam," the man said in accented Galean. "We are not to be looking for trouble." They moved almost in sync, and Cordelia shuddered. She'd heard that pairs lived together from birth, did everything together because that was how their gods operated. As if their gods even existed.

"And you're about finished, yeah?" Cordelia asked.

Edwina glared over her shoulder before beaming at the pair. "Let us speak later."

They nodded, laid a metal coin on the table, and hurried out the door.

"Try not to glare too hard, pally," Edwina said. "You'll chip the varnish on my bar."

"I didn't know you traded with heathens."

Edwina set a glass of dark red mead in front of her. "It's not against the law."

Liam strode through the door before Cordelia could retort. "What's not against the law?"

"Trading with Sun-Moon worshipers," Edwina replied.

Liam removed his helmet, shaking free his light brown ponytail. "Yeah, I saw them as I came down the street. What did you get?"

"I'll show you." She hurried into her stockroom.

"Fucking Sun-Moons in our city," Cordelia mumbled.

"Ease up. Fighting's done for the day."

"I guess you're right. How did it go with your damsel?"

He took a swig from Cordelia's glass. "She gave me her address."

"You do move fast."

"Your jealousy is delicious. Have I ever mentioned that?"

"If you like that, you'll love the taste of my fist."

"You know I like the rough stuff. Speaking of." He craned his neck toward the stockroom. "What exactly does one have to do to get one's own glass of mead?"

"Coming, coming." With a flourish, Edwina set a glass of frothy yellow liquid on the bar. "Try this first."

Cordelia choked on her mead. "Ed, that is a glass of piss."

Edwina glared at her. "It's called beer, made from grain. On the house for you, Liam."

"Looks…tasty," he said. "What shall we drink to?"

"To the Pickled Prog," Cordelia said, "where every paladin gets a free glass of urine just for coming in the door."

In the face of another glare, Liam took a careful sip. "Not bad."

Cordelia drained her glass in one gulp before Edwina could gloat. "I'm off to the keep. Find me after your date. I want to hear all about your damsel's disappointment."

"Fuck off," he said, their usual parting words.

Cordelia sighed and stretched as she took the road to the keep, her steps heavier than when she'd marched into the swamp. All that stood between her and a restful evening was a damned report. Face-to-face meetings with the captain were the only drawback to promotion.

She passed under the crest on the keep's bailey, a mailed fist clenching a lightning bolt, and climbed up the first staircase. Off to the right of the entry hall, the barracks were a warren of closets and cubbyholes. Lieutenant Jen Brown leaned against Cordelia's cubby, arms crossed, and a frown so deep, her face would stick in that pose if someone thumped her on the back.

Her dark eyes narrowed as Cordelia gave her a languid smile. "Where the hell have you been?"

"Afternoon, Brown. Pissed-off looks good on you."

"Don't give me that half-assed-compliment crap. You were wasting time in the pub with Carmichael the younger, weren't you?"

"You know, he really hates it when people call him that."

"Honestly, Ross—"

Cordelia undid the clasps holding her breastplate together and set it on a bench with a small thump. "I am all of two minutes late, Brown. Lighten the fuck up."

Brown pulled the armor toward her and adjusted the buckles. "This thing smells like a sewer." Cordelia helped her give it a quick clean, and then she donned each piece, adjusting them for her slightly shorter frame.

"Take care of yourself out there, Brown, you delicate flower."

"I will bust you in the mouth, Ross, Storm Lord be my witness."

Cordelia snorted a laugh as she dressed in loose-fitting trousers and a plain shirt. Brown hustled out the door, muttering to herself, though Cordelia didn't know why she was in such a hurry. Her partner wasn't even there, knowing how late Liam tended to be. Cordelia turned the slug over to the quartermaster, then handed him her sidearm for recharging. He held the slug between two fingers and raised an eyebrow.

"Don't ask." But as Cordelia climbed farther into the keep to the captain's office, she almost wished she'd lingered in the barracks. Captain Carmichael was intimidating enough on her own, but she also talked to the Storm Lord on a regular basis, and someone who spoke with God had to have nerves of liquid steel.

The aide's desk outside the captain's office stood as empty as ever. Carmichael said she didn't need a buffer between her and her people. No one started up those stairs without a reason.

"In!" her voice called when Cordelia rapped on the door. She sat at her small, plain desk, writing in long slashes on a piece of parchment. She glanced up with the same green eyes as her son but without any of his easy joviality. "Sit."

Cordelia dropped into a chair, and Carmichael finished writing within moments, dropping her pen into a ceramic inkstand.

"Report."

"Fourteen boggins dispatched. One shot fired."

Carmichael leaned back in her chair. "My son?" When Cordelia nodded, Carmichael stood to pace. "That boy will never learn."

"He thought he was saving my life."

"From a handful of boggins? You've never had any trouble before."

"Squall is so close to the swamp, and these boggins seemed…"

"Yes?"

Cordelia fought the urge to squirm. "Smarter."

Carmichael stared at her for a few long seconds. "Where is Lieutenant Carmichael now?"

"Um, I'm not sure where he is at the moment, Captain." Probably the bar, but maybe with the damsel.

Carmichael sighed. "I don't want to know. It's not your problem, anyway."

Cordelia tried to think of something that would get Liam off the hook, but before she could figure it out, Carmichael barked, "Dismissed!" Cordelia fled, happy to not be drawn into a heart-to-heart with God's mouthpiece.

CHAPTER TWO

Carmichael let out a long breath after Lieutenant Ross departed. She had a brief thought about sending someone to find out who her son was fucking this time, but she had too many other problems to handle first.

Augmented boggins in the wild, attacking her people. How many times had she warned the Storm Lord about that, asking over and over what would happen if his goddamned science project got loose? She grumbled to herself as she locked her door and lifted away a section of disguised wall, revealing a hidden space behind. Sitting inside like a prog about to pounce was one of the last functioning pieces of tech on all Calamity.

The transmitter, always ready to wake and crap all over her day. To think, she'd been happy when her predecessor had picked her to be the next captain. She had the brains, the intestinal fortitude. A good fit for the job, old Captain Pendell had said. But he'd given her a look of such pity. That should have been a clue.

He'd shown her the transmitter, and while she'd stared like a first-year grunt with a new helmet, he'd sighed. "The Storm Lord is human," Pendell said, "just like us. He has these powers, is all. And you'll have to communicate with him regularly, arrange to pick up the godsends when he dishes them out."

She'd just kept staring. "He's a human, not a god?"

"Might as well be a god. And he does give us clear skies and things we need."

"But." So much didn't make sense: The length of time the Storm Lord had been alive, the variety of gifts he'd given them, and not just tech. Their super-powered assets, the yafanai, were a gift from the Storm Lord, too. "How?"

He'd shrugged; the weariness in his shoulders seemed to grow the longer the hidden door was open. "You'll be contacted at least once a month, always near dusk. It's best not to ask too many questions. If you've got a problem, send him a signal, but it better be big. He's got some scheme in the works, supposed to put us ahead of the game."

"What kind of scheme?"

Another shrug. "Metal."

And she'd latched on to that. They all knew the stories. They'd seen the paladin recruitment vid, the artifacts of the first landing. On another planet far away, humankind had achieved incredible wonders, but metal was so scarce here, though the other resources were plentiful. Her head had danced with visions of skyscrapers and spaceships.

And now they had smart boggins, and relations with the drushka were always tenuous, despite the ambassadors and the trade agreements. At any moment, the drushka might again decide that they wanted humans the hell off their planet, and now humanity would have two intelligent species to fight if things turned nasty. She sat down next to the transmitter and keyed it on.

Dillon stared out the window, forehead resting on the cool slope of the *Atlas*'s wall. He was so *bored* these days. Living for three hundred years had taught him some patience—he could sit and stare at the planet for hours—but as soon as he realized he'd been sitting and staring for hours, he got so depressed.

But his own special chunk of Calamity was just now rotating into view, so he settled against the bulkhead again, not liking the look of the clouds heading toward his people. A little focus, shift the electro-magnetic current, pull like to like, and voila.

The clouds spiraled away to become a hurricane on some other shore, but who cared about other shores? His people would get the rain they needed and no more, and he got...

What? A little less bored?

The comms on his desk pinged, and he stared at it, thinking the sound might be an artifact from his power use, but no, there it came again. Someone on the ground was signaling him, and only one person knew where he was.

"Well, well." He scooted over to his desk, leaned back, put his feet up, and tapped the receiver key. "This is Papa."

On the other end, Captain Carmichael sighed. God, she was so much fun. "Storm Lord?"

And she *loved* calling him that; he could hear it. "Speaking."

"Your experiment, sir. Something's gone wrong."

For a moment, his brain had to catch up. "Right, the swamp creatures."

"Boggins, sir."

"Did you get word from the research station, Captain?"

"No, sir. My officers report boggins using unusual tactics, and I thought—"

"But no word from the station?" He rubbed a spot of dust off his desk. They were in fucking space; how was there still dust?

"Not in a few days, sir, and I thought…"

It was probably dead skin floating around. Lazlo could regenerate all of them, but that didn't stop the shedding. "Yes?"

"Well…"

The only one who wasn't shedding anymore was Lessan, out there orbiting the planet just as they were, unless the gravity well had gotten her. "You want me to lead a squad into the swamp for you, Captain?"

She sputtered, and he bet she hated stumbling over her words, hated that she couldn't come out and say she wanted to cancel the whole boggin thing or that she hated his guts. She'd been reluctant from the beginning, but his people needed metal, and they needed help to get it. She knew that.

A knock came from the door.

"You're a soldier. If there's a problem, handle it." He disconnected. Only one person *knocked* on his door. "Come in, Marie."

She stalked into his suite, her plump cheeks purple with anger. She'd cobbled together some flight suits into a huge, cleavage-baring dress that showed off her lovely curves but still made her look like a weather balloon.

"*Contessa*," she said. "I know you haven't forgotten."

He pointed past her. "How come you never use the chime, Marie?"

"You call me Contessa, and I call you Storm Lord. That's the deal."

"We don't have to be so formal when it's just the two of us, sweetheart. We've seen each other naked *and* upside down. What's a first name here or there?"

She went even redder, and he wondered if a person could choke on her own rage. She'd never forgiven him for not giving her any respect as the requisitions officer. She should have learned that he didn't give anyone on this shit-ship more respect than they deserved.

She took a deep breath, and his gaze strayed south. "Too many supplies," she said in a lower tone. "You're sending too much to your pets."

"Only what they need."

"My people manage with very little."

"Five people live on the Deliquois Islands, and they're all related."

And back to purple again. "Just because you're not a telepath and have to use tech is no reason why your people should get more gifts than ours!"

"We can't use half the stuff I send." He raised the pressure in the room just a little, filling it with the scent of ozone.

She stiffened, and her eyes narrowed. "Power cells are useful no matter their form, and other tech can be cannibalized for its useful parts."

He splayed his hands along the metal surface of his desk, little arcs of electricity jumping from finger to finger. "Oh, I don't think we're to cannibalism just yet."

She laid her palms on the desk as if daring him to shock her. "I'll go to the others."

He nodded behind her at the door, and she stormed out as huffily as she'd come in. He could fry her, space her, and be done with it, but the others would turn on him, all the breachies she bullied into her way of thinking. So far, Christian, Marlowe, Dué, and Lazlo had ignored her, but if any of them turned against him, it could be lights out.

Well, not Lazlo, never him. And Marie would never get Dué to participate in some petty scheme. Dué never participated in anything except cackling to herself. God, she freaked him out. Her one eye was always tracking things no one else could see, and if you caught sight of her empty socket, it flared with light, some telepathic trick. She spouted prophecies, moved random shit around like Marlowe could, and once, she used pyrokinetics like Christian's to burn all the oxygen out of several compartments; no one knew why. She had telepathy like Marie and some of the breachies, like Marlowe and Christian, too, and sometimes she replied to thoughts, spying like the rest of them had agreed not to. Lazlo didn't have to regenerate her; she did it herself. The only power she hadn't yet displayed was Dillon's. Of course, no one had Dillon's power. He was unique, a special fucking snowflake.

Of course, Dué was the only one on the satellite with the gift of prophecy. She'd once turned to Marie in the middle of the mess hall and said, "You'll die wearing something red." That had shut all of them up for days. After Dillon's electrokinesis, prophecy was the rarest gift. Only one of his yafanai had it, and from what he'd heard, she used it for some kind of fortune telling, a way to make some money for the temple.

More power to her.

His comms pinged again, the internal line this time. With a sigh, he answered, sounding just as Captain Carmichael had earlier. Served him right, he guessed.

"The Contessa has been here," Christian and Marlowe said, talking on top of one another.

"So?"

"You know what she wants."

"Again, so?"

They sighed in unison, and he felt a prickle along his scalp as they pinpointed his location with their telepathy.

"I'm in my office. Stay out of my head."

The tingle stopped. "Just cut back on your drops."

"Because a fucking breachie said so?"

"For the peace." The signal cut out.

Dillon glanced over his shoulder again, out the window at the planet. Leading an expedition into the swamp sounded better and better.

❖

Lazlo lost himself in the plants, the life flowing through stalks and stems. The botanical habitat was filled with the scent of them, the perfect communion of root to soil. Without thoughts, without reasons, they could just *be* together.

Across the room, a minute cry of almost-pain made him doubt that philosophy. The yafanai-makers. Again. The plant that enabled Dillon's followers to have their own powers was his forever problem child. He sent out a tendril of power and soothed away the corruption.

Luckily, he didn't have to deal with each plant long. He'd harvest their blooms, distill those into the sticky, gritty paste that Dillon called the yafanai drug, and then send the drug to the planet. The plants tended not to live long after that, and he'd start a new batch. Dillon had asked why he couldn't send seeds so the yafanai could make their own drugs, but Lazlo didn't like the idea of the ground dwellers messing with something they didn't quite understand. He was always tweaking his formula, trying to see if he could predict what powers a person might manifest. So far, it was a crapshoot between telepathy, macro- or micro-psychokinesis, pyrokinesis and prophecy. Only Dillon had developed electrokinesis through the accident that had given the bridge crew and the breachies their powers. Prophecy and pyrokinesis were also pretty rare, though some on the surface had them. Telepathy seemed the most common, though people differed in range and strength and whether they could send thoughts or simply receive them.

It was enough research to last a lifetime, several lifetimes. Lazlo stared at the plants and wondered if such studies could sustain someone for all eternity. God, that was a miserable thought.

Feet pounded down the stairs from the lift, and even without the micro-psychokinetic powers that let him manipulate matter on a cellular level, Lazlo knew who it would be, the only person who ever came to see him between regenerations.

Dillon ranted about the crew, sprinkling his tirade with fucks and goddamns and sons-of-bitches. Lazlo had to smile, even after all these years. He was just so entertaining, and anger made his eyes sparkle, though Lazlo told himself not to go there again.

"Did she talk to you?" Dillon asked.

"Who?"

"Marie fucking Martin, who do you think?"

"No one comes to talk to me except you."

Dillon had said that the others claimed Lazlo made them uncomfortable, though Lazlo didn't know why. He wasn't Dué. One of the men, Kenneth, had even shared his bed on occasion, though such occasions were few and far between. Maybe it was the fact that he kept them all alive that unnerved them.

"Are you listening to me, Laz?" Dillon's hand rested on his shoulder, and Lazlo resisted the urge to lay his cheek on it.

"No one talks to me," Lazlo said. "I haven't told anyone about your schemes. I haven't told anyone about the plants or the yafanai."

Dillon drummed his fingers on the tabletop. "They're going to find out someday. They'll pry into my head. They won't be able to help themselves."

"Not everyone is obsessed with you."

Dillon flashed a smile that made Lazlo's insides lurch, no matter how many times he told them not to. "Why don't you wear your glasses anymore?"

"I fixed my eyes a long time ago, and then you made fun of me."

"What can I say? I'm a dick. Everyone knows this."

Lazlo snorted a laugh and let a little tendril of his power wander over. "Your cells need redoing soon."

"That time again?"

"Anger uses you up faster."

"Better pencil me in for every other day, then."

Lazlo reached out with his power, scanning for weak spots, old cells, degeneration. He repaired or replaced the flaws, delighting in the corridors of a body he knew so well, at least from this angle.

Dillon closed his eyes, a dreamy smile on his face. "That's some good shit, Laz."

A blush was unavoidable. "Nice to be appreciated."

"Anyone who doesn't is a fucking moron." He clapped Lazlo on the shoulder and squeezed, violence and tenderness in one act.

CHAPTER THREE

Cordelia stumbled home late to a summons pinned to her door. The captain wanted her in the morning, an urgent meeting with Paul Ross, the mayor of Gale—who happened to be Cordelia's uncle—and the drushkan ambassador, Reach, who happened to be a pain in the ass. Well, they were both pains in the ass, but it was more socially acceptable to think it of Reach.

She imagined that Edwina had gone crying to Paul about how Cordelia chased the Sun-Moons out of the bar. Come to think of it, opening trading relations with outsiders had probably been Paul's idea in the first place; extending hands and opening minds, his usual feel-good, modernist bullshit. She'd have to get a good night's sleep and steel herself for the crap he'd dish her. Luckily, Carmichael would also find trading with the Sun-Moons a terrible idea, if that was what they were going to debate about.

And then there was Reach. Storm Lord help her, Cordelia had nursed a huge crush when they'd first met. She could easily summon the image of Reach's willowy body swaying as she walked. Her whorl-covered brown skin seemed to soak in the light, and her hair, a riotous blend of red and orange, turned heads wherever she went. Her eyes were light yellow and missed nothing, and she smelled like new spring growth.

And then she'd started calling Cordelia "Paul's metal-skinned niece" as if Cordelia didn't rate a name. Reach always made certain everyone got a good view of her long fingers with their extra joint, particularly the poisonous claw atop her middle fingers, a not-so-subtle threat. Cordelia had been mystified by her antagonism at first, but when she learned that Paul and Reach had become lovers, everything became clear. Cordelia had been a little jealous of her uncle at first, but when she saw what a pain Reach could be, she changed her mind. Reach thought Cordelia was too hard on her uncle, too defiant. She'd once told Paul that he would get more done if he'd thrash those with contrary opinions instead of arguing with them.

Cordelia leaned back on her narrow cot, resting against the wall of her room. Just big enough for the cot, a trunk, and a lamp, the room seemed like a cage at times, but she never spent much time there, just enough in the evenings to remind her why she left in the mornings. She wondered if all drushka were like Reach, if she'd ever meet any others. She shifted forward and rummaged in her trunk, tugging clothes out of the way until she found the journal, the work of her many-greats grandmother, Jania Carruthers Ross, whom the drushka had called Roshkikan. She'd lived among the drushka, studied them, and ultimately caused their people to split into two groups, one deciding to trade with humans and the other trying to wipe humanity from the face of the planet. The latter half had destroyed Community, though since then, they'd been quiet.

Quite the legacy. Cordelia looked at the names written inside the journal's front cover, a tree of ancestors who'd been anthropologists or ambassadors working with the drushka. Paul had certainly followed in their footsteps, somewhat. Cordelia's parents had invited her into the legacy, giving her the middle name Sa, the drushkan word for rain, but that was as far as she went into the family business. After her parents had died in the swamp, it had been paladins all the way.

She didn't need to read the journal. She knew all the words, and there was nothing that would help her get along with Reach, nothing that outlined the best way to kill a drushka, if it came to that. With a sigh, Cordelia sank down on her bunk and drifted to sleep, the journal resting on her chest.

In the morning, after a quick scrub in the barracks, she stomped up the stairs to the captain's office. Twice in as many days was unfair. And now she had to meet with her uncle *and* Reach as well. It hadn't been an easy night, filled with dreams of sinewy bodies who yelled at her for not visiting her uncle more.

Paul stood as she entered. "Cordelia, how have you been?"

"Uncle…Mayor. I'm good. And you?"

"Never better."

"Everybody, sit," Carmichael said. "We've got a problem."

Reach tapped her poisonous middle claws together. "The *chanuka* grow bolder." Her accent was thick around the words, her voice deep and smoky. "That is why my brethren were only able to deliver half the *hoshpis* we agreed to, and now Paul's metal-skinned niece confirms it."

Cordelia resisted the urge to roll her eyes. "What's a chanuka?"

"Boggins," Paul said. "Loosely translated, chanuka means 'mud people.'"

Which made her wonder what hoshpi translated to. She knew them as giant bugs that kind of resembled old pics of cattle. Gale had managed to wring quite a few resources from them. "But the boggins are animals, not people."

Reach just stared. Paul cleared his throat. "The drushka call any creature that eats meat a person." He glanced at Reach. "Well, person isn't really the right word. It's more like—"

Carmichael cleared her throat. "Let's get back to the boggins attacking hoshpis."

"The latest report from my people," Reach said, "tells of the chanuka attacking while the hoshpis were being gathered."

Cordelia had to smirk. "Can't handle a few mud people?"

Reach smiled, showing Cordelia her sharp teeth, but she didn't wrinkle her long, narrow nose in drushkan affection. "It seems you cannot as well. Your captain tells us you had to use one of your coveted bullets yesterday."

Paul brushed Reach's wrist with his fingers. "We don't want anyone, drushka or human, to be hurt if it can be avoided. One of our scientific research stations is also overdue to report."

Carmichael frowned hard. "Three days overdue. Lieutenant Ross, I'm sending you to find out what the hell happened, see if these smart boggins are involved."

"Agreed," Reach said.

Paul nodded. "What do you need from me?"

"A couple of yafanai would be nice."

He looked up as if doing figures in his head. "I can spare a couple."

"The day after tomorrow at daybreak," Carmichael said.

"Ambassador, get word to your people to meet the lieutenant and her squad on the Oosjani Road."

Reach spread her hands. "We will show you what there is to be seen."

"I'll contact you if we need anything else."

Reach stood and headed for the door. Paul seemed as if he might say something else, but Carmichael turned her attention to the papers on her desk. With a shake of his head, Paul shot Cordelia a smile before following Reach.

"Lieutenant, thoughts?"

Cordelia shifted in her chair. "Dank, endless swamp, dangerous creatures. Sounds like fun." It was also where her parents had died, but she tried to keep that from showing.

Carmichael leaned back, a little smile playing about her lips. "Get your gear together and select a team. You'll be the only armor. No more than five leathers." She scribbled a few words on a piece of parchment. "Give Sergeant Preston this order. He'll be your trail master. Rendezvous with the drushka, and they'll take you to the research station. You be damn careful with those yafanai, Ross. They're hard to replace. Dismissed."

Cordelia saluted and left. The trail masters lingered out back of the keep, so she took the long staircase to the bottom, where all the other pathways branched. They called it the ambush room, so she wasn't surprised to find her uncle waiting there.

Paul smiled in his serene way, the same disguising expression he'd worn the whole of her childhood. The one time she'd seen it unintentionally slip was when she'd told him she was going into the paladins instead of politics or science.

"I was hoping to catch you." He gave her wide eyes, just creased at the corners as if barely containing hope. "It's been a long time since we've seen each other. I've missed you."

An old ploy, but it almost made her wince. Sometimes, he looked so much like her father. "Save the guilt for the guildmasters, Uncle Paul."

His hangdog expression transformed almost at once. "Fine, but I do want to see you more often. No one knows me like you. You're my favorite sparring partner."

"Your favorite? What about Reach?"

He ignored that completely. "And I want you to leave those who trade with the Sun-Moon worshipers alone."

"Ah! Edwina complained to you."

"She won't be the last if you take your armored carcass around terrorizing people."

"Just thought I'd let my opinions be known, in case you forgot to ask the populace."

"Wait, who am I?" He felt around his clothing as if looking for a pen. "Oh, right! The mayor of Gale, the one who decides Gale's trading partners, among other things, and I'm qualified to do it alone."

"Everyone has the right to an opinion, you always say so."

"You don't have the right to be a bully."

"I have to go, Uncle Paul. I have duties."

"Don't we all? If you want to protest trading with the Sun-Moons, don't buy from the people who buy from them."

Her favorite bar and the Storm Lord knew where else, but she wanted him off her case. "Fine."

He gave her a wry smile. "I've made contact with the plains dwellers, too, and I hope to move out farther from there."

"Plains dwellers? Don't they live in tents? What could they have—"

He grinned, and she knew he'd be happy to stand there all day and argue with her, but she had places to be. She gritted her teeth. "We'll have to save this for another time."

"Dinner when you come back. I'll hold you to that."

"But—"

"It was your idea. Be safe out there." He smiled and turned away before she had a chance to respond.

Lydia kept her serene mask in place as the petitioner backed out the door into the temple proper, bowing as he went. They were always bowing and scraping and smiling too widely.

She really wanted to jump from her cushions and shout, "Boo!" But that would make most of them bolt, a few cry, and some might soil themselves. Or maybe a handful would laugh, forget that she was the all-seeing prophet of Gale, and just have a conversation with her. That would be nice.

Freddie stepped out from behind a curtain, tablet in hand. "Stop that."

"What? I didn't say anything."

"You had your mischief face on."

"I was wishing some of these people would talk to me instead of staring at the floor, asking their questions, and then running for their lives."

Freddie planted a kiss on her forehead. "You don't need them. You have me."

Lydia captured her hand and nibbled the knuckles. "I'd like to."

"After we're through. Only thirty-five to go."

Lydia groaned and stretched her back. "Why can't we do this outside? It's a lovely day."

"No privacy. And half the population doesn't believe you can use your gift unless they sit on pillows in this dark room and choke on the stench of flowers."

"From a prophet who is sereneness incarnate." Lydia took a few deep breaths and made her face settle again. "Let's do this, sweet baby."

Freddie snorted a laugh and called the next name before she disappeared behind the curtain.

The door banged into the wall as the next petitioners fumbled through, a young couple; farmers, if their clothing was any indication. Lydia knew their question already, no gift required. All farmers asked for the same thing.

"Honor to the Storm Lord," they muttered. Both knelt and stared at the floor.

Averting their gaze, the one thing she hated more than bowing. "What's your question?"

Behind the curtain, Freddie cleared her throat softly. The farmers didn't seem to hear. They fidgeted before one blurted, "A new crop, O Prophet Yafanai. We want to know if the seeds we purchased will flourish in our fields."

Lydia couldn't help a quirk of the lip. O Prophet Yafanai was a new one on her. She focused on the couple's mental energy until her consciousness floated above them and sound fell away to nothing. The future was always mute.

She glimpsed her own body sitting still, saw the tops of the farmers' heads. Time gained substance around her, coalescing like a ball of thread, surrounding her, spinning out to touch everything, living or lifeless, but she kept her focus on these two. She willed minutes to tick by like seconds and saw herself give the couple their answer, though she still couldn't hear what she said.

As the couple walked from the temple, her spirit followed, and she willed the hours to hurry, saw the farmers return home, passing before her faster than they could ever move. Days flew by, and the farmers planted. Days became months as the plants grew. Sun and stars and moon wheeled across the sky, and the crops shot from the ground as if catapulted from the soil.

A simple question answered, and she should have let time wind up again, but boredom prompted an extra peek. Years spun away. The farmers had a child, and Lydia slowed time as the boy, at four years old, wandered away from his father during a trip to Gale. A stack of crates teetered, fell. The farmer tore at them, trying to shift their weight, shredding the skin of his fingers, but too late. Oh, how they mourned.

Lydia let time wind faster again, seeing another child, one that grew into a healthy man who founded a new settlement, and they celebrated, sadness in their faces as if remembering. Lydia let their lives wind back into the ball of time until she sat in front of them again, safe in the Yafanai Temple, their children years in the future.

Seconds had passed since they'd asked their question, and Lydia burned to warn them, but the future could never be changed, ever. The populace just liked to believe it could, but everything was fixed, whether they believed it or not.

"Your crops will do well."

They jerked, startled, probably expected more time to pass; then they grinned at one another, bowed, and dropped their coins in her bowl before they fled, just as she'd already seen them do.

Freddie stepped out, holding a cup of water. "Was it bad?"

Lydia sighed a laugh. "I don't suppose we have anything harder than water on hand?"

"You shouldn't look beyond the question, Lyds. No life is perfect."

Lydia winked at her. "No life without you, I'll grant that."

"I'm going to kiss you when we're done."

"Bring on the next, then!"

A well-dressed woman barged through the door as if she belonged there, dark green vest embroidered with silver thread. She not only met Lydia's eye, she raised an eyebrow as if surprised Lydia could meet hers. Still, she had to kneel like all the rest, and it was hard to contain a smirk.

"What do you wish to know?" Lydia asked.

The rich woman had a furrowed brow, and the slight redness around her eyes spoke of recent trouble, never mind the stiff-backed pride with which she knelt. "I haven't heard from my brother in a few days. He's a researcher, works with the yafanai from time to time." She paused, and Lydia wondered if she thought all yafanai knew each other.

"And you wish to know…"

"What happened to him? He went on some swamp expedition, and I haven't had word in almost a week."

"I'm sorry. I need someone to follow into the future. I can switch from person to person if they meet each other while I'm looking."

The rich woman's eyes blazed before they glittered with tears.

"Describe him to me," Lydia said. "Then I can follow your future and watch for him."

She did, and Lydia followed the long skein of the rich woman's life, business deals and lovers, a great fire that left her stock untouched. She became wealthier until she died.

When Lydia came back to herself, the rich woman was still staring. "I didn't see him. I'm sorry."

"Do you mean I'll never see him again? That's unacceptable!"

"You're going to get richer, if that's any consolation."

The rich woman opened and shut her mouth a few times. When she stood, she flipped several coins into the bowl. "Something extra for your trouble."

She stalked out as determinedly as she'd entered, and Freddie slipped out from behind the curtain again. "Well, well. I thought I might have to get violent for a moment."

"We should put out a sign. Mind your manners or the prophet's sweet baby will hurt you."

"Utterly terrifying. Thirty-*three* to go."

Lydia sighed and stretched. Would there ever again be a day as long as this? She could have gone into the future and looked, but the idea that there might be a longer one was actually terrifying.

CHAPTER FOUR

Cordelia situated her pack atop her armored shoulders. She watched from the corner of her eye as Sergeant Preston badgered Privates Clemensky and Carter about the sizes of their packs, asking if they were smuggling lovers into the swamp along with their gear. They hid their eye rolls and fussed with their leather armor, all of them starting to sweat in the morning sun outside Gale's western gate.

Private Jacobs whistled softly and gestured toward Gale with her chin. Cordelia turned as a young man and a slightly older woman marched toward her, more purpose in their stride than if they were just family saying good-bye. They had a relaxed air, the man sporting an overconfident smile, and the woman with half-lidded, bored eyes. They might as well have been wearing signs that said "yafanai," though they'd traded their ritual robes for plain trousers and shirts.

The man gave a wave. He stood several inches shorter than Cordelia, but most people did, and his partner was even shorter than that. His light brown hair fell over his brows, making him seem about twenty. Her red hair had been pulled back in a severe bun, sharpening the already severe angles of her face.

"We're ready to go." He slapped a small bag that hung from his shoulder. The woman tossed hers at Cordelia's feet.

Cordelia had to smile. The pissing contest had already begun. "Jacobs, take the yafanai's bag. What are your focuses?"

She raised an eyebrow, but he said, "I'm micro-psychokinetic and a little telepathic." When his companion stayed silent, he cleared his throat. "Natalya is psychokinetic. I'm Horace Adair, by the way."

"Macro- or micro-psychokinetic?" Cordelia asked.

"Both, from the large to the microscopic." She sighed during the last word, not so subtly stressing that she was macro and micro bored, too.

Horace thrust his hand out, and Cordelia shook it. "Lieutenant Cordelia Ross."

He squeezed before letting go, and as Natalya moved toward Sergeant Preston, Horace leaned close. "Don't mind Natalya. She's a little stiff, but once you get to know her, well, try not to let her annoy you."

"I'm not annoyed."

He smiled, and a little tickle passed over Cordelia's scalp. "You can't fool me."

She leaned forward, bending at the knees, and his eyes widened, but she put a hand on his shoulder so he couldn't step away. "Think hard before poking around in my head, Mr. Adair. The swamp's a big, dangerous place, easy to get lost in." He paled, and she maneuvered him into line before she took her place at the head of the column.

It took all morning before they were truly within the forest, not yet in the great swamp but among the large trees that heralded its presence. Cordelia kept them on the track the drushka called the Oosjani Road and wondered how long it would be before their hosts revealed themselves. All her pondering about meeting other drushka made her impatient to get it done. If they reached the true swamp and still had no escort, she'd be forced to turn around.

The wind rustled the trees, making the branches clack together and shaking the leaves in a papery hiss. Some insect took up orbit around Cordelia's head, and she tired of swatting at it. The squad muttered together as the morning wore on with the occasional bark from Sergeant Preston when they became too loud.

When Jacobs muttered, "Did you see that?" Cordelia turned. Before she could ask, a boggin sprang from a clump of bushes, leading with a long, crude spear.

Cordelia whipped out her blade and chopped through its neck. The squad cried out as more boggins rushed from the undergrowth, silent, all of them with spears. Damn. She'd never fought so many armed boggins at once.

"Truncheons!" Cordelia called. "Form a circle." But they had to struggle to stay together. There wasn't even time to throw javelins before they were surrounded.

Four boggins rushed Cordelia, all in a line. She braced her feet, but another boggin hurtled out of the melee to knock the other boggins prone. Before they could rise, an invisible force slammed them into a nearby tree, and they fell to the ground. The squad dispatched most of the others, but some fled into the forest, chased by flying debris.

Natalya knelt among the leathers, gaze following the boggins, her entire body tense. When Cordelia offered her a hand up, she took it, a smirk on her face.

"An ambush," Sergeant Preston said. "Boggins putting together an ambush?"

Or a test of their strength. Cordelia shuddered. "Throw the bodies away from the road." Private Clemensky sat in the dirt, blood streaming down his arm. Cordelia knelt at his side while Horace stitched his shoulder with needle and thread. "All right, Clemensky?" When he nodded, Cordelia looked to Horace. "You're a medic, too?"

"Telepaths can tell where it hurts, and as a micro, I can deaden the pain a bit." He tied off the line of stitches and cut the thread. "Of course, with our micro powers, Natalya and I can keep the wound closed while I stitch."

"Could you keep it together until it heals?"

Natalya leaned over Horace's shoulder. "No one could keep that kind of concentration for days. Horace is good at what he does. You should trust him."

She shrugged. Any trust came from the fact that Gale had strict laws against telepaths prying into heads whenever they pleased. She was just lucky she was sensitive enough to know when it was happening. She hauled Clemensky to his feet by his good arm. "You gonna make it, grunt?"

"Point me at them, Lieutenant."

"Good man. Keep toward the middle. Let's move out."

As the squad moved deeper into the swamp, solid ground grew rare. The squad followed long sandbars through mud and grime, wading from island to island. The world became a tangle of greens and browns punctuated by wandering shafts of sunlight that turned the pools of water into burnished gold. The surrounding trees had gone from large to massive, stretching up until the canopy was a blur overhead. The ropy branches tangled and became lost in one another, curling together in midair, connecting each tree to its fellows and making the swamp into one huge organism. Insects hummed everywhere, creating a background tempo for the clicks and whirrs of unseen animals. When the wind gusted, it carried the cries of thousands of birds that nested in the faraway canopy.

It was beautiful, just as her parents had described it before it had killed them.

Cordelia called a halt on a large piece of dense ground filled with underbrush. They'd lost the Oosjani, muddy as the way had already become, and the drushka hadn't shown. She wondered who was going to have the fight with Reach, her or Carmichael? And what would Paul say?

Something whistled from the trees, and Natalya and Horace dropped to the ground, unmoving.

Cordelia whipped out her sidearm. "Circle the yafanai!" The squad hopped to obey. The swamp had fallen silent but for the faraway whoops of some animal and the sound of ragged breathing. Cordelia thought again of Community, how the only people who'd survived were those who'd managed to run fast enough. The drushka had pulled the houses down, scattered the stone walls. She was amazed they hadn't salted the earth, but they liked growing things.

"Anyone see anything?" A chorus of nos answered her. "Clemensky, check the yafanai. Be ready to—"

"I do not trust humans," a voice called, the accent even thicker than Reach's, a throaty purr. "Without your mind throwers, we are on level ground."

Not unless they also had guns. "Fucking drushka," Cordelia muttered. She cleared her throat. "You bring us out here to attack us?"

"To talk. As equals."

"Funny way of showing it," Sergeant Preston muttered.

A clatter of branches, followed by a sharp yelp, came from the trees. Someone stumbled from the underbrush soon after, hands over his head. "Don't shoot! I'm human. I'm coming out." He gulped for air as he stumbled forward, wiping sweat from his bald head. "Higaroshi Adan. Sorry about the scare. I tried to hurry down, but I fell instead." He smiled and stretched his back before reaching out a hand.

Cordelia just blinked at him. He stared for a few seconds, smile failing. He glanced at Horace and Natalya, still lying unconscious before his arm dropped to his side. "I told her this was a bad idea.

They're not here to hurt you. Reach sent word. The hunt leader just doesn't like yafanai."

"The who?"

"Me, human," a new voice said.

Cordelia brought her gun up. A drushka crouched upon a branch behind Higaroshi, in plain sight, though Cordelia was certain she hadn't been there before. Her hands curled over her leather-clad knees, giving Cordelia a good view of the poisonous middle claw, the only sure way to tell a female drushka from a male.

The drushka sat on her heels, bare feet curled over the wood, the bark of the tree as dark as her brown skin, though just as lined with whorls. Her short, unkempt red hair looked as if it had been styled by the wind, and her lichen-colored eyes watched with unrestrained curiosity. Her leather shirt and trousers were unadorned, just lighter than her skin, meant to blend in.

Cordelia kept her gun up, and the drushka grinned into it with sharp teeth. She wrinkled her narrow nose in affection. Cordelia lowered her gun a fraction, and the drushka leapt from the branch to land at Higaroshi's side.

"You always greet visitors this way?" Cordelia asked.

"*Ahya*, if they are dangerous. Your mind throwers will recover soon. They were not struck hard." Her hands rested on her hips, near two wooden knives that hung from a string around her waist.

"You might have killed them."

The drushka spread her hands as if to say anything was possible. "Your people taught us the ways of the sling. Do you doubt your own teachings?"

Cordelia tried to remember everything her uncle had taught her about diplomacy but came up short.

Lucky for her, Sergeant Preston called, "Yafanai are coming around, Lieutenant."

She holstered her sidearm. The drushka smiled wider as if this whole predicament was the funniest thing in the goddamned world. It'd be a shame to have to shoot her.

Higaroshi cleared his throat. "I'm guessing you're Lieutenant Cordelia Sa Ross?"

"That's right."

He stuck out his hand again. "I'm pleased—"

"Sa?" the drushka asked. "You have a drushkan name mingled with your human one? Who gave it to you?"

"My mother. It's been in my family since—"

"Roshkikan, yes? The one you called Jania. The drushka have long memories."

Cordelia lifted her eyebrows. "Then maybe you can remember never to attack someone who only came to talk to you."

The drushka touched her forehead, an apology, if Cordelia remembered right. "Do you know what Sa means?"

"Yeah. So, now we know who I am and who Higaroshi is, do you mind telling us who you are?" She kept her voice light, mockingly sweet, and several of the squad snorted.

If the drushka noticed, she didn't show it. She gestured toward one of the spinier plants that clustered around the base of a tree. "I am named for this."

It looked painful and irritating, a good choice. "Are you going to tell me what that's called, or do I have to guess?"

"Um," Higaroshi said, "the drushka prefer to be called by the human words for their namesakes until one establishes trust. I've been calling her Nettle, and she seems to like it all right."

An eye roll would have felt so right at the moment, but Cordelia resisted again. Fucking diplomacy. "Sounds good to me."

Private Clemensky helped the yafanai to their feet. They steadied each other, and Horace muttered something about helping them both with his power.

"And now they are well," Nettle said.

"No thanks to you."

She wrinkled her nose. "We saw the fight with the chanuka. We knew they would recover."

Higaroshi groaned, and Cordelia took another deep breath, fighting the urge to smash in the drushka's narrow nose, spoil her nice-looking face. "Saw that, did you? Didn't think about helping at all?"

"Humans need drushkan help whenever they enter the swamp?"

"Hunt leader—" Higaroshi started.

Cordelia pushed past him. "It'd be nice, asshole. Are we supposed to be allies on this mission or not?"

Private Carter whispered, "Movement to the left, Lieutenant."

Nettle touched two fingers to her cheek, and her gaze lingered a moment on Cordelia's lips. "I have told them not to attack, even though we are standing so very close to one another now." She smelled like new leaves with just a tiny hint of something floral.

"I can take the two on the left," Natalya said.

"Muzzle that," Cordelia said softly. "We're still talking."

Nettle smiled again, her gaze traveling Cordelia's face and showing something like approval. "Shall we go?"

"Sure. Lead the way. The sooner we're done, the sooner we can get the hell out of here."

Nettle spread her hands again and whistled into the trees.

Higaroshi smiled. "That went well!"

Cordelia wondered what he thought a situation looked like when it went poorly, but he'd probably seen Community's ruins.

More lean figures came out of hiding, ten in all, regarding the humans with what seemed like simple curiosity. As the squad gathered their packs again, a short drushka with a female's claw strode toward them. Her green hair was shorter than any of the other drushka, most only a quarter inch from her scalp, though a longer stripe started from the center of her brow and continued over her head to her nape.

"You are not like Higaroshi," she said to Cordelia. "You are a warrior, a metal skin."

"Lieutenant Ross," Higaroshi said, "this is—"

The drushkan girl laid her index finger across his lips. "No. I want her to name me."

Cordelia looked from one to the other. "I'm going to need a hint."

The girl reached to her belt and pulled a small knife. The squad shuffled, but Cordelia held up a hand to still them. The girl was as tall as her chest and thinner than the other drushka. Cordelia was pretty sure she could chuck this one far into the swamp if necessary.

The girl glared at her knife. Unlike Nettle's weapons, this one wasn't sleek or sharp-looking. No longer than her hand and scarred with nicks and gouges, it seemed a desperate weapon. "I made this myself," she said. "The only weapon my mother would allow." She slapped her thigh, frustrated. "I am named for it. Would you call it a knife?"

"I'd call it a shiv."

The girl repeated the word several times before beaming. She wrinkled her nose away and turned to Nettle. "I like this name."

Nettle spread her hands and smiled. "Ahya, I can see. Now, we must have our mouths speak to our legs—"

"And teach them to move," Cordelia said loudly, remembering that phrase from Jania's journal. "Some of us have been studying."

Nettle regarded her a moment, head tilted, before she signaled her people to move out. Cordelia ordered her squad to follow, all of them grumbling, and she didn't blame them. The drushka led the way as the ground turned to liquid, and the humans clambered onto the huge branches that curled through the swamp like cables. The drushka leapt from limb to limb above their heads, effortlessly graceful. Cordelia stepped carefully, knowing that the sucking morass beneath her could pull her to her grave.

As they passed farther into drushkan territory, Cordelia thought through her ancestor's journal and tried to recall everything Paul had told her about drushkan ways, trying to figure out if she should have known the drushka would greet her squad so drastically. They seemed far from the threatening ambushers now, laughing and speaking to one another in their hissing language. They seemed very flexible, far more than a human could be, and Cordelia wondered if their bones or joints were just that different. Nettle seemed the most graceful of all, sometimes twisting in midair as she leapt.

"They're quite beautiful," Horace said.

She glanced over her shoulder. "Why are you up here behind me?"

"Preston thought it best to put me at front and Nat at the back. We could help if someone falls in the water." He chuckled. "Though, please don't take this the wrong way, Lieutenant, but there's no way I could lift you. I could probably keep you afloat long enough for the others to pull you out."

"Probably?"

"The Storm Lord knows there are no guarantees in life. Maybe I should switch places with Nat."

"She has to keep an eye on the whole column. That's why Preston put her in back."

"But your armor alone…"

"Isn't worth lives, though some might disagree." She looked back again, and he shrugged with a happy smile.

"You are slow, humans!" one of the drushka called. "Can your mouths not teach your legs to move faster?"

"We're keeping up," Cordelia said. "We don't fancy a swim."

Nettle dropped down to walk in front of her, backward, fucking showoff. "If you leave your metal skin, you will go much faster."

"Thanks for the tip, but I think I'll keep it."

"You are stubborn."

"One of my many admirable qualities."

She grinned. "Luck is with you. The way is not long to our first campsite."

"Then on to the research station?"

"Where human and chanuka lived together."

"The humans were living with boggins?"

Nettle spread her arms. "So it appeared."

"That doesn't make any sense."

"It is out of our territory. We hoped you could explain it."

Cordelia thought hard but came up with nothing. Carmichael could figure it out.

The drushka led them to a small island among the mire, not much more than a bare patch of dirt, but after marching along the branches, it seemed like paradise. The drushka started a fire as night fell, and Sergeant Preston helped Cordelia out of her armor. She stretched and swung her arms, conscious of watching drushka.

Shiv moved toward her slowly, gaze swinging between the humans and the drushka where they were parted by the fire. "I would like to wear your metal skin."

"It wouldn't fit you." And no way in hell would the captain ever okay it.

Shiv narrowed her eyes before studying her own smaller, leaner body. "Ahya, so I see. I will survive without it."

"I'm sure. I like to have it around." When Shiv continued to watch her, Cordelia cleared her throat. "It's saved my life before."

She poked Cordelia with a non-poisonous finger. "You will not break so easily, I think."

"Thanks. You're also...not very breakable."

Nettle stepped around the fire. "Are you having a bother from this girl?"

Shiv whirled to face her. "I am not a bother, hunt leader! We are making ourselves excellent good friends."

Nettle's eyes narrowed, and her hands curled into fists.

Cordelia cleared her throat again. "It's all right. I'm happy to talk." She put on what she hoped was a convincing smile, but they fell into drushkan and ignored her. She shifted closer to her people, leaving them to it.

"Drushka are weird," Private Jacobs said.

"Just let them get on with it."

Horace craned his neck, looking around her. "I wonder what the problem was."

"Maybe they're a couple," Natalya said, "and the bigger one thought the little one was coming on to you, Lieutenant."

The squad chuckled. Cordelia snorted but snuck a peek at the two, hoping they weren't a couple. Shiv seemed far too young, but Nettle? Of all the women Cordelia had spent time with, the dangerous ones were always the most attractive, and her ancestor had written about having a drushkan lover.

Best to keep to the mission, though.

Nettle broke from Shiv and faced Cordelia again. "Your forgiveness." She touched her forehead. "That one is young."

"There's nothing to forgive." She couldn't help letting her gaze linger, though, as if she'd already planted a seed, and there was no stopping it growing.

Nettle looked up and caught her staring. They shared a glance, and Cordelia admired the marks on her skin, how they added depth to the plains of her face.

"She should not..." Nettle's gaze traveled over the ground as if it held an answer she could find. "Bother anyone." With a shake of her head, she moved away.

B46 touched her mouth, working it up and down as she watched the tall creatures on the forest floor below. They hooted and squeaked and rumbled at each other. In the before times, B46 had sounds, too: a shrill call for danger, a growl to claim a meal. But this was so much more.

Some of the tall creatures smelled similar to her kind. Others smelled like meat and stink, plus a harsh tang from the one that gleamed like a pond in midday. There was nothing like that smell in B46's memory, not in the before time and not from her days spent captured by the tall creatures, caught like a youngling in tree roots.

A large male crouched beside her, picked a bloodsucker off the back of her arm, and tossed it in his mouth, grinding its spongy flesh. She nuzzled his neck and saw in his eyes that he had a knowing like hers. The tall creatures had called him C28 and used something to mark his arm, just as they had hers.

She listened to the tall creatures again but could understand nothing, just as she couldn't when the tall creatures had held her, marked her, and hurt her. She'd had to wait until one of them had come close enough to grab, then she'd pushed against her bonds and broken free. She'd clawed the tall creatures then, tore them, and ran.

She looked to the kin that had run with her, now scattered through the trees. Squat, thick bodies, eyes on short stalks, claws on hands and feet, and mouths with many teeth. They'd all been caught by the tall creatures, beaten, poked, and prodded as she'd been. In the before time, she'd been drawn by the scent of her kind, but now the knowing kept them together, made them kin. Some were missing. They'd attacked the tall creatures while she'd watched and seethed and remembered.

The peace of the before time had vanished, taking with it the flavor of each moment. Rage filled her every corner now, driving past hunger, past want, becoming need. The others waited, silent, watching her with the same knowing she felt. She grunted and slapped the tree, and they shuddered, snarling, their rage filling the air between them.

The male offered her the bag, and drool filled her mouth. This was from the place of hurt, the only good thing to come of it. She dipped her claws in and licked them clean of the sticky grit. Deep, dull sounds filled her head, made her chest heave, and the calls of the birds sharpened. She could feel the heartbeats of her kin. Each bump of C28's skin stood out like pebbles, and she saw the jagged edge of a broken tooth far back in his mouth. Every moment since the tall creatures had first given her meat laced with the sticky grit replayed in her mind. The tall creatures had weaknesses, and she would find them all. No nest could hide them from her claws; no arms could shelter them from her rage. She flexed her claws, driving deep gouges into the bark.

The sticky grit would hurt her later. Her body would ache, and she would moan, but while it was upon her, she would take its strength.

When she climbed, her kin followed. They would seek out more of their kind, those who didn't have the knowing, but perhaps they could be taught. The tall creatures would learn from her as she had from them. They would know cries of terror, the cold dash of fear, and the rush of blood when life ended forever.

CHAPTER FIVE

Nettle pointed ahead through the trees, and Cordelia squinted, trying to see through the swath of greens and browns. "I don't see anything."

"It was well hidden."

"And it's stayed that way." They'd traveled through the morning, and the stress of trying to keep her footing on the slick branches had made a knot between her shoulders. All day, they'd had nothing under them but deep, moss-covered water, and it was starting to wear on her something fierce. "How did you find it?"

"The stench."

As if summoned, the wind shifted, and the smell settled over them like fog: the heavy, pungent scent of dead flesh and the metallic tang of blood. The swamp suddenly felt all too humid, and Cordelia's stomach shifted, bile rising. She pressed a hand to her mouth. Behind her, Private Carter threw up into the water. Cordelia shuffled away so she wouldn't follow his lead, but others sounded less fortunate.

"Lead on," Cordelia said, trying to keep her teeth shut.

The drushka climbed to a tree-borne encampment, huts built around sturdy trunks with bridges connecting them and ladders leading to the lower branches. It looked as homey as a person could get in the swamp, except for the bodies caught on railings or tangled in hanging vines. Some lay along the branches and bridges.

Cordelia thought the air particularly hazy until she realized it was thick with flies. "What the fuck?"

"Look quickly," Nettle said. "The stronger the smell, the bigger the predators that will come. My people have kept them away but not for much longer."

But every place she looked, Cordelia saw a body who'd been someone's parent or child or lover or friend. They'd been ripped apart, Storm Lord help them. One of the closest had bite marks on his chest and limbs. His face had been torn away in five bloody strips, leaving his lips untouched, but the rest was a ruin of flesh and fluid.

Blood lay in crimson pools along the branches, too much to dry, and she tried to step around it, but it was everywhere, and clouds of bugs rose around her, disturbed from their feast. When she came to a boggin body, she noted a slash across its chest. She looked for a blade, but the only weapons she saw in human hands were pieces of splintered wood, as if they'd tried to defend themselves with bits of furniture.

Higaroshi was so pale he looked ready to pass out. "I told them to leave everything as it was."

"Were they all killed by boggins?" Cordelia asked.

Sergeant Preston knelt over a nearby body. "Most of them, looks like. These are claw marks, the right height for a boggin, and this is a boggin bite."

"We know this man," Horace called from one of the huts.

Cordelia crossed over to him. "Yafanai?"

"No, a researcher who worked with us."

A fact to file away for the captain. But everyone out here had been studying something. Her parents' faces rose in her mind. They'd also been researching the swamp, and just like these people, they'd never go home again. At least her parents had fallen to their deaths instead of being torn apart. Childhood anger tried to rear in her again, but she pushed it down. Time enough for that later. "Spread out. Pick up anything valuable. Sergeant Preston, collect descriptions and search the bodies. Their families will want their things."

"Lieutenant." He nodded.

"What happened here?" Cordelia asked as Nettle moved up beside her. "What's happened to the boggins that they'd do this? They've never attacked a human settlement this large."

"I do not know, and this causes me worry."

"Why didn't Reach tell us about this?"

"We discovered these bodies just as we got word to meet you. She is being informed now." She paused, making that same head motion as if searching for something to say. "There was one other body that we did remove. Drushkan."

"One of yours?"

"Not my band, not my tribe. He was of the old people."

"The ones that destroyed Community?"

Nettle sucked her teeth in confusion.

"The first human settlement, the one that Roshkikan belonged to."

"Ahya, this is not far from their territory. The drushka was killed by a chanuka."

"Maybe he tried to help these humans."

"*Ahwa*, no. If the old drushka had helped these humans, some would have survived. But if there were other dead drushka, they were carried away. We found this one because a *saleska* was trying to pull his body from the roots of a tree."

"Saleska?"

"The water people." She mimed a long snout and snapping teeth.

"Oh. Progs. So, you think a member of the old people was here because…"

"I do not know. There were more humans along the branches in that direction that were killed by drushkan weapons, killed as they fled this place. We could not protect their bodies, not so far from the shelters. The saleska do not often climb or leap, but for this feast…" She spread her hands as if to say anything was possible.

"The old drushka could have been protecting their territory. Or I guess they could have had some deal going, but from what I know, no humans have spoken to the old drushka since my ancestor's time."

Nettle spread her hands again and walked away. Higaroshi took her place. "This whole thing upsets them. They don't know why humans were here. They don't know what's gone wrong with the chanuka, and the old drushka haven't been to this part of the swamp in years, since just after the drushka split up."

Jania had written that the drushkan schism was caused because some wanted to trade with the humans, and the others wanted to destroy them. Though after the old drushka had destroyed Community, they'd seemed to have changed their minds.

Higaroshi wiped the sweat from his bald head. "Maybe these researchers attracted the old drushka's attention somehow. What's clear is that they didn't have permission to make contact at all. Come, look at this." He led her inside one of the huts.

People littered the floor, clawed and bitten almost beyond recognition and turning the air so foul she could almost see it. She pressed a hand to her mouth and tried not to breathe. Sergeant Preston was propping open the shuttered windows with long poles. He pointed toward the tree trunk where rows of mesh boxes stood atop one another.

No, not boxes. They had doors held shut by a series of wooden fasteners. "Cages?"

"Seems like," Higaroshi said. Boggin bodies hung from some, the fasteners still secure, but the wooden mesh had been ripped open from the inside, turning into barbs that snagged the boggins who'd tried to escape. Other boxes had their doors torn off completely.

"I've never seen this type of wood," Sergeant Preston said. "It's not woven. Looks like it grew in this pattern."

Cordelia touched it, a sinewy fiber that seemed strong enough, but when she peered closely, she saw discolored spots, lighter than the others. She tugged on one and felt it give. "It's brittle in places." Another cage gave toward the middle, the edges bloody where its occupant had climbed out. "Who'd design a cage with weak spots?"

"Nettle is convinced these have something to do with the old drushka. They were all very upset by this whole scene."

Cordelia tapped the mesh. "This wood is the same color as the drushkan weapons, but they don't look brittle. Is there any way to contact the old drushka?"

"I think contact between the two groups is forbidden."

"Because some of them talk to us, and the others don't want anything to do with us." She took another slow look around. "Until now."

Private Carter met her when she emerged. "We finished our sweep."

"Descriptions?"

"Best we could. Some of them were too…" His jaw trembled.

Cordelia clapped him on the shoulder. "Good work." She turned to the rest of the squad as they gathered around. "I'm proud of you, grunts. You did your duty as paladins should, and now we can do right by these people. The Storm Lord would be proud of you."

"Yes, Lieutenant!" they chorused.

"One thing left to do." The horrible part. "Horace, Natalya, we'd appreciate your help."

"For what?" Horace asked.

"Burial detail, such as we can give them. We'll move the bodies to the lower branches first."

"What will you do when you have them there?" Nettle called.

"Give them to the swamp."

Nettle looked to the other drushka, who wandered out from the trees at her glance, Shiv at their head. "We will aid you."

Cordelia nodded, touched. Everyone shifted the bodies, human and boggin, down to the lower limbs. They pushed the boggins in without ceremony, but Cordelia led a moment of silence before they placed each human in the water, letting them drift slowly. They didn't stay long, didn't want to watch the bodies be consumed by the denizens of the swamp, but there was no other way to honor them; there were too many to carry out.

The drushka led them away from the research station, back to what they still called the Oosjani Road, though Cordelia still didn't see any path to speak of.

In the late afternoon light, Nettle approached her. "Our leader wishes to see you."

Cordelia cracked a wry smile. "Are you talking about yourself in the third person now?"

Nettle sucked her teeth again, a trait that Cordelia was finding endearing, even a little sexy, as if utter confusion was a turn-on. "The third person?"

"I'm going to get sick of saying never mind." She chuckled without much humor. "Which leader?"

"The one who commands all my tribe."

Cordelia heard a gasp and turned to see Higaroshi standing close enough to eavesdrop.

"But no one meets the leader," he said. "I mean, even I haven't."

"The ambassador doesn't get to meet this person, but I do?" Cordelia asked.

Nettle spread her hands. "You are the only one. Higaroshi will come back with us to our home, but only you will meet the leader."

Higaroshi hung his head. Cordelia considered her options and bit her cheek. Carmichael had told her to find out what was going on, and maybe this leader could fill in some gaps. She'd have to send her squad on without her, but she'd still have a pack of drushka for backup, providing they helped instead of just watching. As the drushka had guided the humans, though, she got the impression that now that they'd all met, the drushka would fight beside her. And they wanted to find out what had happened to the boggins, too.

"Sergeant Preston, get everyone back to Gale, and tell Captain Carmichael that I'll be a guest of the drushka for a little longer."

"Lieutenant." He lifted an eyebrow and sidled close. "Are you sure?"

"I have to find out all I can. Keep the squad together and get back to Gale as quickly as possible."

He thrust his chin at the drushka. "Can we trust them?"

"We don't have much choice, and after that first dust-up, they've been helpful."

He nodded and hustled everyone together, and after a nod from Cordelia, they followed their drushkan guides, heading for the edge of the swamp.

"Good luck, Lieutenant," Horace called over his shoulder.

She waved and then gestured for the drushka to lead the way. As before, they leapt between trees, but Cordelia walked carefully along the branches, Higaroshi behind her.

"Haven't perfected your leaping?" Cordelia asked.

"I'm an anthropologist and a diplomat, not an acrobat. Watch that slippery patch, there."

"Don't worry. I have no intention of hurrying."

"Um, I hope you don't mind me asking, Lieutenant, but did you say your ancestor was Jania Carruthers Ross? Roshkikan?"

"Yep."

His voice pitched higher, getting excited. "Do you know her journal is required reading for anthropologists?"

Maybe he'd ask for her autograph next. "A lot of people have read it."

"Have you? I mean, hearing the thoughts of one of her descendants—"

"Being related hasn't given me any special insight, sorry."

"I just think it's fascinating that—" He yelped, and she turned in time to see him fall sideways. She grabbed for him, snagging his shoe as he tumbled from the branch. It slipped from his foot, and he splashed into the water a few feet below them.

"Man down!" She knelt, searching, but he bobbed back to the surface in half a second, sputtering and treading water.

When he saw her face, he grinned. "Don't worry, Lieutenant. I don't sink."

One of the drushka lay down and reached out a hand. He said something in drushkan, smiling as he did, but as Higaroshi reached for him, he cried out, eyes wide.

A dark shadow glided under the water, streaking for them. "Pull!" Cordelia shouted. She leaned forward to help just as the drushka heaved. Higaroshi shot out of the water and slammed into Cordelia. She toppled backward just as the long snout of the prog broke the water's surface.

Enormous jaws clamped around her thighs as brown murk closed over her head. The prog swung her back and forth, teeth squealing dully against her armor. She pounded on its hide, mouth clamped shut to hold in air that wanted to scream forth.

Terror tried to grab hold of her, but she summoned the heady joy of the fight, the anger that had been lurking in her core. Boggins couldn't kill her. People couldn't kill her. She damn sure wasn't going to let a piece of fucking nature kill her! She bent across the prog's snout, drew her sidearm, and felt for the spot between the prog's eyes. She pressed the muzzle down hard and fired, once, twice, again.

The sounds were only dull pops, and the powered weapon kicked against her hand. The jaws went slack, and she plummeted downward to sink into muddy silt. She floundered to her feet, stirring up gunk in the already yellow haze. The surface wasn't far—a few feet above the prog's gently sinking body—but it might as well have been the surface of the moon. The prog settled into the silt beside her, a long dark shadow, and she cast about for some way to pull herself up, her lungs aching.

Something tugged on her shoulder, and she swung for it, thinking of another prog, but a hazy drushkan face filled her vision. Long fingers pulled her close, and another hand pinched her nose shut. She forced herself to stand still while the drushka formed a seal between their mouths. It slowly pushed air into her mouth before swimming for the surface.

Other hands fumbled with the straps of her armor, but she shook them off. Removing it would take too long, and they might drop some plates in the process. She knew metal wasn't worth another person's life, but this was hers, and she'd be damned before she'd leave a suit of armor at the bottom of the swamp. The drushka began to push her while others towed her, leading her toward something large and dark, a tree trunk.

She trudged through the mud while the drushka dove like fishing birds, feeding her air after she exhaled streams of bubbles. She thought only of one step after another, telling herself she could do this. She would not panic. She would not break, nor would she stop. She was not her parents. She would find a way out.

Finally, she reached the trunk, and the drushka pulled her upward while she clung to the slippery bark. When her head broke the surface, she sucked in breath after breath, and when they pulled her onto a wide branch, they collapsed together, all of them gasping. The drushka held tight to her as if afraid she'd fall again. Shiv smiled, wrinkling her nose, and Cordelia saw a milky, nictitating membrane covering her half-closed eyes.

Cordelia felt for her sidearm. Right in its holster. She must have stowed it from memory. Even underwater, even after a prog had tried to eat her, she'd remembered her training. It made her want to laugh. Dimly, she thought some people might have wept, but fuck that.

Nettle leaned into view, hair plastered to her face, and her brow wrinkled in concern. A drop of water slid down her cheek like a caress before it dropped to Cordelia's chin. "Are you well?"

"No." She reached for another drop before it could fall, and it rolled down her palm. "That was the closest I've ever come to dying." But she hadn't died. She thought of her parents again. Maybe they should have tried harder.

"Give her some air," Higaroshi called from beyond the sprawl.

Nettle looked that way, and Cordelia watched the drops slide down her graceful neck. The drushka stood together, hauling her upright.

Even if she fell again, she would survive. Fucking swamp couldn't kill her. "Do you think your people could get the bullets I fired?"

Nettle wrinkled her nose and held them out. "Did you think we would not know how precious metal is to your kind? Must I remind you of drushkan memories again?"

"Thanks," Cordelia said. "Everybody, thanks."

They patted her armored shoulders. "And thank you for helping me," Higaroshi said.

"I lost your shoe."

"One of the drushka grabbed it. There's little they miss."

"Thank the Storm Lord for that."

As they walked for the rest of the day, Cordelia's mood swung like a pendulum, elated and victorious to moody and depressed. She didn't think she'd been in the grip of so many damned feelings since she was a teenager. When they reached solid ground as night fell, she almost whooped in delight.

Higaroshi called it the drushkan enclave, a close gathering of trees holding small wooden houses, a true gift from the Storm Lord. As other drushka swarmed around the returning band, Cordelia followed Higaroshi to his little house, stripped off her armor, and passed out on his floor, too tired to even think about the day, let alone talk with anyone.

In the morning, she groaned as she climbed down the tree. She'd never worn armor from sunup to sundown for days in a row. It didn't help that she'd had a few obvious bad dreams: drowning, monsters, scary big teeth. But when she woke, she forced herself to try to be happy about the fact that she was alive. Everything else could wait until she wasn't in the damned swamp anymore.

Nettle reclined against the trunk below, her arms above her head. Cordelia's gaze wandered along the sinewy line of her thighs. She'd factored into a few other dreams, her muscular body shrouded in shadow, but Cordelia had known she was naked, bright eyes inviting. The sight of her now made Cordelia tense in a good way, but it only served as a reminder that her entire body felt like one big knot.

"Our leader is not far, an hour at most," Nettle said. "My band will remain here while I escort you."

"An hour at your speed or mine?"

She smiled, but the look evaporated when Shiv approached them.

"Hunt leader," Shiv said. "I am ready."

"I have told you, young one, only Sa Ross and I will go."

Shiv tossed her head. "And I have chosen not to listen to you."

Cordelia looked from one to the other as they stared each other down. Shiv's fingers twitched, and Nettle's open hand shot out and struck her stomach. Shiv grunted, reaching for her carved knife, but Nettle's fist arced out and caught her in the jaw.

Shiv fought to rise but slid to the ground. She wiped a golden trickle of blood from her mouth and grinned. "You hit like a tree, hunt leader."

Nettle chuckled. "If you live long enough, you will make a fine queen."

Cordelia lifted her eyebrows, frozen between the desire to reach for a weapon and stay the hell out of this. "Um?"

Shiv walked away, and the drushka continued about their day as if one of their hunt leaders and someone who might one day be a queen—and what the fuck was that about—didn't just have a fistfight.

"Are you ready to leave?" Nettle asked.

"Is there an answer that might get me punched?"

"If you say you are ready to leave, we will go. If you are not, I will wait." She spread her hands. "If you were to say, 'I will be ready to leave once I am punched,' ahya, I would help you. But I would think it very strange."

Cordelia had to laugh. "Well, if I ever need a punch, I know who to turn to." Late-night, drunken street brawls with Liam at her side flashed through her mind, but she shook them away. "Lead on."

Nettle walked beside her on the firm ground, this haven of packed earth in the middle of the swamp. They traveled without conversation, and Cordelia let herself enjoy the sounds of nature without the clatter of voices. When she sighed, Nettle glanced at her. They shared a smile, one that lingered, and Cordelia recalled the water rolling down Nettle's neck. In one of her dreams, she'd chased it with her tongue.

"Have you ever thought about—"

Nettle's eyes widened. "Down!" She hauled on Cordelia's arm, and a spear sailed through the air where their heads had been.

Boggin howls rang through the trees. Cordelia drew her blade as hordes of the little bastards swarmed out of the underbrush, too many to count. She'd never seen a pack so large, so armed, and since when did they throw their spears?

Nettle pulled her two daggers. "Run!"

Cordelia drove her blade into a boggin's neck and kicked it out of the way. She and Nettle turned in circles as they hurried through the trees, trying to watch each other's backs.

"They should not have gotten this close without us hearing," Nettle said.

"How much farther?"

"My people are just over that rise."

"Run for help."

"You will be killed!"

"Not with my armor!" If they pulled her down, got to her face, she'd be in trouble, but she could keep them off for a few moments. "You're faster than I am!" A boggin flung itself at her, and she stabbed it in the belly, but it caught her blade in its claws and clung on. She kicked to keep the others at bay, but the impaled boggin weighed her down. Hefting the blade in both hands, she swung hard, sending the dying boggin to crash into its fellows.

"Watch out!"

Cordelia stumbled as Nettle shoved her. A spear glanced off Nettle's forehead and slid across her temple. She fell to her knees as golden blood gushed from the wound. Her daggers hung from her wrists by wooden tendrils, clinging to her as she slumped to the side.

"Fuck! I told you not to worry about me!" But that spear would have hit her face, a weakness she'd hoped the boggins hadn't figured out yet. She sheathed her blade and hauled Nettle's limp body over one shoulder. As she struggled for the ridge, she freed her sidearm and pulled the trigger as fast as she could.

Two boggins died, and the others scattered. She jogged, Nettle thumping against her back. She shot another boggin that dove from the pack, making the rest scramble behind one another. She crested the ridge, imagining a hollow full of drushka ready for a fight.

No one waited there, no encampment, no sign that there had ever been one. The boggins had scoured Nettle's people from the face of the planet.

A boggin crashed into her before her heart had time to sink. She staggered, and her sidearm flew from her hand. Nettle pitched over her shoulder to roll down the hill. Cordelia whipped out her blade and cut the boggin's arm off before stumbling after her.

The ground shuddered as long brown vines broke the surface, undulating like dancing snakes. Horror shuddered down Cordelia's spine as the vines curled over Nettle, wrapping her limbs and tugging her downward. Cordelia leapt, grabbed Nettle's arm, and lifted her blade high, aiming for the vines.

One shot from the rest and grabbed her arm. Another wrestled the blade from her hand. Cordelia held tight to Nettle, but that didn't stop the vines, and Cordelia had to let go or they'd both be buried alive.

"No!" Cordelia spotted her sidearm and lunged for it, but the vines grabbed it, too, and now one curled around her free arm and another around her leg. "Fuck you!"

They pulled her down, and visions of the prog's teeth reared within her, but there was nothing she could do, no strategies that would help. The boggins huddled along the ridge, watching, chattering. "Fuck you, too!" she yelled.

She pictured some monstrous creature below waiting to eat her and Nettle both. But her blade and sidearm were down there, too. All she had to do was get to them, and she could go down swinging.

Cordelia took a few deep breaths, made her body go slack, and gave herself up to the hungry earth.

B46 watched the tall creatures sink into the ground and chittered her rage. She'd known this would happen. Every time her people attacked this spot, the roots had stolen her prey. She scratched in the dirt and rested on her haunches. Beside her, C28 grunted and patted the ground.

His aggravated scent stung her nose, but she waved his reaction away and flicked her hands toward the trees. They would have to come back later. At least they now knew more about the tall creatures' weapons: sharp ones, like short spears, and a small thing that roared and killed her children in an instant. More knowing could only help them now, even if some of the duller children had to die for it.

B46 caressed C28's arm, and he yawned, calmed. He yipped at the others, and they melted back into the trees. The younglings that had just hatched, laid just after her freedom, were such beauties; they grew far faster than her young in the before times, though they were still small. They had a knowing, too, though not as great as hers, not as great as those who ate the sticky grit.

As she climbed among them, she patted her lower belly. She would lay again soon, as would many of the others, and these new younglings would be even smarter, faster. They all laid quickly now, another gift of the grit. A feeling grew in her, as strong as the rage, but just as sweet. Happiness, something to savor. The tall creatures could never escape her, not truly. Soon, she would have enough younglings to cover the ground, and no corner, under or over it, would be beyond her reach.

Chapter Six

D illon ran his fingers along the cool hallway wall, pressing down hard enough to make his skin squeal against the metal. Life aboard the *Atlas* had been more boring than usual the past few days. Ever since Marie had finagled Christian and Marlowe on to her side, everyone had given him a wide berth, even the ladies. He'd had sex with nearly every woman on the satellite—all but Marlowe and Dué—but they were staying away now no matter how much fun they'd had in the past. That was Marie's doing, too, he was sure. Maybe he shouldn't have made that crack about her worshipers, never mind that it was fucking true.

And Carmichael hadn't contacted him since he'd hung up on her. He wanted to know how the swamp expedition went, if she'd even sent one. He bet it was muggy in there, hot as hell, but freeing in a way. He'd been on different planet-side missions in the past, could acutely recall the feel of powered armor around his body, a weapon in his hands, and soldiers at his command. It sounded like fucking paradise now, even with the bugs and the sweat and the drugs he'd have to pound down so he didn't get some alien parasite.

Anything would be better than these sterile hallways and petty fights and school-like bullshit. There were drop pods in the hangar designed to get a person to the planet. He could leave, but then he'd age and die like any regular chump, just like his worshipers, who might not be too happy to find out he was as human as they were.

Now, if he could get Lazlo to come with him… He snorted. Lazlo lived for this sealed environment. He didn't even like people touching him, most of the time. He'd freak out if a bug jumped on him or some stranger wanted to have a conversation. No, he would definitely prefer to remain here, where everything always stayed the same.

Like Lessan, floating out there in space.

Dillon wandered to the lift, heading for the botanical habitat. When the lift doors opened on the habitat level, Dillon paused. Voices. In Lazlo's lair? And more than one, so Lazlo wasn't talking to himself. Dillon crept to the doorway and peeked through.

Christian and Marlowe stood side by side, like always, hands touching, but they were always touching. His blond head and her dark one moved in sync as Lazlo gestured toward the wall.

"I don't need much," Lazlo said, "just a nook here. Some of the new growth needs to stay separate from the others."

Dillon craned his neck and spotted the yafanai-making plants where they usually were, where anyone could see them, but the lieutenants wouldn't know what they were, just as no one else knew. But Lazlo's fucking console was live, so anyone who wandered over might see what he was working on if he'd left it open.

Dillon took a deep breath and told himself not to worry. If they wanted to snoop, the lieutenants wouldn't need computers, and they wouldn't need to run experiments on a handful of plants. They'd just dig around in heads. With his powers, Lazlo might be able to stop them, but few others could. Dué probably, but not Dillon. Goddammit, no one was supposed to be snooping. They'd made a fucking pact!

Dillon took a deep breath and made himself calm down again. After all, it seemed as if Lazlo had invited them.

The lieutenants nodded to Lazlo, and the walls glowed as Christian poured power into them, heating them until Marlowe could stretch and bend them. They formed a bubble in the wall, and Marlowe lifted a section of glass with her mind. With Christian's heat, they molded it into shape and melted it to the metal, making a new room with one clear wall. They burned a door into the new room, and Lazlo smiled, thanking them. Heat billowed up the stairs, carrying the stink of hot metal.

Dillon pressed his nose to his sleeve. Fuck, but they were good. They could do the whole station like this, make it look like the Taj Mahal if they wanted to. If it came to it, how could he fight them? Maybe he could suggest they practice against each other, like some kind of gym or a gladiatorial arena where they could test their powers. Marlowe might be able to knock aside a bolt of lightning and give Christian the chance to fry him. He'd have to surprise them with a little jolt that they'd both feel, and while they staggered, he'd hit them with a bigger bolt.

Then he'd lose control like with Lessan.

The lieutenants climbed the steps. "Waiting for us?"

"I don't need anything redecorated, thanks."

They passed him, one on each side, and it gave him a shiver, as if their connection ghosted through him. "Can't find something useful to do with your time?" they asked.

"Oh, piss off, the both of you." He waited until they'd gotten on the lift before he crossed into the habitat.

"You didn't have to skulk in the doorway," Lazlo said.

"Didn't want to intrude with your new friends."

"Oh, tell me you're jealous."

"You wish."

Lazlo's eyes crinkled a bit as if the comment pained him. Great, one of his sensitive days.

"What's the new space for?" Dillon asked.

"What do you think? Your new schemes, your new plants. You, you, you."

Dillon winked. "Gives you something to do."

"Why do you have to tamper with the planet all the time?"

"Gives *me* something to do."

"I should just tell everyone I made it possible for your people to have abilities via the plants, and then their people can all have powers, too."

For fuck's sake, it was a *very* sensitive day. "And why would you do that?"

Lazlo shuffled things around, not looking at him. Lazlo had never made a true pass at Dillon, but sometimes he acted as if they were married. Dillon resisted the urge to sigh. There was a reason he'd never gotten married, a good one. This one. But he'd had enough angry girlfriends to know how to fix this. He put his hand on Lazlo's shoulders, digging in his thumbs.

"I know you like to test yourself, Laz, to see just how much you can accomplish. Hell, you studied our brains and made a fucking drug that can replicate what we do. You're a genius. And that's not even your greatest accomplishment. Without you, we wouldn't have coffee."

Lazlo snorted a laugh, still not looking at him.

Dillon rubbed harder. "And you work with me because I may be a dick, but on this boat, I'm the least of the evils." He thought for a moment. "Unless you count Dué. I don't know if she's evil, but she's definitely nuts."

Lazlo moved out from beneath his hands, shuffled a few more plants around, but he didn't seem angry anymore. "With her around, we're all going to wake up as throw pillows one day."

"Well, at least it'll be interesting." Dillon toyed with something's leaves a moment. "Have you ever thought about going down to the planet?"

Lazlo gave him wide eyes. "God, no!"

"Yeah, that's what I thought."

Lazlo had tried all afternoon and couldn't forget the feel of Dillon's hands on his shoulders. It was an old tactic, well recognized, but damn if it didn't still get him. Dillon was both the carrot and the stick combined in one person. Lazlo had told himself a hundred times, a thousand times, that Dillon would never love him, not the way he wanted. In two hundred and fifty years, Dillon had only ever swung one way.

Why then did he dream of Dillon? Why was he comfortable around the man, more so than with anyone else? Lazlo had told himself many times that they were friends, and that was all. He'd told himself he could live with that, but feelings were feelings, just as his mom had always said. If they'd been on earth or anywhere in the galaxy where they could get away from each other, Lazlo would have cut ties long ago. Here, all he could do was give himself the same speeches, take from their relationship what Dillon was willing to give, and glean scraps of affection where he could.

He put down his tools and looked at his plants, the ones he'd been shifting into the new room. The place still carried the heavy tang of hot metal, but any little damage it did to Lazlo's lungs, he could repair. It couldn't hurt him as much as his own head could.

Too much thinking for the day. It was making him tired of himself. A break was past due. He'd go to the mess hall, have a nice cup of coffee, stare at the window, and think of anything but Dillon. Maybe he'd go to his quarters, watch a baseball vid that he hadn't seen two or three hundred times and have a nap.

And dream of Dillon.

"Oh, pathetic," he muttered as he waited for the lift. He scrubbed his hands through his hair and missed the shift of glasses on his face. He couldn't let go of anything today.

When the lift came, he stepped inside and laid his head against the cool, slick walls. The entire station was the same, all gleaming like a morgue table. If Dillon's people wanted metal as much as he claimed, they'd lose their minds over the *Atlas*.

Nope, that thought was adjacent to Dillon and therefore much too close. He thought instead of the people on the planet, how everyone on the *Atlas* had worshipers but him. If he did have some, he'd have to use a transmitter to contact them like…some did. One of the crew had once asked why he didn't demand worshipers as his fair due, but he wasn't able to give an answer. The breachies had whispered—where he could hear, of course—that he must just be content to share followers.

But the breachies took every opportunity to gossip, to manufacture squabbles, to decide who was in and who was out. And he wound up as their target many times, except when it was time to regenerate them. Then they were all smiles and compliments, the bastards. He should have denied them, made them wet their pants a little, but he didn't. Because he was a pushover.

If he had followers, he supposed he could have sent them the yafanai-maker plants, could have given them superpowers. He liked to think they would have been a peaceful people.

People who would've gotten mowed over by everyone else.

The lift stopped at crew quarters, and Lazlo's mood plummeted further as he wondered which of them it would be. His mouth fell open when Dué's jerking steps carried her inside.

Lazlo eased into one corner. "Ms. Dué. Afternoon."

The lift doors shut behind her, but she didn't turn to face them like a normal person. She didn't give the lift a command. Her remaining eye shifted here and there as if chasing an invisible fly.

Lazlo's gaze traveled to her empty socket, and he slid his thumb along his palm, thinking how quickly he could heal her but remembering her words when he'd first thought to try. Years after that, he'd felt powerful enough to try again, but as soon as he'd brushed her with his power, she'd flung him down a hallway and pinned him three feet above the floor, yelling, "Wicked children get no sweets!"

Still, it was hard to resist that gaping wound, no matter that it had sealed. He could feel her empty socket at his core, waiting. He crossed his arms to avoid reaching out to her with his mind. Maybe just a pat on the shoulder to show her that—

Her eye fixed on him with lightning quickness. "No one gets to touch me."

"Sorry."

"Naughty," she said, an impish smile curling her lips.

He tried to fit tighter to the corner. "Yep. Sorry, again."

"Oh, destiny." Her eye slipped shut as she stepped closer. "They will follow you. Peace, finally." She slammed a hand into the wall near his head, and he ducked away to the other side of the lift. She didn't follow, only leaned against the wall as if he was still standing there, and she was going to speak in his ear.

"Prepare for unleashed knowledge," she said. He would've sworn she'd said it right beside him, would have sworn that was her breath tickling his cheek.

The lift doors opened, and he leapt out, not caring where they were, not caring if it was open space. She looked over her shoulder with her empty socket as the doors shut again, and he knew it was watching him.

CHAPTER SEVEN

Cordelia fell into darkness. The vines withdrew, and she froze, waiting for claws or teeth. After several moments of silence, she felt around with one foot.

"Be at ease, metal skin," a voice said, a sibilant, drushkan hiss. "You are not harmed."

"Who are you?"

Soft light grew around them, revealing a bowl-like cavern with vines stretching across it like webs, exposing glowing moss as they moved. The mass of vines led to a solid base of wood that took up the whole of the cavern's ceiling. Not vines, then; the roots of a massive tree.

A drushkan silhouette sat atop a mass of undulating roots as if they were a throne. "I am Pool." She held out hands tipped with two poisonous claws. Her leaf-green hair and eyes nearly glowed in the soft light, and her deep brown skin had so many lines and arcs and whorls that she seemed tattooed all over. "Do you not recognize me, Sa?"

Cordelia froze, searching her memory. "No. Have we met?"

"I knew Jania, our Roshkikan."

"But that was two hundred years ago!"

Pool's mouth twitched into a smile. "I am a queen."

As if that answered everything. "Okay."

"Truly, you have not heard of me?"

"No, sorry. Where's Nettle? Is she okay?"

"The hunt leader's wounds are being tended. I thought that Roshkikan might have violated my request to leave me from her story.

I feared she might have written about me, at least to her kin. I am glad to hear she did not."

"Right." Cordelia nodded slowly. Should she bow? That didn't seem right. "Um, I'm honored to meet you." She looked at the green hair, remembered Nettle's words about Shiv one day being a queen. "I've met your daughter, I think, or at least your heir."

Pool inclined her head. "My often disobedient daughter." She rubbed the bridge of her nose, reminding Cordelia of Carmichael. "Do you have offspring?"

"No. I don't think I'm cut out for it."

"Ahya, only you could say. I was not supposed to breed. Sometimes, we must choose the unexpected path." She stood, and Cordelia had to look up at her, a thing she didn't often have to do. "Perhaps you can tell me, Sa, why humans have contacted my former family, those you call the old drushka."

Cordelia rolled her lips under and tried to re-summon any lessons Paul had given her on diplomacy. "Are you talking about the humans at the research station? Are you certain they contacted anyone? The old drushka could have attacked them for any reason."

"A good assumption, as she who was seventh during Roshkikan's time has become ninth."

When Pool stared at her, Cordelia shook her head. "Is that another test? I don't know what it means."

Pool chuckled softly. The roots lifted Cordelia's blade and sidearm from out of the mass and laid them in Pool's hands. "She really told her family nothing." Her gaze drifted over Cordelia's shoulder as if lost in the past.

"Just like I said." Cordelia tried to keep her voice neutral, but she was bruised and sore, she'd been attacked by boggins, and then she'd been pulled underground by a monster tree. Diplomacy was coming harder and harder. She eyed her weapons, but Pool held them loosely, not threatening. "Something you want to tell me?"

Pool strolled around the cavern, and the roots followed, coiling around her, stroking her waist, and hanging like large fringe from her leather shirt and trousers. "The seventh and the ninth are two queens of the old drushka. Before the drushka split, I was the first queen." She gestured above her to the massive tree. "I was Anushi, the sapling, youngest and smallest of the nine."

Cordelia's gaze flicked to the huge trunk. "Smallest?"

Pool flashed a grin. "The ninth is called the Shi, the leader of all our people, above all other queens and their tribes. The size of her tree is beyond your imagination." She trailed her long fingers down her roots. "Each queen has her own tree, and when a Shi dies, those queens below her move up to the next largest tree, so that each queen will one day be Shi." Her gaze went far away again. "All but me. When I split from them, I became the hole in their heart."

Cordelia nodded slowly, trying to picture it. "So, the queen who was in the seventh tree during my ancestor's time is now the ninth queen? And it's her turn as Shi?"

"Ahya, but we queens lead long lives, and so the seventh should not have become the Shi so quickly. But one of the queens died in tragedy. In a storm, so they say."

Cordelia shuffled her feet. If the Storm Lord had caused that, they might be in deep shit. "And to know that, you'd have to be in contact with the old drushka."

"I severed my mind from their call when I attached my tribe to the humans, but I still feel their pull. Sometimes, I hear their words, their lament." She pinned Cordelia in place with her cool gaze. "The new Shi hated Roshkikan and all your kind, and her fervor has not cooled. I fear she plots against you and hopes to draw me back into the fold."

"So, maybe she contacted the people at the research station. She could have pretended to be friends with the humans and then, what?" Cordelia shook her head. "Made some kind of pact with the boggins? I don't even know what people were doing out there." But Carmichael would. She might even have known that the research station was in contact with the old drushka. But why risk alienating the drushka who were already their allies? "Wouldn't the old drushka kill us on sight if they hate us so much?"

Pool spread her hands and shook her head, the gestures of two peoples. "I feel their ill intent. It was why I wanted to speak to you, Sa." She walked forward slowly, moving with effortless grace. Even above the smell of wet earth, she carried the scent of greenery in the sun. "If you cannot tell me why the humans were speaking with the old drushka, then perhaps you are split as we are. How strongly does the blood of Roshkikan run in you?"

Cordelia swallowed, wondering what Pool was asking. "All I can do is take this information back to Captain Carmichael. I don't make decisions for my people."

"And if I ask you not to tell your captain of me? That you only tell her you spoke to a drushkan leader?"

Cordelia tried to think of a way that could hurt her people and came up empty. "I can leave it out if you think it's necessary."

Pool wrinkled her nose. "What do the ambassadors say? For the betterment of diplomatic relations?"

Cordelia shrugged, but her mind was racing. If Carmichael had approved a meeting with the old drushka, and the old drushka were trying to suck Pool back into their fold, Pool certainly wouldn't want Carmichael *or* the old drushka to know where she was and what she knew. But now Cordelia had agreed to keep a secret from her captain, for the sake of the drushka. But if the humans were already keeping secrets, she supposed she owed them that for showing her the research station, for saving her life.

Blood of Roshkikan indeed.

Pool held the weapons forth, and Cordelia put them away as the roots danced around them both. "The chanuka are withdrawing." Pool looked upward as if she could feel it. She put a hand in a pouch hanging from her waist and brought forth a handful of bullets. "From the bodies."

Cordelia took them, breathing a sigh of relief. "Thank you. Will Nettle be coming with me?"

"When she recovers."

"Good, that's good. Glad to hear that."

Pool smiled, a look that grew as Cordelia cleared her throat and fought the urge to shift from foot to foot.

"She's, um, a good hunt leader," Cordelia said. And pretty sexy, but this wasn't the time for that thought.

Pool was still smiling. "Do you care for her?"

"I...haven't known her long."

"Sometimes it does not take long, or so I have observed."

"Well." And now what was she supposed to say?

"Roshkikan had a drushkan lover."

"She, uh, she wrote something about being close to the drushka, yeah."

"Close to?" Pool laughed. "Such tame words for such an intimate dance."

Cordelia just nodded. "So, time to go?"

Pool looked up and away again. "The *shawnessi* have sung Nettle's pain away. She will join you soon."

Cordelia took a slow look around but saw no one else. "Shawnessi? Sung the pain away?"

Pool touched her forehead. "Forgive me. You look so much like your ancestor, for a moment, I thought you the same." She lifted a hand, and the roots reached out.

Cordelia braced herself for the slide through the earth again, but it was mercifully quick. A new guide waited for her on the surface, a male who said that Higaroshi named him Smile. As they walked quickly through the trees toward the enclave, his happy-go-lucky nature reminded her of Liam, but he was still serious enough to watch for boggins. Maybe Pool would keep more of her warriors closer, to protect her. Maybe they'd send Higaroshi away, and all live together again, though why it was so important to keep Pool a secret, Cordelia didn't know.

They were determined; that was certain. Maybe Nettle had knocked the yafanai out for a deeper reason than just ensuring the drushka and humans were on even footing. Maybe she feared that yafanai telepaths could read drushkan minds and wanted to see if they'd spot an attack before it happened. Pool had communicated with someone who wasn't in the room. Maybe there were drushkan telepaths, too.

One of the dead men at the research station had worked with the yafanai but wasn't a yafanai himself. He could have been trying to figure out a way to listen for drushkan telepaths, and the old drushka had caught him at it.

And the boggins? How did they fit in? So far, they'd led her into a trap, set up two ambushes, and slaughtered a research station. They'd attacked in very large packs, armed more of their numbers, and had learned to throw their spears. Something had been done to them, something requiring a yafanai researcher. If toying with human minds could grant them powers, how much harder would it be to train boggin brains to be smarter?

"How many humans are there?" Smile asked softly.

Cordelia shook herself back to the present. "I don't know for certain. Why?"

"I hope to one day go to the human place, to your Gale, but there are other humans, ahya?"

"Yep, a lot more, living in other cities or villages. Do you want to be an ambassador like Reach?"

"Ahwa, no. I am not so knowing."

"Well, my uncle is the mayor of Gale. He could arrange for some of you to visit."

"The queen says better if we do not."

"Why?"

He spread his hands. "So the secret will stay."

"And why is the secret so important?"

A soft whistle made them turn, and Cordelia reached for her sidearm.

Nettle jogged up behind them, stern gaze flicking between them. "Too much talking. I could have killed you."

Smile grinned. "We were looking for chanuka, not drushka."

"Yeah," Cordelia said, "what he said."

Nettle stalked past them. "You should not speak so loudly."

"We'll try to keep it down," Cordelia said.

"Keep what down where?" Smile whispered.

"Our noise, or Nettle will remind us again."

"Ahya, I would rather hear it from her than from the chanuka."

Nettle grinned over her shoulder. They hurried to the enclave but arrived too late in the day to start out for Gale. Even with all her new questions, all the info she had to report, Cordelia didn't mind a chance to rest. At least she could take the damn armor off sooner.

She staked out a spot in the middle of the camp and shucked her armor piece by piece, piling it up on the ground and dumping her pack next to it.

Higaroshi sidled up to her with a non-convincing smile. "I see the leader didn't invite you to stay the night."

"That's right."

"Uh-huh." He crossed his arms and glanced around, rocking from foot to foot. "So, how was it?"

"Classified." She stared him down, stone-faced and leaning forward with implied menace, as if he was a new recruit.

He paled, lips shaking. "I'm sorry." He hurried away.

She chuckled, torn between the desire to collapse laughing and chase after him to calm him down. Instead, she sat, took a few rags from her pack, and started wiping the armor down, humming as she did.

Nettle sat on the other side of the armor pile, one arm resting on her knees while her long, sensuous fingers traced the edges of the armor plates.

"Fully healed?" Cordelia asked.

"Ahya." She didn't even have a scar where the spear had struck her. "Is your metal skin hot to wear?"

"Sometimes."

"Do other humans wear it besides your people?"

"No, Gale has all the armor from the first landing. It's one of the gifts from the Storm Lord."

"Your god. Are there other human gods?"

Cordelia shrugged, wondering where this was going. "Some people claim there are, but the Storm Lord's real. He controls the weather."

"None of my people knew of this god before the humans came."

"So, what do your people believe in? Like, how do the drushka believe this world was created?"

She spread her hands. "There was a great tree who grew too big and crumbled, becoming the world. Its seeds split open, spilling out the world's creatures, and new trees sprouted from the bark of the old."

A nice enough idea, even though their great tree would have to have been growing in space. Still, she didn't want to go poking Nettle's beliefs. She finished cleaning one plate and set it aside, and the pile between them grew shorter. Nettle leaned back on her elbows, one leg cocked up. Cordelia kept hearing Pool in her head saying, "intimate dance."

She tried to think of any of her old lines, but she couldn't invite Nettle out for a drink or give her a little gift she'd "just happened upon." She had the strangest urge to fall sideways and rest her head on Nettle's long torso.

Nettle caught her glance and looked away quickly, smiling. Then she frowned and knocked one hand against the ground. "You must know, Sa, I do not like lying."

Cordelia kept cleaning, waiting for more, her libido briefly suspended.

"No drushka likes speaking falsehoods, but I do not like when I must keep from saying a thing, as when I had to say leader instead of queen. It has the feel of lying to it."

"A lie of omission, we call it."

Nettle's gaze locked on hers again. "Do you know of the scent?"

"*The* scent?"

"I have never encountered it, but some drushka tell stories." She spread her hands. "They say humans sometimes wish to mate with drushka because of this scent, that it makes drushka tempting to certain humans, very much so. I had to speak of it to you, so that you know that when you look at me, it could be the scent instead of—"

"You think this scent is controlling me? That I'm irresistibly attracted to you because of the way you smell?" Now that would be embarrassing, but in their brief time together, there'd been a few looks going the other way as well. Maybe Nettle just wasn't willing to admit it.

"I thought we should speak before you were tempted."

"To what? Lose control?" When she didn't answer, Cordelia leaned over, stopping a hair's breadth from her neck, and inhaled deeply, moving until they could stare eye-to-eye. "You do smell nice, but I can keep myself in check. If one of us is tempted, maybe it's you."

The nictitating membrane at the corner of Nettle's eyes twitched, and her mouth hung open a fraction, just enough for a glint of sharp teeth. "I wanted you to know of it before anyone lost anything at all."

With a slow smile, Cordelia straightened and went back to cleaning her armor. Nettle moved away, and Cordelia watched her go, but now she had doubts. What if nothing Cordelia felt for her was real? But wasn't all attraction just random chemicals? Did it matter if some of them were alien?

Shiv plopped down in front of her. "Are you speaking to your metal skin? Can it hear you?"

"No, I was grumbling out loud."

"About what?"

Cordelia paused. This was probably the most willing source of information she'd get. "Do you know anything about the scent?"

"Ahya. The elders say it makes your people have the liking of my people. Why?" Her eyes grew wide, and she clapped. "Do you have the liking of someone? Ah! Is it me?" She wrinkled her nose so hard her face seemed to turn inward.

Cordelia sputtered a laugh. "No, sorry."

Shiv slapped her thighs. "I would like a human lover. Who is it you want?"

"I just wanted to know if the scent was real or not."

"Only you could say. Do you have the liking of many drushka?"

"Just one, and now I'm not sure about her."

"Tell me who. If she is ugly, it is the scent."

Cordelia sighed and leaned forward. Shiv leaned in as well until their faces almost touched, grinning. "Nettle."

Shiv sat back, tapping her chin. "The hunt leader does have a nice stride. She is too hard at times, too much the tree. She will not let me do as I please."

Yep, that punch, that smile, that take-no-shit attitude, even the way she'd struck first and asked questions later. Yum.

Shiv poked her in the arm but kept the claw curled into her palm. "You do have the liking. I see it in your face. Ashki is her name, as the drushka say."

Cordelia said it in her head but not out loud, not yet. "How do you know what a human looks like when she 'has the liking'?"

"Higaroshi used to look at a drushka that way, but she had the liking of someone else."

"Was he affected by the scent?"

"Who can say? Listen, Sa." She grabbed Cordelia's shoulders and put on a serious face. "Do not let it stop you."

"I never said I would."

"You should speak to others and see if you have the liking of them, too. Then you will see it is not the scent, and you can bite the hunt leader's ears all you want." She stood and smacked one fist into her palm, face set in steely resolve. "Then you can make the hunt leader take me to the human lands, and I can find my lover. Ah, Sa! We will sing stories to each other then!"

Cordelia sighed. Seeing if she was attracted to any other drushka was worth a shot, but she wasn't up to biting anyone's ears just yet.

The next morning, Nettle's band escorted Cordelia toward Gale, traveling swiftly along the ropy branches. Cordelia split her time among the drushka, mingling even with those who didn't speak Galean. She excavated the few drushkan words Paul had taught her from the depths of her memory, and with a little pantomime, she could communicate well enough.

Some were standoffish, some talkative. Most were attractive enough, she supposed, but none as much as their hunt leader with her sideways smile. None of them seemed inclined to talk about the queen or the boggins. Maybe someone had told them to keep their mouths shut, another lie of omission.

As she watched them, Cordelia thought of how humans would have called the scent love at first sight or soul mates or some other crap. Leave it to the less technologically advanced species to reduce it to chemistry. Whatever it was, she forced herself to keep her mind on her feet rather than her fantasies. They camped for the night on another sparse patch of ground, and Cordelia curled up to sleep alone.

They followed the Oosjani Road the next day, coming ever closer to solid ground. One of the scouts reported an armored paladin waiting just outside the swamp, and Cordelia was left to advance alone, the drushka preferring to hide during first meetings. When Cordelia spotted Liam waiting for her, she grinned, waving.

Liam waved back as Cordelia jogged through the sparse trees. His heart relaxed to see her. She could take care of herself better than anyone he knew, but still, he worried. He'd been surprised when his mother didn't send her any backup, but she trusted Cordelia, something she'd never say about her own son.

"Don't tell me you've marched through the swamp by yourself!" he called. "Did the drushka abandon you, or did you scare them off?"

She slapped his shoulder, the armor too bulky for hugs. Her dark brown eyes sparkled as she grinned. "They're around. They like to watch first."

"Kinky. What did you find out?"

"I'll give my full report to your mom, don't worry."

"She'll end up telling me, you know that, probably while yelling at me for something else."

"My squad get back okay?"

"Without incident. So, give us a hint. Where are the drushka hiding?" He glanced around, thought of everything he knew about the drushka, including their arboreal nature, and glanced straight up.

A green-haired drushka lay on a branch some ways above his head, the bright sparkle of its green eyes giving it away as alive. He followed the lines of its sleek body to where its hands curled around the branch, middle fingers tipped with poisonous claws, a female.

She rolled from the branch and landed on another, just beside him, without a sound. Cordelia didn't seem to notice, but Liam couldn't take his eyes off her. Tiny shells sown along the edges of her leather sleeves glinted in the sun. She lowered her face, twisting side to side like a serpent, hypnotizing him.

Liam liked to think he could resist his nature, resist all the pretty men and women who crossed his path, but they lingered inside him and treaded across his senses, and he always gave in, could no more resist them than he could resist breathing.

The drushka didn't tread. She charged, her brightness clouding his vision, the woody scent of her lodging in his throat like candy. Her face hung in front of him, and he memorized the marks upon her dark brown skin. He tilted his face up, just to say hello, but she darted forward and took his lower lip between her sharp teeth. She bit down slightly, a row of sweet agony. He shuddered and closed his eyes.

"Liam," someone said, maybe the voice of God.

"Yes, Lord?"

Cordelia turned him roughly. "Wake the fuck up!"

He shrugged out of her grasp. "What?"

She gave him a nasty look, her cheeks a little pink, but he never saw the point in shame, not anymore. Rustling leaves made him turn. The green-haired drushka stood on the ground now, beside another female with short red hair.

"Forgive us, please," the red-haired one said. Her hand was wrapped around the upper arm of the green-haired one as if holding her back.

"No need to apologize." Liam grinned. "I'm Liam Carmichael."

When the drushka didn't speak, Cordelia cleared her throat. "I call them Nettle and Shiv. They like to let other people name them."

Liam's grin widened, and he winked at the green-haired drushka. "I'm guessing you're named after the knife."

She tossed her head, her gaze kicking him in the gut. "Ahya."

"Let's get moving," Cordelia said. "Nettle, are you coming with us?"

"Ahwa. We will remain in the swamp."

Shiv glared, her mouth a thin, angry line.

Liam opened his mouth to argue, but Cordelia gave him a look of pure buzzkill, and he shut up.

"Will you tell Reach of all that has happened?" Nettle asked.

"I'll tell my captain," Cordelia said, "and then she'll decide what to do, but I'll mention that you want Reach to know."

"Then we will send word on our own," Nettle said.

Liam winked at Shiv again. "I know just the messenger."

She licked her teeth, but Cordelia tugged on Liam's arm.

"Good-bye, then," Cordelia said, "and thanks." She marched Liam along, her face twisting between lots of emotions. It burned in him to ask about everything that had happened, but she'd talk when she was ready. He was happy to let her lead, giving him plenty of chances to look over his shoulder.

CHAPTER EIGHT

Cordelia hustled Liam out of the thick woods, practically towing him toward Gale to keep his feet moving.

He whistled, still casting looks over his shoulder though Shiv had been lost from view for some time. "I never thought anyone could be so intoxicating."

Cordelia fought visions of Nettle and failed. "According to them, there's a smell that makes them irresistible, like a drug or something."

"And it makes you want to have sex with them?"

"I'm not sure how it works or even if I believe it."

"Finally! Ever since I hit puberty, Captain Mom's been telling me I'm weak-willed, can't say no to some down and dirty sex. Now all I have to do is date drushka, and she can't hold me responsible."

"So, you want some alien sweat gland dictating your behavior?"

"Eh, being in love feels like being drunk anyway." He eyed her, smiling. "How did you find out about this smell?"

She shrugged, but his grin was inching up, forcing hers to do the same.

"What did you do, Delia? Or should I say, whom did you do?" When she shrugged, he cried, "Drushka lover! One trip to the swamp, and your trousers fall right off."

"Look who's talking! You fuck anything that looks at you twice."

"Anytime. Anywhere. So..." He prodded her arm.

"I'm not telling you shit."

"Oh." He put a hand to his chest and staggered as if she'd shot him. "Here I am, at the threshold of knowing everything there is to know about sex, and you deny me the final piece: sex with an alien?

You should feel happy, nay, honored, at the chance to complete my bevy of knowledge."

She sputtered a laugh. "Complete your bevy by yourself. I didn't have sex with one. It wasn't even a near thing."

He rested a hand on her shoulder. "Tell me what happened, and I'll tell you where you fucked up."

She slapped his hand away but told him all the personal things, knowing he wouldn't repeat it and knowing he'd sympathize where she needed him to. Their talk lasted all the way to Gale and through it, him nodding all the while and clutching her shoulder when she told him about the prog.

"I'm fine," she said. "I'm alive."

He nodded but the tightness in his face spoke volumes.

When she told him about Nettle, he said, "If she doesn't want you, her loss. There are plenty of lovely ladies to choose from."

She gave him a sideways grin. "Like Shiv?"

"If she ever comes to Gale or I go to the swamp, I am making my play, sweat glands or not."

"I admire your tenacity. Listen, I'm going to report before I change, get it over with. Meet you at the pub?"

"I'll go with you to Captain Mom's office."

"She's not going to let you in."

"That's okay." He followed her into the keep and up the stairs, and she wondered if it was her near-death experience that made him unable to leave her side.

"Liam, I'm fine. She's going to yell at you."

"She doesn't need an excuse to do that." He knocked on the captain's door.

"Busy!" Carmichael yelled.

"Guess I'm getting changed first," Cordelia muttered.

Liam leaned around her. "Lieutenant Ross is back from the swamp." He waited a heartbeat. "Captain."

The door flew inward, and Carmichael raked the two of them with her gaze. "Ross, inside. Lieutenant Carmichael, since you clearly don't know the meaning of the word 'busy,' report back here in an hour so I can educate you."

Liam's salute was crisp enough to make any superior officer

proud. Cordelia slipped inside the office, and Carmichael slammed the door so hard, the walls rattled.

"Report."

Cordelia told her of the cages, the dead boggins and humans, the theories of the drushka, and how the drushkan leader thought that the humans had contacted the old drushka. She kept Pool and her tree out of it, though she thought of them often, reliving the feel of the roots pulling her underground.

Carmichael paced slowly, showing every expression from thoughtful to thunderous. "Conclusions?"

"I think those researchers were doing something to the boggins, maybe with drushkan help, maybe at the request of the yafanai."

Carmichael lifted one eyebrow but didn't offer anything. Cordelia couldn't shake the feeling that she knew exactly what had gone on out there. Now everyone involved was dead.

"Captain, am I right?"

"Oh, I'm sorry, Lieutenant. I forgot I was supposed to report to you." She paused, tapping her chin as if thinking. "Oh wait. I'm not."

Cordelia swallowed. "No, Captain."

"Are you sure? You are a member of the esteemed Ross clan, niece of our mayor. Are you sure you're not in charge?"

"Yes, Captain."

"So glad to hear it. Now, with your permission, you're dismissed."

On her way out, Cordelia said, "The drushka asked if their ambassador could be kept in the loop."

"And what did you say?"

"I said it would be up to you."

"Well, thanks for that. Dismissed. Again."

Cordelia stood outside the door, took a deep breath, and wondered if that was what Carmichael looked like when she felt guilty. But she was the captain. Even if she'd made a plan and it had gone sideways, she didn't owe anyone an explanation.

Even if it fucked up relations with the drushka? This could be the end of their alliance with Pool, and then everyone in the swamp would be intent on killing them. Carmichael might only have to answer to the Storm Lord, but she would have to answer.

Liam waited on the stairs. Before he could speak, she said, "We've got time for a drink before you have to report. Let me get the hell out of this armor and do a quick scrub-down."

"Naked pub visit. I like it."

"Depending on how tired I am after I peel this shit off, it might happen."

He followed her to the barracks, and they both stripped, though Cordelia didn't know if Liam was off-duty yet. As she scrubbed in the washroom, she decided it didn't matter. He seemed to think that if he was going to be in trouble anyway, he might as well make it worse.

"How was your talk with Captain Mom?" he asked.

"As you'd expect."

"So, are we getting blind stinking drunk to help you recover?"

She snorted a laugh. "A quick glass. You have an appointment, remember?"

"But if I'm drunk, maybe she'll finally…" He chuckled. "I don't know."

"Just follow orders. It's not that hard!" Easy to say, but she was the one keeping secrets. She shook the thought away. "Come on. One small drink to strengthen your spirits, go take your licks from Captain Hardass, then we'll drink until we're intimately acquainted with the floor."

He grinned. "I take back every bad thing I've ever said about you. You have the best ideas."

❖

Carmichael stared at where the transmitter was hidden. The Storm Lord had already told her to handle his mess, and he'd probably tell her the same now, even after his scheme had gone cockeyed, and everyone associated with it was dead.

No. *She'd* gotten those people together. *She'd* ordered them not to tell their families where they were going. *She'd* given them permission to contact the old drushka without informing the drushkan ambassador, and *she'd* passed them information and boxes of tech from the Storm Lord. *She'd* known it was too dangerous. And it hadn't been faith that made her do it. Her thoughts had been filled with the promise of metal and everything else a slew of augmented boggin servants could get them.

Anger stung her temples, and she went from pacing to stalking the room like a cage. She lifted the false wall. She could bash the transmitter to pieces, never take orders from that bastard again, but what hell would that bring down on their heads?

"Fuck!" She slammed the false wall back into place.

Running footsteps paused outside her door, and she waited for a knock, anything to turn her wrath on, but the steps bled away again.

Now the boggins had escaped, and humanity had one new enemy, maybe two, if the old drushka had been leading them into a trap the whole time. Maybe three enemies, if their drushkan allies decided they'd been betrayed.

Carmichael sat at her desk and pulled out some parchment. Deal with it? Well, he could bet his ass she was going to deal with it, her way. She'd put it right.

She listed her soldiers, dividing them into squads. Cordelia Ross would lead one. A good soldier, and the troops liked her. If Carmichael had her way, Ross would be her successor to the captaincy. She jotted down Brown and Lea at the heads of their own squads, even as she wished she could replace them with her son.

But Liam couldn't lead a squad. She'd raised him after his father ran for the hills, and she knew everything he wasn't capable of. She'd wanted him to follow in her footsteps, wanted to be the first captain in Calamity's history to pass her position to her child. But no, he fucked up as often as he could and then smirked about it. She should have tossed him out on his ass long ago but couldn't make herself do it. What would become of him? A long slide into alcohol and sex until he became a waste of oxygen?

Not while she drew breath. As tough as she'd been on him, maybe she hadn't been tough enough. When he swaggered into her office a half hour late and tipsy, she wondered when he'd lost his fear of her. "You're disgusting, Lieutenant."

He paused, halfway to sitting, then eased down. "That has occurred to me."

"Why can't you do as you're told, boy?"

"And what have I done wrong now, O Captain?"

Carmichael slammed the desk and surged out of her seat. He leaned back, and she kept her angry mask, happy she could still scare him.

"You only obey when you want to. I'm surprised you met Ross at the swamp instead of drinking yourself into a stupor."

"I care about her, and I wanted to find out what happened at the research station."

Hope bloomed in her that he might be taking an interest. "Ross said you met some of the drushka."

"Two of them, briefly."

"Thoughts? Impressions?"

"They were very...attractive."

Hope sank to the pit of her stomach. "Are you serious?"

"Well—"

"The aliens weren't put here to be one of your conquests!"

"I didn't say that!"

"Oh, you don't have to explain how you fuck everything that moves, how you're looking to leave a swath of bastards in your wake just as your father did. Do you need the company?"

He didn't speak, only stared with nostrils flaring.

"You're on cleaning detail for the rest of your life. Get out of my office."

He left without a word, and Carmichael barely resisted throwing something at the closed door. She went back to her list and put her son under Lieutenant Ross's command. It seemed the only place for him.

Cordelia stumbled down the street, leaning on Liam as he leaned on her. It had gotten dark while they'd been in the Pickled Prog, later than she'd thought. After Liam had returned from the captain's office, Cordelia had thought it best to get as drunk as they could as fast as they could. As the pinched, angry look had slipped from Liam's face, replaced by drunken bliss, she'd known she'd made the right decision.

There were still lights flickering in the Prog, not quite closing time, but their loud rants about "barrels of piss" had gotten them tossed out on their ears.

Liam mumbled snatches of a song in Cordelia's ear. She'd already gone through the bliss stage, and now the haze was beginning to clear. A headache built in her temples, and her face hurt. The streets had gone dark with shadows, and every hard edge reminded her of the prog's teeth, making her hands twitch.

"*And I will always be yours,*" Liam sang, "*and you'll be mine.*" He looked at her, song failing as he peered at her in the glow of the streetlamps. "Ooh, someone is angry."

"Shut up." She left him to stumble along on his own, but he caught up with her quickly.

"You're mad because…because…" He blinked slowly. "Because you couldn't get laid in the swamp!"

"Shut your face, Liam. I mean it."

"If that's not it, tell me why. Tell me. Tell me, tell me, tell me, tell me—"

"Fuck off!" Her head swam, and she had to take a deep breath. "All this crap with the drushka, and no one will say what's going on." She rolled her shaky hands into fists. "Fucking tree grabbed me." But she wasn't supposed to be talking about that. "Fucking prog tried to eat me. Goddamned parents died."

He squeezed her shoulders. "You can't die because I love you." He held her at arm's length, and she didn't know which of them was swaying. "Please, please, please don't die."

"Okay."

Tears swam in his eyes. "I mean it. If you die, I'll burn this fucking town to ashes!"

"No, you won't. Shut up." She pulled him to her, and they staggered along again.

"Why am I crying? We should celebrate!" He looked around. "I know what we should do. We have to find someone."

"Stop it." But her pulse quickened. There was one cure for black moods that was better than any drink, but they hadn't done it in years.

"I know what Cordelia wants," he said in a singsong.

"No!" But by the Storm Lord, she wanted it bad. She couldn't encourage him, though. That wasn't how this game was played.

A group of voices echoed up the empty street. Liam picked up speed. A group of people, drovers by their dress, gathered under a streetlamp, their laughter bouncing off dark storefronts. Cordelia tried to catch Liam, but he'd already spotted them. Her pounding heart drove away visions of the prog, Pool's roots, or her parents. The song of battle always cleaned out the corners of her mind.

"Oh yes, oh yes, oh yes!" Liam said.

"Don't." But it sounded halfhearted, even to her.

"Hey, you hoshpi fuckers!" Liam shouted to the drovers.

They turned as a pack and glanced at one another.

"Get the hell off my street!"

Cordelia took a deep breath. It could still be stopped, and if it could, it should. Those were the rules. "He's drunk," she yelled.

"Shit, no. I'm just reeling from the fumes coming off these dirty bastards." Liam threw a grin over his shoulder and kept walking. He wanted this as much as her. The drinks might dull his mother's words, but this could erase them.

One of the drovers stepped up, hand out. He said something soothing to the drover pack, and then called, "We don't want any trouble." Ah, the Peacekeeper.

Liam pointed at him. "I want you animal-smelling fuckers to get out of my sight and go back where you belong, on your knees behind your animals, pumping away."

Brows darkened further, casting faces with more shadows. Cordelia expected someone to step around the Peacekeeper and take on the role of the Puncher, but as sometimes happened, the Peacekeeper's face contorted into rage, and the Puncher was born.

Liam took the first hit in the chin, rocking back on his heels. He shook his head. "Not in the face, please. Your daddy likes my pretty smile."

The Puncher hit him again, right in the gut. One of the others kneed him in the groin, sending him to the ground. The rest laughed.

Cordelia couldn't move, not yet. He'd insulted them, and they'd delivered a couple of hits. He'd been expecting that. Well, maybe not the shot to the nuts. But now he was down, and they could walk away, but if they chose not to…

The drovers teetered and swayed, calling insults. It seemed as if they might leave, but the Puncher turned back, and the others egged him on. He lifted Liam by the shirtfront, free hand curling into a fist. Cordelia's feet began to move.

Liam coughed a laugh. "Oh, my new friend, you have done it now!"

Cordelia hit the drover hard, sending him flying. The others leapt for her, the one who'd kneed Liam throwing an arm around her neck, but a quick elbow to the gut threw him off.

The others seemed to move through sap, so clumsy in the face of her training. All she knew about combat came boiling out in an explosive rush, so terrible and joyful to be used. A grin stretched her face, making it hurt in a different way. Liam rocketed to his feet, always a good one for taking a punch.

One of the drovers launched a haymaker. She ducked and came up with an open palm to his jaw. He fell, but someone else kicked her in the crotch from behind.

The ache spread through her core. "Son of a bitch!" She spun, grabbed a drover—the same one that had kicked Liam—and pulled him closer.

"Lemme go, lemme go," he squealed.

"Let's see." She kneed him in the groin. "How you." And again. "Like it!" One final time, and his face squeezed so far shut he looked like a wrinkled fruit. She tossed him away and caught another coming for her, the Puncher. She slammed her forehead against his nose, feeling it crumple and spread blood across her hairline. He fell like a rag doll.

Cordelia punched another drover as she ran past. When she staggered and tried to swing back, Cordelia hit her again. The rest were lying still or long gone. All were breathing, no one with a broken bone except for a nose. It would have been easy to snap fingers or destroy knees, but where was the fun in that?

"Are you all right?" she asked Liam as they turned for home again.

"Just bruised."

"I hate it when you do that."

"Liar, liar. We both need this."

"Blow me."

"As you wish, so shall I provide." He made as if to drop to his knees.

She pushed him to keep walking. "Not even if I really wanted it. I got kicked, too."

"So? You don't have balls."

"Still hurts, asshole."

"I bet if drushka girl were here, you'd let her downstairs."

She snorted a laugh. "She could come around that corner with gifts of candied fruit and fully charged armor, and I would shut the door in her face."

"Wow. That must really hurt."

"Damn straight." She hugged him from the side, planted a kiss on his temple, and steered them toward the keep.

CHAPTER NINE

Usk tracked the chanuka through the swamp, watching them from the high branches. The ninth queen, the mighty Shi, had told him that the creatures had become smarter. As he watched them chatter and rut, the host of smaller ones flocking around the large, they seemed the same disgusting, mud-eating chanuka they had always been, born below the branches and meant to stay there.

But they seemed more alert, as the queen said. He had gathered them for the humans, at the queen's order, and the humans had done something to them. Now their journey through the swamp, revisiting the place where the humans had imprisoned them, seemed to have some purpose. Maybe they mourned where so many of their kind had died. Maybe they celebrated their escape from the brittle cages. Maybe they plotted. Only the Shi knew.

The wind shifted, and the chanuka fell quiet. Usk knew they'd scented him and his band. If they were the same as they had been, they would have fled. Instead, these smarter chanuka gathered in large circles, the better to see in every direction. Before, they had been somewhat clever, hunting in packs, using broken branches as spears, but now they seemed to have...purpose. They took up their spears and howled, a beastly noise that might flush prey from hiding.

But he was not prey. He signaled to his band to stay where they were and handed his weapon to Nata, his second. "Be ready."

She had her own weapon out, eyes on the chanuka. Usk stepped into the open and clapped his hands. Several chanuka hurled spears, and he leaned out of the way. They had learned to throw their weapons. Clever. The largest female chanuka bellowed at the others, and they held their spears in front of them. It seemed they had also learned to obey.

The Shi had warned Usk they might attack, but that he must find a way to communicate. He held his palms up to show he had no weapon. The large female growled at her fellows, and no more spears flew. Usk descended slowly, warily, but they let him climb down unharmed.

He reached the female's branch and held his hands up again. She shuffled forward, snarling but waiting. He opened his belt-pouch with painstaking slowness and took out the sticks the Shi had shaped for him. He knelt and arranged them on the branch: a circle for a head, a long stick for a body, smaller ones for arms and legs.

The chanuka cocked her head, eyestalks white around their bases as she strained. She grunted, and those behind her shifted, snuffling. She waved at them, and they quieted. Her stare at Usk seemed to say, "And? What now?"

Usk took a final item from his pouch, a piece of metal pilfered from the human settlement in the swamp. He placed it over the figure's body, and the chanuka took a half-step forward and licked her lips.

He laid a bit of dried grass over the figure and showed the chanuka his fire lighters: two sticks, one slotted. He rubbed them just so until the grass ignited. The fire consumed the stick figure in moments, even under the metal that protected it.

The chanuka watched with unblinking eyes. She prodded the blackened spot with her spear before looking to Usk again.

He swept the remains of the fire into the water and laid the fire lighters on the limb. With one final show of his unarmed hands, Usk backed away and climbed high, whistling for his tribe.

B46 peered at the sticks, at the blackened spot. She sniffed where the hard, foul-smelling stuff had been, the same substance that some tall creatures draped over their bodies like shining skin. Her spear couldn't hurt it before, but now she knew how to get inside.

She'd known fire in the before times. Her people had learned to fear it as it streaked from the sky, blasting trees to pieces and eating and eating until water killed it. But this tall creature had taken fire from these sticks, fire enough to eat wood, even inside the shining skin.

Her mates gathered around her. If she moved her hands as the tall creature had, she could make fire, control it. She rumbled deep inside, her happiest sound, and heard it spread to her mates and children. Oh, this was good.

But the tall creatures would not wait and watch fire be born. Those who lived inside the swamp could kill it with water. Best to save it for those who lived outside the trees, those her mates had followed. They gathered far from the water, made their nest far from the trees.

Perhaps the creatures who'd given her fire wanted her to leave the swamp, but she was not finished here. She thought of the roots that had stolen her prey before. There were still many creatures to kill there, more that gathered far from the bothersome roots. Better for the children to cut their teeth in their home, no matter what these creatures wanted her to do.

She would make a plan for the other nest, the place of the shining skin. And she would need more children. They would need room to breed, and perhaps they could find other creatures in the swamp to aid them.

❖

Lydia sat up in bed, gasping. She hadn't followed random futures in her sleep since she was a novice, still trying to master her power, but the many minds she'd touched in her dreams had all carried a common future that towed her along. All of them, one by one, had been engulfed in flames that roared through Gale like a winter wind.

The dreams were already fading, faces gone, details drifting away. She closed her eyes and told herself it could have been a simple dream.

Beside her, Freddie shifted, and Lydia eased from the bed. Dim light peeked around the shutters, dawn or just before. If fire was in Gale's future, the dreams would keep happening. She could run through the town, warning everyone, but it wouldn't do any good. The future couldn't be changed. A great fire would take who it would, and nothing she could do would stop it.

Freddie curled on her side, a tiny smile on her full lips. Lydia could follow her future, but changing it would still be impossible. If she decided they should run from Gale, then she would see them running. If

Freddie refused to go, Lydia would see that, too, and whatever she saw would be the way that it happened.

And if she saw Freddie die? Lydia shuddered. She'd be forced to march toward that fate, waiting for it, letting it color everything that happened to them before then. She crept back into bed, curled around Freddie, and kissed her forehead. Better not to know.

CHAPTER TEN

Dillon watched the planet again, and it felt as if the whole station was waiting, but for what he didn't know. It had been nearly three weeks since Marie had turned the others against him, but things still hadn't gone back to normal. Hurried conversations turned to whispers or petered out when he entered a room, and when the breachies had to share the mess hall with him, their glances were almost predatory.

Lazlo had told him of Dué's odd behavior, but when was she not odd? More unnerving, Marie had visited the botanical habitat since then, and she didn't need cell regeneration yet. She'd said she'd come to check on Lazlo, though she'd never done so before. Dillon knew she was snooping, but Lazlo's work seemed undisturbed. It didn't matter. Even if Marie found out about the swamp creatures or the yafanai, what could she do?

Send him floating out with Lessan? No, never. Marie's breachie cronies were a bunch of sycophantic fucks, but murderers? He couldn't see that. Unless they'd gone as crazy as Dué, or they managed to convince Dué to kill him. Even in all of his fight fantasies, Dillon never imagined going against her.

Imprison him? What would be the point? He supposed they could try to drive him out of his fucking skull, but he already felt that way half the time, had been feeling that way for a long time, and it was getting worse.

No, there was a third option. Exile. Goose bumps sprang up over his arms as he moved closer to his window. They could send him down to the planet, watch him wither and age, all of them immortal as long as they had Lazlo.

Dillon shook his head and told himself not to be so paranoid. They were punishing him; that was all, freezing him out. And if he was getting jumpy, that meant they were winning. It was just more of their bullshit, more games they had to play to keep from being so bored all the time.

His door chimed, and he stared, wondering if this was it.

"Dillon?" Lazlo's voice.

Dillon had to laugh at himself. "Come on in, Laz."

The door slid open. "Do you want to get some coffee?" Lazlo had been sticking to him like glue lately. He'd felt the shift in the winds, too, but he'd never been comfortable anywhere.

"Have a seat, Laz."

Lazlo sat slowly. "What's going on? You look more irritated than usual."

"You know something's up."

"Please don't tell me you're letting the breachies get to you."

"It's different this time."

Lazlo didn't bother to argue, but he picked at his sleeves, a true tell if there ever was one.

"Can you tell where they are right now?"

Lazlo sighed but closed his eyes. "I expect they're scattered like they usually…" He frowned, head turning.

Dillon's heart thumped harder, and he licked his lips. "What?"

"Well, the breachies are often in groups."

"But now they're *all* together."

"Yes."

"Even Christian and Marlowe."

Lazlo opened his eyes. "And Dué."

Oh shit. "I told you they were plotting something."

"With *Dué*? No, this has to be some kind of coincidence."

"We have to know what's going on in that room."

"Why wouldn't they call me?"

"Come on, Laz. They know we're friends."

Lazlo frowned so hard Dillon bit back a laugh. "You mean they think I do whatever you say whenever you wave your hand!" Lazlo said.

No, it took a lot more than hand waving most of the time, but Dillon didn't mention that. "They just see you as life support."

"Bastards."

Dillon nodded. "Can you sense anything from them?"

"I can't risk scanning the lieutenants or Dué. The others seem agitated. Marie seems gratified. There's lots of high emotions, lots of adrenaline."

"They're about to act."

"Dillon, we don't *know* anything!"

"I do. I know." But he wasn't going to let them get away with it. He'd fight. He'd fuck up the satellite if he had to. He'd space them all!

But, a little voice inside him said, why should he let it come to that? There were other options, far more satisfying ones. Certainty flooded him, greater than he'd ever known. They were plotting to exile him, and he was going to let them, but not like they thought. "If anyone tries to listen to us, can you block them?"

"Not directly. I mean, I could attack the source of their power, but—"

"If they try to hear us, even on the sneak, would you know?"

"Definitely."

"Good. Tell me if they try. Come on." Dillon strode past, not waiting to see if Lazlo would follow because of course he would.

"Where are we going?"

"Botanical habitat."

"What for?"

"They're going to send me to the planet, Laz. That's what their little meeting is about. I've read mutiny reports. I know what it looks like." The lift opened, and they hurried inside.

"You are jumping to conclusions," Lazlo said.

Dillon took his shoulders. "All of them meeting together? You know I'm right."

Lazlo's face shifted through expressions, disbelieving to horrified, and finally, his cheeks flushed with anger again. "I won't let them."

Dillon patted his shoulders, touched. "Don't try to stop them." The doors opened at the habitat, and Dillon strode out, pounding down the steps. "I've just got a few things to take care of first."

"I could stand in their way! They wouldn't do anything to me. I'm too valuable to them."

Dillon gathered all the yafanai-maker plants and threw them into the incinerator. "Where are your notes?"

"In my…" When he trailed away, Dillon looked. Lazlo was staring at his console in horror. "I logged out before I left."

Dillon nodded slowly. "Someone's broken into your files." Luckily, Lazlo had created his files so they couldn't be copied. Anyone who wanted to access them would have to use this console. Dillon laid his palm flat on it and pumped electricity over the surface until the console crackled and popped, surface splintering into a spiderweb of cracks.

Lazlo stared at it, stricken, as if his child had died. Dillon gripped his arm. "I'm sorry, Laz. You won't need it anymore. Gather up anything else about the yafanai and chuck it. They won't get your research."

Lazlo slammed his hands on the table, his eyes shiny, face bright and angry. God, Dillon didn't want to see him cry. "You're just going to let them—"

Dillon barked a laugh. "Grab any of the drug you've already harvested, as well as any seeds, and come on."

❖

Lazlo had tears in his eyes, but he tried to fight them down. Dillon hated tears, and Lazlo didn't want their last few moments together tainted by too much emotion.

Last moments together? What the hell was happening? Someone had broken into his console; that was a fact. Dillon was convinced everyone was turning on him, and everyone's secretive behavior the past weeks seemed to back him up. But exile? There had to be another explanation, and if there wasn't, there had to be some way to stop it.

Dillon seemed almost happy. His jaw was firm with resolve, eyes glittering with life. He had a mischievous smile on his face. As they hurried from the botanical habitat, Lazlo told himself he would help fight the others, if it came to that. They couldn't just turn on Dillon and get away with it.

But with every step, his knees grew weaker and his vision hazy. He wasn't a fighter, damn it! "Dillon, where are we going?"

"I'm taking one of the pods and getting the fuck out of here."

Lazlo stumbled. "You're giving them what they want?"

"No, Laz, I'm taking charge of my own fate before someone

decides it for me. They'd hurl me down to the ground with nothing. I'm taking what's mine and getting ahead of them." Dillon gave him another fond smile, and Lazlo returned it, but his heart was pounding, and he didn't know what to do. He couldn't think.

They made it to the hangar, and Dillon started fiddling with the controls in one of the pods, a bigger version of the little drop-and-carries he used to send supplies. This one could carry a person, as many as four by the look.

"Dillon—"

"Hmm?"

But what could he say. Good-bye? I'll miss you? Kiss me, you fool? He felt a gathering of many heartbeats, all converging on the hangar. "They're coming."

"I need a little more time."

"Okay." Lazlo took a deep, shuddering breath and turned toward the doors. He kept telling himself that the others wouldn't hurt him, and even if they did, he could fix anything.

Then why was he shaking so badly?

They came in as a pack, Marlowe and Christian leading the way with Marie just behind them, and the others huddled close by, all but Dué.

"Naos," her voice said in his mind, and he knew she was watching. "Why don't you ever call me by the right name, Simon Lazlo?"

Lazlo licked his lips and tried to stare everyone down. "Go...go away."

"Come out, Storm Lord," Marie called.

Lazlo tightened his jaw as they stared past him. He pulled himself straighter, lining up a row of Dillon's favorite swears in his head.

Dillon put a hand on his shoulder and stepped out. "What's this? The villagers come to roust the evil monster out of the castle?"

Marie leaned forward, and Lazlo wondered why she hated Dillon so much. *When* she'd started to hate him like this. A miasma of power hung around her, a greater power than hers. "You've dug your own grave," she said. "We know about those creatures you've tampered with."

Dillon sighed, and Lazlo felt his power flow. The air tingled with a tinny smell. "So?"

A slug of power shot from Marlowe, and Dillon staggered. That miasma hung around all of them, and it seemed to make all their tempers sharper.

Lazlo stepped forward. "Stop this!"

Dillon rubbed his chest. "I was going to leave peacefully—"

"You'll get nothing," Marie said. "You'll be lucky if we let you leave with the clothes on your back!"

"You shouldn't have changed the planet," Marlowe and Christian said. "We agreed not to, to let our followers do as they will."

"Oh please," Dillon said. "Tell me you're not doing the same. I love a good lie."

Lazlo felt their emotions peak, and he shouted at them to stop, that something was wrong. They fell silent and slowed, like a vid at half speed. Their mouths kept moving, fingers pointing in accusation, hurling insults back and forth, but he was outside their slowness.

Dué stepped through the door, winding through the pack at a normal walk, her one eye locked on Lazlo, and her power tingling through his skull. "Why do you stand for this?" her voice said in his mind, her mouth still. "You are so much larger than they."

"I can't just go around hurting people," he said. "I'm not a…"

She smiled. "God?"

"Are you doing this? Making everyone angrier than they should be?"

"Prophecy makes slaves of us."

"It's not prophecy if you make it happen!"

She laughed. The sound and movement of the others came back in a rush, angry voices subsiding as they realized who stood in their midst.

"What—" Marie took a step back.

"Go," Dué said, aloud this time. "I'll hold them."

Lazlo blinked at her. Christian, Marlowe, and the breachies stopped talking, stopped moving, as if someone had hit pause. Only their eyes moved, bulging in disbelief. Power roiled off Dué and scattered around the room.

Dillon laughed, and the sound had a tinge of evil. He blew her a kiss. "Thank you, you lovely nutter!"

"Remember to duck," she said.

Dillon spun Lazlo around. "Laz."

Lazlo couldn't breathe, was amazed he was still on his feet. What in the world was even happening? "Good-bye? Is this…"

"I hope you haven't had lunch yet." Dillon lurched backward, hauling Lazlo with him. Lazlo stumbled over the lip of the pod. Dillon lifted him, plonked him down in one of the seats, and activated the safety webbing. It slithered over Lazlo's body, holding him in place.

Lazlo squawked as Dillon punched the control panel, and the door hissed closed, the pod vibrating as it slid through the airlock. Dillon leapt into his own seat, and the crow of his voice drowned out Lazlo's protest. The sound of the pod's engines firing silenced both of them, and they hurtled toward the planet.

CHAPTER ELEVEN

After two weeks, Liam's bruises had almost faded, leaving just a smudge of yellow around his chin. Cordelia eyed it from time to time as they stood in the mess at the back of the keep and watched the recruitment vid along with the day's batch of children.

Goddamned waste of power. They barely had enough juice for their sidearms, but the Storm Lord had decreed that the children of Gale would watch this vid when they reached a certain age, so watch it they did.

It *was* impressive. Soldiers leapt from Pross Co. carriers, traveling the galaxy and kicking ass. When the vid told them they'd "Meet exciting alien species!" the teacher reminded them that they wouldn't, unless they counted the drushka.

Who were impressive on their own. Cordelia shook the thought away. Well, she tried. Nettle had made several memorable appearances in her dreams, usually naked, Cordelia's brain blurring information she didn't have. One time, Nettle had been dressed as a baker with a tray of sweet rolls, and Cordelia didn't even want to wonder what that was about.

The kids oohed and ahhed as the vid highlighted guns and armament. They cheered as a soldier almost twisted a man's head off when he came through her door uninvited. Her family stopped her, introducing the man as a guest, and the vid proclaimed that Pross Co. soldiers gained "catlike reflexes." The vid family looked at the camera with giant grins and put their thumbs up, just as they did after every segment.

Cordelia snorted a laugh. The kids chattered when the vid was done, probably more excited to watch their first vid than anything, especially after the exhaustive tests the yafanai had put them through the day before.

Liam elbowed Cordelia in the side. "Nearly twisting that guy's head off is my favorite part."

"All the grinning, though. They look crazy." She pulled her mouth into an insane smile and gave him a thumbs-up. "I've had severe skull trauma!"

He returned the look. "I carry around a head in a bag!"

Brown crossed the hall behind them and paused when they grinned crazily at her. "You fuckers are weird." She watched the kids file out. "I love that vid. It made me the woman I am today."

"Now who's weird?" Cordelia said. "I wanted to be a paladin long before I saw that piece of shit."

"That makes two of us," Liam said. Though his reasons were different from hers.

Even after Cordelia had passed the yafanai tests for strength of will and mental stability, she'd chosen the gun. She'd been a scrapper at school, and a wandering paladin had broken up one of her fights one day. He'd laid a heavy, armored arm across her shoulders, helmet shining around his face. He'd been proud. Uncle Paul had yelled at her that night, but she'd smiled through it, knowing there was someplace that fighting was welcomed *and* celebrated.

A leather hurried over to them. "Lieutenant Ross, a letter for you." He pushed a thick, reed-made card into her hands.

"Dismissed," Cordelia muttered. Fine paper, heavy ink. She knew it was her uncle's doing before she noted his perfect handwriting.

"To my dearest niece, Cordelia Sa Ross," it read. "You are invited to dine this evening with your uncle, who is taking time out of his extremely busy schedule to visit with his only remaining relative. Dinner will be served at dusk. Don't make me send Reach after you." It was signed, "Paul Philip Ross, Mayor of Gale (A man of some importance.)"

"La-di-da!" Brown said. "Damn, Ross! Sometimes I forget you're royalty."

"Shut up."

"Yeah, Jen," Liam said, "you should feel humbled that her golden majesty deigns to speak with unwashed lackeys like us."

Cordelia held up a fist. "Do you want some of this?"

"She offered to touch you!" Brown said. They bowed in sync.

Cordelia read the card again. "Not fair of him to threaten me with a diplomat."

"Dusk is in a few hours," Liam said. "You better get ready."

"You'll have to get your hair done," Brown said. "Polish your shoes."

Liam nodded. "One of your servants will be happy to lick them clean."

"Fuck off, the pair of you." Cordelia stomped up to her room. Luckily, she wasn't in armor that day, so she only had to find something suitable to wear. She dug through her trunk, picking out loose-fitting mauve trousers and a matching shirt. The shirt had the fewest holes, and the trousers were comfortable, though she'd chased a thief down while wearing them two days ago. She'd meant to sew up the rip at the knee, but there hadn't been time. Armor might have made a better choice, but Paul would just make her take it off.

With a sigh, she took the trousers off and tried on her second-best pair, tan to go with the mauve. These had a hole near the crotch, but no one would notice when she was sitting down. She dug an embroidered vest from the bottom of the trunk, not even remembering the last time she'd worn it. It wouldn't quite stretch over her shoulders. A relic from before armor training, then, when she'd packed on her current muscle.

"Fuck." She could go buy something else, but she liked to save her money for more important things, like mead and gifts for the occasional fling, as rare as those were. Nettle wandered through her head again, but there wasn't time to dwell. If her uncle was going to embarrass her with fancy invitations, she was going to show up at his house far too early. That would set the evening off on the right, annoyed foot.

She set off for the finer part of Gale, all well-maintained houses and shops of every variety. Rickshaws rumbled through the area night and day, so she kept to the side of the road, trying to arrive at her uncle's house not coated in dust. She was nervous, though she didn't know why. She knew all of her uncle's tactics, all his guilt trips, but she wasn't looking forward to diatribes about how she should and shouldn't conduct herself. It felt too much like being a kid again. At this rate, she'd need another fight before Liam's bruises had even faded.

She passed near the market and stood clear while several rickshaws clattered by. A few notes of eerie singing made her turn, looking deeper into the alley. Someone was moving, and she heard faint crying, a child's voice. She tiptoed closer. If someone was hurting a kid, Paul would just have to accept fresh bloodstains on her clothes.

Reach knelt in the middle of the alley, singing softly. A boy stood in front of her, about two years old and dressed in a simple shift. His feet were bare. As Cordelia came closer, her own shoulders relaxed, her anticipation for a fight bleeding into calm as the melody washed over her. The little boy's tears faded into snuffles, and his stare went dreamy.

"What harms you, *isa*, little one?" Reach asked. "Why do you cry?"

"Mama," he said softly.

"She has lost you?"

The little boy nodded, and Reach lifted him into her arms. "We will find her, *isa*. Do not fear. Let your sadness cease." She crooned again. When she saw Cordelia, she froze but relaxed quickly, her usual haughty expression taking over. "Paul's metal-skinned niece."

"Paul's drushkan lover." Cordelia looked Reach up and down and put several random pieces together in her head. "Pool said something about healing songs. Was that what I heard?"

Reach blinked rapidly, and Cordelia tried not to grin, glad to have something that put the ambassador off her game. "You should not speak that name where others can hear."

"Relax. No one knows who I'm talking about. So, you're a healer. Or what did she call it? Shaw-something?"

Reach's chin lifted. "A shawness, as my people say. Shawnessi for more than one."

"Can you really heal with those songs or just—"

Reach stepped past her. "I do not know what all of my songs could do for a human besides soothe them." The boy stirred in her arms, and she hummed.

"What are you planning to do with that kid?"

"Find his mother."

"Good. I'll help." When Reach gave her a glance, she grinned. "If we're both just looking out for the kid, we should get along fine."

"The baker, Gerard, knows many people on this lane."

And many people seemed to know Reach. They smiled at her,

inclined their heads. If they thought it was odd to see her walking around with a human child, no one said anything. Cordelia noted that she kept her poisonous claws tucked away from the boy's body. She also smiled at everyone they met. A friendly Reach, who would have thought? Maybe that was just her ambassador face. There had to have been a reason the drushka had picked her to speak for them.

Gerard, a man with the largest jowls Cordelia had ever seen, knew the boy right away. "His parents work a booth in the market. His grandmother is supposed to watch him, but sometimes she falls asleep. Here, I'll take him."

Reach handed the boy over and then slapped her thighs, her mouth turned down. "Careless."

"Can you watch him until his parents come home?" Cordelia asked.

"My brother can. He's got three kids of his own that he minds while his wife pulls a 'shaw. He offered before. Guess they might take him up on it now." He laughed, belly shaking. "They'll be so embarrassed at the drushkan ambassador minding their kid."

"It is no bother." Reach smoothed the boy's hair, and Cordelia wondered if she had children of her own she was missing or if she just liked them.

They walked toward the mayor's house together, and Reach grumbled about the boy until Cordelia sighed. "Maybe you should offer to babysit," Cordelia said.

"I would be more successful."

"I don't doubt it."

Reach eyed her up and down. "You know you are early for dinner with your uncle."

"I like to surprise him. Will you be joining us?"

"Ahwa, no! Paul says you like to 'verbally spar.' When a drushka fights, she uses her hands."

"A people after my own heart."

"Ahya, our minds are alike." She walked in silence for a moment. "Perhaps you will tell him why your captain or those under her command contacted the old drushka."

Cordelia thought fast. "Sounds like a conversation you should have with the captain."

"If she did not inform me before, why should she now? Something tells me the coming days will teach us much about trust."

"What does that mean?"

Reach spread her hands, but Cordelia noted the tightness in her face. She was angry. Well, if Cordelia had the same suspicions, she'd be angry, too. They said nothing more as they reached Paul's house, and Reach continued through the street, not waving good-bye, if drushka even did that.

Cordelia stood on the stoop and combed her fingers through her hair. She knocked, and when her uncle opened the door, she gave him a wide grin. "I'm early."

"Cordelia, welcome." He stood aside so she could enter, not showing a hint of being rattled, the bastard. He even squeezed her shoulder, very drushkan.

"I ran into Reach on the way here."

"Did you?" Still not a twitch. He wore loose white trousers and a long red vest over his shirt, plain like hers but in much better repair. He had a lot of potted plants dotting his house, and she wondered if that was Reach's doing.

He led her to a small dining table. "Reach wanted to give us some space, since you've been far too busy to eat with me for such a long time."

"Put away the artillery, Uncle Paul."

"Oh, come now. That was an easy one. Getting a reaction out of you isn't going to be any fun if you cave that quickly."

"Or was that my evil plan the entire time?"

He snorted a laugh. "Our late lunch is almost ready. Or early dinner, if you like."

She nearly tripped over her chair. "How? Liam sent word to you that I was coming early? Or was it Brown?"

He shrugged and sat. After a few moments, his housekeeper brought in two plates of food. "Roast *joora* meat and cattail grass," she said.

Paul bent over his plate. "Smells delicious, Katey. Thank you."

She smiled before hurrying back to the kitchen.

"Fancy," Cordelia said.

"Nothing but the best for my seldom-seen niece."

"I'll have to ignore you more if you're going to tempt me back with food like this. Or just let me know when you won't be in, and I'll drop by."

"Funny." He cut into his meat and popped a piece in his mouth. "So, what's Carmichael going to do about this research station, the boggins, and the old drushka?"

"Why don't you ask her?"

"She isn't here."

Cordelia jerked her thumb toward the door. "I could go get her, and the two of you could have dinner."

"We're having candied berries for dessert, your favorite."

"Damn." She took another few bites. "You said something before about trading with plains dwellers, and I still think that's a terrible idea."

"A change of subject as subtle as a hammer. I don't know why you became a paladin when you could have been a *terrible* politician."

"What can I say? I'm an overachiever."

Paul spread his hands, another drushkan gesture. "We'll never know what the plains dwellers can offer until we open communications."

"They don't have any metal."

"No one said they did."

"And what would they want from us?"

"I won't know until I ask."

"And then you'll let them wander around Gale like the Sun-Moons."

He lifted his cup. "One big happy humanity. Speaking of humanity, what about those researchers, the ones who were killed by the boggins?"

She leaned back and put her feet on the neighboring chair, watching his eyebrows twitch. "You know, I think most families don't talk like this. They say, 'How have you been?' and…" She trailed off, not having any idea.

"We're far more interesting than most families. We put our feet on the furniture and everything."

"Ha! I knew that would get you."

"So teenage of you."

"You know, if the Storm Lord was here, I'm sure he wouldn't approve of trading with the Sun-Moons or the plains dwellers."

"Oh, Delia, as grateful as I am for the Storm Lord's bounty, he is not here. You never know who can be your ally until you ask."

"You've certainly made allies with the drushka."

He leaned forward. "From what I hear, so did you."

Nettle flashed before her mind's eye, and she blushed a little, more out of surprise than anything. Paul sat back with a satisfied smile.

"Did Reach tell you about the scent?" she asked.

He paused chewing, and she smiled so hard it hurt. "Drushkan superstition," he said.

"Yeah? Or would people say you've been manipulated?"

"People will say anything. I'm quite in possession of my faculties."

"Sure?"

He ate a few more bites. "I'm sure Liam would agree with me about making allies."

"Liam would agree with any arrangement that includes the chance for new sex partners."

"And what could my trading partners offer that would tempt you?"

She thought of everything from the recruitment vid. "Tanks. Mobile artillery from the paladin vid. A metal vehicle, big gun."

"You're scary enough in armor. I can't bear to think of you in anything more frightening." He snapped his fingers. "The Sun-Moon worshipers mentioned something about a ballista, a weapon that throws big spears. They use them against raiders."

"Raiders." She rubbed her chin, picturing the rush of battle day after day.

"If I get you a ballista, you can tell people, publicly and in armor, that trading with outsiders is a grand idea." When she stared at him, smiling wryly, he shrugged. "Give and take is what politics is all about."

"Fine."

He pointed. "You cannot go throwing spears inside the city."

"I'll take my toys outside. I promise."

He smiled, and it had a tinge of genuineness. "I'm glad you came."

"Me too. All it took was good food and bribes."

He lifted his cup again. "To politics."

"To alien sweat glands."

He glared at her.

Katey came back in, brows drawn. "Sorry to disturb you, Mr. Ross, but the delivery boy told me that people are talking about a strange light in the sky. They're very agitated."

"What kind of light?" Paul asked.

"Big, sir, so they say. I thought you might want to know."

Paul looked to Cordelia, and they both stood. "I'll get to the keep," Cordelia said, "see what I can find out."

"Be careful."

"You, too." She caught herself before she could tell him to fuck off, certain he wouldn't appreciate the farewell she shared with Liam. "You, too."

CHAPTER TWELVE

Lazlo stumbled out of the pod, his ears ringing, eyes watering. He'd thought the ride down was bad, shaking and shuddering, the roar of noise, his power keeping him from blacking out. But now he was on the *surface* of the *planet.* Birds and insects shouted around him, the sun pounded down on his shoulders, and the pod ticked like a clock as it cooled. He smelled dirt and hot metal. And grass! A field of sickening green stretched away into forever, and it smelled so strongly he could feel it. But that wasn't just the smell. He could feel every weed, every flower, all pulsing in time with his power. Trees waved and rustled, the sound playing up and down his spine, and he knew not to keep looking, but his gaze shot to the horizon, ground meeting sky in such awful finality.

He fell to his knees, dry-heaving. The station was always in motion, but down here everything was so still and so hurried at the same time, scudding clouds and waving grass and fluttering leaves and noise on top of a planet that he couldn't feel shifting under his feet. Bile filled his mouth again.

He fought through it all and let his power flow, creating a feedback loop with his own body until he could only feel himself.

And Dillon, who whooped like a crazy person. He was breathing hard, too, but his manic smile hadn't slipped. He only looked a little green. Lazlo let his power flow over both of them, adjusting their lungs, but he still had to fight back the desire to retch.

"I bet they are pissing themselves right now!" Dillon said. "Screaming and clutching each other and wondering how long Dué has been in collusion with us. I bet that's just what Marie is saying, *collusion*. I hope she tries to blow Dué out an airlock and winds up smeared across the deck."

The image made Lazlo shut his eyes again. Breathing, that was the most important thing.

"They'll be driving themselves fucking insane trying to figure out how to get you back."

"You." Lazlo took a few deep breaths. "You grabbed me. You forced me down here."

Dillon muffled his smile, folding his hands together. "Laz, buddy—"

"Don't you dare! Oh, don't you dare, you arrogant prick! You kidnapped me!"

"You're a little old to be kidnapped, aren't you?"

Lazlo flung a handful of grass at him. "You didn't even ask!"

"Would you have said yes if I did?"

"That is not the point, asshole!"

"All right." Dillon lifted his hands. "All right, Laz. You're right. I'm sorry."

"Oh, well, if you're sorry, then it *must* be okay." He flung more grass, a bit of dirt mixed in this time. "What the fuck are we going to do down here?"

Dillon licked his lips, and his eyes widened as if finally seeing that he couldn't just "buddy" his way out of this, that it was more than a snit. "We'll take shelter with my people. Everything will be all right, Laz. Don't tell me you weren't as bored up there as I was."

"There are worse things to be than bored. They're going to notice that you're just a man, Dillon, when they thought they had a god."

"I'm still powerful. You're powerful. Even with the yafanai, no one down here can touch us. I'll just keep trotting out the old rhetoric: humans came to this planet via a ship, some of us became gods, and some went to the planet. The end."

Lazlo stood on shaky legs. "Living on a satellite for two hundred and fifty years is not godlike."

"So don't mention the *Atlas*. Only answer what you want to answer." He laid a hand on Lazlo's shoulder but tensed as if he might get bitten. "Living for over two hundred years is going to be the only part anyone hears."

Lazlo groaned and walked a small circle, one hand on his hip and the other rubbing his forehead. He forced himself not to look at the horizon again, told himself to just keep breathing.

"We should get going," Dillon said.

"I'm not going anywhere with you." He couldn't live on the surface with all these people.

Dillon frowned, a skeptical look instead of an angry one, and Lazlo knew they were thinking the same thing. Where else could Lazlo go? He couldn't even look at this place, let alone find his way around, and the pods weren't two-way vehicles. The *Atlas* wasn't equipped with any kind of shuttle. They'd planned to construct a space elevator at their original target planet—the materials were already there—but there was no way to escape Calamity's gravity well.

"Gale is that way," Dillon said, pointing. "We can make it before nightfall."

Oh hell, nightfall. Calamity wasn't just noisy and bright and vomit-inducing. It was dangerous, too. And Lazlo had helped Dillon make it more dangerous.

"Look, Laz, I'm sorry. I know that was a jerk move, but I can't live without you."

And now they were in some romantic vid, and Lazlo knew it was a calculated phrase, but his heart still lurched. Double, triple, quadruple damn. "You mean you can't live forever without my power."

"While that is true, you are the best friend I've ever had."

"And you're the most manipulative jackass I've ever known."

"Hey!" And now Dillon had that wounded look, the real one. He was a schemer, and he knew it, but having it spoken aloud by someone he cared for still hurt him.

Lazlo would have to add quintuple damn to his litany. "No more schemes, Dillon."

"Done."

"I mean it. I'll come with you now, but that doesn't mean I'm staying."

"I know. I'm sorry. It was a shitty thing to do, spur of the moment, I promise. I will prove to you that life down here with people who appreciate you is worlds better than being up there with those leeches. And you don't have to be scared of anyone or anything."

Lazlo snorted. "We'll see."

"No, I mean it." He looked sincere, but he felt sincere, too, as Lazlo touched him with power. "You feel threatened by anyone or anything, call me, and I'll come running. If anyone gives you so much as a look you don't like, I will roast him, hand to God."

Lazlo had to snort a laugh. On the satellite, everyone had to be civil to avoid all-out war, but they found ways to be snide, and though Dillon often put them in their place, he had to toe the same line. Here, though? Well, it could be advantageous to have a god on one's side.

Dillon had forgotten how fresh and clean everything could taste. Every gust of wind, every insect hum made him want to shout with joy. He'd been caged too long. And he didn't have to worry about parasites or nausea or any of the old ailments that used to plague him on planetary missions. Now he had Lazlo, the fucking wonder cure. It had been a little hard to breathe at first, and then it hadn't. Lazlo. When he'd inhaled a burst of pollen and started to cough, the feeling had eased at once. Lazlo again. He could eat anything he wanted, and any bug could bite him, and he never had to worry, all because of Lazlo.

Dillon was tempted to pick him up and swing him around, but Lazlo wouldn't like that. He was still angry and frightened, if his hunched back was any indication. Dillon walked a little closer, so his taller frame shaded Lazlo from the sun. Lazlo would get over his anger, and then he'd realize what a strong goddamned team they'd make down here! Dillon knew they should have done this years ago, but he didn't dare say that, not yet.

Dillon saw the taller of Gale's buildings first, one of which would be the Paladin Keep, those that walked in the footsteps of his old squad, his pride and joy, and he hoped they'd kept up some of the old traditions. Some captains had been better about it than others.

Carmichael! He'd get to meet her in person, see if she was as easy to antagonize face-to-face. If she didn't like doing things his way, he supposed he could replace her, but he didn't want to do that, didn't want to come in and start shoving people around, especially if the troops adored her. He wouldn't take up his old rank as colonel. God was so much better.

The yafanai would be all over him. He grinned. Better to stay in the temple, then. He'd heard it was pretty opulent, and living in a barracks was something he didn't miss from the old days.

They soon came close enough to see the palisade, but the people standing behind it on platforms were still tiny ants.

"Are you going to march up to the gates and say, 'Hi, I'm God'?" Lazlo asked.

Dillon took a deep breath and sent his senses out, reaching for nearby weather systems. "I think a bit of a show is in order, don't you?"

Lazlo rubbed his arms as the wind picked up. The air turned sharper, heavy with the scent of rain, and thunder rumbled in the distance. "A few tornados?"

"Not that dramatic. Keep an eye on my blood pressure, will you?"

"Thank you so much for the privilege."

Dillon laughed, but as he poured more power into the storm, his sinuses clogged, and he felt pain build behind his eyes. Before it could become annoying, the feeling eased. Lazlo again. Dillon kept walking and held his arms out, letting arcs of electricity jump between them. The people above the palisade were scurrying now, and others were pouring out the gate, pointing. He heard the swell of many voices.

The sky darkened. "Stay close to me, Laz, but don't touch. I don't want to catch you in the strikes."

He felt Lazlo just behind and kept his power tight to his own body. When he was close enough to the gate, he tried to think of something impressive to say. The citizens of Gale were huddling from the wind, shielding their faces. Well, maybe one more display would be enough, and then he wouldn't have to say anything.

He pulled at the clouds, aligned the charged particles just so. Lightning forked down around him, crashing to the earth in five points as Dillon lifted his arms. He made the bolts skitter around him in a circle, tendrils reaching to each other, crisscrossing, filling the air with a white-blue glow.

The people of Gale fell to their knees, crying out to him, naming him Storm Lord. He smiled and let his lightning dissipate, let the storm settle in.

At his back, Lazlo coughed. "Well, I don't know what I was worried about."

❖

Carmichael pushed outside the Paladin Keep. The streets were crowded with people asking if the paladins had seen the Storm Lord, if he'd be coming to the keep. Others asked what was happening, and some were just hanging around as if it was a festival day and they had nothing better to do.

Carmichael ground her teeth and barked at people to get back. Her spotters had reported a godsend, one of the packages from heaven that everyone thought were mystical, but that she knew were drop-and-carry pods from the satellite above. For all she knew, the general populace thought of them as shooting stars, but when the spotter had mentioned how large this one seemed, she'd known it was him, but she hadn't wanted to believe it.

"Captain!"

She looked for the voice and spotted Lieutenant Ross pushing through the crowd. Tall and muscular, she'd always made a good crowd breaker. Carmichael thought to use her to push to the temple, then thought better of it.

"Ross, hold the fort while I'm gone. Don't let any of these people inside."

"What's going on, Captain? I heard some people talking. They said the Storm Lord is here." She laughed as if it had to be a joke, but her expression fell when Carmichael didn't join in. "Are you fucking kidding me?"

Before Ross could lose it, Carmichael grabbed her arm. "We don't have enough intel. Just hold here until I come back."

"But if it's, I mean, the Storm Lord!"

"I know who he is, Lieutenant." And boy, did she ever. "Do your damned job like I told you."

That put some starch in her spine. "Yes, Captain." She took up her post in front of the doors, under the bailey, and barked orders at those around her, whipping them into formation, the better to keep stragglers out. Several leathers reassured the crowd that the Storm Lord wasn't inside, and Carmichael thought they might believe it. But he had to be in town if the sudden storm and the stir of the populace was any indication. There was one way to make sure this wasn't a trick. She needed to find the bastard.

She took alleys and side streets, navigating around the mass of people that grew larger the closer she came to the temple. Luckily, many seemed to know her, from a distance at least, and she used her fame to clear a path to the temple gates. A few yafanai stood in front and shooed people away from bothering God. They gave her a haughty look, but she returned it with blunt hostility.

For a moment, she thought even that wouldn't work, but someone in the back of the crowd muttered her name, and the yafanai guards glanced at each other. She leaned close. "I'm told our god wants to see me. Do you want to keep him waiting?"

That did the trick, and she had to wonder if this was the last time having a god would be useful.

She passed the gates, took a few short turns, and she was in his presence. He was a little older than she'd imagined, grayer around the temples, but still good-looking. His gray eyes would have made her look twice if she didn't know what a prick he was.

The yafanai had dressed him in golden robes, and she wondered what they did to the fabric that made it shine. With all the embroidery, it reminded her of a fancy tablecloth, but she didn't say that, wondered if she dared think it, wondered how great his power was. The storm that rumbled outside suggested great power indeed.

"Storm Lord," she said. When he stared blankly, she realized he'd never seen her either, but he hadn't been looking for her. Still, if he didn't know her at once, it meant he couldn't read her mind. "I'm Captain Carmichael."

He snapped his fingers and gestured for everyone to leave. They did so, giving her jealous looks that nearly made her laugh. "You're different than I pictured," he said.

His voice was the same, at least, testifying that he wasn't some yafanai trick. He had the same subtle accent she was used to, though they spoke the same language. The words had no doubt shifted from what their ancestors had spoken on Earth, but the Storm Lord had kept up with them.

"For most of my life," she said, "I pictured you as a god."

He held out his arms, and the sleeves of the robe swept the floor. "I do what I can."

Nope, still a man with pretty powers and a terrible attitude, proof that a nice face didn't equal big brains. "Is there something we can do for you, Storm Lord?"

He gave her a wry smile. "As if I just dropped by to borrow something? I'm here to stay, Captain."

She tried to keep a neutral expression, but some of her disappointment had to be creeping out. "I see."

He took a step. "Are you going to ask me why?"

She didn't move away, even when the hair on her arms stood up. It was a good threat, and he no doubt wanted to know if she was going to reveal his humanness by asking the wrong questions at the wrong time. "Not my business."

"Good. Very good, Captain. There are going to be some changes around here, but there's no reason your position should be one of them."

She didn't know what to say, but she wasn't going to give up her captaincy without a fight. He didn't respond to that thought, and no one came bursting in. So, the other yafanai weren't telepathically eavesdropping around their god. They probably thought he'd sense it. That was very useful information.

"How did it go in the swamp?" he asked. "How's my research station?"

"Everyone's dead."

He froze for a second. "Shame. And the swamp creatures?"

"Boggins, Storm Lord. They're loose. They're a threat." She took a deep breath. "I'm handling it."

The Storm Lord took a long pull out of an ornate cup and licked his lips. "I'm going to love it here." When she didn't respond, he smiled again, and she knew he was delighting in the fact that she feared mouthing off. "What say we pay a little visit to the Paladin Keep, eh? Can't keep the public waiting."

She put on a slight smile, eager to see what he did with a crowd, and if there was anyone obvious that could be turned against him, should the need arise.

❖

Lazlo had fought not to frown while Dillon basked in the Galeans' adoration. When they'd first come to the Yafanai Temple, he'd wondered if there was a corner he could hide in, a place to curl up, bemoan his fate, and think about how unfair life was.

But Dillon had kept him close, waving away those who tried to touch him, pushing people back when they came too close. Lazlo's heart had pounded so hard he could count the beats in his ears. He'd been so close to panicking many times, and only Dillon's strong presence had kept it at bay.

At last, in the temple, Dillon had hidden him in a small room. "Laz, just breathe."

"I don't know if I can do this."

Dillon's strong fingers had dug into his shoulders. "Deep breaths, one after another. Listen, I have to go back out there, but I want you to stay in here and find your calm, yeah?"

"Yes." And then he'd shut the door, and Lazlo had never been so happy to be alone. When Dillon had come back dressed in golden robes, they'd laughed together. Dillon had offered to find him something equally ridiculous, but Lazlo had wanted to keep his green flight suit, one of the many he'd had for a long time.

Dillon had shaken his head. "You need to fit in if you want to avoid attention, buddy."

True, but he'd still picked something plain and light blue, very soothing. He'd thought he could get a slow handle on things as long as he could be alone with Dillon nearby.

Now, Dillon came back into the small room, and Lazlo sensed his agitation. "Captain Carmichael's here. We're going to take a trip to the Paladin Keep with some of the yafanai."

Lazlo's fear came rushing back. "Now?"

"Just stay here, Laz. I'll be back for you."

"No!" He hated the panicked animal sound in his voice, but he couldn't help it. Everything was happening too quickly. "I want to go with you."

"You sure? There'll be a lot of people." Genuine concern radiated from him. Lazlo could have bathed in it.

"I'm sure."

Dillon gave him a proud smile and led him into a room full of yafanai. Everyone had this adoring look on their faces except one woman who stood near the wall, scowling. She was dressed as plainly as he was, and a quick scan revealed that she had no extraordinary powers. Her short hair was iron gray, and her green eyes pinned him to the spot. She was the same light brown as most of Gale's inhabitants, and her build was slight but muscled. She looked as if she could take care of herself, and he envied her so much in that moment.

"People," Dillon said. "This is Lazlo. You, you, and you, you're going to walk next to him on our way to the keep. Make sure he doesn't get lost or trampled. Captain Carmichael is going to lead the way."

The stern woman nodded and shot Lazlo a curious look before she led the way out, Dillon just behind her. The three yafanai Dillon had selected surrounded Lazlo and kept him in Dillon's wake. He tried not to think of them as babysitters. They were shields. Dillon was protecting him. He repeated it over and over as they walked down hallways of dull stone instead of gleaming metal. He stared at Dillon's back and made himself breathe.

When they emerged into bright sunshine and the roar of the crowd, Lazlo's knees nearly crumpled. How did Dillon stand it all? People were clamoring around him, kept off by Captain Carmichael, a host of yafanai, and now some armored figures who appeared out of the crowd as if by magic, Dillon's famous paladins.

Lazlo felt his gorge rise and used his power to soothe himself, trying to recall if he'd been this bad on Earth. His anxiety disorder had always been pretty crippling. Why else had he volunteered for a small colony job on a backwater planet?

But this was the wrong planet, and while it had been small at one time, it wasn't any longer.

"Are you all right?" one of his escorts asked.

"I'm…"

She moved, and he pulled back, thinking she meant to take his hand, but she offered her arm instead, leaving the choice to him. He took her elbow and looked into a pair of dark, kind eyes.

She was a little shorter than him, with dark hair the same shade as her eyes and a soft smile. She looked young, maybe early twenties, but many of the people on the *Atlas* had looked young. She didn't have the same air, though, with the experience of centuries and the petty cruelty that came from a small number of people locked up together for so long.

"My brother had trouble with crowds," she said. "He used to get terribly anxious, had to go home more often than not. You're doing well."

He laughed and knew it sounded breathless. "Thank you."

"Your name is Lazlo, right?"

"Yes." The crowd roared, and he jumped.

She stepped so that her face was in front of him again, and he had to focus on her. "Just Lazlo?"

"Um, Simon Lazlo. But everyone calls me Lazlo or..." He was about to say doctor, but he didn't even know if they used that word anymore. He only knew their language because Dillon had him keep up with the changes they made, the better to communicate his research to them.

She laughed lightly. "Only paladins call each other by their last names, Simon. You don't seem the paladin type." When he blinked at her, she winked. "That's a good thing."

"Don't like soldiers?"

She shrugged. "My name is Samira Zaidi."

"Zaidi?" And just like that, he was back on the *Atlas*'s bridge, before the crash, chatting with the real bridge doctor, the one who was supposed to help people. Lazlo could still picture his green flight suit, the name *Zaidi* stitched across the breast. He'd mentioned that his children were among the colonists, a boy and a girl, grown up now and on their first mission. And here was one of their descendants, far removed.

"Please, call me Samira. I'm not a paladin, either."

"No, I just knew someone named Zaidi once."

"But you've been with the Storm Lord in heaven, right? The unwinking star?"

Right, the cover story. "Well, you see, when humans came here, he...became a god—"

"And my ancestors were here on the planet. Were you watching over them?" She looked excited by the prospect of a personal guardian angel, but Lazlo's stomach shrank.

Maybe Dr. Zaidi's children had assumed he'd died when the pods landed. Or maybe they'd thought that his pod had been one of those that the *Atlas* had to space. Lazlo wondered what Dillon had told his followers about that and was ashamed that he'd never given it much thought.

Samira's gaze flicked to the Storm Lord, and she spoke softly. "We thought you might be his servant, but are you a god, too?"

"No! Absolutely not, and I'm not a servant, either. I just handle some things for him. Like the yafanai." He winced. Dillon was supposed to have created the yafanai, not Lazlo. "I mean…"

She continued to watch him, but he didn't want to dig himself in any deeper.

"I'm a healer," he tried.

She nodded slowly, but he wondered if she'd let it go.

Dillon pushed toward them. "I have to go inside the keep, Laz, and it's getting pretty rowdy out here. I need you to stay."

"What? Can't I—"

Dillon bent close to his ear. "Use your power and keep the crowd calm. There's something I need to do." He led Lazlo and the entourage closer to the keep, clapped Lazlo on the shoulder once more, and pushed his way inside.

Lazlo turned to the crowd, barred from the keep and not loving that. There were angry mutterings, the beginnings of frowns. Lazlo focused on their many minds, coaxing out endorphins and dopamine, but in small amounts, enough for the crowd to sigh in bliss without realizing they'd been tampered with.

Samira whistled softly. "Wow. Was that you?"

He scanned her quickly, finding macro-psychokinetic abilities. "Hopefully, most people won't realize anything happened at all."

"Very subtle. You're not just a healer, Simon. I think you might be *the* healer."

He chuckled. "You have no idea."

CHAPTER THIRTEEN

Nettle stared at the latest dead body. Step by step, her people had been pushed to the center of their territory, chased by chanuka whose numbers were greater than seeds scattered in a high wind. One at a time, they were no match for a drushka, but they attacked in hordes now, mixtures of large chanuka who clawed and bit while their smaller brethren threw spears. Not so long ago, they had been timid creatures, their weapons nothing more than found sticks, but now they seemed to take care crafting sharper spears, shaping them so they could be thrown. And they worked together as never before, charging from the water in packs, grabbing drushka and forcing them under. They crept through the undergrowth and hacked at ankles and knees. Whatever the humans had done to them had turned them into masters of the kill.

A brown root snaked up from the soil and dragged the dead drushka under, making her one with the planet again. Nettle held out an arm, and another root coiled around her. She felt her queen's sorrow through that connection, felt the worry for their people. Nettle shared the feelings, but what could they do?

Pool sent a picture of Sa Cordelia in her metal skin. Chanuka spears could not pierce a metal body. But would the humans help, even if the chanuka were a problem they had created? And if the humans ventured into the swamp in great numbers, would they leave again willingly? What would they want in exchange for their aid?

Pool's laughter bubbled in Nettle's mind. Reach had said that if given a patch of ground, the humans would spread like ivy. Pool's memories called them a courageous people, often foolishly so, who would give their lives for those they cared for. Roshkikan had been so. But humans also blundered into danger without thought. Time always seemed to be hurrying away from them. Roshkikan had needed to know too much too quickly. She had been in love with change, and that had turned the bulk of the drushka against her, against all humans. And some humans did not know how to stop a fight once it had begun. A few punches, and they were ready for war.

But Sa had not been like that. She had not responded to the downing of her mind-throwers by trying to kill the drushka. She had accepted the test for what it was, had showed restraint while making it known that she would only be pushed so far. Nettle could easily summon the memory of her proud, defiant shoulders, the angry flash of her dark eyes or the quickness of her smile. Her emotions changed as quickly as a beetle's shell, but she had not let her feelings rule her.

But Sa was young. She might make a good ally now, but her thoughts could change, steered by those who commanded her, like her Storm Lord. True, Nettle thought, but they could still use her help if she would give it now. Perhaps she could convince other metal skins to aid the drushka, and then she could command them to leave the swamp once the chanuka had been dealt with. She was true as well as fierce.

And her form was as pleasing as her presence: the strong play of muscle under intriguing curves. Nettle's temples tingled, and her chest tightened. Pool's mind shivered as she delighted in the desirous sensations. Nettle grinned. Sa knew about the scent. Anything that happened between them now would not be tainted by lies, whether there was any truth to the scent or not, as long as both of them were affected. The next time they were alone, Nettle would let her desire show, would act more like young Shiv and let her wishes be known.

Irritation thrummed down Pool's connection at the mention of her rebellious daughter, a thorn hidden among soft leaves. Before the schism, queens were born to random parents, so that there was always one queen-to-be who learned among her fellow drushka before her time as queen began. Another queen was born just as a Shi died, and then the queen-to-be became Anushi, sapling. Pool had been a queen-to-be during Roshkikan's time, knowing a human before she took her place as Anushi. And once she had become a queen, she had broken her people in two.

And queens of the old drushka did not have children, for the child of a queen would be a queen, and they could not risk having more queens than trees that could bear them. But Pool had missed the company of other queens, the harmony that only their minds could provide. She could speak with all her drushka, but she could only commune with another queen. It had been a secret ache, deeply harbored. She had shared it with Nettle many times, until she could no longer bear it.

And now they had Shiv, who had no tree to look forward to until the day long in the future when her mother died, and then she would be alone.

"Not for long," Pool thought, the words clear in Nettle's mind.

Nettle paused, waiting for an explanation, but none came. The root released her, leaving her wondering if Pool pondered having another child.

A cry of alarm sounded from the trees. Nettle put her hands down for her daggers, and the tendrils of wood that kept them at her waist flowed over her wrists and secured the handles to her palms.

She ran toward the sound and saw a drushka pulled into the underbrush by a multitude of chanuka arms.

"To me!" Nettle called. Other hunt leaders echoed the cry around her. Nettle leapt for the chanuka, but another group of them rushed from the low brush.

Nettle skewered one in the belly and dodged a spear from another. She kicked a chanuka in the face and slashed at a large female. All about her, drushka were locked in combat, but they were pushing the chanuka back. Perhaps the creatures had finally overreached. Whether they had or not, Nettle knew the drushka had to push them back or give up what remained of their ground.

❖

B46 watched her children and trilled in glee. The sticky grit quickened her breathing, and she memorized the moves of the tall creatures, watching the way her children died. She signaled to the high branches where the bulk of them waited like coiled vines, covering the trees. Her muscles jumped, and she dug her claws into her thighs to keep from crying out. They were so close.

C28 waited on the branch below, sending children trickling into the fray. When he'd left her, his eyes already enormous from the grit's effects, she'd known they'd win this day. The tall creatures drew closer, led by the promise of slaughtering more of her children.

She smeared more grit along her gums. The bag held crumbs now, but it would be enough. She heard the shredding, ripping sounds of enemy flesh being torn from its bones. It would be easy to give in to bliss, but she held to her anger. Rage ebbed but didn't quit the field of her mind.

The tall creatures passed far beneath her hiding place, and she unleashed the children waiting above her, dropping them on enemy backs. She sent groups of them to both sides of the fight, surrounding the tall creatures so none could escape. Soon, pockets of tall creatures fought for space as well as lives, but for every child of B46's that fell, two more took its place, then three more, four. She leapt to join the fray as her children closed about the tall creatures like a fist, stabbing and clawing and biting. The taste of their flesh complemented the bitterness of the sticky grit, an intoxicating combination.

❖

Shiv listened to the sounds of combat that echoed through the trees. She wanted to run into its teeth, to put her sorry knife to chanuka throats.

Higaroshi pulled at her arm again. "Please, young one, if you leave, I will have no one to protect me."

She slapped her thighs. Nettle had only told her to protect Higaroshi in order to keep her from the fighting, but he *would* die if left alone. Perhaps the chanuka would not come this close to the enclave, but why not? They had already ventured too close to her mother's hiding place. They had already killed many drushka and lost their fear.

"Shi'a'na," Shiv called with her voice and her mind. If her mother would reveal herself, Higaroshi could hide in the branches, and Shiv could join the fight.

But her mother did not answer. Shiv slapped her thighs again and took another step toward the sounds of combat.

Higaroshi screamed. Shiv whirled and spotted a chanuka creeping through the underbrush. Its eyestalks bulged at the sound of the scream, as if it was as surprised as Higaroshi. Shiv leapt for it, her carved knife streaking forward. She bent away from its spear and tore her blade across its throat.

"Shiv!" Higaroshi yelled. He pointed to brush that now seemed alive with creeping chanuka.

She pushed him toward a tree. "Climb!"

One of the chanuka dashed at them, and she clawed its face. It clutched the wound and shook, falling to its knees as the paralyzing poison coursed through it. Higaroshi yelped and fell from the tree. Shiv glanced up to see the fang-filled mouth of a chanuka smiling down at them.

She hauled Higaroshi to his feet and tried to find somewhere to run. "Shi'a'na!"

Nettle leapt the closest bushes, several drushka beside her. A whirlwind of blades, she turned the chanuka into meat within seconds. She and the others had golden wounds marring their bodies, leaking over their clothes. One had an arm that hung uselessly, blood streaming from a bite in his shoulder.

"The queen is coming," Nettle said. "You and Higaroshi will go with her."

"Who?" Higaroshi asked.

A branch snaked from the trees and curled around his waist, lifting him screaming into the air. Shiv leapt along with him into her mother's tree, landing near where her mother sat in a little shelter of bark.

Shiv held tight to Higaroshi. "You must hold on!"

"A drushkan queen?" He pointed to Shiv's hair and then to her mother's, the same bright green, though her mother's flowed over the trunk, held by tiny wooden tendrils. "Is this your…"

"Hold on," Shiv said again.

The roots of the Anushi tree wrapped around other trunks in the swamp, and it pulled itself forward. It flung chanuka far into the distance or crushed them where they stood. Its leafy branches swung through their ranks, collecting drushka and holding them close.

❖

B46 hurled a spear at the walking tree, but the tall creatures huddled too far into its branches. Her children balked, terrified. They scattered, but the walking tree killed them faster than they could run. She howled her rage at this thing that had disrupted all her careful plans. Every creature in the swamp would have been hers, and from here she would have moved on to the stinking nest outside the trees, but she'd never expected this.

Trees weren't supposed to move, not in the before times and not now. She remembered the roots that had taken the tall creatures from her before, but nothing like this had happened, and that had been far from this spot.

She would have to plan again.

Or perhaps it was time to abandon these tall creatures and turn her gaze to the others, those she could kill with fire.

As she fled into the swamp, she knew one thing for certain: she would have to collect the panicked children and then make more, but she could always make more. She would make another plan, turn her thoughts again, and make them into a weapon.

The chanuka had fled, but the drushka stayed aboard the Anushi tree or kept close, scanning the swamp for danger. Shiv watched as the hunt leaders gathered the dead, what was left of them, so their bodies could rejoin the soil.

The branches lowered her mother to the ground, and Shiv hopped down, too. "Shi'a'na?"

Her mother waved her to silence as Nettle strode over to them. Golden blood still streaked Nettle's body, some of it cracking open as she moved.

"How many dead?" Shi'a'na asked.

"A fourth." Nettle's eyes closed in pain. "A fourth of our tribe."

One of Shi'a'na's roots curled around her own waist and another around her shoulders as if comforting her. Shiv turned away; she would never feel the comfort of a tree while her mother lived.

"I will speak to my daughter alone."

Nettle moved away, though Shiv could have spoken to her mother privately through the roots. She tried not to curl her lip at the thought. Her mother preferred to speak to her face because the roots reminded them that their communion could never be pure, that Shiv was not a real queen.

"Are you going to chastise me for fighting?" Shiv asked. "Or for something else?"

"I cannot be angry with you for doing as I did."

"You can do whatever you want. You are queen."

Shi'a'na sighed both with her mouth and her mind. Everyone in the tribe could probably feel her aggravation with her wayward offspring. Again. "We are important, daughter. Drushka will die to protect our lives above theirs. We make them reckless."

Shiv slapped her thighs. "I have no tree. I hold no importance. If we were part of the old drushka, we could have ruled side by side!"

"If we were part of the old drushka, you would not exist." She laid her hands on Shiv's shoulders, stopping any hasty response. "And I would not wish that."

Shiv wanted to sink into the warmth of that voice, but the words did not reflect her mother's actions. "You never crafted a living weapon for me, though you gave one to every other member of our tribe. They have pieces of Anushi bark, your very self, to defend them, and I have this." She flung her knife to the ground. "Dead wood."

Her mother straightened, and Shiv prepared herself for wrath. To Shiv's surprise, Shi'a'na touched her forehead. "I am sorry, my daughter. I thought that having to craft your own weapon would make you strong, independent from me, and it has, ahya, but I wonder if it is worth the price of your anger. Since you would one day rule alone, I thought…" Her smile was sad, thoughtful. "Now I see that ruling alone was always the problem. We were not meant to be queens alone."

"And so?" She felt her mother's call and looked up. Her breath stuttered as the Anushi tree lowered a stick to the ground. Small roots bunched on one end, and a smattering of branches graced its crown. It touched the soil and dug in, no taller than Shiv, but she felt it standing there as if it was one of her own limbs. She called to it with her mind, and it tottered to her, swaying, forcing her to jump forward and catch it. It laid its branches over her in an embrace, and like root to soil, they were one.

"Shi'a'na," Shiv said, joy quaking her voice. She hugged the tree carefully, scared of fracturing this joy.

"Too young to carry you, but ahya, it will not always be so."

With a sob, Shiv threw her arm around her mother, holding the young tree in the crook of her other arm. "I am so sorry, Shi'a'na, for ever being a thorn to you."

Her mother clutched the back of her head and pressed their foreheads together. "The wind has not blown in our favor. These chanuka grow ever stronger, some doing of the humans, but I see the hand of the old drushka as well. There are rumblings in my mind. They are coming."

Shiv caressed her little tree and knew it was so. She sometimes felt the pull of the old queens, but she had never touched their minds as her mother had. And through this tree, she touched her tribe in a way she never had either, always having to go through her mother before. They were all connected, made one through the queens, and without the queens, they were alone. "I see now why we must survive. We are the drushka."

Her mother wrinkled her nose. She had created a child when it was forbidden, created a queen, and now she had made a queen's tree from her own branches. Nothing was impossible for her. She would save them from the chanuka and the old drushka both.

And Shiv would help her.

Her mother laughed. "Yes, daughter. You will help. You will go with Nettle to the human place and learn more of them. If we are to remain free from the old ways, your path will stay close to the humans." She gripped Shiv's chin. "But you will obey the hunt leader as you would me and do as she says."

Shiv let her chin rest so her mother could see her obedience. "I will do as she says." She clenched her jaw, letting her spirit shine through. "But I will not enjoy it."

Her mother smiled and wrinkled her nose again.

CHAPTER FOURTEEN

Cordelia stared at the palisade, wondering if she should go around to the gate or just jump over. She laughed at the thought, earning her a few funny looks from passers-by. Her cheeks were hurting from the grin she'd sported for two days, ever since the Storm Lord had joined his chosen people and charged their armor.

It sent shivers down her spine just thinking about it.

When she'd first seen him, her heart had hammered so hard she'd felt it winding into her belly. The Storm Lord on Calamity, among his people. She knew the old story: he'd become a god after humanity had reached this planet, but how had he come back to the planet as a human?

Well, nothing was impossible for him. He'd been dressed in golden robes. She'd wondered why he hadn't come to his people in armor, but all thought scampered from her mind as he passed within two feet of her, casting a joyful smile at his people.

She'd followed in his wake, sliding in behind Carmichael, who hadn't seemed as if the Storm Lord's arrival rated any particular ecstasy. Liam crowded in at Cordelia's side, and she grabbed his hand, squeezed it as Carmichael showed the Storm Lord around the keep, coming at last to the armory. He paused in front of the armor racks, where they stored the suits when not in use.

But it had another function once.

The Storm Lord had bent and arranged the old batteries, the heaviest part of the armor that no one bothered to wear anymore. He asked if those were all the batteries, and the crowd of paladins gasped as they realized the power he meant to give them on top of everything else.

Cordelia had clutched Liam's hand until he'd whined. The Storm

Lord warned them to stay back. A buzz filled the room and several tiny clicks came from the racks. The batteries rattled, and when the Storm Lord hooked them into the armor, it glowed so softly Cordelia thought she was imagining it. The paladin recruitment vid kept playing in her head, the soldiers of Pross Co. doing the impossible, the leaps and the lifting that powered armor could give them.

The Storm Lord had caught Cordelia's eye and smiled, and she didn't think she'd ever forget his first words to her: "I had that same look on my face the day I joined up."

He'd asked for her name, but Carmichael answered and threw out that Cordelia was the niece of the mayor as if she needed that connection to protect her. The Storm Lord gave her a shrewd look but didn't lose his smile. Carmichael's frown deepened when the Storm Lord began to train them. He taught them how to leap, how to keep their balance, how to take advantage of their new speed and strength. He showed them how to raise and lower their ultrathin visor, how to use the targeting functions and how to make the armor glow. Cordelia thought she might collapse from sheer joy, but the armor would hold her up.

"You should have seen the real suits," the Storm Lord had said. "The battle armor and not these dress pieces. This is damn fine tech, but it was sent as a show to make the original colonists feel protected." He touched it fondly. "And it makes for good vid, but the battle armor was for business."

They'd sighed with him. The battle armor featured prominently in the recruitment vid, but the suits they had were impressive enough, as far as Cordelia was concerned.

People had so many questions about what the armor was made from and how they could make more, but the Storm Lord said they couldn't, not without metal and someone who knew how to recreate the components inside.

When it had been time to give someone else a turn, Cordelia wandered toward the front of the keep, her mind whirling. With powered armor, the paladins had even less to fear from Calamity. Nothing could stop them, not the swamp, not the Sun-Moon worshipers. She'd spotted her uncle lingering at the edge of the crowd that waited peacefully for the Storm Lord to reemerge.

When she'd asked the reason for his frown, he said, "Questions, Delia. Use your head. Why is he here now? How did he get here? Where has he been?" He frowned harder. "And what need will Gale have for a mayor with their god around?"

She'd rolled her eyes, asking why the Storm Lord should want his job. She'd mentioned that Carmichael was as disappointed as he seemed to be, and his gaze had gotten shrewd again. Before he left, he gave her a long look and told her to keep questioning everything.

"I know a showman when I see one," he'd said.

As she stared at the palisade now, she decided it didn't matter. So what if it took Carmichael and Paul a little time to get used to things. Cordelia knew what her god wanted from her. He wanted her to do her job, and he'd given her an easier way to do it.

"Go around," Liam said as he caught up to her. "Don't show off. You're like a kid with a new toy."

She grinned anew. "How are you not freaking out about this armor?"

"When we're out in the field, go nuts. What if you squashed someone now?"

She snorted a laugh but did as he said, waiting until they were in the field before running, her armor propelling her faster than she could ever go before, doing most of the work for her so she didn't get tired easily. They split up for long patrol, once around the city, but they caught up to each other long before they would have in the past.

"Want to take another lap?" she asked.

He shrugged. "We could turn it in early, go to the pub."

"You can if you want. I'll finish the sweep."

"The one we just did?"

"We're supposed to go carefully."

He sighed but started around again. She went slower this time, scanning the distant tree line. They were supposed to be looking for boggins or old drushka. Whatever had happened to the boggins, she knew they were going to come calling sooner or later. Or maybe the old drushka would come pick a fight. Something had to come now that she had powered armor. Otherwise, she might just explode.

Movement among the trees caught her attention. She lowered her visor, and her vision zeroed in on that point as if she'd gone flying across the field. She staggered even though she wasn't moving. A clump of underbrush rustled, and Higaroshi tumbled out, followed by Nettle and Shiv.

Cordelia put her visor up and ran, scanning the ground for obstacles. She imagined falling head over heels at top speed and then rolling to a stop at Nettle's feet, the epitome of grace.

They turned her way, and she raised a hand, calling out. Instead of answering, they ran toward her, and she wondered if something was chasing them. The thought made her grin even harder.

She slid to a stop, and Higaroshi barreled into her, his sweaty face tight with panic. "Ambassador," she asked, "what is it?"

He shook his head. "There were just so many."

"We must speak to your leaders and to Reach," Nettle said. Her smile seemed almost shy, a contrast to her words. Maybe she was just distracted. "There are too many chanuka. The queen is in danger. We all are."

Cordelia looked to Higaroshi, but he didn't seem confused by Nettle's choice of words. That particular secret must have gotten loose. "You're in luck. We've got the leader of leaders available. The Storm Lord is here."

Higaroshi gaped. Shiv and Nettle sucked their teeth. "The god who lives in the sky?"

"I'll explain on our way to the keep."

❖

Carmichael glared at her closed door, imagining she could see the man on the other side. She'd never had an assistant. She'd never wanted an aide. If anything needed saying to her people, she would say it, but now this bastard had shown up on her doorstep.

Marcus. She could almost see his patronizing smile. "The Storm Lord commanded me to assist you," he'd said.

Oh, she just bet he had. He might as well have used the word spy. The Storm Lord didn't trust her. He didn't need telepathy; she couldn't keep her disdain in check. For once, she wished she was a better actor.

She tried to keep her surface thoughts generically antagonistic. The law forbade telepaths from prying into heads at random. She remembered hearing once that untrained telepaths developed shields to keep from being bombarded by the surface thoughts of others, and after they learned, they always kept those shields in place. And digging into someone's head, actively using their powers, produced a feeling in some targets, a tingle in the head. If Marcus wanted to pry into her head, maybe she would know, but she'd never felt the tingle before. She didn't know any telepaths. If she did feel it, though, she could take his ass into custody.

And then what? Arrest God? Haul him before a judge? Maybe the mayor would side with her. She hadn't seen Paul since she'd sent Lieutenant Ross into the swamp. Maybe it was time for another meeting, just to see if he was as happy about the Storm Lord's presence as...

"Shit." She forced the thoughts away. This far from other people, Marcus could probably lower his shields enough to hear her, and she hadn't felt anything. She couldn't even think to herself anymore! She stomped to the door and jerked it open.

Marcus jumped to his feet. The drawers of the desk were half-open, as if he'd been rummaging through them. "Captain?"

"You're fired."

"What? The Storm Lord said—"

"Close your mouth, follow me downstairs, and then keep going out the front door. Unless you'd like to be *helped* out?"

She started down the stairs without waiting. For a few steps, she heard nothing, then his footfalls echoed behind her. When they reached the main floor, she turned, and Marcus gave her a confused glance before he left.

Carmichael let out a breath. Now what? Would the Storm Lord come himself or send a lackey? And would she admit her disobedience or try to lie and smooth things over? Would he strike her down?

She snorted a laugh and surprised herself with how much the thought didn't scare her. Let him take her out in front of her people and see where that got him. He was their god, but the paladins wouldn't stand for that, not without some words, at least. He'd always encouraged them to be loyal to one another. Now he'd have to deal with that.

Raised voices from the courtyard caught her attention. Lieutenant Ross was leading two drushka and the human ambassador through the main doors, collecting a small crowd of paladins as they went.

Carmichael shoved forward. "Report."

Ross saluted. "Captain, the boggins have attacked the drushka."

Good thing she'd already started planning for any boggin trouble. The Storm Lord would have to wait. "Put them in the meeting room on the second floor." They headed off, and she summoned a leather from the pack. "Go to the mayor's house. Tell him we need him and Ambassador Reach for a problem with the drushka. Keep it quiet." She pointed at everyone gathered around. "That goes for all of you."

After they murmured assent, she took the stairs to the second floor two at a time. Maybe they could get something going before the Storm Lord even heard about Marcus. Then when he came calling, she'd be off dealing with real problems.

Halfway to the meeting room, she noticed that Liam had trailed her from the ground floor. "Weren't you on patrol with Ross?"

"We split up to do the rounds. I saw her come in with the drushka."

"The attractive drushka?"

He didn't even have the sense to look sheepish. "What's up?"

"Find Sergeant Preston and Brown and Lea. Tell them to double-time it up to the meeting room."

To his credit, he didn't argue, though he did cast one wistful glance at the closed door. She resisted the urge to kick him in the ass. He'd be in that room later whether she wanted him or not.

All chatter ceased when she opened the door. She strode around the long table and sat at the head. "Report, in detail this time."

The ambassador licked his lips, and a smile wobbled into life on his face. "I'm Higaroshi Roya, Captain. The ambassador to the drushka? We met when—"

"I remember."

"Well, these are Nettle and Shiv, and they, well, perhaps they should…"

Nettle laid a hand against Higaroshi's chest and pushed him gently into his chair. She perched on the edge of hers as if ready to leap to her feet. "The chanuka have attacked our home, hunt leader. We drove them away, but many drushka are dead. Our leader thinks we may not survive another attack, not now that the chanuka have seen every way we can fight. They are too smart, made that way by you, we believe, and now we ask for your help with the trouble you have wrought."

Carmichael stood to pace. Higaroshi stared at the table, but Ross and the other drushka kept their gazes on her, Ross expectant and the drushka with a steady, unreadable stare.

"The trouble we've wrought?" Carmichael asked.

"You know of what we speak. Our leader thought that Sa Cordelia was ignorant, but you, the hunt leader?"

Carmichael's lips quirked up. "Well." But how could she just admit it, even when they knew, and they wouldn't let her worm her way out of it? "We'll help you. I was already planning on it."

It was as good as an admission. Ross looked away, and Carmichael knew she was ashamed. Well, why shouldn't she be? There was enough shame to go around.

"Why did you tamper with the chanuka?" Shiv asked, eyes bright with confusion or anger. "Did you wish us dead? Did you wish your own kind dead?"

"Of course not!"

"Then why? Or should we wait for Reach, and you will tell her?"

Carmichael sighed. "You understand orders, yes?"

Ross crossed her arms, and Carmichael saw much of herself in those broader shoulders. "The Storm Lord didn't order this."

And if Carmichael argued, how much would it look as if she was passing the blame? "You'll have to make up your own mind, Ross."

The door opened, framing Paul Ross in the dimness of the hall. "I didn't realize you'd borrowed my brain, Captain."

She had to smile, even with everything. "Mayor." She nodded past him to Reach. "Ambassador. Sit. We have a lot to talk about."

But how much to tell them? Whatever was needed to kill the boggins, she supposed. After that, she had her troops and her town to think of. She hadn't forgotten the Storm Lord's threat to keep his story quiet. If it got out, she didn't think he'd keep the casualties to her. And what good would it do if anyone found out he was human? It could tear apart everything they'd built. Circumstances weren't dire enough to risk that. Yet.

CHAPTER FIFTEEN

Dillon leaned back on a pile of cushions. This was the life. He'd been a soldier since he turned eighteen. His old man had been a soldier, and his mom, though he barely remembered her, and his old man had kept their lives sparse, befitting Pross Co. grunts, with plenty of vids to make up for what they didn't have.

Dillon snuggled deeper into the cushions and bit into the soft flesh of a piece of fruit. "To hell with vids when you can have this." He pushed off his slippers and rubbed his toes together. Maybe he could wrangle a foot massage out of someone.

"Did you say something?"

Dillon glanced over to where Lazlo sat beside a pile of books and papers. He didn't use the cushions but a hard-backed chair, and all he'd done since they'd come back to the temple was read. He didn't look up from his work but kept messing with his face as if adjusting glasses that weren't there.

"Why don't you relax, Laz? Have some fruit."

"How much of this did you know?"

"You're going to have to be more specific."

"These people recorded everything from the first landing, on computers at first, until someone realized no new power cells were coming, and then they copied their words onto whatever paper they had, like the margins of this old novel. Who even thought to bring something like that?"

Probably someone like Lazlo, but Dillon didn't mention that.

"Then they used cloth until they figured out paper, which was hit or miss. Some used clay tablets. Clay tablets!" He stared as if they were having a revelation.

"And?"

Lazlo shook his head. "The colonists landed with practically nothing. They had a whole infrastructure waiting at the target planet, everything they'd ever need. All that was lacking was them. And then they were stranded on a planet with some hostile alien species, and they had to dig up some pretty ancient ideas, had to learn to make *paper* all over again. And every time they made another leap in technology, they were careful to copy what they'd learned so it couldn't get lost again."

Dillon nodded slowly. "Impressive."

"Extraordinary. And all while having no clue what might happen to them. They hoped for rescue." He waved one book and then set it aside. "They thought they were going to be wiped out." He held up another. "With dying transmitters, they shouted into the dark."

"We answered when we could."

"I didn't. I hid in the botanical habitat and put the planet out of my mind." He hung his head a bit. "I'm ashamed of that."

Dillon turned his head so his eye roll would go unnoticed. "We couldn't talk to them until we'd gotten the knack of our abilities, until we'd gotten our stories straight." He stood and crossed to read over Lazlo's shoulder. "If you admire them so much, go out and talk to some of them."

Lazlo snorted. "I almost gave the game away last time. Maybe I'm just not cut out to live in Dillontown."

Dillon barked a laugh. "Talk to them about their wondrous history. I'm sure they'd love the opportunity to brag. And you could tell them about you, just not all that you've done for them. It's a thin line, but you can walk it."

One deep sigh later, Dillon knew he'd caved, but he still sat there, bringing down the room.

"Start small, Laz. Walk around the temple. Say hello to people." And maybe pick his spirits up for once.

Lazlo stood, clutching the table as if afraid he'd drown without it. "I guess I could."

"Or maybe just go for a walk."

"Okay, all right, I'm going."

As Lazlo opened the door to leave, Dillon added, "And see if anyone around here gives foot massages."

Lazlo paused, shoulders tight, and Dillon thought he might have a sarcastic retort, but he hurried through the door. Maybe he was just tired.

Or still angry. Sometimes, it took him a while to get over things. Well, being around others would help that, give him something to occupy his mind. Lazlo didn't like talking to people, but he'd never learn to like it if he didn't get out and fucking do it.

And babysitting him all the time was getting exhausting. But he was scared, and he'd get even more scared if Dillon started pushing him away. Dillon looked to the door, ready to call Lazlo back, tell him to hide in the room and read. Maybe he'd take his own advice and meet some new faces. There were some lovely ladies in the temple. The whole city held untold bounty.

A tentative knock came from the door. Dillon smiled. "Come on back, Laz, I—" Marcus walked in, and Dillon shut his mouth with a snap. "Didn't I send you to Carmichael?"

"She threw me out, Storm Lord, threatened me if I didn't go."

Dillon clenched his fist, and a tingle ran through his body as he bottled his power. "She what?" When Marcus opened his mouth again, Dillon sliced a hand through the air. "I heard you." A spark leapt from his skin and singed the wall.

Marcus fell to his knees. "Forgive me, Storm Lord!"

Dillon blinked at him, so surprised that his power shut off like a switch. "Get up, man! I'm not angry with you." Marcus sagged, and Dillon didn't know whether to yell at him or pat his head. "Just go. I'll sort this out. Get yourself together."

Marcus fled. Dillon took a deep breath. He'd have to be more careful with his power. He hadn't realized he could terrify them so easily. Well, some of them. Carmichael had fired Marcus even after she'd known who'd sent him. It was almost as bad as telling Dillon off in person. He even admired her for it. After the breachies had come at him sideways, such a blatant fuck-you was refreshing.

It still had to be dealt with, and her position made it tricky. On the one hand, he couldn't let her get away with anything. On the other, he didn't want to punish her too harshly, at least in the public eye. The troops respected if not liked her. He'd seen that during armor training. They hopped when she said hop, and none of them had cast hateful, mutinous glances when her back was turned. If he stripped her title, they might turn on him, but if he let her skate on petty shit, they might think they could do the same.

"Fuck." If this had been any of his old commands, he would have given her such a tearing down that the rest of the unit would have been trembling. Maybe that was what was needed, a bit of a tear-down, something that would make her fuckup known, that would teach the rest of the soldiers to toe the line, but not make them lose all respect for her.

And he'd thought Lazlo had a thin line to walk.

Step one, change out of the goddamned gold robes. They were impressive, but for a dressing-down he wanted something a little more down to, well, Earth.

❖

It was the foot massage comment that made Lazlo want to punch the wall. That was so Dillon. So much on Calamity to wonder about, to think through, and Dillon focused on his freaking feet.

And that after he'd practically muscled Lazlo from the room so his relaxation time wouldn't get muddied with something as trivial as history. Lazlo should have known this would happen, should have known that all of Dillon's promises to look out for him would fade in the middle of these enamored people.

Not completely fair. Dillon had looked out for him, had kept people away from him, and had spent time with him. Their rooms were right next to each other, though Lazlo bet Dillon hadn't lain awake listening to all the sounds that weren't the *Atlas*. He'd probably slept like an innocent.

"Simon, are you all right?"

He glanced up to find he'd nearly collided with Samira. "What?"

She smiled brightly. "I came looking for you."

"Oh, well, um, if you need the Storm Lord, he's..." He waved down the hall.

"I know. How are you? You look upset."

He barked a laugh and covered his mouth. "It's a long story."

"A great philosopher whose name I can't remember once said, 'All we have is time.'"

Some more than others. "Is there something I can do for you?"

"No. Why?"

"Well, you came to see me."

She laughed as if he delighted her. "To see how you are! The question is, Simon, what can I do for you?"

"People don't ask me that." The words came out unbidden, and he wished he could stuff them back in.

She frowned as if that was the saddest thing she'd ever heard. He scanned her quickly, looking for deception and found none, his touch so light he didn't think she could detect it.

She rallied, shaking her head and smiling again. "Do you want to meet some other healers? I don't think any of them can match you, but you might find something to talk about. They're usually in the courtyard this time of day. Have you ever communed?"

He had a sudden vision of people frolicking through trees and talking about their oneness with Mother Earth. He chuckled, and she seemed to take that as an invitation.

"This way."

With all of his books back with Dillon, all Lazlo could do was shrug. "Why not?"

She led him down a hallway. Maybe finding someone to talk to was a good idea. Samira seemed kind enough. Dillon would have seen her as a willing source of information. Well, that and a collection of attractive body parts.

"Do you know how to make paper?" he asked.

"Uh, no." When he didn't answer her curious glance, she shrugged. "I know where you can get some. If you're looking to learn, I'm sure the guild would be willing to teach you."

"I'm just thinking of everything that can be forgotten, remembered, and then forgotten again. Enough people learn a thing so it doesn't get lost, but not everyone has to know it."

She nodded slowly. "True, at least until you don't need it anymore."

He asked her more questions about the people of Gale, and his fear ebbed away, so much so that when they stopped in a large courtyard, he had no idea where in the temple he was.

Panic tightened his shoulders, and his heart thudded in his ears. Several people sitting on benches around a wooden table glanced up, and as he used his power to calm himself, they studied him closely. He felt tendrils of their micro-psychokinetic powers slinking toward him, not intruding, just hovering. He gave their powers a little push, a subtle threat, and several of them stood, mouths open.

Samira touched his shoulder. "Everyone, this is Simon, the man I told you about."

Two men and two women, they wandered closer, but they didn't seem offended by his rejection, more curious. One of the men even smiled brightly. "You can scan us if you want. We don't mind."

It was like offering to grope each other, but he sent a soft brush of power their way, reading some telepathy to go with their micro-psychokinetic powers. They stared at him as if waiting.

"I, um, I just did."

They shared another of those astonished looks. "I didn't feel anything!" one said.

They babbled on top of one another, and he stepped back from their collective voices. Samira held up her hands and leaned in front of Lazlo, shielding him. "Give him some air!"

They laughed and stepped back. "You have to commune with us!" one woman said.

And there went the visions again. "I don't know what that is."

Curious glances this time. Samira gestured to them one at a time. "This is Leila, Horace, Will, and Kessy." They nodded with their names, Kessy waving hello.

Horace gestured toward the others, a bright smile on his handsome face. "We're the yafanai healers, though most people go to the regular doctors in town."

Will rubbed his fingers together. "We only get the big money in here, though the docs will call us in for messy problems."

"That boy with his ankle bone hanging out of his leg." Kessy stuck out her tongue in disgust.

Leila shivered but said nothing.

"When we commune," Samira said, "we use our powers together, let them flow." She waved. "It's hard to explain, much easier to do. Those with similar powers commune together, but I can stay with you. I've communed with almost everyone anyway."

Kessy winked at her. "You make it sound dirty."

Samira gave her a playful shove and looked back to Lazlo. "We'll get started, and you just jump in when you're ready. It's very relaxing."

He nodded slowly, but he was enjoying watching them. He kept his senses open for deception, for innuendo, for the sniping and politics that were always at play on the *Atlas*, but he kept coming up empty. They sat around the table again, Samira beside him. They didn't link hands as he expected, but they did close their eyes, and he felt their power flow. He studied their faces, lingering on Horace's: the curve of his jaw, the way his dark lashes lay against his cheeks.

Lazlo shook his head to get it together. He couldn't go falling apart every time he saw a handsome man. He focused on their powers instead. Their abilities hung in the air without purpose but full of potential, winding together as they flexed their mental muscles. Weak, not a tenth of what he could do, but it must have seemed miraculous to them. He didn't want to overwhelm them, so he let his own power trickle amongst theirs and kept his eyes open, studying each of them. They seemed so relaxed with each other. Horace even sighed, the soft planes of his face relaxing to the point where he seemed almost asleep.

At first, they didn't seem to notice Lazlo's power. He let himself be known slowly, not wanting to swamp them. He could shut off their abilities with a snap. They gasped and explored his power, not following it back into him but sliding over and around it, and he felt their awe. With a relaxed chuckle, he closed his eyes and let himself bask in their adoration.

❖

Dillon made himself stroll through the doors of the Paladin Keep. He shook hands with soldiers and slapped backs. He'd collected a few people on his way through the city, and he had them wait outside so as not to crowd everyone. They seemed happy to obey without Lazlo's help this time. Maybe he'd proven to them that he was always coming back.

The soldiers greeted him warmly, not yet tainted by Carmichael, but who knew how long that would last? "Which way to the captain's office?" he asked.

They pointed up the center staircase from the large central room. "But she's not up there right now, Storm Lord," one said. "There's some problem with the drushka, and she's meeting with them."

Drushka, eh? He had yet to see one, though he knew Gale had an ambassador. He wondered if this new problem had something to do with the boggins and the research station. Probably. Maybe Carmichael was paying the drushka to wipe the boggins out rather than going in and doing it herself. That could have been what she'd meant by "handling" it.

He followed the directions and made the room in time to see three paladins going in, people he vaguely remembered from armor training, though he couldn't recall their names. Two men and a woman, all young and strong, exactly what soldiers should be, even though they were meeting behind his back at Carmichael's direction. He caught the door to their room before it could shut and stepped inside.

At the head of a large table, Carmichael's eyes went wide before she brought her cool expression back out. He'd enjoyed watching her struggle to keep her face neutral in the Yafanai Temple, and she'd either been practicing, or being on her home turf made her more relaxed.

Nearly everyone else in the room gawked, from the three soldiers he'd seen to Lieutenant Ross—the mayor's niece, that he remembered— to three more human men. The three drushka stared, no emotion he could read on their narrow, lined faces. They made the whole room smell like plants.

"Storm Lord," Carmichael said, "what can we do for you?"

The bald man made a strangled noise and nearly fell out of his seat. It took the red-haired drushka's arm to keep him in place.

Dillon motioned for everyone to stay seated. "Just here for the meeting. I like to keep abreast of current events."

Carmichael's eyes narrowed, and he could almost see her trying to figure out what he knew and how he knew it. "Please, sit." It sounded a little strangled as she gestured to the other head of the table. "Storm Lord, this is Mayor Ross and Ambassador Reach. Nettle, Shiv, and Ambassador Higaroshi. Lieutenants Ross, Brown, Lea, and Carmichael. Sergeant Preston."

He lifted an eyebrow when she indicated the man who shared her name, probably her son. There were probably lots of family professions in Gale, never mind that there was one Ross paladin and one Ross mayor in this room alone. He wasn't surprised to find Rosses in politics. They'd held positions of power all over space. It was where the ross in Pross Co. came from, after all.

"Catch me up," he said.

"Well," Carmichael said, "Storm Lord, the boggins have now attacked the drushka in their own home." Her accusatory glance rested on him until Ambassador Reach struck the table.

"Killing a fourth of us." Reach curled her hands into fists, and he wondered if her claws could puncture her skin. She glared at Carmichael. "You have done this."

Interesting. Carmichael hadn't told them about her orders. "A fourth of your kind are dead?" he asked.

"Ahwa, just of our tribe," Nettle said. "If the old drushka are plagued by the chanuka, we do not know it, but as we are, we cannot stand alone."

Reach slammed a hand down again, and Paul Ross took her wrist, rubbing it. Well, well.

"How did you get away?" Dillon asked. "You didn't kill them all, or you wouldn't be here asking for help."

"The swamp saved them," Reach said.

He nodded slowly. "Cryptic. I like it." They gave him unreadable looks, all except for Reach, who glared like rage incarnate. They didn't seem weak. The boggins must have gotten smart indeed. What a boon they could have been if they'd been brought to heel. He wondered whose fault that was, what fuckup had let them loose.

Carmichael cleared her throat. "Four squads led by Ross, Brown, Lea, and myself." She handed a piece of paper to Preston. "Get your gear together. Pick your grunts. Lieutenant Carmichael, you're with Ross."

Lieutenant Carmichael nodded, didn't seem to care that he was the only lieutenant in the room without a squad. Dillon could have had one, too, if he wanted. All he had to do was give the word, and he'd be leading an armored pack into the swamp tomorrow.

Without Lazlo? There was no way in hell he could convince Lazlo to march into a mire with dangerous alien creatures, and without Lazlo, Dillon would be susceptible to everything this planet had to throw at him. He pictured making everyone wait while he threw up into some sinkhole because the wrong mosquito had bitten him.

Carmichael stood as if to dismiss everyone.

"I will not leave until I have my answer," Reach said. "Tell me what you have done to these creatures and why you have done it."

Carmichael's gaze flicked toward Dillon. He waited, wondering what she would do.

Paul Ross cleared his throat. "It was supposed to be a swamp study. That's what we all signed off on."

"It was a study, in a way," Carmichael said. "We...I wanted to know if we could increase the intelligence of the boggins. I ordered the researchers to feed them the same drug that gives the yafanai their abilities."

Dillon almost leaned forward as she took all the responsibility on her own shoulders. She could have blamed him without revealing his human nature. Was she afraid he'd demote her? Kill her?

Had he ever mentioned Lessan to her?

"For what purpose?" Reach said.

"Gale needs metal." To her credit, she met everyone's gaze. "And we need help to get it."

Cordelia Ross frowned hard. "You were going to get them to work for us?"

"Slaves?" Paul Ross said. "Just smart enough to follow orders."

Carmichael sighed. "We didn't know how violent they'd become."

They all sat silent, digesting this. A soft sound, as if someone ran a brush over the walls, grew into a drumming. Rain. He hadn't heard the rain in so long. Did he call it without realizing?

"So," Carmichael said, "now you know."

"I should take your miserable head," Reach said.

Carmichael sat back in her seat. "You can try."

Reach leaned forward, and Paul and Cordelia Ross called for peace at the same time.

"We've got a plan," Cordelia said. "Let's just do it."

Paul nodded. "Right. We make sure the drushka are safe, and then there will be plenty of time for discussion."

"What of the old drushka?" Nettle asked.

Carmichael shrugged. "They contacted us, offered to catch the test subjects we needed. They said they wanted to make peace."

Dillon frowned. She had told him something about the drushka, but he hadn't paid much attention.

Reach lifted her hands and dropped them. "You should have told me! They hoped you would create your own destruction, and so you have."

Right, there was some kind of schism in the drushkan ranks. "Do you think they wanted to get rid of you at the same time?" Dillon asked.

They all looked at him as if just remembering he was there. The three drushka sucked their teeth, a sound and sight that almost made him laugh. "Well, if your former comrades wanted to kill the rest of you," Dillon said, "maybe they sabotaged the experiment."

"The brittle cages." Cordelia looked to Nettle, who sat forward eagerly.

"Ahya. They wanted the creatures to get loose, but to wish our deaths?" Nettle stared along the table. "Our leader thinks they want us to return to them."

Dillon shrugged. "Maybe they thought that if there were only a few of you left, you'd have no choice but to come running back." He lifted an eyebrow at Reach. "Sounds as if they're just as responsible for your current predicament as we are. And we'll help without trying to keep you under our thumb, or whatever your old comrades want to do with you."

She sat up straighter but said nothing. Good, maybe she'd have something to think about besides revenge. Carmichael might be a pain in the ass, but she was a human pain in the ass. He had to take her side in any species disagreements.

"Well, now that we've got that sorted out." Dillon stood. Funny how he'd originally come to give Carmichael a dressing-down, but he couldn't do that now that she'd taken all the heat. Maybe that was why she'd done it, to appease him. Or maybe she would remind him of this moment if he tried to give her another aide. Well, he'd just done that to see how she'd react anyway. He'd have to try to find her amusing again, not let her bother him.

"Let me know how it goes," he said. "Captain, care to walk me to the door?"

She stood warily, and he almost grinned. He'd keep her waiting for the other shoe to drop, make her good and nervous, and keep her from fucking with him again.

Chapter Sixteen

Cordelia watched her god walk out the door and hoped he wasn't disappointed in his paladins, their captain, or her. Carmichael had finally admitted that she knew what had gone wrong with the boggins, that she was responsible. She'd fed them the yafanai drug when she hadn't known what the results would be. She'd trusted the old drushka. And all so Gale could bend another race to their will? What the fuck had she been thinking? It made Cordelia's stomach turn, made her ashamed to be a paladin, and that hurt her even more.

Reach paced beside the table until Paul led her to a corner and spoke softly to her. Preston read over the papers Carmichael had given him. Higaroshi was staring at nothing, his lips pressed together in a pale thin line. Lea and Brown sneaked peeks over Preston's shoulders.

Shiv and Liam seemed to be having their own sexy version of a staring contest. They exchanged such heated looks, Cordelia wouldn't have been surprised if the whole room got pregnant. Nettle also watched Liam and Shiv, her expression somewhere between worried and amused.

Liam got up and slinked to a small table. He poured himself a glass of water and took a sip, and Cordelia would have sworn he was a sex ad.

"Anyone else?" he asked.

"Depends," Brown said, "you offering water or a piece of your ass?"

Cordelia snorted a laugh.

Liam chuckled as he rejoined them. "And how much would you pay, Jen?"

"Why buy when I've had the free sample?" Brown nodded to Shiv. "Not that you should turn it down. It is nice."

"Thanks," Liam said just as Lea muttered, "He's not a piece of meat."

Shiv wrinkled her nose. "Ahya." But what she was agreeing to, Cordelia had no idea. "Perhaps I will have the water."

Liam got up again, staring after her as she crossed the room. "I'll help you." He bent to Cordelia's ear. "And you should have your own conversation before Carmichael comes back."

Cordelia looked to find Nettle watching her. They both looked away at the same time, and Cordelia wondered if Nettle felt the presence of others as keenly as she did. Brown was watching, too, so Cordelia got up as non-sexily as she could manage, walked around the table, and plopped into the chair next to Nettle, leaning in so Brown and Lea couldn't hear.

"Hi."

"I was wondering if we were to speak," Nettle said.

"I'm sorry to hear about your people. I wish I could change it." She rubbed her forehead, certain this hadn't been the kind of conversation Liam meant.

Nettle squeezed her wrist. "Thank you for your grief. We gave them to the swamp, much as you did your people."

"Pool warned me that my captain might have known what happened, but I didn't want to believe."

"Will the knowing help us?"

Cordelia glanced at Reach. "I don't know. I'll leave the diplomacy to other people."

"But you are so good at it." She wrinkled her nose. "When I told you of the scent, it was not to keep you away. I did not want a falsehood between us."

"Well, I wasn't exactly truthful when I said you were the only one who was tempted."

Nettle turned, long legs crossing at the knee as her slow gaze traveled up Cordelia's body, leaving Cordelia feeling quite naked, other people in the room be damned. She flushed from the heat radiating through her body and wanted nothing more than to slide her hand along Nettle's thigh, to feel those muscles tighten.

Nettle's mouth parted slightly. "Perhaps there should be nothing between us, no clothing, no air."

"Sounds nice."

Brown cleared her throat loudly. "If everyone is pairing up, that leaves the sergeant and the ambassador together. That good with you guys?"

Preston laughed. Higaroshi seemed to turn even paler. From the corner, Paul chuckled and muttered something about young people.

Carmichael barged through the door and walked to the head of the table again. She stared at all of them as if trying to remember where she'd left things. "You've got your squads. We leave tomorrow. Any questions?"

"Do you want any yafanai for the expedition?" Paul asked. "I mean, I don't know if I can get you any now with—"

"We're good." Carmichael gestured at Nettle and Shiv with her chin. "Can you take us to meet your people?"

"Ahya," Nettle said.

"Good. Ambassador Reach, you should stay here in case any more drushka trickle in."

"Do not tell me my business," Reach said.

Carmichael lifted an eyebrow but didn't respond. There was going to be bad blood there for a long time.

"Captain?" Higaroshi said. "What should I do?"

She shrugged. "Why are you asking me?"

"I'm sorry." He looked to Nettle. "I don't think I can go back. Those creatures, their mouths…" He wiped his lips.

Reach moved to stand behind him. "Rest with us. Let the warriors fight."

He nodded.

"Dismissed." Carmichael strode for the door.

Liam gave Cordelia a pointed glance before he followed Carmichael out. Shiv stared after him.

"It's all right, Shiv," Cordelia said. "You and Nettle stay with me."

Reach led Higaroshi out. Paul patted Cordelia's shoulder before he followed. Preston left right after, but Brown lingered a moment, giving Cordelia a slow smile.

"Shut up, Brown," Cordelia said.

She laughed and left with Lea on her heels.

❖

Liam trailed his mother's stomps, just as he'd done as a child. But instead of waiting in the hall for her to notice him, he pushed into her office behind her.

"What are you doing?" she asked.

"I'd like to talk to you."

Her face screwed up, and she leaned away. "About what?"

"Nothing personal. Don't worry."

"I don't have time for—"

"I'm not staying in the rear on this expedition."

She sat behind her desk, leaned back, and fixed him with a scrutinizing stare. "You want to lead a squad?"

"No!"

"Figures. You're Ross's problem. She'll put you where she puts you."

"And I'll ask her to put me up front. I just wanted you to know, in case you were surprised to see me there."

Her eyes narrowed. "What are you up to?"

He shrugged, tried to keep his expression neutral, but there was no hiding from her.

"You're trying to impress the drushka? Which one?"

Another shrug.

"I could order you left behind, give that pretty armor to someone else, and see if that gets your brain to overrule your dick for once."

"You haven't given my armor away yet. Why start now?"

"Don't push me, boy."

But who was pushing whom here? She'd never throw him out of the paladins. He knew part of her wanted him to quit, to walk away so she could say she'd done all she could, but he wasn't going to cave. "I just wanted you to know."

She continued to stare, and he had a flash of memory: he'd sneaked out of the house after she'd yelled the roof off one night. He'd gone to Cordelia, said he wished his mother was dead, and she'd punched him right in the mouth, telling him not to wish for things he knew nothing about.

But had Cordelia's parents ever looked at her like this?

When he didn't respond, his mother started shuffling papers. "Anything else?"

"No." He forced back his need for her approval and walked out.

He couldn't go to Shiv with this mommy shit clinging to him. Normally, he'd just go drinking with Cordelia and banish his ghosts, but they both had other things to think about.

He opened the door to the meeting room slowly, wanting his third sight of Shiv to be as savory as possible. She turned toward the movement, and he bit his lip, remembering when she'd done the same.

She stood, graceful, as if springing in slow motion. The look she gave him said she wanted more than just amorous glances, and she wanted it soon. Many people had looked at him with lust, but none had made him feel like prey before. He returned the look as best he could.

"Any news?" Cordelia asked.

He shook his head. "Everyone else is gone?"

She gestured at the room. "Didn't notice, huh? Come on. We have to figure out what to do with these two."

He was going to say he had a few good ideas, but as much as he wanted Shiv, he didn't want to strain things between Nettle and Cordelia, not knowing what they'd agreed to. The glances they gave each other said they had some ideas, too.

Shiv growled, and Liam's gaze snapped back to her. Her predatory look had gotten even sharper, and though he still wanted her, he almost took a step back.

Nettle hissed something in drushkan. Shiv responded in kind.

"Well," Cordelia said, "we can show you a bit of Gale." As they went out the door, she asked, "What did you say to her, Nettle?"

"I told her not to injure anyone."

"Don't worry. Liam can take it."

He grinned over his shoulder. "And what did she say?"

"That I promise nothing!" Shiv called from the hallway.

They descended the stairs together, and Liam walked beside Shiv through the courtyard. She craned her neck, gawking. Liam glanced back to find that Nettle and Cordelia had followed, but where he hoped to see some touching, maybe a few kisses, they both had worried looks.

"Great," Liam muttered.

Shiv followed his gaze. "Nettle is worried for our people." She slapped her thighs. "I am as well. So many are dead."

"Yeah. I'm sorry about that."

She stood on tiptoe and put her palms to his cheeks. "But you are lovely. Your eyes are like mine."

"Thanks." Though he had to wonder if she just called herself lovely, or if that was a language snafu. "I like to look at you, too."

She wrinkled her nose away. "I would very much like to be lovers with you."

It almost made him stutter. "I know where we can—"

She stepped away and slapped her thighs again, looking to Nettle. When she stomped that way, Liam followed. He caught Nettle saying, "I would like to stay with you, Sa, but perhaps it would be better to be within the trees."

Cordelia chuckled. "I'll be thinking about you whether I can smell you or not." They both laughed and turned to Shiv with surprised looks.

"I know your mind, hunt leader," Shiv said. "You are thinking we should stay closer to the trees, where my mother can reach us if she needs us."

"Ahya, young one. Is that why you are angry?"

"No, my thoughts are the same. I have been in your presence too long!"

Both Cordelia and Nettle laughed. Liam opened his mouth to protest, but Cordelia shot him a warning look.

"When the sun comes," Nettle said, "we will meet you."

Liam gave Cordelia a look of his own. "You'd be safer in Gale."

"Two drushka can hide in the trees," Nettle said. "The chanuka will not find us."

Shiv grabbed Liam's neck and forced his head down. She kissed him hard, all greedy nibbles and probing tongue. When she released him, his head swam.

"Do not forget me," she said. And then she and Nettle were walking away, Nettle casting a smile over one shoulder.

"Great," Liam muttered. "That did wonders for my erection."

Cordelia sputtered a laugh. "Drinks?"

"Yes, please."

CHAPTER SEVENTEEN

Carmichael watched her troops with a glow of pride. The silver silhouettes of the armors glinted in the sunlight. The leathers marched in orderly rows, pure business—even with a bit of chatter— ready for anything. The powered armor felt good around her shoulders, one thing she could thank the Storm Lord for.

Inside the forest, Nettle and Shiv led the squads to a host of waiting drushka. The tallest stepped forward, her hair as bright green as Shiv's. It cascaded over her shoulders, but still seemed thicker than a human's, each strand more like a plant stalk than a lock of hair.

Ross pushed forward and pointed to her. "Captain Carmichael, this is Pool, the leader of the drushka."

Pool inclined her head, and Carmichael followed suit.

"I'm sorry for your loss," Carmichael said. "What kind of numbers are we looking at?"

Pool spread her hands. "Difficult to count, both the chanuka and our dead."

Carmichael fought the urge to wince. Had Reach sent word? Did they all lay the blame for their dead at her feet? Most of the drushka stared with an intensity that could have been anger or anticipation for battle.

"How many of your people are going in with us?" Carmichael asked. "We'll need trackers."

"You will have them, but I will keep the bulk of my people with me."

Carmichael nodded, expecting that.

Pool gestured Shiv forward. "My daughter will accompany you, to see what is to be seen."

"Will she stay in the rear where it's safe?"

"She will do as I say."

"Ross," Carmichael said, nodding at the girl. Ross took Shiv and fell back with her squad. Scouts split off from the host of drushka and scattered. "We'll be back," Carmichael said. "Paladins, move out!"

They headed for the drushkan home, where the attack had taken place, though Carmichael doubted the boggins were still there. She hoped for a trail. The troops kept up a good pace, the armors far outpacing the leathers; everyone had to slow to keep together. When the massive trees of the swamp began, the armors flitted through the branches with the ease of drushka, while the leathers were left to clamor along the lower routes.

They camped for the night and continued their march the next morning, finding the drushkan home as abandoned as Carmichael thought it would be. She set the trackers on finding a trail, and they quickly sought one out. Broken branches and leaves marked a clear, obvious path, not in keeping with everything she'd heard about these new, smarter boggins.

Unless they'd been sloppy on purpose. When the trackers found no other trail, Carmichael decided it didn't matter. If they had one way to go, they had to go that way, but she reminded everyone to keep their eyes open. The squads fanned out, in earshot of each other but with enough distance that they couldn't be surrounded.

They kept quiet enough to listen, but the swamp was alive with sounds and tiny movements: the slurp of creatures slipping into the water, the buzz of insects, the waving of leaves and vegetation, and the rattle of many-legged things clattering over bark. The boggins could be on top of them, and they wouldn't know, though Carmichael hoped the drushka could warn them. Of course, if that were true, a fourth of the drushka wouldn't be dead.

One of the trackers whistled. He knelt on a low branch, pointing into the distance. Carmichael leapt and landed at his side, her stabilizers keeping her balanced. She zoomed in on where he pointed and spotted a boggin standing in the open as if waiting. Not that smart, then.

There were more beside him, standing casually as if for a surprise party. She scanned for others, looking up and down as well as around, but there were only a handful, under fifty, not the hordes the drushka had described. Of course, the drushkan fighters had killed more than a few. Maybe this was all that was left.

As the paladins drew closer, the boggins formed ranks. Carmichael lifted a hand and dropped it, signaling the charge.

❖

Liam tried not to laugh when Cordelia howled and darted for the pack of boggins. Most of the squad streaked forward with her, shrieking like the unquiet dead.

She leapt without a seeming thought for her safety, but her armor kept her upright, though with the odd wobble that made Liam's heart jump. He hung back and watched as her powered swings split boggins down the middle in a spray of blood and viscera. She sheared through weapons and limbs and lopped off heads as if mowing grain.

In seconds, her shoulders sagged as if the urge to fight went out of her. As Liam skewered a boggin, he understood. There was no challenge here, no bite. There weren't enough boggins to test the leathers, let alone those wearing powered armor. He'd expected scores of them, but it seemed only these few had survived. He wondered if the drushka would even thank them for this.

A few of the boggins had climbed high, and the armors leapt after them. Liam followed and shoved a boggin off a higher limb. He leaned over and watched it fall, arms and legs flailing. He scanned the branches below for Shiv, wondering if she was staying away from the fighting. Nettle fought alongside a group of leathers, and Liam thought to make his way there, maybe find Shiv nearby.

Something heavy dropped onto his shoulders. He lurched forward, his stabilizers whining, feet sliding. The faraway water loomed, but there were so many branches in the way. Would his armor save him if he hit every one on the way down?

Long claws grated on his helmet. He dropped into a crouch and reached back. His head wrenched backward, threatening to send him over. He stood and tottered in a circle, flailing, reaching, and wondering if he could swing at it without clanging himself in the head.

The crack of a gunshot echoed above the sounds of combat. Everyone, human and boggin, turned toward the noise. The weight fell from Liam's shoulders, and he nearly followed it, but Cordelia grabbed his arm.

"Thanks." He clutched her shoulder and tried to smile through the panic still gripping his chest.

"Wasn't me." She nodded into the resuming battle.

His mother put her sidearm away as he looked. She hated wasting bullets, and she'd spent one on him. "Mom."

She turned away, and the fight was over soon after, everyone looking for a new target and not finding one. Liam's mother marched toward him, her face grim. She'd saved him. She loved him. She couldn't say it, but it had to be true.

When she stalked toward him, he raised his visor and whispered, "Mom—"

"Follow me."

When they were away from the others, she turned, her own visor up. "Why the fuck did you let your guard down?"

"I wasn't—"

"You endangered your whole squad by letting a boggin get that close to you. Do you think trained soldiers grow on trees?"

He blinked. Trained soldiers?

"I can't lose a single blasted one of you!"

"One of me?"

She slapped him hard, sending him reeling for the second time that day. Ache vibrated through his skull from her armored swing. She had to have pulled it, could have broken his jaw. Her face was blotchy and crazed, and if she hadn't been wearing her armor, he bet he would have seen her chest working like a bellows.

"You shouldn't have come," she said. "If you can't do the job right, you shouldn't have come. I thought Ross could mind you, but no one can."

"It's not my fault that—"

She hit him again, and all he could think was that a normal person would be crying, but when had either of them been normal?

"I'm sorry," he said.

She lifted her hand again, but Cordelia barked, "That's enough, Captain."

Liam looked over his mother's shoulder to see Cordelia standing a few feet away, hand not on her sidearm but close.

His mother turned slowly. "What did you say to me, Ross?"

Cordelia's shoulders squared as if this was one fight she could get behind. "Respectfully, Captain, you should take a walk."

They stared each other down, and Liam got the impression they'd forgotten he was there. That was fine. He wanted to be forgotten. When he began to wonder if he should walk away, his mother marched back to the squads.

Liam let out a breath. "My hero."

"Are you all right?"

"I'm always good for a punch." But he couldn't contain a warble in his voice.

She clapped him on the shoulder, and the motion combined with the shock was enough to make him sit. "I'm fine."

She knelt beside him. "You're not."

"Just leave it."

"I can listen."

He shook his head.

"Look, Liam, um, lots of people like you."

He laughed, knew it was bitter, and hoped it had enough enthusiasm to put her off. "Just fuck off, please?" He said it with a smile, one she returned, but hers had a pitying tinge.

"I'll be right there if you need me."

She moved off, and he watched her go, all confidence, something he'd always admired, something he tried to copy when he could.

Shiv dropped from the branch above, and he started, the sight of the beckoning ground looming in his mind.

"Shit!" he cried. "Don't do that!"

"Do what?"

"Be so quiet."

She tilted her head. "Is there another way to be?"

The question was so absurd, it floored him. "Loud and obnoxious?"

"Why would anyone wish to be so?"

"It's a joke."

"It is not funny."

He picked at his boots. "Sorry. A boggin landed on me, and it freaked me out."

"I heard. And then your hunt leader thrashed you for being careless."

He stared. "Is that what happened? I thought my mother hit me for no good reason."

"Your mother and also your hunt leader?" She sucked her teeth. "You should have another hunt leader. Or you should learn to duck her strikes."

It had never been more apparent that they were two different species, and even though he still desired her, he felt the space between them. "I don't understand what happened."

She spread her hands. "One of the trackers said you looked as if you did not wish to fight. You did not watch the battle, and the chanuka nearly killed you." She touched his wrist. "I am happy it did not."

"Thanks."

"And then your hunt leader punished you, and now you will better see the enemy."

It sounded so simple, but his mother had never hit him before, no matter how much he'd disobeyed her, and there had been more than disappointment in her crazed eyes.

"Why did you come if you did not wish to fight?"

He shrugged. "To see you."

"Then why did you not stay in the back with me?"

"I…" How could he say he wanted to impress her now that he'd done the opposite?

She stroked his chin. "You did not fight, yet you did not stay back. Then your mother had to save you. Mother and hunt leader, she cares twice whether you live or die, but she has more to tend to in battle than you."

He thought about his mother's comment, about not being able to afford losing one, her son or her squad. It'd been a long time since any paladin had been killed, and he knew she felt bad about the researchers who'd died, though she'd never admit it. She never admitted to any feelings but anger and disappointment.

"She's never cared this much."

"Has your life ever been in danger before?"

He thought of all the times he'd been beaten up, tried to remember if he'd ever thought it was the end, but no, not until that thing had perched on his head, and he'd seen the drop. The memory came back like a hammer, and even in the armor, he started to shake.

Shiv sat in his lap and folded her long arms around his shoulders. "You have much to learn, but ahya, so do I. All life is folded together, like new soil flowing over old."

He held her but not too tightly, aware of the strength in his powered limbs. If only he could take it off, hold her for real, but that would piss his mother off more. "I wished her dead once."

"Truly?"

"Well, maybe not dead but somewhere else, out of my life."

"Ahya, I know this feeling."

"Well, a week later, some thief broke her arm, some of her ribs. If she hadn't been so stubborn, he might have beaten her to death." He'd been at her bedside, and she'd shamed him into holding back his tears. He'd sneaked out that night, had sex for the first time, an older girl who'd offered to soothe him. He'd forgotten how close those two events were.

"And you think your wishing brought about her injuries?" Shiv asked.

"Not logically, but at the time, I felt so guilty."

She tilted his chin up and nibbled his lip. "You are not a mind thrower. You do not cause such things to happen."

"My brain doesn't always obey logic."

"Then we will distract it." She rubbed her cheek against his and whispered in his ear. "My mother tells me some of you will stay in the swamp overnight. Insist on being one of these." She stood. "And if your hunt leader should strike you again, hit back!"

He stood with her, and they moved to the squads, Shiv taking up her place at the rear of the column. His mother called for them to move, not looking at him, stalking among everyone like a wild animal. Soon after, she called a halt and moved off by herself. After a glance at Liam, Cordelia followed her. Liam sidled close, keeping out of sight.

"Captain?" Cordelia asked.

"Don't worry, Ross. I'm not losing my mind."

Liam peeked around a tree. His mother paced up and down a short branch, Cordelia waiting on one end.

"I hit my boy."

"I know, Captain."

Liam's mother nodded, but there were no tears, only an angry look, but maybe she was angry at herself this time. "I keep seeing him in my mind, playing with my helmet when he was four. I had such hopes."

And he dashed them every chance he got. He clenched a fist and told himself he would not feel guilty for being who he was.

"You know you've got the captaincy after me, Ross?"

Cordelia gawked. "What?"

"Going deaf?"

"No, Captain!"

A knot in Liam's chest loosened. He'd been terrified she'd pick him even though he knew she wouldn't. Logic again.

"The drushka have requested some of you stay in the swamp overnight," his mother said. "You'll be in charge."

"Captain."

"I'm guessing my son will stay with you?"

"That…would be his choice, Captain, I'm sure of it."

His mother paused, and Liam wondered if he should step out. "Fine. Well, come on, Ross. We haven't got all day. Time to get moving."

"We've only been resting a few minutes, Captain."

"Move your ass!"

Liam hustled back toward the squads and tried to look as perplexed as everyone else at the shortest rest they'd ever had. His mother had saved him and struck him all in the same day. Maybe it still meant she loved him. He told himself that from now on, he wouldn't be everything she wanted him to be, but he'd stop rubbing her nose in that fact at every opportunity. They'd never be a storybook family, but maybe they could have an uneasy peace.

❖

The stomping feet echoed in B46's submerged ears. The water hid her from the tall creatures, leaving her eyes and nostrils free, but the tall creatures did not look for her or her children among the floating logs.

Difficult, but she'd managed to gather her children after the tree had attacked them, and then before they were ready, the tall creatures in their shining skins had found her again. Some had to be sacrificed, the children that had watched her eagerly, and it was harder this time.

These children had such intelligence, such speed, and such obedience. They looked to her in all things. But if any of them were to survive, some had to die, enough so that the tall creatures would think them all dead. She'd chosen among them, given them their task, and then forced herself to watch and remember.

She shifted away from the moss and logs, her children following as the tall creatures retreated into the distance. She climbed among the branches and found the slaughtered children while her mates gathered those that floated below. She pulled two into her arms, sniffing their carcasses, tasting their wounds and seeing her life without them.

She wanted to howl, but that would bring the tall creatures back. She held them close, their rage stolen from them. But they would not be wasted meat. She called to her mates and her remaining children, called that they should consume their dead kin, absorb their rage. They would have a purpose, even in death. The taste of their flesh would spur her anger, and she would not forget, but for now, she would mourn.

CHAPTER EIGHTEEN

L azlo wandered through the temple museum and didn't know whether to laugh or cry. The yafanai had allocated only two small rooms for so much history. They'd enshrined what they could from the original landing: bits of plastic, a small vial of bug spray, shreds of old flight suits, and other bits of flotsam they hadn't been able to repurpose, all with careful, handwritten labels inside wooden cases.

Samira had steered him here after his interest in Gale's history, and the first room proved enough of a marvel to keep him busy for hours. It was also empty of people, a good place to hide.

The healer communion had gone well until Dillon had found them and lured Lazlo away. He'd stalked up and down his room, complaining about Captain Carmichael until Lazlo calmed him with power.

Communion had been so soothing, and Lazlo knew he'd sported a relaxed, sleepy look that made Dillon laugh. When Lazlo had spoken of what he'd done, Dillon had gotten excited, asking eager questions.

Lazlo had told him about communing, feeling a warmth between him and Dillon like they'd occasionally had on the *Atlas,* when Dillon had been interested in what Lazlo could do for no other reason than that it was interesting.

"Do you think you can use this communion to make some of them stronger?" Dillon had asked.

And there went that bubble. Lazlo had railed about tampering with people *yet again*, after everything that had gone wrong with the boggins, after some of the initial experiments with the yafanai had gone horrifically wrong, too.

But Dillon had persuaded and smiled and rubbed Lazlo's

shoulders. He'd made promises and played on their history. And Lazlo had seen right through that bull, but he'd still melted like wax. In the end, he'd agreed that if some of the yafanai were willing to be stronger, he'd see what he could do.

And if they'd been on the *Atlas*, he would have gotten to work, but now there were so many places to hide, so many ways to delay. It gave Lazlo a naughty feeling, like hiding from the teacher, and if he could enjoy himself while hiding, well, why not?

It might have been the coward's way out, but it was a way out, and the museum was a perfect place to lay low. Dillon wouldn't go into a museum unless forced.

Lazlo wandered into the second room and stopped, his heart thudding. His drawings, his tools, and his ideas shone from every wall. It wasn't just a shrine to Gale; it was a shrine to him, to the creation of the yafanai.

His carefully drawn brain diagrams hung in elaborately carved frames. Those had come first, along with his drawings of the plants that would become the yafanai-makers. When he'd sent them the refined drug, they'd tried eating it at first, but the results were too unpredictable.

He moved to the next case. For permanent abilities, the drug had to be injected into the brain. The long, thin needles he'd shaped with his power were pressed into the soft red fabric of a display case. He'd designed them to traverse the eye socket or sinus canal. It must have hurt like hell. Still, he ran his fingers over them, remembering the happy hours he'd spent in their meticulous creation. Once the Galeans had a few micro-psychokinetics, the drug could be introduced into the blood and then guided to the brain via power, and there had been no need for the torture devices he'd created, beautiful as they were.

He hadn't thought of the pain of Gale's citizens. He'd been happy to be busy, to bask in Dillon's warm approval. He almost tore the frames from the wall, but he had to face these truths, to look at all he had done, the good and the bad. It would be too easy to lay it all at Dillon's feet.

He stopped in front of the next drawing, a sketch of an apple tree. He'd done it from memory, but everyone on board the *Atlas* had excellent memories, a side effect of his treatments. Had he sent the drawing by mistake, or had Dillon grabbed it with the others?

It took him back to the botanical habitat, where he'd grown an apple tree eventually, as well as coffee plants. He'd loved them, but sometimes he'd wanted to get away from them and enjoy their fruits, sitting in the mess hall nursing coffee and staring out the window.

He couldn't help thinking of one day in particular, when a group of four breachies, Lisa and her three-man harem, had come in while he was alone. They'd smiled at him, said hello, but there was a rudeness about them, as if they were looking for a fight but not daring to actually provoke him. They'd put together trays of food, vegetables he'd grown, and sat at the table in front of the window, blocking the view.

He'd stared into his coffee and listened to their low voices. They sneaked the occasional glance his way and tittered, about what he didn't know. He'd heard his father's voice saying he wouldn't get picked on so much if he didn't look like such a target, but he didn't know how to look like anything else.

He almost chucked his lovely cup of coffee and stormed back to his hole. The door opened before he could, and Dillon strode inside, a genuine smile flashing Lazlo's way. Lisa laughed, and the others shushed her. They glanced at Lazlo again, smirks in place.

Dillon's stare landed on the breachies, and they fell into silence. He crunched into an apple, his strong jaw working up and down as he strolled toward the breachies and sat, facing them but looking out the window. Their smirks wavered and died.

Dillon leaned back and plopped his size-twelves on their table. They frowned at his boots, at each other, but said nothing. Lazlo had grinned. It still made him smile. He never knew if they were so afraid of Dillon because of his rank, his strength, or the fact that he could turn them into rotisserie chickens.

Or maybe they knew they were outclassed in the bullying game. Dillon didn't bother to treat them like shit. Worse, he acted as if they weren't even there. And as they squirmed, Lazlo could tell they were starting to *feel* as if they weren't there, either.

Lisa stood, her food barely touched. "I have to go." She stepped back over the bench and started for the door, but her fork slid off her tray and bounced with a metallic ting on Dillon's bench.

Lazlo sensed it as she held her breath. All the breachies froze, but Dillon picked up the fork and held it out. As she took it, he slid his index finger over hers, and she blushed like a schoolgirl even though she'd been alive for over a hundred years.

She fled, and the others followed soon after. Dillon didn't spare them a glance. "Hey, Laz, come look at this view."

It was a good view, even with Dillon's big feet in the way.

Someone cleared her throat from the museum doorway.

Lazlo whirled, hand on his chest. "You startled me."

A young acolyte hurried forward. "I'm sorry, sir! I didn't mean—"

He waved her back. "What do you need?"

"It's the Storm Lord's new project, sir. They're ready for you."

He blinked. "I'm sorry?"

"The yafanai who want to get stronger? The first one is ready."

Lazlo shut his eyes and counted to ten. And here he'd thought he could hide, but of course Dillon would just set it up and tell him when they needed him. He could refuse. But Dillon would keep on, carrot and stick, and bring him around again, and he'd end up doing it.

"Enough," he muttered. The acolyte opened her mouth, but he gestured ahead. "Lead the way."

She led him to a bedroom where two yafanai waited, one resting in a chair while the other stepped forward.

Lazlo recognized one of the healers, the cute one. "Horace." He was disappointed but couldn't say why. "Is it you, or…" He looked to the red-haired woman, someone he hadn't met.

She arched an eyebrow. "It's me."

"My friend Natalya," Horace said. "Never satisfied." He gave her an affectionate smile which she barely returned.

"Fine." Lazlo knew he was angry, knew he should put this off, but better to just get it over with. "I'm going to put you to sleep. Do you want to lie down?" He gestured to the bed in the corner. Other than that, there was just a dresser, and he wondered which of their rooms it was.

"The chair is fine." She relaxed into its padded embrace. "I'm ready."

Lazlo put her into a coma too quickly, but there it was. She was already strong, both a macro and micro-psychokinetic, but she must not have felt strong enough. He knew the feeling.

"Do you mind if I stay and watch?" Horace asked.

"Fine."

Lazlo found Natalya's power center and set about expanding it, changing her brain, feeding it as he would a plant.

"Can I help?" Horace asked.

Lazlo was in too deep to answer, but he sensed Horace's power trying to follow. Lazlo slapped it away. This was already delicate. He didn't need an amateur fiddling around. He let his concentration slip enough to growl a warning.

Horace said something else, but Natalya mewled, pained at the interruption. Lazlo dug back in, trying to see what the problem was.

"You're hurting her!" Horace said.

No shit, but Lazlo couldn't speak, looking for the source of the discomfort and finding her power expanding where he'd set it in motion, synapses in her head rewiring, but it was happening too fast; they needed his guidance. Horace's power came pushing in again, but the delicacy of this work was beyond him.

Lazlo couldn't slip again, not enough to tell Horace to get out. He tried to wave the man away, but Horace's power still crept forward. Stubborn ass. Maybe if Lazlo focused, he could just put Horace to sleep. As he tried, Natalya jerked at them both, lashing out with her ballooning power. She cried out as their abilities entwined as if communing, but her power grabbed and pulled at Horace and Lazlo both.

Lazlo tried to shut her down, to shut the whole thing down, but her panic infected him. Natalya drew him out while Horace tried to push both of them away and made Natalya as strong as quicksand.

As he had the thought, Lazlo felt their confusion, their abilities so far linked that one of them was reading his mind, and he couldn't have that. He tried to jerk away, but his body was strangely heavy. His eyes were shut, and he commanded them to open to see himself staring down at him.

He cried out, and the vision went hazy, and then he was looking at himself through Horace's eyes as well as through Natalya's and his own. His brain tried to process input from three different sources, but they were all shrieking so loud! Stabbing pain chased him through three brains, and he couldn't tell what belonged to whom.

Lazlo tried to access his power again, to separate them, but that caused a cascade in Horace's brain as he tried to match Lazlo's ability. Horace's legs buckled as his power center expanded. Lazlo tried to stop himself, but Horace's power kept ballooning, siphoning off Lazlo's inexhaustible reserves. Lazlo screamed in rage, at himself for doing this so half-assedly and at Dillon for pushing him into it.

The anger helped ground him, and he latched on to it, fighting for his own body, letting rage propel a burst of power, hoping they wouldn't be killed as he hammered all three of them into unconsciousness.

Lazlo came back to himself slowly. He was staring at the ceiling, the rug bunched beneath him. Horace was asleep, eyelashes dark against his cheeks. His brown hair lay tousled as if he'd just run his fingers through it.

Lazlo resisted the urge to touch that hair, wondering how soft it would be, and climbed to his feet. Natalya was still asleep. They couldn't have been out long. No one was beating down the door yet, and someone had to have felt what they'd done.

Tentatively, Lazlo probed their powers and gasped. Natalya's macro powers might rival Marlowe's, and her micro powers had grown threefold. Horace could match him with the right training, but he couldn't begin to think about the ramifications of all that. He went to the door to call for help.

Dillon tried not to brood. Of all the colossal fuckups, this one took the cake and the prize and whatever else there was to take. When Dillon had suggested Lazlo augment some of the yafanai, he had thought the word "careful" to be implied, doubly so for Lazlo, who was usually careful about everything. He had to have been distracted, and strong feelings would only distract him further.

Lazlo's shields were probably wide open as he eased Horace awake. It was a delicate process, if the concentration on his face was any indication. Lazlo had to bring Horace awake by degrees, wait to see if he lashed out with his power, and then bring him along a little further. Fucking baby steps.

Lazlo glanced up from where he sat on Horace's slender bed. "It's going well."

Dillon nodded and kept his swears to himself. They were already light-years further along than what they'd been able to do for the other one. When Natalya first awoke, the smaller items in her room had drifted upward as if someone had switched the gravity off. As she'd focused, she'd thrown Lazlo across the room like a goddamned rag doll. Dillon had caught him and taken them both to the deck as walls of energy shattered Natalya's dresser to kindling and cracked the plaster on the walls. She'd made a funny, hiccupping sound, chest heaving before she began to shriek. Lazlo had jumped on the bed, and everything crashed to the floor as he'd put her under again.

So far with Horace, everything was better, if painfully slow. If these two were burned, that was a fucking shame. Lazlo hadn't even had a chance to start a new crop of plants yet.

Horace's eyes slid open.

"Horace, you're in your room, safe," Lazlo said.

"I feel different."

"Your powers have grown, but you're going to be all right." He looked to Dillon helplessly, but Dillon waved him to continue.

"I can feel everyone. All the people." Horace's eyes widened, and he grimaced.

"You can block them out. I'll show you." Lazlo took Horace's hand, and calmness flowed from him like waves.

"Better," Horace said.

"You need to learn to rebuild your shields. It'll take time, but it's a gift!" He gave Horace another of those awkward pats. "A wonderful gift." He cast another panicky glance at Dillon.

"I'll get out of your hair," Dillon said.

Lazlo made as if to stand. "What should I—"

"Fix it. You'll be less distracted if I'm not here."

Lazlo winced but turned back to his patient. As Dillon left, he heard Horace ask about Natalya and knew he'd chosen the right time to leave.

Without Dillon radiating disappointment, it was easier to concentrate, but it left too much room to think. Lazlo patted Horace's back in halting little circles as Horace wept in his lap. Shields were a must, and Lazlo kept his own tight, hoping Horace couldn't feel just how uncomfortable he was.

Lazlo didn't know if it was an overabundance of hormones or worry for Natalya, but Horace seemed determined to be as sad as possible. Lazlo couldn't leave. He didn't want to think of Horace crying alone. But emotions could be tempered and brain chemistry retuned so the sadness wouldn't be so crippling.

Horace sat up. "Are you altering my feelings?"

"Just a bit, so you won't—"

"Don't do that. I want to feel."

"I'm sorry." Lazlo folded his hands on his lap.

Horace frowned hard. "I can feel how embarrassed you are. I can feel the people in the hall."

Lazlo strengthened his shields, setting them around both of them. "It will get better, I promise."

"Will I wind up like Nat? She's not going to die, is she?"

"I…don't want to lie to you."

Horace sobbed again and leaned forward to rest on Lazlo's knee as if the weight of the idea was too much. His emotions were so bald, naked. Lazlo wondered how long it had been since he'd seen someone so open. Ever? He'd seen inside the cells of everyone on the *Atlas*, but it wasn't the same. They'd never seemed vulnerable.

He patted Horace's hair, finding it silky, just long enough to stick up through his fingers. "We won't give up on Natalya. Maybe if you and I work together, we can wake her safely, mute her powers enough for her to gain control."

Horace sat up and sniffed. "I hadn't thought of that." He wiped his cheeks. "You're right. I can be strong if it'll help her."

Lazlo smiled. "You must care for her a great deal."

"We've known each other a long time." He caught both of Lazlo's hands in his. "Please, teach me."

The tears made his dark eyes shine, and the color in his face brought out high cheekbones. His hair had fallen across his forehead, and Lazlo fought to keep from brushing it away. A jot of desire surprised him. He kept his shields iron tight so it wouldn't get out, though he didn't damn it away.

CHAPTER NINETEEN

Cordelia settled beside Liam on the solid patch of ground, watching the swamp darken into twilight. Even though they could sleep in their armor, they'd taken it off. Cordelia tried to tell herself there were myriad reasons for doing so, but sitting with Liam, waiting for Nettle and Shiv, she knew there was one overarching one: sex was impossible with it on. Liam wasn't trying to fool himself about it. After all, they'd already put Preston in charge of the squad for the night.

Shiv and Nettle had gone scouting, promising to return soon. Cordelia knew they were talking to Pool somehow and didn't ask questions. She expected Liam to complain about the wait, but he just watched the swamp with a smile. He'd been quiet ever since Carmichael had hit him, his cheeks bearing dark red bruises. Maybe the whole incident had shocked him into silence.

Or maybe he was just occupied with thoughts of Shiv. "I'm feeling kind of nervous," he said, "like it's my first time."

"Unusual for you, O expert."

"It's nice, even if I might jump out of my skin."

When Shiv leapt from a tree to land nearby, Cordelia started along with Liam, and they laughed together. Shiv ignored Cordelia and kissed Liam until he moaned. Cordelia tried not to stare, wondering if they were going to do it right there, if she should leave, but after a caress that made Liam shudder, Shiv led him into the trees.

Cordelia chuckled and relaxed as Nettle settled beside her.

"Is your smile for the fighting?" Nettle asked.

"I didn't like it as much as I thought. I'm happy about those two."

"I hope nothing foolish comes of them."

"They're worth a little foolishness."

Nettle wrinkled her nose. "Ahya, you are right, maybe. And I like the light it puts on your beautiful face."

Cordelia ducked her head and laughed. "Nice line." But Nettle didn't feed people lines. Her whole race disliked falsehoods, and flattery probably didn't come naturally to them. When she met Nettle's confused look, she knew it was true.

She pressed her lips to Nettle's, finding them thin but soft. They gave under her gentle pressure, and she cupped Nettle's cheek with one hand while Nettle caressed hers.

When they parted enough to speak, Nettle said, "Should we find a secret place of our own?"

Cordelia took another kiss before she answered. "That's the best idea I've heard in a while."

Weak dawn light barely penetrated the thick trees. A pattering of rain, shaken from the faraway canopy by the shifting wind, fell across Cordelia's naked body. She shuddered, though it wasn't cold. If she'd ever been naked in the rain, the memory was buried in childhood.

Nettle reached up from their little nest in the hollow of a tree and let the rain run down her bare arms. Her skin absorbed some of the water as bark might, but Cordelia licked a few drops off her stomach. As they'd explored each other's bodies, Cordelia had noted the roughness of Nettle's skin and the way her spine could bend and flex farther than any human Cordelia had known. They'd quickly learned how best to pleasure each other.

Nettle kissed her as if chasing the moisture. "The sky calls your name."

Cordelia's parents had told her that Sa meant rain as soon as she was old enough to understand it. They'd thought it a gentle name, but Paul had said the drushka didn't see it that way. To them, rain was something that couldn't be fought, only avoided. "I've always liked that name."

"It suits you. You are as inescapable." She trailed a finger down Cordelia's neck. "And as satisfying to my thirst."

Cordelia had to kiss her, both for her own desire and to stop the words that could lead her toward uncharted emotions, given enough time.

"The troops will be up soon," Cordelia said.

"We have a little time."

"And I haven't noticed how uncomfortable this branch is until now."

With a laugh, Nettle flowed to her feet, pulling Cordelia up, too. They pressed together, not leaving room enough for the rain to slide between them. Cordelia broke their kiss long enough to bite Nettle's chin.

Nettle shuddered and growled, the nictitating membrane sliding over half her eye. "You do that like a drushka."

"I'm a quick study."

"You said we should rise, and now you bite me?"

Yeah, she had said that, hadn't she? "I couldn't resist."

"I can keep my body between yours and the uncomfortable branch."

"Maybe we have a *little* time."

Nettle fell, taking Cordelia with her until they heard the calls of human voices. The squad was up and looking for her. And whether they thought she was in danger or they just wanted to rouse her from her love nest, they wouldn't stop anytime soon.

She and Nettle dressed and descended. Liam was waiting, already in armor, and by the time she donned hers, he had the troops ready to march.

"Does sex with a drushka come with a dose of initiative?" she asked.

He chuckled. "Yours clearly didn't."

She gave him the finger, and as they marched to the head of the squad, he mumbled, "Shiv had to rejoin her mother. I didn't have anything else to do."

"I knew it had to be something like that."

Though her armor still held a charge, she marched along the lower branches with the leathers as Nettle led them back to the Oosjani Road. Cordelia walked beside Nettle when she could and had to fight to keep her hands to herself. They were already sneaking constant glances.

Cordelia had to shake her head to stop staring at Nettle's lips, her thighs, the line of her neck.

"What does oosjani mean, anyway?" Liam said loudly.

Nettle glanced over her shoulder. "Path is how you might say it."

Cordelia frowned. "So, this is the Road Road?"

"Humans asked for a word that meant path. We did wonder when they put their own word on it as well."

Cordelia laughed, but as she realized that the end of the Oosjani would mean parting from Nettle, she sighed. "Where will your people live now?"

"There's room in Gale," Liam said.

"Only Pool can say for certain."

When Shiv leapt to land beside them, Cordelia started again, but everyone else seemed to have gotten used to how abruptly she appeared. "My mother has said nothing to me about where we will live."

"Does that mean you can come back with us?" Liam asked.

"Ahwa, no! The drushka must remain together inside the trees. It is our home."

It was a quiet march after that, Cordelia trying to watch her surroundings, trying not to focus on saying good-bye. As the trees began to thin and the swamp turned into forest, Liam and Shiv embraced enthusiastically, sharing another of those kisses that made everyone turn away.

Cordelia glanced at Nettle. "Our turn? Just how uncomfortable do we want to make everyone?"

"More jokes. It is how you guard your emotions, ahya?"

"Definitely."

"Then, my laughing one, I will simply say good-bye." She squeezed Cordelia's hands once before gathering the rest of the drushka and melting back into the trees.

Cordelia turned to see the squad grinning. She took a deep breath, fighting a flush, ready to shout at them to get their asses moving, but Liam cleared his throat.

"Column, march!" he barked. The soldiers moved out, staring forward. He gave Cordelia a shrug. "As I've always told my mom, there's no need to get loud."

Sometimes getting loud did the work for you, but she didn't mention that, content to let Liam steer the column so she could remember all that had happened between her and Nettle without thinking too hard on what it all meant.

By the time they reached the keep, the leathers were exhausted. Even Cordelia was starting to feel some strain. The armor made a long hike infinitely easier, but she couldn't keep walking for days and not feel anything. She took her helmet off inside the courtyard and stretched as the column marched past, all of them dismissed to rest.

A leather on guard duty waved to her. "There's a delivery waiting for you, Lieutenant." He gestured at a cloth-covered lump.

She reached for the card on top. "For my niece," it read, "Your ballista."

With a whoop, she yanked the cloth away, revealing a collection of wooden parts and a long length of sinew. Her fatigue forgotten, she waded in, picking up parts and trying to figure out how they went together. Leave it to the Sun-Moons to give her a disassembled weapon.

"Building a home of your own?" Liam called. He'd sneaked into the keep at some point and now reemerged wearing only trousers. His hair was wet, and he had a towel around his neck.

"It's a weapon, not a house."

"Looks a bit unwieldy."

She picked up a large pole. "Hold this."

"I hope you're joking! Just how heavy is that?"

"Why the hell did you take your armor off?"

"Some of us like to bathe."

"So, find someone who's armored."

He rolled his eyes but fetched Brown and Lea.

"What the hell, Ross?" Brown asked. "Drushka give you that?"

"It's a ballista, and you can help me put it together, or you can leave."

Lea's stern face lit up, and he climbed into the mess at Cordelia's side. "Like the wooden models I used to build with my dad."

"Here," Cordelia said, "this looks as if it fits in that slot. Come on, Brown, get your ass to work."

She sighed but pitched in, and with three of them building and Liam directing, they had it together in no time. About seven feet long, it rolled on wooden wheels and had a boxy contraption at the front with a hole facing outward.

"It launches a spear?" Lea asked.

"As big as a small tree trunk," Cordelia said with a grin.

He studied the mechanism. "This crank pulls back the sinew, you put the spear in, and you pull this lever."

Cordelia pulled the lever, and the sinew made an echoing "pong" sound. She grinned harder.

"Did they send the spear?" Lea asked.

Cordelia shook her head. "I'm sure we can find something."

"Not me. I'm going out on patrol," Brown said.

Lea waved her away. "I'll catch up."

She grumbled as she left, but Cordelia ignored her. She and Lea rooted around the back of the keep while Liam made fun of them. They found a small beam, wheeled the ballista outside the palisade, and watched it hurl the beam far into the fields.

"Unwieldy but impressive," Lea said. With a nod of good-bye, he left.

Cordelia grinned at Liam, who nodded toward the keep. "Now will you bathe?" he asked.

"Fine. Since you keep harping on it." She wheeled the ballista back inside Gale.

"I'm only thinking of you. In the armor, you don't smell bad, but I doubt you'll want to wear it to the Prog. And if you take it off without bathing, you'll bleach all the wood in the place."

"Now you're just being mean because you don't have a big phallic toy."

"Oh, but I do. I just don't share it with you. Keep moving."

She parked the ballista in the keep's courtyard and patted it. She'd have to drop by her uncle's and thank him. Or send him a note. Yes, a nice, avoidant note.

❖

B46 grunted as she laid her latest clutch of eggs in a tangle of underwater roots. She never would have laid so close to the clutches of others in the before times, but now she knew to post guards. All the children could be born together.

She trailed her claws along the hides of the guards as she passed. They grunted, keeping watch on the swamp. They were so clever. She'd never known she could be content just by staying close to those she'd borne.

In the before times, she'd always made her nests near her clutches, staying near the water, the source of food. She'd huddled inside holes in tree trunks or nestled inside tangles of branches that could shield her from predators. She'd never climbed high, never wanted to be far from her next meal.

Now she swung through the branches with ease, with no fear of leaving the water behind. She reached the sinkhole her people had constructed, a deep pool guarded on all sides by branches threaded through the roots of trees. It reminded her of the place her kind had been held; it kept the occupant of the sinkhole from wandering off before they were ready to use it.

The water creature rolled its black eyes to watch her. She saw no glimmer in it like some of the children had, like her mates had, that marked them as more knowing than before. Her children had looped vines around its limbs to keep it from thrashing and breaking free. It could do no more than stare.

B46 touched its pebbled skin, one finger skirting the teeth along its snout. It snapped lightly, four legs pumping while the slender arms in the middle of its torso wriggled.

B46 chittered, mocking it. It had power, but it could not use it until her say-so. It had anger, and she could focus that. She left it, climbed higher into the branches until she could see the other sinkholes her children were preparing, so many they dotted the landscape.

❖

Usk knelt before the writhing roots of the Shi, so large they took up the entire cavern underneath her enormous trunk, a roiling mass as large as three entire tribes of drushka.

He could not see the Shi herself, the woman who'd cast off her name when she became the eldest queen. She was lost somewhere in the mass of roots, never to see the sun again. But as he thought this, the roots coiled around his body, and he gave his mind over to his queen.

She wanted to lead all of the drushka, but there was a hole in their midst, something the Shi before her had tolerated, but now they would be whole again.

The roots lifted Usk, and he let his body go slack in trust. "What must I do, Queen?"

She sent him images of the chanuka fighting the humans. That had delighted her, but when he saw the chanuka fighting the renegade drushka, her anger flashed to the fore. It deepened into rage as the Anushi tree attacked the chanuka forces. The tree was too important. Even if none of the renegades survived, the tree must.

The Shi had hopes, vague imaginings of the renegade tree rejoining the drushkan whole, of the renegade queen kneeling at the Shi's trunk, brought there by Usk, favorite of the Shi.

"My queen, I do your bidding in all things."

He felt her love, her mind's caress. The renegades would be one with them, and the chanuka would kill all the humans, and life would become perfection again.

CHAPTER TWENTY

Horace had always liked strolling the roof of the Yafanai Temple, the second highest spot in Gale. He liked how the wind toyed with his hair and how the city spread out below him. Most of all, he'd liked how he could drop his telepathic shields because everyone, else was so far below.

Now, with his augmented abilities, the thoughts and feelings of Gale hammered through every shred of shield he could muster. The aches and pains of each citizen gnawed at him, beating behind his forehead. He sensed the movement of every drop of blood, the mix and swirl of every hormone. The pulse of the city threatened to suck him in, scatter him among them. Pain turned to panic, and it was all he could do not to tear at hearts and brain stems just to make them leave him alone.

As he groaned, eyes rolling back, a cool hand wrapped around his arm, and an echoing coolness spread through his veins. The touch pulled him away from the city pulse and rooted him in his body. He gulped in air and sagged to his knees, opening his eyes to Simon's kind face. When he tried to speak, he could only manage, "Mmph."

"Turn your power inward," Simon said, "focus on your own body, and breathe."

Horace found his own pulse and followed it until it rang in his ears. "If that's what I feel through my shields, how am I ever going to use my power?"

"Practice. Pretend you're an acolyte all over again."

"I was never this kind of acolyte. Is this what it felt like when you were learning?"

Simon looked away. "You've become very powerful."

Horace would have loved to open up his power, see what Simon was feeling, but he didn't dare, knowing he might lose control again.

And he probably couldn't get through Simon's shields anyway.

"Don't get discouraged," Simon said. "You'll be able to help Natalya soon enough."

Horace almost laughed. Simon always seemed to misread people, even with his great power. Samira said he kept asking what she wanted from him when all she wanted was to help him. But Samira loved bringing shy people out of their shells and nursing "wounded birds," as she called them. Horace had once asked if she'd ever let someone take care of her, but she'd laughed.

And Simon was her latest bird. She'd done a bit of spying, had told Horace she thought Simon might have feelings for the Storm Lord, based on how he was always staring. Horace had said, "Who doesn't love the Storm Lord?" and she gave him one of those you-know-what-I'm-talking-about looks.

Horace didn't know if any of that was true. The way the Storm Lord behaved toward many of the female yafanai and none of the males had revealed where his interests lay. Poor Simon, if he was stuck there. He was appealing, and not just in a wounded way. The way he bumbled about with emotions was endearing, and though he was smaller than the men Horace usually went for, he had a nice face: sharp features, those kind eyes, and a mop of tousled blond hair.

"You've never discouraged me." Horace reached for Simon's hand, but he backed away. "What's wrong?"

He laughed softly, as if afraid someone was going to shush him. "What happened to you and Natalya is my fault, and I wanted to say I'm sorry."

"You've said that."

"Not enough. I can never say it enough."

"Simon." Horace took his hand this time, gripping it so Simon couldn't pull away. "Look at me. Natalya volunteered. You didn't know what was going to happen. I stuck my nose in where it didn't belong. We were working without a map; you told us that. Things went wrong. It happens. And you let me cry in your lap for almost a whole day. I think we're even." He tried for a joking smile that went half returned.

After a sigh, they shared a long glance. Simon looked away,

flushed. "I'm supposed to be making you feel better, not the other way around."

"You have, and you are. Now, no more blame. I have to practice." He held himself straighter and strengthened his defenses. "Drop your shield, please."

❖

Lazlo did as he was asked, letting his power slough away from Horace a little at a time, letting Horace test his own shields.

He remembered this feeling when he'd learned to control his power, but he hadn't been so brave, hadn't had this many people to keep out. Horace marched steadily forward and took the time to make sure Lazlo didn't feel guilty.

And that look they'd shared! Lazlo had felt it through all their shields. There was a blip of attraction on Horace's part, and Lazlo didn't know whether to feel joy or horror. Nice to be noticed, he supposed, but what if Horace wanted something from him? Could he have a lover on this planet? Would it be like Kenneth, the man who'd sometimes shared his bed on the *Atlas*, a casual thing he didn't talk about, or would Horace want something more? Could Lazlo give him something more? What would Dillon think?

Lazlo clenched a fist. Why should he care what Dillon thought? Dillon had no right to an opinion where Lazlo's love life was concerned. But Dillon was Dillon, and anything that distracted Lazlo from working on Dillon's projects wouldn't be tolerated; Lazlo was certain of it.

Horace's grunt brought Lazlo out of his reverie, and he realized the sensations of Gale were slipping past Horace's shields. Quintuple damn. He should have been paying attention!

He wrapped his shields around Horace. "Sorry, I'm sorry. I was preoccupied."

Horace gasped, but he didn't fall to his knees again. He wiped the sweat from his forehead and grinned. "What did I tell you about apologizing?"

"Sorry." When Horace raised an eyebrow, Lazlo had to laugh. "Force of habit."

"We'll have to think up a punishment, some kind of tax every time you say you're sorry."

"Put a coin in a jar, that sort of thing?"

"Something like that." He winked, and Lazlo felt that tendril of attraction again. His body responded, and Horace's eyes widened. It had just slipped through, and now they both felt what the other was feeling. Horace took a step forward, staring at Lazlo's lips.

Lazlo stepped back so quickly, it was a wonder he didn't trip. "I'm over two hundred years old," he blurted.

Horace blinked and then shook his head. "You don't look it, and I don't care."

"You should. I'm old and jaded. You should enjoy your youth. No arthritis or anything." He knew he wasn't making sense, just throwing words between them as obstacles.

Horace stepped forward as if the words weren't even there. "You don't have arthritis. I would have felt it."

There came that attraction again, and Lazlo knew Horace was putting it out there intentionally, making the promise that if they were together, each would feel what the other was feeling, passion squared.

Lazlo didn't retreat as Horace took another step. Their hands found each other. Horace moved forward slowly, his gaze holding a question, asking permission. With a sigh, Lazlo tilted his head.

The kiss came quickly, the world contracting into a tiny bubble with just the two of them. Horace's free hand cupped Lazlo's cheek, and he couldn't help leaning into that caress. It was tender, and Lazlo should have enjoyed it with every fiber, but when he opened his eyes, Horace's face wasn't the one he most hoped to see.

He stepped back. "You're going to be mad, but I have to say sorry again."

"Look," Horace said with a sigh, "if you don't want—"

Lazlo barked a laugh. "Oh, there's want, believe me. It's just, well, you don't deserve this, Horace. You don't deserve all my baggage and bullshit."

"I think you're worth a little angst, if that's what you mean."

"I don't know if I even know how to be close to someone anymore." Oh, the drama. He was back on the *Atlas*, unable to stand his own company.

But Horace laid a hand on Lazlo's shoulder that promised companionship at least, with the offer of something more. "What did you tell me? Practice. Pretend you're an acolyte again."

Lazlo laughed, starting softly and building until the sound rang around them. It felt good, really good, and overdue. Horace was smiling, waiting, and damned or not, Lazlo kissed him, reveling in the heat between them but breaking away before he could get lost again, before he had a chance to picture Dillon's face.

"Now." Lazlo gestured toward Gale. "More practice."

Horace gave him a knowing look. "I thought that's what we were doing."

"Practice that will help Natalya, please."

That got Horace to focus, and they practiced for the next few hours until Horace was too tired to continue. Lazlo sent him off with orders to rest; he wouldn't hear any other suggestions. Still, he nursed a happy glow that grew when he met Samira in the halls of the temple below.

"Samira, where are you off to?" he asked.

"To get something to eat. You're not going back to your room, are you?"

"Why? Should I?"

"No reason!" She radiated false cheerfulness. "Come with me."

"What's wrong?"

"Why should anything be wrong?"

He gave her a look that he hoped said it all.

"Please, Simon. Come have lunch with me. There's cobbler."

"Did someone rob me? Is someone waiting to kill me?" He pushed past her. "What could be so bad—"

He felt it then: Dillon's presence, which he was always aware of, and someone else, enveloped in feelings that could only be sexual. And Lazlo had trouble even kissing someone without wondering how Dillon would feel about it.

He plastered on a smile. "That's fine. It's fine. We're not a couple or anything, so it's fine. Really, really fine."

She frowned. "I saw the way you looked at him. I'm so sorry, Simon." She smiled and projected so much pity it was a wonder he couldn't see it.

"He can do as he likes. He has before."

She nodded. "Well, there's still cobbler, and the kitchen is all the way over on the other side of the temple."

Where he might not feel them. "Sounds delicious."

She threaded her arm through his and led him away, asking about

Horace. Lazlo tried to wrap himself in the remembrance of Horace's lips, though the whole experience felt tainted now.

❖

Caroline was a ball of energy and a flexible one at that. Dillon thought she would have happily shared his bed until the proverbial cows came home, but he knew he should get up before his stamina flagged. He supposed he could have gone to Lazlo for a shot of adrenaline, but Lazlo wouldn't have appreciated that one bit.

As Caroline nuzzled his neck, Dillon asked, "Want to show me around the city?"

"If that's what you like, I'm game." Her smile backed up her words, and he gave her another kiss, a promise for later. He would have made her breakfast if he had any idea how such things were done down here.

At the thought of breakfast he realized he had no idea what time it was, but luckily, the sun was bright when they left the temple. Without escorts, fewer people noticed him, and the way he and Caroline strolled through the city didn't catch many people in their wake. He shook hands or patted shoulders as he wanted. A farming couple begged for rain, and he guided a little drizzle their way. He relaxed, having a fine time, Caroline on his arm, her blue eyes twinkling at him as they talked of this and that. This was what he'd been missing for years, just a normal life.

They wandered to the east side of town, toward the warehouses and hoshpi pens. He gawked at the strange, almost spherical creatures that Gale managed to squeeze so many resources out of. Someone had told him that the leather armor junior paladins wore was made from hoshpi carapaces. He wondered if that still technically qualified as leather but decided it didn't matter. Someone else had said the local mead was made from liquid that the insects secreted, and he hoped he'd managed not to look too horrified. After all, they ate the meat from the things, too. Still, he'd pledged to never drink a glass of the stuff if he could get out of doing it.

The hoshpis bumbled along behind wooden railings, their dome-shaped bodies knocking into one another. They keened and shuddered as they tried to flap insect-like wings held tight with straps. One of them waddled near them on its six legs and appraised Dillon with one large, watery brown eye.

"Hello, ugly," he said.

Caroline snickered. The hoshpi snorted and wandered away.

"Did I offend?" Dillon shared a chuckle with Caroline until he saw two robed figures talking to one of the hoshpi drovers. A man and a woman with symbols embroidered on the back of their robes, a sun and moon, and he knew who they must be.

"I'll be damned," he said.

Caroline followed his gaze. "Sun-Moon worshipers," she said with a sigh. "As if the sun and moon are anything more than astrological bodies."

"Uh-huh." He watched the pair as they dickered with the drover and counted their money. "What are they doing here?"

"Trading. The mayor set it up. Some of the paladins have been saying what a good idea it is."

"Paladins." Dillon thought for a moment. "The mayor's niece is a paladin." And then there was the man assigned to her squad, Carmichael's son. If the younger generation was friends, did that mean the mayor and the captain were close, too? He thought back to the meeting. The mayor had seemed surprised by Carmichael's confession about the boggins. She hadn't told him the truth, then, unless the surprise was an act. The mayor had also seemed intimately close with the drushkan ambassador. There might be quite a conspiracy going on, especially if he added the so-called Sun-Moon into the mix.

The robed pair handed over coins and shook hands with the drover. As they moved away from the pens, heads together, they glanced around, gazes passing over him. They paused, staring. Dillon held his breath as their expressions blanked before they smiled, and he knew who he was looking at.

His mouth went dry, and he resisted the urge to just leave, not knowing if they might follow.

"Colonel," they said together as they approached. Caroline opened her mouth, but Dillon laid a hand on her arm.

"Christian, Marlowe. I knew you could talk to your people, but through them? Well done. Guess we were all good at keeping secrets."

"And it seems we have an inroad into your city, and yet you have none in ours." The accents of the two vessels were heavy, their mouths unused to speaking the language of the *Atlas*.

Dillon shrugged. "I have something a lot more valuable than trading inroads."

They glared now, and he knew they were more than a little panicky at losing Lazlo. Caroline gasped and clutched his arm as Dillon felt the merest tingle over his scalp. It faded quickly, and he knew Caroline was shielding him.

"Trying to work through your vessels to attack my mind? Nice try." He frowned mockingly. "Oh, but it looks as if you're too far away to do any real damage. A yafanai was strong enough to block you."

"No matter," they said. "There is more than one way to fight." They walked away, jingling their purse.

Dillon looked to the drover counting his money. He could have the Sun-Moons arrested, he supposed, but how would that look? Christian and Marlowe would abandon their minds, leave them without a clue. He needed a way to jettison all the spies from his city.

Caroline stared after them. "I didn't know Sun-Moons could—"

"They can't. Listen, don't tell anyone what happened. It's god stuff."

She nodded slowly, and he could tell she was burning with curiosity, but she didn't ask.

"Do you know where the mayor's house is?"

She gave him directions, still not asking questions, and he gave her another kiss.

"Go back to the temple. Have something to eat." He didn't wait for a reply before he was off.

This time, as he walked through the crowds, he dismissed people, telling them he was on important business, and those who bothered him warned others away until news spread ahead of him. When he arrived at the mayor's street, it had cleared of people.

He ducked into the shadow of an awning when the mayor's door opened. He stood flush against a storefront, trying for casual while remaining in shadow. Carmichael walked out of the mayor's house, and Dillon's gut clenched. A report? A friendly chat? Something else entirely?

Carmichael didn't seem to notice Dillon or the empty streets as she stalked away. Did she ever just walk anywhere, or did she always look like someone on the hunt? At the moment, it didn't matter. Once she was clear, Dillon crossed to the mayor's front door and knocked.

A young man opened it. "Can I help…" His jaw fell. "You?"

"Yeah, it's me." Dillon stepped past him. It was a nice house, roomy, though it lacked grandeur. "Is the mayor in?"

"Yes, Storm Lord." He brayed a nervous laugh that even Lazlo would have been embarrassed by and clapped a hand over his mouth, eyes as wide as saucers.

"It's okay, son," Dillon said. "Show me in, please."

The young man led Dillon to an office off the side of a large entryway. "Sir, the Storm Lord is here to see you." He stood aside without waiting for orders and shut the door behind Dillon.

Mayor Ross stood from behind a wooden desk, his expression calm, though it had stayed pretty calm through the meeting with Carmichael, too. "Storm Lord, I don't think we've been introduced. Paul Ross." He held out his hand.

Dillon gave it two quick pumps before he sat in one of the chairs facing the desk. "Is the drushka and boggin business all sorted out?"

Paul Ross hesitated a moment before sitting. "I'm surprised you're asking me instead of Captain Carmichael."

"I saw her leaving."

He gave one of those oily, politician smiles. "Very observant."

"I see a lot, including Sun-Moon worshipers in my city."

"Trading partners—"

"Spies."

Paul Ross's mouth inched closed, and he leaned back in his chair. Dillon could almost hear him wondering how he was supposed to deal with an irritated god. Dillon let him work it out in silence.

"I beg your pardon, Storm Lord," Paul Ross said, "but I won't know what you want from me until you tell me."

But would knowing equal obeying? "It's easy. I don't want Sun-Moons in my city, and more than that, any tête-à-têtes between you and Carmichael are now going to be ménages à trois with you, her, and me." He shrugged. "Without the sex part."

Paul Ross looked so baffled, Dillon wondered if it was more than just the French that was confounding him. He took a deep breath. "You want to be present for any discussions between Carmichael and me?"

"You've got it."

"Our jobs overlap a lot, Storm Lord. We have many meetings—"

"I like meetings."

Paul Ross took a deep breath, and Dillon wondered if he was about to get yelled at for the first time by someone in Gale who wasn't Lazlo. On the one hand, he was amused, but on the other, it wouldn't stand. But Paul Ross just took another breath, and another, as if he was counting to ten.

Dillon had to laugh. "Are you trying to think of a way to refuse? Go ahead. Even I'm curious to see what I might do." He laid his palms flat on the desk and pushed to his feet. "The simplest thing would be to replace you."

"Think so?" It was almost a whisper, but it showed balls. He stood, too, but without Dillon's leaning menace. "I've been thinking a lot about gods recently."

"Is that right?"

"It's the power of distance. People judge me, critique me, make their opinions known. I have to earn their respect, their trust, their forgiveness. You…"

Dillon raised an eyebrow. "I have it because of who I am."

"Who you *were*. It's easy to worship an abstract, but a man?" He smiled sadly. "What will you do when they can *see* you letting them down?"

Dillon's chest tightened, and he could feel his anger building. Who the fuck did this guy think he was?

"Go on, replace me," Paul Ross said. "Make Gale a theocracy or dictatorship, however you want to sell it. Let the whispers of dissent and doubt start now."

Power hummed through Dillon, and he threw little sparks that Paul Ross watched closely. "So, that's it, eh?" Dillon asked. "I let you do as you like, or you'll start the 'Let's overthrow the Storm Lord' campaign."

"Such a thought hadn't entered my mind until now."

"Bullshit."

"But I did know a confrontation of some sort was coming."

"You haven't seen a fight yet."

They locked stares, and a small noise came from the door. Paul Ross took a step around his desk, calling, "Blake?" and Dillon didn't know if he was calling for help or a witness. Dillon grabbed him, not thinking, just as he had once before.

He told himself to stop even as he was moving. Lessan loomed in his mind, and he tried to hold in his power, but he hadn't been this goddamned angry in such a long time.

Paul Ross didn't shudder and jerk like Lessan had done. He went up on tiptoe, his eyes rolled, back arching, limbs splayed so hard it was a wonder his joints didn't snap. Instead of horror, Dillon's anger grew at this upstart paper pusher. How dared he lead Dillon down this road again!

Power exploded outward, and Paul Ross went flying, hitting the wall beside his desk hard enough to dent the plaster, little cracks running from it like spiderwebs. The body fell with a pathetic thump. Dillon breathed hard. He closed his eyes, opened them to the body, and closed them again, trying to will it away.

The skin of his temples tightened, tingling as his anger faded and left him gasping, hoping. "Oh God."

Next time he looked, it wasn't just Paul Ross lying there but Lessan, too, her body covering his like a ghost. Both their heads rested upon their chests, arms and legs lying lifeless. As Dillon knelt, heart pounding, Lessan picked her head up, watching him with dead eyes, her lips quirking as if asking, "Is that all you've got?"

The air was filled with the scent of charred meat, and Dillon swallowed, thankful there wasn't anything in his stomach to bring up. He'd have to open a window before he left. The thought made him laugh, a high-pitched noise he didn't recognize. "What the fuck am I supposed to do? I didn't want to rule them with fear."

Lessan pointed over her left shoulder to a wooden poleaxe standing in the corner, almost hidden behind a potted plant. Dillon glanced at it and back to Lessan. She winked, eyes all black like a shark's.

Dillon shut his eyes tighter, pressing a hand over them until red lines streaked across the darkness. When he opened them again, she was gone, but her idea remained. He could make it look as if someone else had killed the mayor, someone who used a wooden poleaxe, whoever that might be.

It would still be murder, but it wouldn't be Dillon who'd done it.

He took the poleaxe and gripped it high on the shaft. With one hand, he hauled Paul Ross's body up until it aligned with the dent in the plaster, head still dangling. Dillon grunted with the effort but stabbed the body in the chest and shook it to get some blood on the wall. Then he let it slide down and stabbed it again, lower, letting gravity do the work of making a nice blood pool. He cast the weapon aside. It was a good idea, never mind that it came from a ghost. Dillon snorted a laugh, opened a window on the far side of the office to let the fresh air in, and moved to the door.

Just as he'd suspected, the young man waited there, eavesdropping, though he couldn't have known all that had happened.

"Your name is Blake?" Dillon asked, blocking the view.

They young man nodded.

Dillon slipped out and shut the door behind him before he laid an arm across Blake's shoulders. "Come with me. There's someone I'd like you to meet."

CHAPTER TWENTY-ONE

Halfway back to the Paladin Keep, Carmichael realized she'd left her sidearm behind. She didn't go about armored as her lieutenants did, but several incidents with thieves and such had gotten her into the habit of going armed.

But Paul Ross didn't like guns in his house, so his aide had put it somewhere, and her head had been so full of everything they'd spoken about that she'd marched out without it. If she'd let the aide show her out, he probably would have reminded her, but she'd been in too much of a hurry.

A day had passed since all the squads had returned from the swamp. Carmichael wanted to fill Paul in on what they'd found, and as they'd talked, she'd blurted out what she knew about the boggins, the Storm Lord, everything. The Storm Lord's experiments were probably going to get worse now that he was on the planet, and she'd wanted to warn Paul about that. While she was warning, she'd spilled the biggest secret she had: the Storm Lord was human.

Paul had taken it well, with only a modicum of surprise, but that was more than she could usually get him to show. She wished Reach had been there. Then she could have smoothed things out between them by admitting the boggin project had been the Storm Lord's idea. She'd taken responsibility at the time because there'd been too many ears in that room. She had no idea what might happen if everyone knew their god had marched them to war with the boggins. She didn't know what that would do to morale. But now that the Storm Lord was among them, and he could do whatever he pleased, Carmichael thought the people in charge should be prepared.

Paul had sat in silence a long time, finally asking what she thought the two of them should do.

She'd admitted she hadn't taken the news well when she'd first heard it. That her god was human had set off a cascade of betrayal within her. She'd loved the idea that a person could transcend their humanness and become something greater. "I suppose it's the breaking of the illusion I can't forgive him for," she'd said to Paul. "I built up a god in my mind, something distant, other, not someone like me. I guess I'm pissed he dashed my expectations."

Paul had given her a bigger smile. "Rude of him. It won't take the populace long to figure out, you know. They'll start making comparisons between him and the yafanai. It won't happen overnight, but it will happen."

"And what will he do then?"

"Do you think he'll go on a killing spree if challenged?"

The thought had given her chills. "He'd target us first. Our families, our friends."

"The whole damn town if he has to?"

She'd shaken her head. They didn't have enough information to predict what he'd do. They'd have to keep their ears open, that was for damn sure.

No one answered her knock on the mayor's door. She raised the latch and poked her head inside. "Hello?"

No answer. The aide stayed close to the front door at all times while the mayor was open to visitors, but no one came bustling forward, and she heard nothing from inside.

She stepped in, shut the door, and inched toward the office. "Paul?"

When she opened his office door a crack, she smelled it: a sharp, coppery tang, carried on a draft through the window.

"Paul?" Standing to the side, she pushed the door open and saw him.

Not her first dead body, probably not her last, but the violence in the room took her breath away. He lay in a crimson pool, a gore-stained poleaxe beside him. His chest was still, face pointed down. She tiptoed forward as if he might awaken, but when she pushed his head up, his slack eyes stared at nothing.

"Holy hell." She picked up the poleaxe and studied the end, looking for any clues about who might have used it.

A shriek from the doorway drove her to her feet. Reach stood there, baring her sharp teeth as she screamed something in drushkan and leapt forward, leading with her poisonous claws.

Carmichael jabbed, more interested in driving her away than hurting her. "Stop! It's—"

Reach pulled up short and hissed. The poleaxe writhed in Carmichael's grip as if alive, and she threw it behind her. Reach darted forward again, and Carmichael swung a fist. Reach ducked under, claws up. Carmichael fell back against Paul's desk and kicked, catching Reach in the stomach, though her claws left a deep groove in Carmichael's boot.

"I didn't kill him, Reach!"

When Reach leapt up again, Carmichael darted out of the way, but Reach sprang past her, grabbing the poleaxe.

"Shit." Carmichael moved to keep the desk between them, wondering if she could risk a mad dash for the door. Maybe Paul's aide had left her sidearm somewhere obvious.

Movement came from the doorway. Reach didn't give it a glance, but Carmichael spotted someone running away. "Somebody went for help," she said. "If they tell people you're attacking me—"

"I do not care if I am killed." Reach jabbed, and Carmichael ducked, still on the other side of the desk. "I will have your blood."

"I didn't kill him!"

"He was a warrior of the mind, not the body! You did not have to slay him!" She leapt on top of the desk and stabbed.

Carmichael went flat, rolling. She grabbed the chair and used it as a shield. Reach's next thrust skewered it, and Carmichael tried to hold on, but Reach levered the chair out of the way. When the poleaxe came darting back, there'd be nothing to stop it.

The crack of a gunshot made them freeze, though Reach's stare didn't leave Carmichael.

"Stand down, Ambassador!" Ross's voice from the doorway.

"Paul's niece," Reach said, her voice still tight and raw, "stand with me. We must avenge him!"

"I said stand…" Her voice trailed away as if she'd spotted the body. "What the fuck is going on?"

Carmichael risked a look.

Ross had her sidearm out and her gaze locked on Paul. Her free hand flailed toward Reach as if seeking to pull her off the desk. "Reach? Captain? What the fuck?"

Reach clambered down. "This *shach* has killed Paul!"

"He was dead when I got here!" Carmichael stood and marched around the desk, taking Ross's sidearm and pointing it. "Back the fuck up, Ambassador."

"You will not live to—"

"Everybody, shut up!" Ross tore her gaze from her uncle and looked at Reach, her shoulders heaving. "If Carmichael wanted him dead, Reach, she would have shot him!"

Reach breathed hard for a moment before she rested the butt of the poleaxe on the floor, the best they would probably get from her.

Ross turned crazy eyes on Carmichael; she looked like someone half an inch from losing it.

"Take the ambassador outside, Lieutenant," Carmichael said. "I've got this."

With a tight nod, Ross ushered Reach outside, both of them shaking. Maybe they could lean on each other. Carmichael knelt and closed Paul's eyes.

❖

Cordelia kicked the side of the house until her boot went through the wood, and her foot felt as if it might come off. Reach watched her closely, as if wanting to join in the show of grief but not sure how.

"I keep thinking of the ballista," Cordelia said. "I was going to write him a thank-you note. A fucking note! I couldn't be bothered to tell him in person." Her voice cracked, and she felt the tears start. She tried to wipe them away, not wanting anyone to see a paladin in armor bawling her eyes out.

"Sa—"

"He deserved better than that, Reach!"

"Sa!"

Cordelia turned to look. Reach had Paul's housekeeper by her side. "You're…"

"Katey." She didn't bother to wipe her tears away. "Is it true? I saw the captain kneeling over him. Poor Mayor Ross." She put her face in her hands again.

"You could be mistaken about Carmichael, Sa," Reach said. "If she wanted to turn suspicion away from herself, the shach would not use a gun."

"Carmichael isn't like that. You don't know her."

"I do not need to know her!" Reach shouted. She didn't cry, but Cordelia had never seen a drushka cry, didn't even know if they could. "She is made of secrets. She contacted the old drushka, changed the chanuka for her own ends, and then they killed so many of my kind. How can she be the same in your mind as she once was?"

Cordelia took a deep breath. Carmichael had smacked Liam around, too. At the time, she'd seemed to be coming apart at the seams. But enough to kill Paul? Cordelia shook her head. "She didn't have a reason."

"None that she has shared." Reach lifted her arms and dropped them as if the will to fight was leaving her.

"I'm all over this, Reach. I'll find out who did it."

"Where's Blake?" Katey asked. "Is he dead, too?"

"Paul's aide," Reach said at Cordelia's questioning look.

Cordelia nodded. "Let's search the house."

❖

Dillon hummed with nervous energy as he guided Blake through the streets. He kept one arm tight across Blake's shoulders and put off anyone who stopped to speak with them. He couldn't stop thinking of Lessan's ghost, even though ghosts didn't exist, couldn't exist. He had to have been imagining things. He would have felt any telepathic attack.

Unless the attackers were capable of being so subtle he wouldn't notice. He hadn't met all of the yafanai, didn't know what everyone could do. He shook the thought away. He needed to trust someone, and so far, the yafanai hadn't done anything to earn his ire. "I was imagining things." He held Blake tighter.

"Storm Lord?"

"Shut up, son. God is talking. Everything would have been fine if the mayor had just remembered that."

If Blake had a comment, he wisely kept it to himself. Caroline was at the temple, just as Dillon had told her to be. At least someone knew how to follow a fucking order.

"Is there somewhere we can be alone?" Dillon asked.

"Um, my room? Yours?" She cast a skeptical, worried look at Blake, probably wondering if Dillon was asking her to have a threesome.

The thought made him chuckle. "Not that kind of alone, baby. Telepathically speaking."

She sighed, a relieved sound, and nodded. "The roof. But no one would listen to your thoughts anyway."

"Better safe than sorry. Lead the way."

When they emerged onto the abandoned roof, Dillon noticed that morning had become afternoon. Funny, he hadn't thought that much time had passed. Dillon still had one arm around Blake, who was looking more and more concerned, but good for him, he didn't try to run.

"My friend here needs a new memory," Dillon said.

Blake tried to push away then, and Dillon swept his leg out from under him. When he tried to scramble upright, Dillon snaked an arm around his neck. "Son, whether we do this the easy way or the hard way is nothing to me." He looked to Caroline. "Just take the last few hours from him, everything with me."

She nodded and closed her eyes, a good soldier.

Horace bent over Natalya's bed, all his energy focused on keeping her power locked down. He'd had a nap at Simon's insistence, but when he woke up, he felt strong enough to try to help Natalya. The thought that he might have healed his own mind in his sleep was intriguing.

Simon sat beside him, helping him focus. When they'd first seen each other again after their kiss on the roof, Simon had seemed shy, and Horace had nearly been overwhelmed with the desire to kiss him again. Restraint was important, he told himself. They had work to do.

Natalya blinked and opened her eyes. "Horace?"

"You're all right, Nat. We're holding your power back."

"I can feel it waiting." She smiled, and it had none of the panic

Horace remembered. A little creepy, but Natalya had always been enamored with power.

Horace and Simon lowered their shields by degrees, seeing if she could contain the power. Simon instructed her on how to breathe, and with their shields, she slowly got ahold of herself.

"Can you keep me shielded on your own?" she asked Horace.

He glanced at Simon. "With you awake and helping, I think so."

"Good." She nodded toward Simon and then at the door. "You can go."

Simon stiffened, frowning.

"Nat!" Horace said.

"No, it's fine." Simon straightened his shirt and walked toward the door. "I'll be around if you need to summon me again."

"Thank you," Horace called as Simon shut the door hard behind him. "Nat, that was so rude!"

"Forget about him. Do you know what this means?"

"You're still a little crazy?"

"With the gifts the Storm Lord has given us, we can do anything!"

"Right," he said slowly.

"Drop your shields a bit."

He did so, ready to snap them back if need be, ready to put her out if she needed that. She tested her limits slowly, containing the great power within her, and he felt joy radiating from her in waves.

As his shields slipped further, he had to focus more on himself, trying to shut out those around him, but someone in the temple was using strong telepathy, too much to ignore. He thought he might have felt it with his shields up, as powerful as he'd become. The telepathy was going on above him, would have been out of his reach before, but not now.

He couldn't help looking, curious to find out what was worth so much output. He wouldn't pry, he told himself, just a casual glance, a little nosiness that wouldn't hurt—

He felt new memories, someone erasing old thoughts, a delicate practice, hardly ever used unless there was lots of money involved, and then never like this. A man was struggling, and the Storm Lord ordered his memories to be erased against his will. But why command something so illegal? Horace could sense the blood slowing in the man's body as the Storm Lord's arm tightened around his neck, his gaze locked on Caroline's face.

Horace kept his power away from her, knowing the only reason she hadn't sensed his intrusion was because she was so focused. And if she was busy, she wouldn't be able to stop a peek into the Storm Lord's head—so forbidden—but everything that was happening between the three of them was forbidden.

The Storm Lord's thoughts were so loud, beating at Horace's head: the mayor stiffened by lightning, dead on the floor; the cracks in the wall; the blood; the ghost girl; head tingling now; someone in his head, maybe the same people who'd shown him the ghost; *who the fuck is in my mind?*

"Horace!"

Natalya shook him, and he focused on her frown, his shields slamming down again.

"What were you doing?" Natalya asked.

"The Storm Lord is on the roof."

"So?"

"He's…"

She gripped his arm hard. "If you were spying on our god, the one who gave us such gifts." Her fingers dug in harder, but he couldn't drop his shields to will away the pain. "I won't be able to forgive you."

Horace looked into her eyes and didn't recognize the zealot he saw there. "Nat?"

She released him and then gestured for the door. "Whatever he's doing, it doesn't concern mortals like us."

"Mortals?"

"You can go." But her gaze still pinned him to the spot. "Don't let me catch you snooping again."

When she released him, he hurried from the room, wondering if it was the new gifts that had changed her or if the Storm Lord had done something to increase loyalty, maybe when he wasn't killing politicians and covering it up. Horace looked for Simon but saw no one. He couldn't keep what he'd seen to himself, no matter what Natalya said. He had to tell someone. Murder couldn't just go unpunished.

He flashed through all the people he knew and landed on the capable paladin who'd led the expedition to the research station:

Cordelia Ross, the mayor's niece. If anyone wanted to know, it would be her. With his shields tight, he hurried from the temple, heading for the Paladin Keep.

Lydia sat on her cushions and let her head sink against her chest. Freddie had cleared the rest of her appointments, telling everyone that the prophet of Gale was too exhausted to see any futures that afternoon.

She'd had night after night of bad dreams, that same fire wiping out future after future. She'd seen it in the futures of some clients, had resisted the urge to follow Freddie's future or her own. She was thankful she hadn't followed either of them in her sleep. Knowing what was coming was just too hard sometimes.

She fell sideways on her cushions and curled into a ball. As sleep towed her downward, Freddie covered her with a blanket and brushed her shoulder. Lydia's power sleepily wound around her.

The skein of Freddie's future whirled out of control, pausing as night fell to show Freddie standing at Lydia's side on a platform behind the palisade. As slowly as if moving through sap, Freddie leaned far forward and peered into the darkness beyond, watching boggins rush Gale in the deepening twilight.

Lydia jerked awake. "We need to warn everyone!"

Freddie leapt back. "What?"

"Come on. We need to find the Storm Lord. We need to tell everyone." She couldn't prevent whatever was happening, but she'd be there to meet it. Whatever else happened, that was certain, and now she had only to follow in the footsteps of the future.

CHAPTER TWENTY-TWO

Carmichael couldn't stop staring at the body. It looked wrong somehow, and not just because she'd rather Paul be alive. Movement near the door caught her attention, and Lieutenant Ross stepped inside, looking at Paul's body as if locking on a target. Carmichael had heard her yelling outside, but she seemed to have gone from anger to shock. She'd moved through the whole house, but if she'd found anyone, she didn't say so.

"No one answered the door," Carmichael said. "But I didn't look everywhere. Someone could have sneaked out while I was in here."

When Ross didn't respond, Carmichael snapped her fingers. "Wake up, Lieutenant. We've got a murderer to find." Ross still didn't move, didn't even have a hint of anger anymore. Carmichael sighed. "I met him a long time ago, you know."

"I know. Liam and I—"

"No, before Liam and you, when I'd just made lieutenant, and he was a mayor's aide, before he worked for the guilds." She tried to focus on his face and not the hole in his chest. "I was on guard duty at the keep a lot, and he was always running errands for the mayor. We didn't talk much, but when we did, he moaned about all the shit the mayor had him do, including her laundry. He annoyed the hell out of me."

Ross frowned as if wondering if this was the right story to tell over a body.

"I remember one day he was whining about some stain on the mayor's jacket, telling everyone he had to figure out a way to get it out or be fired, so I said, 'Take a bit of water root, rub it over the spot, then wind the whole thing up tightly, small as you can get, and shove it up your ass.' And he stared at me for almost a whole minute before he laughed so hard he nearly pissed himself." Carmichael chuckled. "He quit that day, and I didn't see him again until after you kids were older and we started working together. He'd learned to keep his complaints to himself by then."

Cordelia nodded slowly. "I'll remember that."

"The story or how to get a stain out of a jacket?"

If that amused her at all, she didn't show it. "We should have a healer examine him."

Carmichael looked at the work the poleaxe had done. She wanted to argue, to say that they knew what had killed him, but something about the body still looked wrong. "I'm going to get some leathers to guard the house, too. See that—"

Someone else moved near the door. Carmichael stepped in that direction, reaching again for a sidearm that wasn't there, but the man who knew where it was stepped into the light, staring at Paul Ross's body.

"Blake?" Ross asked.

"They told me he was dead," Blake said as he nodded.

Carmichael backed him into the hall. "Where did you put my gun?"

He turned a stupid stare on her, and she resisted the urge to slap him. "Your gun?"

"Where?"

He frowned as if searching his memory before he shook his head, moved to a little table, and pulled her sidearm from a drawer. She snatched it from him and stowed it in her holster.

"Where have you been?" she asked.

"I…went out to get something."

She looked to his empty hands. "Where is it?"

His frown came back slowly. "I don't remember."

His confusion seemed genuine, but she didn't know how good an actor he was. "You're coming with me. You and the housekeeper both." Reach would squawk, but Carmichael wasn't letting her best suspects go. "Lieutenant." Ross was still looking at the body with something between sorrow and anger. "Can you hold the fort until help comes?"

"The healer?"

Carmichael licked her lips. "And the leathers. And the undertaker."

Ross made a noise that sounded like a growl blended with a sigh. "I'll hold the fort."

"He was a good man."

"He deserved better than this."

Didn't they all? Carmichael rounded up Blake and the housekeeper, ignoring Reach's glares, and herded them toward the keep.

❖

The house was so quiet. Cordelia tried not to look at him and failed with every breath. Every conversation they'd had, every time she'd insulted him or pushed him to see what he would take, played through her mind. She went through every time she'd blown him off or rolled her eyes or had a snappy comeback.

But he'd loved her snappy comebacks. His little smiles were the most affectionate ones.

When he'd told her that her parents were dead, he'd held her hands. He hadn't complained when she'd raged around the house, breaking everything that would break. He'd held her while she cried, putting his own grief to the side and casting her sadness in the starring role.

Maybe she should talk to his body. She'd heard of people speaking to loved ones after they'd died, but Paul couldn't hear her regret, her sadness. If he could, he'd make it more important than his, even though he was the dead one.

She coughed a laugh that turned into a sob before she muzzled it. Where had Reach gone? Maybe they could share this grief, but Reach was just angry, and her rage would feed Cordelia's own until they did something stupid. Paul would want them to be smart.

Someone knocked at the door, and even though Paul would have urged calmness, she stalked to the door and yanked it open, ready to yell that the mayor was dead, and whoever was coming to bother him should feel bad.

Then she saw the flat, undertaker's cap, and the words stuck in her throat.

"Lieutenant?" he said. "I'm sorry for your loss."

She stood aside. "You can't take him yet."

"I'm to take his measurements before the cart arrives."

The cart. The mayor of Gale was going to ride in the death cart like everyone else. They'd have to save the pomp for the funeral.

No, there was no "they." She'd have to plan the funeral alone, the last of her family. It made her head spin, and her gorge rose before she made herself breathe.

❖

Lazlo followed the young soldier to the mayor's house. After Natalya had *dismissed* him, he'd roamed the halls, looking for something to do. When a paladin came asking for someone to examine the dead mayor, he'd jumped at the chance to leave. But now he hoped the mayor's family knew he couldn't bring back the dead.

An armored paladin let him into the mayor's office where the body was being measured, probably for a coffin. Lazlo didn't come close but let a tendril of power out, sensing the destruction of flesh and muscle. He thought that might be it, opened his mouth to say that the hole in the man's chest was clear for everyone to see, but his power touched something else: charred synapses, cooked organs and muscles. He flashed back to the *Atlas*'s bridge, to his newly awakened power. His senses had been feeding him information he couldn't decipher at the time, but now he knew what he'd felt. An electrocuted body, just like this one.

Lessan and the mayor, killed in the same way. But Dillon had killed Lessan, and there were no live wires for the mayor to grab.

"Well?" the paladin asked.

"He..." Lazlo swallowed.

"Can we remove him?" the undertaker asked.

"No." The paladin moved to look Lazlo in the eye. "He what?"

"He was stabbed."

The paladin continued to stare before she turned to the undertaker and nodded. She didn't watch while the body was bundled out; she stared at the dent in the plaster.

"What have you discovered?" a voice asked from the door.

Lazlo turned and took a step back. "A drushka?" But there was always one in the city; he remembered that. "The ambassador?" Her limbs seemed a little longer than a human's, her skin covered in whorls. She stepped forward with a smooth, gliding gate, and he had to resist letting his power play over her to see how she differed from a human on the inside.

She didn't even glance at him. "What are you doing, Sa?"

The paladin continued to frown at the wall. "It looks as if he was stabbed head on, but Carmichael would have to stab up. She didn't do this, Reach."

"Then whom?"

They both looked to Lazlo. He shook his head and hoped the motion didn't look wildly guilty. "I can't tell who stabbed whom." That was true, at least.

"You can go," the paladin said.

Lazlo tried not to frown. Being dismissed twice in one day was two times too many. He supposed he should forgive both Natalya and this woman. One was injured, and this one seemed more upset than a routine investigation would make her.

"Who was he?" Lazlo asked. "To you, I mean."

"My uncle."

The drushka glanced at him. "My love."

"I'm sorry," he said, anger forgotten. "For both of you."

The drushka inclined her head. The paladin continued to stare at the wall until another armored paladin stepped into the office. "Delia," he said, "I just heard. I'm so sorry."

She nodded at him, her lips wobbling as if her angry look might collapse at any moment.

"There's something happening." The new paladin jerked a thumb over his shoulder. "People are rushing around."

"Any idea why?" Lazlo asked.

He shrugged. "Not sure. If I were you, I'd head back to wherever you're supposed to be."

Lazlo nodded and fled. If there was an attack of some sort, Samira and Horace might need his help. And Dillon?

Lazlo shuddered. Had it been an accident? Then why the blood, the stab wound? What in the hell had gone on in that room? Did he want to know? If it was an accident or murder, what did that mean? Dillon should have been able to keep his powers in check. He'd had enough practice through the years; they all had. Maybe he was coming apart. But did that mean he needed Lazlo's help, or that Lazlo needed to get as far from him as possible?

❖

Horace lingered outside the Paladin Keep. People bustled here and there, and others guarded the entrance. He'd already asked after Lieutenant Ross and been told she wasn't available. They weren't going to let him wander around, hoping to run into her. The few paladins he'd managed to stop didn't know where she was. As time went on, messengers came and went, and the bustling doubled, then tripled.

Horace flagged down a private, one he recognized from the swamp expedition. "Excuse me, can you tell me what's going on? I'm looking for Lieutenant Ross and—"

"I remember you. The yafanai from the swamp."

Horace forced a smile. "Horace Adair, Private..."

"Carter. Lieutenant Ross isn't here. Shouldn't you be at the temple?"

"Why?"

"There's a rumor that the boggins are going to attack Gale."

Horace could only stare. Who would have started such a rumor? The boggins? Before he could ask, someone else called for Carter, and Horace turned back toward the temple, not knowing what else to do. Maybe the Storm Lord would be too busy to look for the person who'd intruded on his mind.

The wind picked up, and Horace shivered, realizing just how late it had become. The lamplighters were passing down the street in the early evening, lights blooming from streetlamps in their wake.

In the tail of a long shadow, someone blocked his path. He stopped, reaching out with his telepathic powers and pulling back as he sensed Natalya.

"Where have you been?" she snapped. "There's an attack."

"I know. I'm headed to the temple."

She stepped into the light and glanced over his shoulder. "Were you at the Paladin Keep?"

"Why?" He tried to walk past, but she grabbed him in a psychokinetic vise. His voice cut short, and he grunted, unable to move.

"First you were acting strangely at the temple, floundering around with your power, and now you're spending time with the paladins?"

She'd never liked the soldiers, thinking them arrogant and

unnecessary in the face of the yafanai, but this anger sounded deeper, as if all her emotions had been augmented with her power. She moved her face to within inches of his, as if she could peer into his brain. "What are you hiding?"

He lashed out, subduing her abilities. She put a hand to her head and stumbled, releasing him. He kept his power waiting, wanting to see what she would do, but she sagged against a wall, clutching her skull.

"Horace?" she asked around a sob. "What's happening to me?"

Pity overwhelmed him, and he soothed the little hurt he'd done. "I don't know, Nat, but I will help you figure it out."

When he stooped to put an arm around her, she threw him away and stood on her own, eyes blazing. "I don't need your help, boy. Get back to the temple. I'm going to the palisade to meet the Storm Lord."

She marched away, and he stared after her. When it rained odd events, it poured. But he was thankful that the Storm Lord wasn't at the temple. Maybe Simon would be there, and he could figure out what the hell was wrong with Natalya.

Lydia stood at the Storm Lord's side. Many of the yafanai huddled behind them, all of them crammed onto a platform behind the palisade. She hadn't had much opportunity to see the Storm Lord in person. He had an easy, commanding presence as he stared into the darkening fields beyond Gale. If he was worried about the boggins she foresaw, he didn't show it.

On the way from the temple, people had crowded around him, asking what was happening. Others leaned out of doorways or huddled in clusters, talking in hushed, almost excited voices. The Storm Lord had reassured them, told them to stay in their homes, lock their doors, and arm themselves with whatever was available, just in case.

His smile assured them that these were merely precautions. The yafanai and the paladins would take care of everything. People hurried away with smiles, and Lydia wondered if they would panic knowing what she knew.

On the platform, Captain Carmichael climbed up behind them in all her armored glory, though she seemed a bit uncomfortable, as if unused to wearing so much gear. The Storm Lord had summoned her, sent for all his paladins, and now they were arrayed along the platforms on Gale's western side.

"Are these future boggins all coming from the west?" Captain Carmichael asked. Lydia had never seen her up close either. The skepticism in her voice made it clear that she'd never visit a prophet unless forced.

"I've followed the futures of some of the paladins," Lydia said. "They all assembled here."

"Wouldn't hurt to spread them out a bit," Carmichael said.

Lydia sighed. What would or wouldn't hurt was irrelevant. She'd seen the soldiers' deployment, so that was how they would deploy. She didn't say that to Carmichael, though. She was pretty sure she'd get a speech about being above fate or not doing things just because a fortune-teller said so.

"Can't argue with prophecy," the Storm Lord said.

Freddie squeezed Lydia's shoulder, and Lydia patted her hand. Good to know the Storm Lord believed in her, but his belief also didn't matter in the end. It just showed he knew that a glimpsed future couldn't be changed. Well, she supposed he would know that, having created the yafanai.

"I can have someone fetch the railguns from the keep," Carmichael said.

The Storm Lord tilted his head as if considering. Lydia had heard he'd charged all the paladins' tech, including some older guns they'd hardly ever used, heavy artillery and the like.

"No need to bust out the big guns just yet." The Storm Lord smiled at those around him. "We've got enough firepower."

"Storm Lord," Carmichael said, "I think—"

"Do your thinking from another platform."

Everyone seemed to hold their breath, but Carmichael climbed down, muttering to herself.

A shrill whistle sounded off to the left. Heads swiveled in that direction. Lydia hadn't known about the whistle—she could never hear the future—but she knew what it meant.

Freddie's hand tightened again. "They're coming."

❖

B46 waited for the sun to drop. She'd snuck close to the stinking nest, circling it until she stood just below the wall, on the far side from the trees. Her children would charge the other side of the nest, running in groups as she had directed, and when one died, they would all feign death. The eyes of the tall creatures would be turned toward them, leaving her to begin the real battle.

When the sun disappeared, she scrambled over the wall, her chosen mates beside her. The tall creatures' nest was a jumble of sights and smells, but she hurried toward the scent she'd already caught on the wind: dried grass.

The tall creatures kept prey milling about, but B46 hurried past them. She loped toward a large structure reeking of grass and dung. It had a hole in the side, winking firelight coming from within where a tall creature chattered to another. One had a long stick in her hand, trapped flame dancing atop it.

B46 slipped through the shadows, her mates around her. They attacked the tall creatures together, tearing their throats out and lowering the bodies to the ground, mindful of the flaming stick. She had come prepared to make fire, but the tall ones were generous tonight.

She crept through the structure and touched her flaming stick to dung and grass while her mates scattered to other structures, using the fire-lighting sticks they had been given. The flames spread faster than an army of insects, eating and eating, with no water around to kill them all.

She ran to another structure and then another, her mates keeping pace. They burned and burned until the tall creatures began to shriek in the night. B46 chattered in glee. Her mates scattered into the darkness, looking to kill where they might, but B46 paused on top of one of the structures, staring at the beauty she'd wrought.

Now all the tall creatures would run this way, leaving her dead children to lie in the field, and leaving those living to spring the trap. The tall creatures would never see the host who waited in the trees, not until it was too late.

CHAPTER TWENTY-THREE

Dillon admired the boggins' bravado. Even though there weren't many of the little bastards, they still charged, screaming at the palisade. Dillon shielded his eyes from the torches, trying to count them, but they ran in zigzagging groups, and he kept losing track. Maybe they thought a serpentine path would make them harder to hit, but they still had a long way to run.

Dillon gestured to his torchbearer. "Give the 'hold your fire' signal."

She nodded and moved her fiery brand in a pattern that was passed along the wall. He tried to see the next platform, to make out what Carmichael thought of that. She'd want to shoot the buggers, but he wasn't going to let her claim one ounce of glory. He didn't want war hero on her résumé when it came time to be rid of her.

"Yafanai, get ready," Dillon said. "When they're close enough, give them hell."

The prophet faded to the back of the crowd, and Caroline took her place. All the yafanai had drawn brows as they stared at the field. The boggins didn't stand a chance.

"Captain Carmichael gives the 'ready, aim' signal, Storm Lord," the torchbearer said.

Dillon chuckled, though he wasn't in a laughing mood. "Pain in the ass," he muttered. "Just more fuel for your pyre."

"Storm Lord?" the torchbearer asked.

"Let it stand. They can pick off any we miss."

And maybe Carmichael had done him a favor countermanding his orders in public. Once he took care of these boggins, people would see who could protect them, who was worth following. Besides, there was no reason to cut the rest of the paladins out of the action.

The hair on Dillon's arms stood up as the yafanai unleashed their powers. Boggins flew high into the air and crashed lifeless to the ground. One collapsed as if punched by a huge fist, dirt flying around its body. Another clutched its head and staggered, rolling to a stop in the high grass.

They couldn't hold a candle to what the satellite pantheon could do, but they were impressive. At the end of the row, Natalya—recovered at last—leaned far out over the palisade, brow creased in concentration, and wherever she looked, boggins were torn to pieces by empty air, guts scattered over the ground. Dillon winced even as he laughed.

The crack of a shot made all of them jump. The torchbearer shrugged. "Captain Carmichael gave the order to fire, Storm Lord."

He couldn't blame her. This had to be the most exciting thing to happen to Gale since…him. And most of the paladins were probably loyal, and he could take care of any who weren't once the fighting was done.

And if any boggins did manage to squeeze past the palisade, the paladins were more suited for close quarters. They'd keep the populace safe. Without worshipers, there couldn't be a god. Best to think of it that way.

Out in the city, someone shouted, "Fire!" and the call echoed from many directions.

"What the fuck is it now?" Dillon asked.

Caroline faced the city, brow wrinkled. "I'm getting many minds thinking about a large fire at the warehouses near the hoshpi pens."

Dillon gritted his teeth. Was it the Sun-Moon? Could it have been them spying on his mind earlier? It would be like them to wait until he was distracted before poking at his city. Maybe when they said they had an inroad, they hadn't just meant money.

Dillon called the nearest storm, yanking on it like a blanket caught on the edge of the bed. It wasn't as close as he hoped, but now it was on its way. "Everyone, stand back." He waited until his yafanai gave him a few feet on each side before he charged the air. Arcs of lightning zipped between the nearest boggins, jolting them into a grotesque dance. He kept a tight rein on it, and pain built behind his eyes. After two arcs, he was breathing hard and wiping sweat from his brow. Where the hell was Laz?

"Come on. The paladins will handle any stragglers. We're headed to the warehouses. Someone go to the temple and collect the healers. They can't wait for people to come to them, not with a fire."

He scanned the crowd, but maybe Lazlo had stayed at the temple with the rest of the healers. As he strode into the city, Dillon thought he glimpsed Lazlo from the shadows, but it couldn't have been. Why the hell would Lazlo hide from him?

Lazlo watched Dillon disappear into Gale. He hadn't been able to climb up beside Dillon, didn't think he could keep himself from yelling, "What the fuck did you do?"

Dillon hadn't even acted guilty. Even Lessan had rated a few dragging steps from him, an air of wrongdoing. Now he looked like a child at play. How could anyone commit murder and saunter away from it? With Lessan, it had been an accident, but with the mayor? Lazlo's core rejected the idea.

Dillon had probably tried to manipulate or bully the mayor, and it hadn't worked. The last time someone had stood up to him—on the *Atlas*—Dillon had run, but he'd been outgunned then. A challenge from a mere mortal wouldn't go unchecked.

"Damn, damn, damn," Lazlo whispered. He climbed the platform and watched the few boggins he could see in the dim light of the moon. He'd heard the calls of fire, knew Dillon had summoned a storm. Hopefully, it would arrive in time.

The torchbearer gave Lazlo a curious look, as if awaiting orders. "The Storm Lord left, sir. The paladin captain took the soldiers soon after."

Lazlo nodded, peering into the darkness. There weren't that many boggins, hardly enough for a rush. Why so few? He'd predicted an astonishing birthrate. When he'd first started working on them, they'd reminded him of his one anthropology course on early hominids, precursors to humans who'd existed somewhere between cavemen and apes swinging between the trees, never mind that the boggins were closer to amphibians than mammals. Given enough time, the boggins would have evolved to be at least as smart as the drushka. They'd already been using crude weapons. He supposed that should have been his first clue that they wouldn't be docile. Maybe he should have smartened up an herbivore instead.

Or he should have left them the hell alone, should have let his reservations overrule his boredom and his need to please Dillon.

"I guess they went to fight the fire," the torchbearer said.

"What? Oh, right. I guess so."

One of the creatures dragged itself toward the palisade. Tenacious and single-minded. It made him shudder. Why couldn't dead things just stay dead? Up and down the palisade, most of the soldiers were indeed gone. Torchbearers looked back and forth, waiting for a signal.

The closest one shouted, "What's going on?"

Lazlo snorted a laugh. He supposed there wasn't a signal for general confusion. The torchbearer on his platform shrugged. Lazlo yelled, "There's a fire!"

"I heard. What's going on with the—" He staggered as something small arced over the palisade and hit his upper back. Lazlo squinted, feeling with his power, but the man wasn't hurt. He wiped something off his head and shoulders and then retched over the side of his platform.

Lazlo looked out into the dark just as something flew toward his head. He ducked, and the torchbearer yelped as she danced back.

"What is that? Oh, it stinks." She covered her mouth and took another step away from what looked like a stomach or some other organ leaking blood and fluid. Lazlo held his own nose as he sent his power out again and detected a boggin clinging to the other side of the palisade.

Out in the fields, something screamed. Small shapes ran through the dark, the sounds of their howls echoing through the blackness. Lazlo's senses told him they were terrified, hearts going full tilt, legs pumping, and adrenaline flooding their bodies. But what in the world were they running from?

He cast his senses further, feeling for what he couldn't see. Long bodies undulated through the grass, large feet pounding, midsection arms reaching for the fleeing meals. Their brains lit up like reactors as they smelled the blood covering the creatures they chased. More gore had been splashed along the palisade, dripping over the people on the other side.

"No," Lazlo whispered. He'd never seen the large predators of Gale's swamp, the alligator-like progs, but he'd heard of them from Dillon, and he knew he was about to get a much better view than he'd ever hoped for. "You have to stop them. They're after the smell."

"Sir?" the torchbearer asked.

"Give the order to fire."

She hesitated, staring at him.

"Do it!" he shouted. "Kill the boggins!"

A prog swept into the light, scooping up a boggin and swallowing it whole, not slowing its charge. Lazlo lashed out at another boggin, stopping its heart, but it wouldn't be enough. The progs had the scent of Gale in their nostrils, and they were hungry, starving, relentless.

A lone pistol rang out, some Paladin who'd stayed on the line, but the progs just snatched up the easy meals and kept coming. For one moment, Lazlo thought they'd smack into the palisade, their charge finished, but a fifteen-foot prog leapt for him, its front feet clinging to the wall as he staggered back. The torchbearer screamed and fell. The prog's back legs scrabbled at the wood, a horrid splintering sound, while its mid-arms reached forward, seeking to pull it up and over. Its glassy black eyes fixed on him, nostrils working like a bellows as its blood-stained teeth snapped for him, foul breath gusting, robbing him of reason.

An invisible hand slammed into its snout, driving it over the wall where it fell with an animal scream. A hand grabbed Lazlo's shoulder, and he flipped over to see Samira on the ladder behind him. "Come on!"

He stood and took another look into the dark. The sound of the prog scratching at the wood below froze his heart, but not as much as what he saw out in the darkness: a sea of boggins flowing soundlessly toward Gale. They must have been waiting in the trees, waiting for others of their kind to get close enough to throw the bags of blood so that still others could lure the progs to the palisade. Astonishing birthrate indeed.

He nearly leapt down the ladder after Samira. All along the palisade, progs were clambering over the wall, and wood cracked and splintered in the distance as a larger prog smashed through.

"Are you all right?" Samira asked.

"We have to get out of here." The palisade was overwhelmed with progs scattering into the city, carrying screams in their wake. "We have to warn people. More boggins are coming."

"Where are the other yafanai?"

"Gone to fight the fire."

Her grin was slightly terrified, but she made the effort. "Good thing I came looking for you, then."

The undertaker had removed Paul's body, but the leathers who were supposed to guard the house never showed. As night fell, Cordelia wondered if she and Liam should just ask Reach to guard the place, but she seemed on the cusp of leaving, too, as if she had no more business here with her love dead.

"Will they put his body in a box before they put it in the ground?" Reach asked.

Cordelia glanced at her from where they all sat around the quiet table.

"That's a hell of a question right now," Liam said.

Reach held her poleaxe closer. "I will take his body. I will give him to the soil the proper way, so he can be reclaimed."

The muscles around Cordelia's right eye jumped, but she couldn't will them to stop. "He would have liked that."

Reach's face twitched as if she wanted to wrinkle her nose, but she couldn't quite manage it.

In the street, someone screamed. A little bit ago, Cordelia thought she'd heard a cry of fire, but when it died down, she thought someone must have taken care of it. She had one duty to attend to already. But someone screaming? She had to check.

As she stood, an animal roar rattled the windows. "What the fuck?"

Reach shot to her feet. "That was a saleska." Tendrils of wood sprouted from her poleaxe and held it fast to her hands.

"A what?" Liam asked as they rushed outside.

A house down the lane collapsed, wood groaning toward the street as walls snapped like kindling. A tail slithered from the wreckage as a huge snout emerged, forcing beams aside like matchsticks.

Saliva flooded Cordelia's mouth, and she fought the memory of long teeth grating over her armor. "A fucking prog in the middle of Gale."

Someone behind the prog screamed, and its head whipped around. It pushed off through the wreckage, following the sound.

Cordelia ran, pulling her sidearm. She fired a few shots into the prog's flank, but it didn't slow. She kept running, holstered her gun, and leapt.

She grabbed the bony plates that followed the line of the prog's spine from neck to tail, and she crab walked toward its head. The pop of a gun sounded behind her, and she put her faith in Liam's aim as she reached the prog's short, fat neck. It slowed and twisted, but she slammed it between the eyes with an armored punch.

It screeched and tossed its head, throwing her into a building, her armor absorbing the impact that still made her teeth knock together.

Liam shot it twice, and it turned, forcing him to leap out of the way. Reach shouted, waving her arms. The prog lunged at her, but she swung her poleaxe around to cling to her back and leapt atop a porch, clambering onto a short roof.

The prog reared, snapping at her. Cordelia grabbed its tail and yanked. It slipped a bit, then slammed her into the ground. The breath whooshed from her lungs, and Liam pulled her clear. The prog was back after Reach in a moment, snapping and drooling, coming ever closer.

Well, that was it. Cordelia had failed her uncle again, and now Reach would be joining him in the afterlife, if there even was such a thing.

The prog's mouth went wide as if to swallow Reach whole, but she rammed her poleaxe down its throat. Before the prog could fall, she jumped on the weapon, clinging to it as if climbing a tree. She sawed back and forth, and the prog gurgled, blood flowing from its long, wide jaws. It toppled sideways, and Reach leapt clear, rolling across the lane as the prog fell to the street, legs twitching with death throes. Its sides worked hard for a moment before the dull, pebbled green hide stuttered to a halt, and it breathed its last. Cordelia couldn't stop staring at the stubby arms that protruded halfway up its side, halfway between its front and back legs. She vaguely remembered hearing that they had something to do with mating, but she really hadn't wanted to know at the time.

Instead, she gawked at Reach, who gave her a tiny smile, cradling one side. Cordelia crossed to the dead prog and pulled the poleaxe free in a rush of blood. "That was impressive."

"What's it doing here?" Liam asked. "Is that the one that almost ate you?"

"I killed that one." But the thought of it following her home almost made her laugh crazily. "Something else is going on."

He prodded it with a foot. Reach took her sticky poleaxe and stuck it to her back again. The street was a disaster, and now that the prog was still, Cordelia heard more screams and the crack of gunshots. And the calls of fire hadn't gone away; they'd just moved through the city, stemming from an orange glow to the east.

"What the *fuck*?" Cordelia gritted her teeth, angry that some city emergency was intruding on her grief, but relief made her pause. If she was fighting progs or fire or whatever the fuck else was going on, she didn't have to think about her uncle. "Let's go."

"Which way?" Reach asked.

"Pick one." Cordelia gave her a nod, grateful she'd still help the city that had caused her so much pain, but maybe she just didn't want to see anyone else suffer. They started down the street together, toward the closest screams, following the path of destruction caused by the prog.

"Everything smells of blood," Reach said. "So much that I cannot…" She tilted her face high in the air, sniffing.

"What is it?"

Reach took off toward a smashed building, leaping up through the debris.

"Reach!" Liam looked to Cordelia. "Should we—"

"Help me, Sa!" Reach called.

Cordelia followed, picking over the largest piles of detritus, trying to keep on Reach's track as she clambered through what used to be a small apartment. Bodies littered the wreckage, and the second floor dangled, exposed to the street.

Reach bent over a body impaled on the wall of a bedroom. "This was his mother."

For a second, Cordelia thought she meant Paul, but his parents had been dead a long time. "Whose?"

Reach sniffed the air again and moved to a small cabinet, its doors blocked by debris. "Here. He is here. His parents must have hidden him before they died."

"Reach, what—"

A little sound came from the cabinet, a child's cry. Cordelia grabbed a beam and lifted it. Reach tore open the doors, and her crooning song filled the shattered space, cutting off the little boy's cries as she pulled him forth.

He looked like the same child Reach had rescued in the alley, and her song calmed him now as it had then. Cordelia grunted as she laid the beam back down. "Kid must have made an impact on you."

Reach pulled down a curtain and bound the boy to her back. "Life means us to be together."

Cordelia didn't know about that, but she couldn't argue it at the moment. Liam was waiting when they came down, and he eyed the boy curiously, giving Cordelia a glance, but he wisely said nothing, and they followed more screams into the night.

❖

When a prog came roaring out of an alley, the yafanai scattered, but Lydia froze. The Storm Lord unleashed his lightning and turned the beast into a pile of charred meat. He stared as if equally amazed by himself, but the skin around his eyes was tight with pain, and his breathing seemed a lot harder than before.

"Look out!" Freddie dragged on Lydia's arm as another prog snapped at them from a side street. They ran, and Lydia tried to warn against getting too far from the useful yafanai, but the prog followed them, and the words died in her throat.

Ahead, a group of people had gathered, talking, shouting.

"Run!" Freddie called.

They scattered, but their noise made the prog roar, and it pushed forward in a rush of speed.

Lydia let time flow away and saw the prog leap, watched Freddie crash into her, sending her flying to the side of the street. She sped through the part where the prog's foot crushed Freddie into the stones before it barreled after the people ahead. As with all futures, there was nothing she could do to stop it.

As the skein of time rewound, Freddie rammed into Lydia's side, knocking the breath from her as she slammed into a wall. Freddie screamed, the sound cut short by a sickening crunch denied to Lydia in her future sight, the sound of bones breaking.

Lydia clambered to her feet, knowing it was bad, that she had to hurry. Freddie sobbed a pain-filled keen as she lay facedown. Her arms flailed at nothing while her motionless legs told a tale of dreadful finality.

"Sweet baby." Lydia fell to her knees, smoothing Freddie's hair and resisting the urge to sink down to the street. "Be still. Try to be still, please. I'll get help. I'll get…"

All the people had fled, chased by the prog. Lydia spied a rickshaw leaning against the mouth of an alley. She stumbled into a run and hauled it over to where Freddie still sobbed.

"I'm sorry, sweet baby. I'm so sorry." Lydia eased her hands under Freddie's body, whispering apologies as Freddie wailed. Sticky warmth coated her hands, but she tried not to think about it. She didn't know how to fix Freddie, but the healers at the temple would. Lydia just had to get her there.

"This will hurt, and I'm sorry. I'm so sorry, but I have to." She kissed Freddie's tearstained cheek. "I have to." She flipped Freddie over as fast as she dared. Freddie shuddered, convulsing, and her lips opened in what would surely be a howl. Lydia pressed a bloody hand over her mouth and leaned over her, muffling the scream.

"You have to be quiet, baby. Shh, shh. You'll bring it back." She sobbed the words, and when Freddie drew another shuddering breath, Lydia lifted her, using the rickshaw for balance, straining and grunting as she hauled Freddie into the seat.

She muffled Freddie's cries when she could. Halfway up, Freddie's eyelids fluttered, and Lydia hoped she might pass out, but once secure, she sobbed again.

Lydia took her place behind the bar and hauled the rickshaw forward. She turned toward the temple, apologizing for every jarring step.

❖

Horace listened to the screams of the city as he paced in front of the temple doors, smacking his hand against the wall. Frustration had been building in his shoulders ever since he hadn't been able to find Cordelia Ross. Now all the healers were ordered to stay at the temple and wait for the wounded to come trickling in. He'd have preferred to be out there, doing something. But at least the Storm Lord wasn't at the temple trying to ferret out who had listened in on his thoughts earlier.

He slapped the wall again, and Kessy glared at him. "Do you mind?" she asked. "Your emotions are leaking everywhere."

"Sorry. It's just, we should be out there!"

"We're supposed to wait," Will said. "The wounded will know to come here, and then—"

"Look!" Kessy pointed into the darkness at someone hurrying toward them.

Horace breathed a sigh. At last, someone to help.

A leather-clad paladin stepped into the torchlight. "The Storm Lord needs you in the city."

"What's happening?" Horace asked.

"There's a fire and something else. Boggins or progs. I'll escort you."

"Shouldn't someone stay to care for the wounded who come here?" Kessy asked.

The paladin scowled. "The wounded are out there! Are you coming, or are you cowards?"

Kessy glared right back, but there was nothing to do but follow the paladin. If the wounded were out there, that was where the healers needed to be. Horace spared one glance back at the temple doors. Anyone who made it there would hopefully be healthy enough to take care of themselves for a while.

CHAPTER TWENTY-FOUR

With the chanuka gone, Nettle knew she should relax, but troublesome thoughts would not be banished easily. The darkening swamp was alive with sound: bird calls fading before the croaks of night creatures, the ever-present insect hum. Standing among the queen's branches, all should have been as it once was, with the drushka content, but Nettle could not make herself forget the lives lost. The swamp had changed. The chanuka had changed it. The humans had changed everything.

And not all for the worse. Nettle's thoughts drifted to the night she had spent with Sa until her body tingled. If the drushka moved closer to the human city, they could have many such nights. The Anushi tree had already come closer to the city than it ever had before, still within the swamp, but now a few hours away. Should they move closer still, into the flatlands? But then the humans would all know of the tree, though they might not realize its importance.

The Anushi's branches creaked, setting Pool down beside her. "I feel your thoughts jangling in my mind, hunt leader."

Nettle dipped her head. "There is much to think about, Queen."

"Ahya, our troubles with the chanuka cannot be over so simply, though the swamp seems quiet tonight. The humans say that too much silence means trouble."

"Like when a predator is near."

Pool rested her head against the bark. "Lately, it seems as if predators are everywhere. Perhaps we should go far from the humans so we will not become ensnared in their plans again. The world is wide, so they say."

The thought darkened Nettle's heart. The world might have infinite possibilities, but there was only one Sa. "Perhaps, or maybe—"

Pool staggered as if struck. She grasped her head, and Nettle grabbed her arm as several branches twined in front of her, shielding her, but from what?

"Queen?"

Pool blinked, widening her eyes as if trying to see past the dark. "What is this?"

Nettle felt something humming through the queen, passing to all her drushka as if her mind was full of wasps. "What is it?"

"They are coming." Pool shook her head rapidly, and the hum of the swarm lessened. "They know we are fewer than we were, and they are coming!"

Nettle gasped as her mind filled with images of leaping drushka, too many to count, all with long, braided hair, the mark of the old ones. Behind them, the roots of the queens whipped to and fro as they guided their massive trees through the forest. Six of the nine queens lashed out with their minds, trying to subdue Pool as their warriors would subdue her tribe.

"Warriors, to me!" Nettle shouted.

"I must remain free," Pool said. "They will not lead me into war with the humans. They will not have me under their sway!"

Her rebellious desires flooded through the mental link, and Nettle snarled. She leaned Pool against the trunk, the better to steer the tree. The warriors readied their weapons, and Shiv climbed to Pool's side, cradling her sapling.

"I will guard my mother's body," Shiv said. "In case the queens seek to harm her."

"If any warriors reach you, call for me," Nettle said.

"You think they would hurt me? Will the color of my hair not stop them?"

Nettle chucked her under the chin. "What there is left of it."

Shiv grinned and gripped her simple knife. The green hair could save her, if anyone took the time to look.

"Mind the queens' limbs." Pool's eyes glazed as she guided the tree. Her snarl had not dimmed. "Do not approach their bodies. They think they will punish us like errant children when they should have forgotten us!"

"Shi'a'na," Shiv said, "should we flee?"

"There is no time, daughter. They will soon be upon us."

Shiv laid her sapling behind her mother. "I wish our armored lovers were beside us, hunt leader."

"Have courage, queen's daughter." But she was right. It would have been nice to feel Sa's armored presence.

❖

If the situation had been less dire, Usk would have felt compelled to simply watch the sight of six queens striding into battle. Their roots and branches whipped around the trees of the swamp, propelling them forward, their trunks swaying and bending, rustling and cracking, and their limbs alive with drushka.

Six queens, more than had ever fought together before. Two had stayed behind: the Shi—far too large to move—and the eighth, who guarded the Shi. Still, their minds were with their drushka, the Shi speaking to Usk through these queens and making her wishes known. She wished the dissenters punished, that the Anushi be gathered back into the fold. The rogue queen would have to submit; how could she not after a sight such as this? Even now, her drushka were probably lying along her branches in supplication, their queen waiting docilely to be guided home.

Nata climbed to Usk's side. "Hunt leader, the renegades are waiting with weapons drawn."

His surprise reached the Shi where she waited far underground, but she felt only satisfaction. A little blood would help the lesson stay learned.

"Let us hope they see their error before we are forced to kill them all." He clapped Nata's shoulder. "Stay with me, young one. We will slip through the guards unnoticed to kill those surrounding the Anushi queen. Then the Shi will be closer to her mind."

Nata looked at the queens arrayed around them. "Will their warriors harm our queens? Have they strayed so far?"

He spread his hands. "I hope not, but if they are willing to fight, who can say what they will do? After being led by a rebel for so long, perhaps they are too unpredictable." They were probably crazed. He wondered if it would show in their looks somehow, if their bodies had remained drushkan, or if their rebellious queen had tainted them. Maybe killing them would be a mercy.

❖

Shiv kept close to her mother, watching the fight through her connection to the tribe, through the tree. All her life, drushka had attacked silently, not howling like humans or beasts as they closed on their prey, but now everyone cried out as if attacking their kind pained them, no matter that the old queens had ordered it.

Nettle gave the call to fire, and a hail of sling stones whizzed through the trees; the old drushka had nothing to match the humans' gift. Many fell to the spinning rocks, but there were more, too many, and soon they drew close enough to fight with claws and blades.

Shiv sought out Nettle again, watched her draw her daggers as she dodged a blade meant for her throat. So, the old drushka wanted corpses rather than prisoners. Shiv's anger mingled with her mother's, and they fed that power to those fighting around them. A pile of dead drushka grew around Nettle's feet until golden blood covered her in a thin sheen.

But not everyone fared as well. Others were hurt, dying. Shiv felt the sorrow of those around them, and though she was still angry, she cried out for all the corpses. This should not be happening. Shiv knew her mother had reasons for leaving the drushka so long ago, reasons that still resonated, reasons so strong her mother could not give them up now, even to save lives. They had to be free. It was part of who they were, part of their core.

Shiv's eyes snapped open as she sensed an unknown branch creeping toward her mother's body. Shiv slashed at it with her knife and felt the revulsion of its owner that anyone would dare to attack a queen.

"I am a queen as well," Shiv said, "with my own tree, and I am free to do as I wish!" She threw her anger at the old queens and hoped they heard her.

The Anushi tree danced through the swamp, trying to keep away from the other queens' branches. She was smaller than they, more nimble, and she had been navigating the swamp for a long time. The others were tired, unused to combat. They tangled in the other trees and seemed confused by the thoughts of their drushka rather than comforted by them.

The seventh queen splashed into the water, ensnared in swamp roots. Another queen and her drushka had to quit the fight to help her. Shiv felt her mother's laugh and joined in until the third queen stumbled forward and wrapped her branches around the Anushi. Warriors poured from her and swarmed the Anushi's limbs.

Shiv knocked a spear out of the air. As another drushka swung at her, she dropped and sliced at his knees. He cried out as his legs buckled, and she shoved him to topple into the swamp.

A line of pain screamed across her back. She turned, swinging her blade in a wild arc. Her opponent stared at her green hair, hesitating as the others had not. She kicked him in the chest, and as he fell, one of the Anushi's branches hurled him into the night.

Shiv knelt at her mother's side. There were too many drushka. She had been wounded; everyone had been wounded. Even her mother had a line of golden blood across her forehead.

"One of the queens lashed me," Shi'a'na said, eyes still unfocused. "They will not stop."

"We will make them pay."

"I cannot let them kill you, daughter, both for my sake and for our people. You must flee."

"I will not leave you!"

Her mother reached forth and brought their faces close. "Bring the humans, daughter. Bring armored Sa and your lover."

"They will see the tree."

Shi'a'na pressed the sapling into Shiv's hands. "The time for that secret is done. We will be free, daughter, or we will be nothing. Do you not feel it?"

Shiv reached for what her mother was trying to tell her. The old queens, the Shi, they did not simply want the Anushi returned to them; they wanted her mind under theirs. As she touched them, Shiv wondered at how similar they were, how dull. Her mother's mind was always bright and alive—even while infuriating—but these queens, they were like an image in a still pond, all copies of the Shi.

"Take care, daughter."

Shiv pressed her bloody knife into her mother's hands. "This will protect you." The Anushi grabbed her and flung her far into the swamp. She kept hold of her sapling and grabbed leaves or small branches as she flew, slowing her fall. When she rolled to a stop along a swamp tree's massive branch, she ran as fast as she could toward the human city.

CHAPTER TWENTY-FIVE

Cordelia, Liam, and Reach had run from fight to fight, mostly boggins, but they were becoming quite good at killing progs, too. Cordelia waved her blade at a small prog, shouting until it turned. Liam emptied his clip into its side—never one for sparing bullets—and it went down. She looked over her shoulder to check on Reach. The little boy tied around her back interfered with her acrobatics, so she guarded their rear and shouted warnings when needed.

The prog twitched, so Cordelia buried her blade in its eye, not stopping until she smacked into bone. She didn't know when she'd started pretending that each monster she killed was the person who murdered her uncle, but the thought made her arm steadier, her aim truer.

"Does being bloody up to your elbows help you somehow?" Liam asked.

She shrugged. "Do you want my extra clip, since you're burning bullets today?"

"They're all in the city. We can dig them out."

Before she could retort, Reach said, "Perhaps we should head toward the fire."

Cordelia shook her head. "We can't do shit about a fire. We *can* kill every boggin bastard in the city." Someone cried out a few streets over, and they headed in that direction.

"If the boggins are bastards, what should we call the progs?" Liam asked. "Should we stick to alliteration, or—"

"I'm not in the mood for jokes, Liam."

He stuttered a laugh. "The world must be burning down, then."

Cordelia could tell he didn't know what to say, didn't know how to comfort her. She wished he'd just give up trying.

Around a corner, a pack of boggins were chewing through a group of townspeople who wielded tools and makeshift clubs. The boggins leapt in and out of reach, luring the humans out of formation and killing them one at a time.

Cordelia shoved her spare clip at Liam and rushed the boggins, howling to draw their attention. A few humans glanced at her as well, and the boggins picked them off. With a swear, Cordelia dove into the boggins' midst, hacking and slashing. Liam's pistol cracked, and two more of them fell.

With the boggins distracted, the townspeople took their revenge, and the pack was dead within moments. Reach pointed the people back to their homes, telling them to remain hidden.

"We heard screaming," one said.

"Barricade yourselves inside," Reach said.

"Is there a fire?" another asked.

"Stay and fight boggins or go fight the fire," Cordelia said. "Do what you want." She started away, listening for screams.

"Aren't you staying?" one of the people called.

She didn't answer, barely heard Liam reassuring them. Reach caught up and looked at her again as if wondering about strange human emotions.

"What?" Cordelia said. "Don't tell me you're already over your anger."

"I am angry about the murder of Paul. It does not stop me caring for others."

"Good for you."

"Perhaps I shall go back to calling you Paul's metal-skinned niece."

Cordelia pulled up short. "What the hell was that about anyway? What changed?"

Reach matched her look for look. "I have never liked you metal-skins. Some act as if nothing can hurt them. But when I saw you grieving at the house, you became Sa."

"Sorry, I'm done crying. This is what my hurting face looks like now."

"You should unleash your anger where it belongs."

Cordelia started walking again. "And you can take your drushkan wisdom and blow it out your ass."

"And now you will feign anger with me."

"Nothing feigning about it."

Liam jogged to catch up with them. "What are we arguing about this time?"

She almost snapped at him, too, but she didn't want to fight them, just wanted to tear more boggins apart if Paul's killer wasn't going to appear before her. "Look, Reach, if you don't want to join the fight, why don't you hide with the townsfolk?"

"My place is by your side."

Cordelia barked a laugh. "Since when?"

"You are the family of my mate, the last of his line. You are in my hands now, as much as he was, whether that appeals to you or not."

"You're going to protect me?"

"However I can."

It made her angrier. "No one asked you."

"That matters as much as a stray leaf on the wind." She held out a hand, and Cordelia flinched away, but Reach only held her palm up. "The sky calls your name."

Cordelia looked up to water pattering all around them. It was probably the Storm Lord fighting the fire, but it made Cordelia think of Nettle. She would give quite a lot to travel back to their night together, much as it had alarmed her when she'd been there, as afraid as she was of feeling anything deeper than lust. But if wishing was enough to make things happen, Paul would be alive.

Who would kill him? After all the arguments he'd had with merchants guilds, with the drovers' council, with Carmichael herself, it had never come to blows. He'd had his assistant and housekeeper for years, no problems there. And a thief wouldn't have left the valuables behind. Who would dislike her uncle enough to march into his office and stab him so hard it left a dent in the wall?

An armored swing could easily do such a thing. But Carmichael hadn't been wearing armor, and why would some random paladin kill the mayor? Unless they were asked to, ordered to. By Carmichael? She'd screwed up with the whole boggin thing, but murder by proxy wasn't her style. When she'd slapped Liam, she hadn't ordered someone else to do it.

A yafanai could hurl a person into the wall hard enough to dent it. That still left why. And there was Blake, who couldn't remember anything. That smelled of yafanai, too. If it had been a paladin or yafanai, who could have given the order to kill? Someone that wouldn't be questioned or ignored.

Cordelia's belly went cold, and it felt as if the street dropped away from her feet. When she stumbled, she didn't shake off Liam's or Reach's steadying hands. Paul had warned her that the Storm Lord's arrival meant trouble. If God had come to see him, he wouldn't have held his opinions in check, even for a deity.

"Sa?" Reach asked.

"Delia, what is it?" Liam said.

"I just…nothing. I don't have any proof."

They exchanged a glance. "You know who Paul's killer is?" Reach asked. "You must tell me."

"We have to wait. Let's finish the fight." She started away before they could ask more questions, her mind whirling. She fought to get her anger back and looked hard for something to kill.

Samira lifted a boggin, but it held tight to its spear, dragging the sharp end from a woman's stomach. Lazlo pounced with his power, sealing the wound so quickly, the woman's grunt of pain and sigh of relief were almost instantaneous.

Samira threw the boggin into a whole pack of them, knocking them flat while Lazlo shepherded Gale's citizens down the road. The one he'd healed mixed with another group, and the tide of them carried her away.

The pack of boggins clambered to their feet just as Samira chucked a fruit stand at them. Several didn't rise again, and those that did were pelted with debris as they fled. Samira breathed hard, sweat beading her forehead. Lazlo eased her fatigue with a passing thought.

She threw her head back and laughed. "With you around, Simon, I could do this all day!"

Dillon had said something similar once, but Lazlo knew Samira didn't mean it the same way. His powers sometimes made people feel giddy. Maybe Dillon was just addicted to it.

No, Lazlo wouldn't blame himself for Dillon's manipulations, his superiority complex, not anymore. Lazlo hadn't made him kill the mayor.

Several citizens waved from a nearby building, shouting for people to take cover in there, but Lazlo shook his head and waved them on. "Barricade the door behind you!"

He couldn't shut himself away. There was too much good he and Samira could do out in the streets, but he dreaded running into Dillon. He had no idea what he would say, so he decided to stay away from him. He rolled his eyes as they ran. Yes, that had worked out so well last time.

"Do you know where the Storm Lord went?" Samira asked.

"Are you sure you're not a telepath?"

"Isn't it him you're trying to catch up to? Or did you have somewhere else in mind?"

He waved at the destruction around them, the bodies. "I just want to be where I'm needed."

"He's probably putting together a plan—"

"You don't know what he's doing. You don't know what he's capable of. You shouldn't be so trusting!"

Her eyes widened. "Of the Storm Lord? Why not? What's he done?"

Anger burned through his temples. Why was it always him that had to defend everything?

"Look, Simon, I know you have feelings for him—"

"Maybe you should mind your own business." He marched ahead, not looking back. Maybe she'd turn down another street, wash her hands of him.

"Oh no, no." She caught up to him quickly. "No way, Simon. If you want to be angry, be angry. If you want to rant, fine. If you'd rather bottle everything up and not talk about it, I will try to respect your wishes and ultimately needle you until you tell me. But I will not be your emotional punching bag." She managed to cross her arms while stalking forward, a pose that would have made him laugh if not for her serious expression. "If I hurt your feelings, I'm sorry, but I know I'm not the reason you're so angry, so it must be *him*. What did he do?"

"This isn't the time." He nodded toward where a lone boggin was sneaking through the night.

Samira smacked it into a wall, and it dropped motionless to the street. "You were saying?"

He chuckled. "I'm sorry I tried to drive you away."

"You're forgiven."

They passed the unmoving boggin, and Lazlo looked to the blood smear on the wall above it. She hadn't hit it hard enough to make a dent, not like in the mayor's house. "He's killed someone."

She sucked in a breath. "The Storm Lord? Who?"

He tried to form the words and couldn't, didn't know if he'd just been hiding Dillon's secrets for too long or if he feared shaking Samira's faith or what. She waited, silent, until they turned a corner and saw the street ahead blocked by a large shadow.

He stopped, hauling on Samira's hand, fearing a prog, but his senses told them it was humans gathered ahead even as one called, "Hold your fire!"

❖

B46 lingered on the walls of the tall one's nest, drinking in the destruction, the carnage and screams. She'd taken the last of the sticky grit and could almost feel it swirling inside her mind. If she closed her eyes, she could feel the children as they clawed and bit, could sense the water creatures as they snapped and dashed. She could taste human blood on her tongue, feel their dying breaths rattle through her.

She sank down in her perch, head resting against her chest as she felt the children fight. She could feel these children as she could no others. They'd grown so fast that they'd howled with the pain of it. She felt the youngest and smallest fighting, clumsy, unproven, but with her presence joining their minds, they fought like leaping waterspouts. She instructed groups on how to fight together, tasted the kill with others, and warned still others when to hide, when to strike. She was everywhere, everyone, all the children connected through her.

Blinding pain roared through her temples, and she sucked in a breath, back in her own body. She thought it might be the smoke wafting over her, prickling her lungs, but no, this was something greater. When she tried to reconnect to the children, the pain came again, and she stopped as her limbs shook, warmth and cold passing over her skin as if the seasons passed in a single instant.

She licked her teeth, her mouth dry. She sometimes felt this way if she hadn't eaten the sticky grit in days, but it hadn't been that long. Or perhaps she'd been eating more and more and hadn't noticed. She longed for the bitter taste, the feel of her mind expanding.

But there was no more. She lifted her nose and inhaled deeply. The tall creatures had first given her the sticky grit. They had to have more. All she had to do was find it. Her stomach rumbled at the thought. She leapt from her perch and wound through the streets, smelling bodies, following her nose, sending out tendrils of her mind so she could check the noses of all the children and search among them past the pain in her mind.

As she got close to one group, her mind reached for them, but the pain became too much, and they staggered along with her. She pulled away, running her claws along their hides as she passed, wishing them a world of killing.

❖

Lydia paused behind the rickshaw's bar, blocking out the sounds of Freddie's pain-filled moans and letting time play out in front of her. She saw a boggin trot down the street, looking for prey but passing her by where she hid in the shadows. She let time rewind and watched it go before heading off again.

For once, her power seemed useful even as it slowed her down. If she hadn't known what was coming, she would have been attacked several times. And once she'd avoided a wide-eyed man who fled down the street carrying an armload of fabric. She hadn't known what he was about, but when he tripped and impaled himself on a piece of debris, it didn't seem to matter.

Lydia pulled the rickshaw forward again, trying to avoid anything jarring that would make Freddie cry out. She kept looking over her shoulder, tried to murmur comforting things, but she'd run out of sweet phrases and now just mumbled, "It's all right," over and over.

Pain had built through her back and shoulders; fear made her clamp her teeth so hard they ached. The streets of Gale stretched on forever, and she wondered if she'd fallen into some parallel world of never-ending nightmare.

When she saw the gates of the temple, she sobbed. "Almost there."

Part of her didn't believe it; she thought the gates would go leaping out of reach, but they stayed put. They were shut, but they would be. The people inside would be afraid of boggins getting in, but the healers were surely just behind, and they would help her. She came out from behind the pole, her fingers cramping from having gripped it so hard, and knocked with the sides of her hands.

No one answered. Well, they were busy tending the wounded. She knocked again. "Hello?"

When no one answered a second time, she pressed her ear to the door and heard nothing. So? Doors were thick, weren't they? She'd just have to be louder. She pounded. She screamed. She clawed at the temple doors and wondered if she could find some nearby building to scale, maybe get to the temple roof, and then find a way down. She could bring someone out to Freddie, someone waiting just inside. Someone deaf or asleep or busy.

Lydia sagged to the ground, sobbing, aching in mind and body. Time played out, and she watched herself rise and cross to the rickshaw.

"No!" She snapped back to the present, and Freddie cried out weakly. Her breath bubbled inside her chest now, a horrid sound, an inevitable sound. Lydia pulled herself up and stumbled to the rickshaw to take Freddie's hand. "I'm so sorry."

Freddie's eyes had glazed over, her face pale and shining with sweat. Lydia clamped down hard on her power to keep it still. She knew what was coming, and nothing in the world would make her watch it twice.

CHAPTER TWENTY-SIX

Carmichael watched the bucket brigades toting water from the city's wells to the blazing warehouse district. She and the other armors had already evacuated survivors and pulled down several smaller buildings to create a firebreak. She'd gotten particular satisfaction from ripping beams out of walls and kicking down supports. It almost made her forget that after all this was over, she'd have to tell the population that their mayor was dead, but there were so many dead. She stepped over a boggin body. Maybe the people would think Paul had been killed by a boggin, but she knew better, and Lieutenant Ross knew better. They still had a murderer to find.

Lieutenant Brown jogged by, pushing a cart full of wounded away from the smoke and drifting embers. The fire seemed contained for now, but one strong gust of wind could pick it up again and spread it faster than they could fight it. They were soaking the nearby buildings as best they could, and everyone, armored or otherwise, sported greasy soot stains on their clothes and faces.

Brown yanked the cart away from an alley, and the people inside cried out. A fifteen-foot prog barreled past them, snapping at the retreating cart but not stopping, running from the leathers that chased it. Brown pulled her sidearm, but the prog's flicking tail flung her down.

Carmichael whipped out her sidearm and planted her feet as the prog rushed her. She let the world go quiet, and with a gentle squeeze, put two bullets in the monster's head. It fell on its chin and slid across the slick ground, tongue protruding. She sidestepped its carcass, not even watching where it came to a stop.

"Brown," Carmichael called, "might want to get out of the way before you shoot."

"Thanks for the tip, Cap. Nice shot."

"Where the fuck are these things coming from?"

"Dunno. I'm almost out of ammo."

Carmichael clucked her tongue and handed over her spare clip.

"I've shot a few, Cap. I just got to the fire a little bit ago. There are boggins in the city, too, you know."

"Where the hell are the yafanai? They were taking care of the boggins when we left the palisade." It had started sprinkling—the Storm Lord's contribution to firefighting—but Carmichael had been hoping for a deluge. Maybe the yafanai were still fighting boggins at the palisade, and there were just too many, more than had been in the field when she'd left. Maybe the yafanai lines had been overrun, and then maybe the progs were attracted by the smell of the boggin corpses.

She looked to the fire. Or this was all someone's plan. "Shit!"

"What is it?"

"This fucking fire started right before we saw these progs, and now there are boggins, too? Fucking boggins started the fire!"

Brown's mouth hung open. "That's really smart."

"Yeah, we've been told that again and again, but have we listened?"

"We thought we'd gotten them all," Brown said. "First in the swamp and then just now in the fields."

"And a smart enemy would make us think that, wouldn't they? And they probably got these progs in here, too." She slashed a hand through the air. "Forget what the Storm Lord says. We're breaking out the big guns."

"The railguns?" Brown's face lit in a smile. "Yes, Cap!"

The Storm Lord had charged the heavy artillery when he'd come to the keep, but they hadn't had a use for them yet. The large bullets the railguns fired only survived until now because they were an amalgam of metal and ceramics, not enough metal to bother with breaking them up, just enough for the magnetic guns to work.

"Where should we deploy?" Brown asked.

"All through the city. Get the first three armors you can find and station them and yourself to sweep the four quarters; kill everything that isn't human."

"Yes, Cap!" She was off like a shot, and someone else took charge of the cart full of wounded people.

A boom shook the right of the square, and Carmichael swung that way, hoping the fire hadn't reached the mead distilleries. A group of robed people stared at a pile of smoldering debris and moved it farther from the fire as if pushing it with an invisible hand.

The fucking yafanai, at last. The rain picked up a bit, and Carmichael spotted the Storm Lord among the other robes. That was a shame. If their line had broken on the palisade, he might have been killed. She supposed he was better for fighting the fire, but he had to be tired if this weak weather was all he could muster.

Whatever he could do now was better than anything she had. Now the soldiers could clean up the rest of this mess. "Paladins, form up!"

The cry passed around the square, and Carmichael divided her soldiers into squads, the better to sweep the city clean.

As the yafanai fought the fire, Dillon watched for any trouble coming from the shadows. Boggins and progs had flooded the city, and he'd figured out that it hadn't been the Sun-Moon worshipers who'd started this fire but the boggins themselves. Little fucking bastards. He was almost proud of them, though he didn't like being fooled. The last thing he needed was to look incompetent, not that anyone would point that out.

Now all he had to do was wipe out the invaders and find out just who'd peeked into his head at the temple. Christian and Marlowe might not have been responsible for the fire, but with Caroline distracted, they might have been able to scan his thoughts.

Not that it would do them any good.

A prog wandered into the square, limping, its tongue lolling. He pumped it full of lightning until it stopped wriggling, though it seemed on its last legs anyway. Even the monsters were getting tired. It had been a long night, never mind that it wasn't that late. Dillon resisted the urge to lean on his knees. The rain was falling in earnest after he'd tugged on it for hours, so between the rain and Carmichael's efforts, the fire couldn't spread, though it was just because of the powered armor that she'd beaten him here. That was okay. It had given him more time to save people as the boggins caught up to them.

He looked to the yafanai just as a macro collapsed. The others gathered around her and tried to help her up. They'd have to save themselves soon, never mind other people. Where the fuck was Lazlo? That question had been running through his head for hours. Lazlo could have fixed them all and not broken a sweat, but he was still nowhere to be found, even after someone had gone to fetch the healers. Dillon fought images of a prog sneaking through the darkness as Lazlo bent over a wounded soul. He'd never hear it coming, and he wasn't fast enough to stop his own throat being torn out.

No, much more likely that he was on his way with the others, safe in a group. He wouldn't need to be the fastest then, just not the slowest. Still, someone should be searching for him.

As he took another weary look around the square, Dillon nodded. The fire was under control with the few nudges the yafanai had done and the townspeople still working steadily. Carmichael was a pain in the ass, but she seemed good at organizing people. He left his one pyrokinetic at the fire and turned back toward the temple. They'd meet the healers, get their energy back, and take on the boggins.

They were a sad, shuffling group, all but Natalya, who stared at Dillon with a half-crazed smile that made her look as if she wasn't used to smiling and didn't quite know how to do it. He supposed she might be awe-stricken or trying to come on to him. She was good-looking, a bit angular, but the weird smile put her out of the running of potential bed partners. He gave her a confident nod, hoping that would make her look elsewhere, but she kept staring.

He nudged Caroline. "What's the story with her?"

"Natalya?"

"I know she's one of the augmented, but is she just weird?"

Caroline looked her way and frowned. "I can't get anything from her, not even surface thoughts."

"Because of her shields."

"Stronger than that. It's as if she's not even there."

Creepy. The augmentation must have given her *very* strong shields. He tried to ignore her and offered comforting words to the others instead.

❖

Lazlo couldn't believe his eyes. It was a ballista. He never thought he'd see anything like it in person, though he also hadn't believed he'd ever see a twenty-foot alien alligator scale a wall.

"It's not mine," Lieutenant Lea said as he invited Lazlo and Samira to take cover with him. Several leather-clad paladins and a handful of others squatted behind the barricade they'd built on each side of the large weapon. "I borrowed it from a friend." He said it matter-of-factly, as if he'd just taken someone's hairbrush. "It's come in pretty handy. We lure the progs down this street and shoot them." The pile of pointy, bloody debris stacked up to the side backed him up nicely.

From the top of a nearby building someone called, "Ready!"

Lea tilted the ballista up, aiming it down the street. "Here we go."

"A prog," the lookout called. "And a pack of boggins behind."

"You're a yafanai, right?" Lea asked.

"A macro," Samira said. "Simon is a healer."

Lea nodded. "You can take the boggins?"

"Sure."

"Good. I'll hit the prog."

Samira leaned close to Lazlo's ear. "Sounds as if he's planning a regular day."

Lazlo would have chuckled, but the roar of the prog made his teeth clamp together. He shuddered, remembering the other being so close.

When the prog rounded the corner, Lea fired, and a makeshift spear punched into its shoulder just in front of its left leg. Lazlo sensed the severed tendons and the broken ribs behind, one puncturing a lung. The prog staggered and fell, flopping but trying to push forward.

Samira lifted the nearest boggins and hurled them into the others. Five broke away, rushing the barricade. The leathers and the townspeople readied truncheons and whatever else they had to hand. Lea pulled his gun. Samira got one boggin before they were out of sight, crouched on the other side of the barricade.

"The prog is still coming!" someone said.

Samira grunted as she tried to shove the heavy creature. Two boggins leapt the barricade. Lea shot one from the air, and a leather hit the other. When it fell, the townspeople gathered around it, weapons rising and falling until it stilled. Another boggin leapt while everyone was distracted, teeth glinting in the dim light. Lazlo paralyzed it, and it fell limply into the crowd of people. One man screamed and pushed it away before he hammered it over and over.

"It's dead." Lazlo tried to catch his arm. "You killed it. You can stop."

"Simon!"

He turned as a boggin reached over the barricade and tore into someone's shoulder. She dropped, shrieking, blood fountaining from the wound. Lea shot the creature, and it fell back, claws catching on the barricade so that it hung like a macabre ornament. Lazlo darted for the injured woman and healed her, but she clung to him, sobbing.

He turned to Samira, his panic rising. "What should I do? I can't put her to sleep out here." He calmed her with his power, but she wasn't annoyed; she was traumatized, and he could only make her sleepy.

"Forget her," someone said. "Where's the last one?"

They quieted, listening. Samira bent close to the injured woman's ear and whispered something soothing, muffling her breathy sobs.

"Can you sense it?" Lea asked.

Lazlo let his senses wander, looking for anything that didn't belong. "On the other side of the barricade. Close." He tried to get hold of it, but there were too many people around, and he couldn't see it. The woman in his arms shifted to latch on to Samira.

A leather peeked over the barricade and was rewarded with a claw across his cheek. He yelped and fell back. Lazlo healed him, and everyone waved at him to be quiet.

"To hell with this." Lea vaulted over the barricade. "Come here, you little shit."

Lazlo grimaced at the screech of claws trying to tear metal and then the wet, thudding sounds of a boggin being beaten to a pulp.

"That's done it," someone said.

Lazlo sagged against the barricade, and Samira squeezed his arm. Everything around him was clear, every sight and sound, the scent of blood. He could almost taste the fear, the heightened senses that kept hijacking his power by their presence. He was terrified, and he wondered how he should react to that, if he should be like the frightened woman and collapse in Samira's arms. He'd been scared all his life, but never like this. What the hell had he been so afraid of? What could be as scary as this?

Dillon? Not even by half. But this was all Dillon's fault. And his own, his inner voice whispered. He'd turned these creatures into killers on Dillon's command. He wished that he *had* been afraid of Dillon. He could confess then, claim he'd done it because he feared Dillon would hurt him or someone he cared about. They'd be angry, but they'd understand.

But if he tried to say he'd done it out of love? Who would understand that? Who would create something so terrible because of love? And if he stayed with Dillon, he'd do something like this again. Natalya and Horace were proof of that. He'd do all this again.

"Simon?" Samira whispered. "Are you all right?"

He nodded, even though the future was more terrifying than the present. He would leave Dillon. He had to. If he survived the night, if any of them did, he had to get as far from Dillon as possible, or history would just keep repeating itself. He'd had this thought before, on the *Atlas*, but it had been impossible then, a comforting lie, but now he had to make it the truth, a fact more terrifying than a thousand boggins.

Funny, he'd never thought fear could make him feel lighter.

When Private Jacobs held up a hand, Horace stopped with the others. Jacobs was supposed to be taking them toward the fire, but they'd taken countless detours, threading around wreckage and destruction and angling toward cries for help.

Horace had healed injury after injury, had soothed the nerves of countless people, including his fellow healers. And he'd eased their fatigue when they'd overused their powers. Kessy had started calling him their little healing battery. His reserves seemed inexhaustible, and the thought made him giddy, even a little fearful, though he couldn't quite say why.

He thought on something Simon had said, about how he had to be careful not to harm instead of heal, that his powers could be flipped to attack the same systems he bolstered. The idea made his stomach squirm, but so far, Jacobs had kept them out of combat, leading them in when the fighting was done.

Now Jacobs crept forward, and Horace followed, the rest of them trailing in his wake. In the next street, Captain Carmichael and a large group of soldiers stood amidst a trail of boggin bodies.

"Captain?" Jacobs called.

The soldiers swung their weapons toward the dark alley, but Carmichael put up a hand. "Easy," she said. "A group of boggins wouldn't call me captain. Come on out."

Horace stepped out before Jacobs could speak again. "Is anyone hurt?"

"The yafanai medics," Carmichael said. "At last."

Kessy held her chin up. "We've had a lot to do."

"I bet. Anyone who's hurt, sound off."

The healers moved through the group, fixing them, soothing them. Horace gave Carmichael an energy boost, cleansing her fatigue.

She breathed deep. "You're the real thing, yafanai."

"Horace. We heard there was a fire?"

"Dealt with, but there are still wounded." She split some of her soldiers up and sent Will and Kessy with them toward the warehouse district. She gestured for Horace to follow her and sent Leila with another group.

She didn't tell Horace where she was going or what they would do when they got there, but he supposed she was used to only explaining when she needed to. He stayed on her heels. He hadn't seen Lieutenant Ross, but maybe they would find her on their way. He hoped she hadn't been killed. Who else could he tell his secret to? Simon seemed too caught up in the Storm Lord, but the idea that he couldn't be trusted sounded wrong in Horace's head.

He stared at Carmichael. He didn't know her, but he'd heard stories about how much of a hardass she was. Did she know people talked about her like that? Would she even care? A true hardass might even be pleased. And she wasn't protecting the Storm Lord at the moment, not that a god needed her help. But maybe she didn't want to protect him.

"Have you seen the Storm Lord?" he asked softly.

"Back at the fire."

"Oh, that's why it's dealt with? Because he took care of it?"

She snorted and gave him a look, as if wondering what he was trying to prove, but that snort said volumes. She wasn't giving the Storm Lord any credit. Still, he waited through two more skirmishes that she waded through easily. He didn't have much to do until Jacobs took a spear to the gut from a boggin she thought already dead.

No one else was near as Jacobs fell back with a cry. She was halfway into an alley, deep in shadow. The boggin twisted the spear inside her, and he couldn't heal her until it was free. And it wouldn't be free until the boggin was dead.

Horace tore the boggin's spinal cord from its brain with one neat flick of power. It dropped, and he stared until Jacobs's cry brought him back to himself. He knelt at her side.

"This will hurt, but not for long." He yanked the spear free, and she screamed, a sound that died as he closed the wound and eased her pain. She gasped, coughing as she drew in too much air.

"Breathe," Horace said.

"Thank…thanks." She stood and wiped the blood from her mouth. "I'm glad you're here."

"You're welcome."

But she was already tottering away to join her fellows.

Horace stared at the boggin, and bile burned his chest. Life could be over this quickly for anyone, Lieutenant Ross or Simon or Natalya, or anyone he hadn't let himself think about since this whole thing started. What the hell was he doing wasting time?

He crossed to Captain Carmichael and leaned to her ear. "I need to speak with you in private."

Her mouth quirked. "We can't exactly go into the parlor."

"I can send you a telepathic message that no one else will hear."

She stared as if wondering what he was playing at. "Well, you asked permission first, so I guess that says something. Go ahead."

"The Storm Lord killed the mayor," he sent.

Outwardly, she didn't change, but Horace's power told him what was happening underneath her skin. Her muscles tightened as if someone had pulled her strings, and anger brewed inside her.

"You're sure."

"From his own mind." He gave her a glimpse of the images he'd seen, including the fact that the Storm Lord knew someone was on to him.

"So you're the only proof?"

Horace went cold, but he gathered his power, wondering how many of them he could subdue if he'd just made the worst mistake of his life.

Something in his face must have answered the question. She nodded. "Stay close to me. I'll keep you alive."

CHAPTER TWENTY-SEVEN

Cordelia kept angling toward the Paladin Keep, leading Reach and Liam. She hoped Carmichael could tell them what had happened to Gale, and she wanted to talk about the Storm Lord. Both Paul and Carmichael hadn't been pleased to find the Storm Lord among them. Maybe she'd already had the same thoughts Cordelia had, and she might have a better idea about what to do.

But what could anyone do to a god? She'd been faithful to the Storm Lord her whole life, and to have that repaid with murder? Even if Paul had done something wrong, he didn't deserve to die for it. That sounded less like a god and more like a monster. Maybe it'd be easier to have a god that didn't exist, as the Sun-Moons did.

The streets were filled with shredded fabric, broken crockery, smashed open boxes, and pieces of wood. Here and there, a body lay among the wreckage. Liam bent over one person who sprawled in the street, her arms outstretched. He felt for a pulse and then opened his visor. "Do you think they—"

A boggin slithered out of the debris on the other side of the body. Cordelia started forward, and Liam went for his sidearm, but the boggin hurled a spear into his open helm. He clutched his face, howling, blood gushing around his clasped hands.

Cordelia cried out. This was not happening again. Her weapons forgotten, she launched toward the boggin with her bare hands. It ducked into a pile of heaped wood and plaster, and Cordelia crashed behind it, scattering debris like sand.

She yelled every obscenity she knew, letting out the rage for her parents, for Paul, for all of Gale. The fucking swamp just wouldn't let them be, and their god might have turned on them. The boggin skipped halfway up a shattered building, but another of its fellows ambled around the corner. Cordelia grabbed the new boggin and swung it into the ground before nearly pulling it apart. It screamed until she planted a foot in its skull and squashed it like an overripe melon.

"Sa!" Reach yelled. "He lives. You must hold him still."

The first boggin still crouched on the building, licking its lips. She could catch it if she—

"Sa!"

She glanced back, but she couldn't let another murderer go free. The boggin scrambled farther up the house, almost out of sight. It was now or never, and revenge was screaming at her to keep going.

With a strangled sound, Cordelia ran for Liam. He rolled on the ground, clutching his face. Reach tried to hold him, and the little boy on her back began to cry. Cordelia fell across Liam's torso, pinning him. Reach fumbled in a pouch at her waist and pressed something to his face. She began to sing, and Cordelia's heartbeat slowed, letting her breathe again. The little boy calmed, and Liam went limp.

Reach eased his helmet off and bent over his face, singing all the while. Time fell away, and the destruction around them seemed to fade. Cordelia pictured her uncle doing all the things he'd loved and thought of her parents sneaking kisses while she groaned at them to stop being so embarrassing. Funny, after losing them, she'd thought she was done with grief, that nothing could ever hurt so badly again. Everyone in her life seemed immortal. They had to be, or she wouldn't survive.

She looked to Liam's face but couldn't see around Reach. "I'm sorry. I almost let you die; I'm sorry." Revenge had made too much sense. If she killed that boggin, she'd thought, everything would have been okay. But that wasn't true, not at all. All the people she'd taken her anger out on over the years, all the fights she and Liam had caused. Had they ever helped?

Reach leaned out of the way. Liam's eyes were shut, but his mouth moved as if trying to follow Reach's song. At last, the notes faded, and Cordelia breathed deep. The clarity receded, and she tried to keep hold of it, but she was only left with: the living were always more important than the dead.

"A large wound through his cheek," Reach said. "I have tried to sing it away, but I have never had to heal this much damage to a human before."

Cordelia nodded. She was shaking, didn't know if she could rise even with the armor.

"Sa, he will live. Rejoice."

"He's lucky."

Reach stood, pulling Cordelia up as she went, stronger than she looked. "Many will live if we save them."

"Right. You're right."

Liam had a small, seeping hole in his cheek, but he blinked and focused on her. "What happened?" It sounded as if he had a mouth full of wadded fabric, and half his face had already started to swell.

She couldn't help a smile. "Can you move?"

"Dizzy. Help?"

She pulled him up. "Clear that head, soldier. We're moving out."

"Fuck off." He swayed but accepted her arm.

Reach held her poleaxe ready. "Someone comes."

Brown dashed around the corner, pulling up short when she saw them. "Where the fuck have you been?" Before Cordelia could answer, she added, "Don't tell me you're going for the railguns too?"

Cordelia blinked before she remembered. They'd all looked hungrily at the heavy artillery when the Storm Lord had first charged it. "I hadn't thought of them."

"Yeah? Well, keep not thinking. Carmichael told *me* where to deploy them, and I get dibs. There might be enough for you if no one else is around." She looked hard at Liam. "What happened to him?"

As if she couldn't guess by everything around them. "He tried to keep me away from a railgun."

Brown sputtered a laugh. "Well, there are four of them. I guess I can share."

As they kept toward the keep, Cordelia's thoughts tried to pull her into another snarl of anger and guilt. She tried to hold on to the purity of Reach's song, but her need for revenge was hard to ignore. She'd been chasing it for so long. And if the Storm Lord was responsible for Paul's death, he had to pay, even if she had no idea how to make that happen, even if it cost her life.

Close to the keep, someone leapt into the street in front of them, and Cordelia and Brown went for their sidearms. Reach cast her poleaxe away and stepped in front of them, leaving Liam to sway on his own.

"Stop, Sa!" Reach said. "Do you not see?"

Shiv stepped around her, and Cordelia pointed her gun at the ground. "What the hell?"

"Sa, the old drushka have attacked us. My mother is threatened. You must come."

Reach sucked her teeth.

"What happened?" Cordelia asked.

Shiv told them of a battle in the swamp, drushka attacking drushka. She peered around the city as she spoke, as they continued toward the keep. "What has happened here?"

"Later." Cordelia's mind was racing. If Pool's drushka were outnumbered as much as Shiv claimed, they wouldn't last the night. And the only way to reach them fast enough was with powered armor. *And* they'd need some firepower.

"I will come with you," Reach said. But as she was, she'd be casting her life away with so many others.

At the entrance to the keep, Cordelia looked back at the city. Maybe Gale would be all right without her. It had the rest of the paladins. It had the yafanai. It had the Storm Lord, who may or may not have killed her uncle. And it had Carmichael, who had gotten them into this mess in the first place, unless that had been the Storm Lord's doing, too. Hadn't she once mentioned something about being under orders?

Cordelia rubbed her forehead. All this mess caused by one order? "I'm coming, too."

Brown gawked at her. "You're abandoning Gale?"

"And I'm taking a railgun." She nodded at Reach. "Two of them, if you think you can handle it."

Reach gave her a flat look. "I am as capable as you."

"You can't abandon your post!" Brown said.

"Well, I'm supposed to be guarding my dead uncle's house, so I already abandoned it." When Brown continued to stare, Cordelia added, "Look, Jen, if the old drushka take out our allies, where do you think they'll head next? How well do you think we could defend Gale from another attack?"

"Oh, but you think you can just march into the swamp and take care of all the drushka?" Brown asked.

"I have to try." There were a lot of people left alive in Gale, but she couldn't stop thinking of Shiv losing her mother and her people.

And she couldn't forget Nettle's smile, her grace, the feel of her lithe body. She pictured Nettle struggling against a horde of drushka until they pulled her down.

A low rumble made them turn, and Lea pushed Cordelia's ballista into the light of the keep. "Thanks for the loan," he called.

Cordelia didn't know whether to gawk or laugh. "I forgot I had it!"

"It came in handy. We ran out of stuff we could use as ammo. I sent some yafanai back to their temple and thought I'd come here. Where are we off to?"

"We're deploying the railguns around the city," Brown said.

Cordelia pointed toward the palisade. "I'm going to the swamp just as soon as I get a gun of my own."

Lea shook his head, and Cordelia thought he was going to try to talk her out of it, but he said, "Railguns in the city won't work. They'll shred walls like paper and hit anyone inside." When they stared, he blinked at them. "All the times you've seen the paladin vid, have you ever really watched it?"

"That's not what Carmichael said!" Brown shouted.

"Swamp it is," Cordelia said.

"No." Brown held up a hand. "We are not marching into the swamp to take on the whole native population."

"Captain Carmichael will figure out about the railguns once she thinks about it," Lea said. He nodded to Cordelia. "Come on. I know where they are."

"I can lead you into the swamp," Shiv said.

Cordelia shook her head as she followed Lea into the keep. "You and Liam are both staying. No arguments, or I will slug you. Liam, you're hurt, and, Shiv, you're too important."

They agreed quicker than she expected. Brown raged at them as they donned the battery and ammo packs for each railgun and then hefted the guns themselves. Reach set her poleaxe and the sleeping boy in the corner. If the gun was too heavy for her, she didn't show it.

At last, Brown shut her mouth with a snap. "This feels wrong."

Lea hefted his gun. "Nothing wrong about it."

Brown eyed the gun with longing and then picked up the last one. "We make this quick. Save the fucking drushka, then come back, and clean up Gale. Can't believe I'm doing this."

Reach listened as Cordelia instructed her in the railgun's use. If she kept the trigger down, the bullets would keep dropping into the chamber, and the magnets—powered by the battery packs—would propel them from the barrel with violent force. "Be mindful of the ammo. You can spend more than you want real fucking quick."

"One of us should carry it for you during the trip," Lea said, "with our armor powered and all."

Reach handed him the weapon. She picked up the little boy and cuddled him close. "Queen's daughter, will you care for my son while I am gone?"

Shiv sucked her teeth but took the boy in her arms. "Yours, *shawness?*"

"Ahya, I saved his life. He is in my hands now." She sang a few notes, and the boy settled deeper into sleep.

"I will do as you ask. His name?"

Reach caressed his cheek with one knuckle. "He cannot speak to tell me, so I will call him Paul."

Cordelia's throat tightened. She would never again be a pain in her uncle's ass. That hurt so much it was hard to breathe. It was easier to focus on the many people she could annoy if they lived through the night.

"He, um, he might have some relatives left," Liam said, nodding at the boy.

Reach glared at him, and Cordelia cleared her throat, warning him to drop it, but he didn't stop his stare.

"I inquired after I found him wandering in the street," Reach said. "A mother, a father, a grandmother, all dead." Her head tilted. "Do you remember where to find their corpses? So you can check?"

"Yep, that's…all right."

Cordelia clutched his shoulder. "Stay safe."

"I'd tell you the same, but you'd ignore me. Come back, all of you."

"It's a promise."

Reach led them out of the keep, claiming she could find her people even if blind. Brown still muttered under her breath, but Lea seemed almost jaunty as they wound through Gale's stricken streets, heading for the palisade. A quick jump and they were over, into the abandoned fields. The sky in the east was beginning to lighten despite the rain, but they still had to use the glow of their armor to light the way.

❖

Everywhere B46 turned, her children were killing and feasting. The water creatures had done their tasks well, battering this nest and scattering its inhabitants. She could not hear their roars anymore, thought them all dead, but the children seemed without number.

She wished she could join the fight beside them, but pain ached through her body, and her thoughts would not stay on a single track. She watched several children die and knew she could have helped them with her body or her mind, but she could not spur her shuffling steps into anything more.

She followed the scent of the sticky grit that drifted through the nest. The children felled a creature that reeked of it, and B46 drank its blood, lapping it from the stones, but it only whetted her appetite. There had to be more.

She stumbled on, and a tantalizing breeze passed over her nose that made her legs straighten a bit and her mind clear a little. Somewhere ahead, the sticky grit called to her in its pure form.

The way was barred—like so many paths in this winding nest—but her claws could always find a way. First, she had to kill the tall creature who guarded this place, who reeked of the sticky grit. If B46 feasted upon her, maybe she would find the strength to get inside to the grit itself.

❖

Lydia's head pounded in time with her pulse. She'd cried every tear she'd ever had, but the sobs wouldn't stop, not since Freddie's breathing had faded away like a snuffed candle. She sat on the steps of the temple and wept, rocking herself and wondering if she should move Freddie's body then wondering what the point would be.

At the end of the lane, someone tottered into the light with halting steps, probably looking for help. Lydia tried to clear her throat to call that there was no help here, but she couldn't make the words.

Licking her lips with a sandpaper tongue, she tried again. The boggin wobbled through a patch of light like something out of a nightmare. Its eyestalks were locked on her, and there was nowhere to run.

Lydia moved to Freddie, thinking the monster had come to eat, but when she let her power play out, she watched the boggin shuffle toward the temple gates, ignoring Freddie, fixed on Lydia like a starving woman.

Time rewound, and Lydia moved into the open, looking for a way to dash around the boggin as it crept closer. It panted, wounded or ill, but its claws and mouth were stained black with blood. She thought to just stand there and be devoured, let her grief end, but something primal raged against that thought. She couldn't run. She would have to fight.

She slid a pole from the rickshaw's torn canopy, though she had no idea how to use it as a weapon. She held it in front of her, thinking to bat the boggin out of the way, but maybe it would be better to jab and hurt it if she could or drive it away if she couldn't.

Well, there was one way to find out.

She let her power hover, going moments into the future before sliding back into place. She lived in two different times, entranced and yet aware. The boggin leapt in the future, and she ducked to the side in the present. The boggin flew past her, and Lydia whirled around, having already seen where it would land. She thrust the pole into its belly, sending it off balance.

It caught itself and raked at her, but Lydia's leg was no longer in its path. She swung the pole around and smacked the boggin in the head. In the future, the claws came up again, and she leaned away, but she didn't go far enough to see that the attack was a feint. In the present, the boggin snapped her pole in half.

Lydia stumbled against the rickshaw and fell. She slid into the future to see where the boggin would attack from, but it put its hands on its head and roared. Lydia cried out with it, shouting Freddie's name.

❖

The pain spread from B46's belly and head through all her joints and muscles, tightening around her chest like a rope. If she could not defeat this creature, she could not get to the sticky grit; she needed this creature's blood! In desperation, she reached for the children, seeking their strength. They heard her call, and she felt some of them racing toward her, but she needed more. She sent her mind to more of them, ignoring the pain beating through her skull. Their will flooded her limbs, and she lunged for this tall creature again.

It flitted out of her way, one step ahead of her. She scored a hit along its arm, and it yelped in pain then danced away. She would need to be faster. She needed more strength, more power.

One of B46's legs buckled. The tall creature cried out, and pain bloomed in B46's chest. She looked down at the length of wood that impaled her, the stick that she had helped turn into a spear. The tall creature was staring at her, still reeking of terror.

The children cried out, and B46 felt their anguish, but she couldn't tear herself away from them, wishing to be with them in the end, wishing she could stay to watch their triumph, but they couldn't pull away from her, and as blackness crept across her vision, she felt them follow.

❖

"What the fuck!" Carmichael yelled as some of the boggins who'd been attacking her squad crumpled, holding their heads and shrieking. Her squad stared in confusion until she yelled, "Stab the little bastards while they're down!"

They obeyed with gusto. The boggins that hadn't collapsed ran, hissing at each other as if they could no longer tell friend from foe.

"Do you know what this is?" Carmichael asked Horace.

"I don't know. I sense something, but…" He shook his head. "They've gone mad."

"Good news for us." She rounded up the squad, and they kept on for the Paladin Keep. Maybe this weird but fantastic crap was going on all over the city. It would explain why she hadn't heard any railguns going off.

Or maybe Brown hadn't made it.

Carmichael gritted her teeth. She'd hoped her lieutenants would be smart enough to stay alive. But alive for what? To live under the murderous Storm Lord's thumb?

A thousand reasons went through her head as she reached the keep, visions of malfunctioning equipment, but the last thing she expected was Shiv and Liam waiting for her in the armory, no railguns in sight.

To their credit, they explained quickly, and Liam didn't give her any of his usual lip.

"And you didn't stop them?" she asked.

"Do you think I could have?"

She put her hands on her hips and breathed. Words like "dereliction of duty" flitted through her mind. Gale could have used three more paladins. It could have used the railguns, except Lea had been right. Railguns would have done a lot of damage to the buildings, to civilians. She'd been looking for anything to even the score.

"If you have anger," Shiv said, "direct it at me, hunt leader. It was I who asked for help, and my people they went to save."

Carmichael let out a slow breath. "Why in hell do you have a human toddler?"

"Long story," Liam said. "He's a rescue."

Weren't they all. She would never have left Gale to help a bunch of aliens, but Ross had been close to them since the mission to the research station. Paul had been the same way, hooked at first sight. And maybe Ross had known Paul would have wanted her to go and save his lover's family.

That didn't explain Lea and Brown, though. They'd gone just to use the guns, or she was a pickled prog. And they had better believe she'd tear them some new ones when they returned. Maybe they all needed to spend some time in the holding cells.

"You wounded?" She'd noted Liam's bloody cheek first thing, and her throat had done an odd little jump, but he seemed fine, walking and talking. Maybe he'd just been scratched. Head wounds took forever to stop bleeding.

"Fine."

"Then get your ass back out there. The boggins are collapsing, but they'll need mopping up, and there are probably still a few progs wandering around."

With a crisp salute and a smile that was only half jackass, he went on his way. Shiv watched Carmichael warily, and she appreciated that. It was always useful to inspire a little fear. Shiv was the only lover of Liam's that Carmichael had ever really spoken to. Maybe this one would stick. Carmichael had already stashed Horace downstairs under guard, and now there was no one in the darkened armory except the two of them and the sleeping boy.

"Do you think your whole group will die without Ross running in to save them?" Carmichael asked.

She frowned hard. "Sa will turn the fight in our direction."

If the situations were reversed, and Carmichael had sent for drushkan help, she'd be desperate for it to come. And the humans had weakened the drushka, killed many of them through the boggins. She supposed they owed the drushka a little heavy artillery. "After the fight is over, will the drushka come here? Maybe we can watch each other's backs." When Shiv sucked her teeth, Carmichael added, "Guard each other."

Shiv wrinkled her nose away. "I will ask my mother when I see her again." She trooped down the stairs with the boy in her arms.

"Don't go wandering around by yourself," Carmichael called. She spied something in the shadows, the bloody poleaxe that had stabbed Paul Ross. Reach had no doubt used it against a few boggins that night. Carmichael touched the end and thought of the Storm Lord jabbing the poleaxe into Paul's body, trying to cover up a murder like a common criminal, like someone afraid.

She ran scenarios: the bloodbath that might happen if only a few people joined in her rebellion against the Storm Lord; the civil war of faithful versus the fallen, yafanai and paladins turning on their own people.

And what was the other option? To keep quiet and let the Storm Lord do as he pleased? How soon before he put a hole in her chest? She was certain he'd find a scapegoat for Paul and one for her, too. Maybe he'd pin it on Blake, who couldn't account for his whereabouts after his memory had been wiped. As for Horace and anyone else who knew the truth, well, people were killed every day by one thing or another. And if the Storm Lord was smart—and Carmichael knew he had *some* cunning—he'd do it before this battle was cleaned up, when any deaths could be explained by the boggins.

No, she had to turn everyone's mind. She had to make the Storm Lord either flee or kill them all. Hell, if they were all fighting against him, he'd lose as long as they didn't turn on each other. She had to act now, before the dust settled, and it would have to be a bloody good plan.

People gathered at the marketplace after a disaster. They waited for a speech from the mayor and looked for lost family. She could tell everyone what the Storm Lord had done, both about Paul and about the boggins, and she'd have Horace to back her up.

She'd need something else. She looked to the bloody poleaxe. Maybe she could cement what she said by having the Storm Lord attack her in public.

And if that didn't work, there was always plan B: shoot him in the back. The people would turn on her then, but she'd risk it if it came to that. Still, better to get through the whole thing alive if possible.

First, the bait. The Storm Lord wouldn't attack her without a reason. She needed to let him know what she knew, needed him to know where she'd be. She took the bloody poleaxe, rounded up a ragtag squad, and sent them to the temple with orders to put the poleaxe in the Storm Lord's room or wherever he might see it. They didn't question her, good soldiers, and she had to swallow a smile of pride.

Next, secure the evidence. She hurried to the meeting room where she'd stashed Horace. He jumped when she came in.

"At ease," she said. "No one's come to kill you yet."

"Thank goodness."

She snorted a laugh. "As soon as my son comes back, I'm sending you with him and his drushkan girlfriend. They'll take you to the marketplace. When I call for you to speak, that's when you pop up. Until then, you wait here, out of sight."

"Hiding and waiting. Fantastic." When she didn't say any more, he blinked at her. "Is that all you're going to tell me?"

"I can't risk the information getting out." She tapped her temple.

"I can hide from a telepath better than you can!"

That might have been true, but the fewer people who knew about her vague plan, the better. Even she didn't think too hard on it, not knowing who might be listening, not that it was even fully formed yet. "I'd appreciate it if you healed my son."

He shrugged, and she read the sarcasm in his pinched lips, but it made her want to laugh rather than yell, the sure sign of a long night.

CHAPTER TWENTY-EIGHT

The heavy hand of fatigue had Cordelia by the metaphorical balls. There had been too many feelings followed by fight after fight, followed by even more fucking feelings, and now she was running along a huge branch in a dim swamp, trying not to think about the drop below.

In the lead, Reach held up a hand and slid to a stop as she pointed to her left. Cordelia knelt, Brown and Lea following her lead. Insects buzzed around them, but nothing else stirred. Maybe Reach was imagining things. They were all tired.

Brown peered into the gloom, head moving back and forth. Drushkan hearing might be excellent, but Brown could hear someone even thinking about moving.

"Anything?" Cordelia whispered.

"Something moving away."

Reach gestured them forward. "I thought I felt something, but…"

"Let's keep on," Cordelia said.

They turned south, farther from the old people's territory. The swamp grew muggier as morning faded, but all stayed quiet. Cordelia feared they were too late, that all the drushka were dead or gone, but Reach signaled a halt again.

Cordelia's nerves stretched as thin as cheap paper, and she resisted the urge to shout at the swamp to just come get them already.

Brown smiled. "Here they come." She readied her gun before Reach could hop back to them.

"The old ones are coming." Reach took her gun from Lea and slung the battery and ammo pack around her shoulders.

Cordelia heard nothing, but she had to trust them. The relief at finding something was too great to be ignored.

"Should we not fire from cover?" Reach asked.

"Nothing's going to get close enough to hurt us," Lea said.

Slapping sounds and rustling came from the trees, too many drushka to run silently. Cordelia closed her visor.

"The queens have a weapon you have not yet seen." Reach's gaze shifted over the ground as if what she knew was too painful to be met head on.

"I've met Pool," Cordelia said. "But isn't her tree far from here?"

"Trees, drushka, whatever." Brown's gun hummed as it powered up. "Storm Lord be with us now."

The words brought a sour taste to Cordelia's mouth. "Lead your targets. Stay in your range." The drushka came into sight, running along the branches. A tree walked in their midst; its branches curled around the swamp trees as it moved. Cordelia's mouth hung open, and her heart pounded even louder than the hum of the guns. She'd known a queen's tree could move, but walk?

"What the shit?" Brown said. Her voice rang through Cordelia's helmet.

Cordelia slid her finger over the trigger, not squeezing yet, just sighting. "I've got the tree." Reach glanced at her, but she shouted, "Fire!"

All other sounds died before the boom of the railguns' bullets rocketing through the swamp. Greenery exploded from the tree, huge patches of bark shaken loose as its limbs cracked under the assault. Drushka were torn apart like paper dolls, their limbs and organs scattered into fine mist.

The remaining drushka dove for cover, and the tree bent double, trying to protect itself as it hurried backward. The railguns hammered into the surrounding trees and shook the drushka loose to fall into the water below.

"Hold your fire!" Cordelia shouted. When the echoes died, she nodded at the fleeing drushka. "They must have come from the larger fight. Let's follow them."

Reach spat over the branch's side and eyed the piles of dead drushka with wide eyes. "This is slaughter."

"Do you want to save your people or not?" Brown asked.

"Save your people by killing your people," Lea said. "Quite a perspective."

Cordelia waved at them to be quiet. "Let's go."

Usk and Nata ran along the Anushi's limbs, killing as they went and working their way toward the queen's guards. Among her high branches, Nata moved toward a lacing of limbs so dense, Usk could not see through them.

A spear jabbed out of the tangle, and Nata dodged, but before she could attack, Usk caught her arm. "Not there, young one," he said.

"But there are enemies."

"That is where the tribe's children are grown."

Nata sucked her teeth, too young to remember a time when each queen was allowed to grow her own tribe, just as long as she had no children from her own body. Now the Shi grew the children for every tribe, a much safer system, as the Anushi would relearn.

"Come," he said, "this way."

She followed him, shaking her long silvery braids over one shoulder, impatience shining in every feature. She loved a fight, this one. She was already fierce, and she would be a warrior for the ages if she would learn more caution.

Or perhaps the time for caution was over, as the Shi had said. Usk felt her waiting in his mind, willing him closer to the Anushi queen. He made Nata hide and let any other enemy warriors pass, wanting to save their strength. Even as he was amused by Nata's impatience to fight, he understood her. He sneered at these renegades, their arrogance and short hair. Long ago, when the Anushi had broken the drushka, her tribe had shorn their hair to show their commitment to the humans, to look more like the invading aliens when they should have been content to be drushka.

"She is close," the Shi said in Usk's mind. "If you must batter her with weapons until she acquiesces, do so."

The thought sent pain through Usk's gut, but he would do as commanded. He spied her through the trees, the Anushi queen, clinging to her trunk, eyes vacant as she watched the battle.

Drushka surrounded her, and one in particular caught Usk's eye, a red-haired female. She shouted orders to those around her, and her wary, confident stance screamed hunt leader. She would be the first to fall.

❖

Nettle knocked a spear from the air and sent one of her guards after the enemy who threw it. The attackers were getting cleverer, launching missiles from the cover of the surrounding branches, but for what purpose? Surely hurting a queen was as terrible a thought to them as it was to her.

Pool sucked in a deep breath. "One of the queens has fled into the swamp."

Good, maybe she would not return. Or perhaps some of the old ones were seeing the folly in this attack. Nettle hurried to Pool's side and lifted a water skin to her lips, but she pulled away with a cry. Her flailing hand caught Nettle's shoulder, and they both cried out as the Shi assaulted their thoughts.

"Why resist me so?" the Shi said, her voice echoing in Nettle's skull. One of her agents had to be close, and her older mind hammered at Pool's consciousness. Nettle tried to pull her back, to keep her in the now.

Pool's teeth clenched so hard, Nettle could hear their grind. "You want us...to have no thoughts...but yours."

"It is my right as Shi."

"No!"

"You must be strong, Queen." Nettle tried to push her will forward, use herself as a wedge between them.

Pool pulled upon her strength and fought. "You agreed. When I followed Roshkikan, when I traded myself for peace, you agreed to let me go!"

"That human is long dead. The agreement was a mistake. Come back to us. Let us be whole, and we will cleanse the humans from our planet."

The other queens' voices joined in, but they were mere echoes, even Nettle could see that. When they attacked, their wholeness made them clumsy, as if they were unused to moving with so many limbs.

She saw them huddled under the Shi's watchful branches, no longer wandering their territory as they did in the days before the schism.

Pool groaned as she jerked the Anushi to the side, away from the other queens, though Nettle still felt the Shi's pull and knew the agent was still close. She broke away from Pool and scanned the nearby branches. A young female launched herself from a tangle of leaves, leading with a fist. Nettle rocked back and kicked her in the stomach.

She grunted and dropped to roll out of the way. Nettle spied movement behind her and readied her daggers. When a spear launched over the female's head, Nettle knocked it from the air and darted forward, leading with her blades.

A male dashed from the foliage and led Nettle away from the young female, his long body snaking to and fro, avoiding Nettle's thrusts. The young female regained her feet and followed, drawing a curved blade that rounded her fist. She punched, making Nettle slow and giving the male time to recover his spear.

Nettle stabbed the young female in the arm, and she hissed, her strike fumbling. Nettle let one of her daggers dangle from her wrist and punched the young one in the face. She fell, golden blood pouring from her nose. She should not have been in this fight, seemed barely out of the branches, and Nettle could not help imagining Shiv in her place.

"Leave this place, young one," Nettle said as she looked to the male. "I have no wish to kill you."

The male jabbed with the spear. Nettle blocked the strike and sought a way inside the spear's range. The male backed away, body twisting as he swept the spear back and forth. Nettle leapt it and risked a look over one shoulder to see that the young female had fled.

Or maybe not. Nettle hit the ground and whirled, trying to keep them both in sight, but burning pain rolled up her back as the young female buried the half-moon blade between her shoulders.

Nettle dropped to her knees, and the blade slipped loose with a ripping sound. She swept her leg behind her, knocking the young one prone. She brought her daggers up, trying to ignore the agony across her shoulders, the river of wetness down her back. She caught the male's spear thrust and heaved him away.

She rolled backward, crying out as her wound stretched and as she flattened the young one to the ground. Nettle looked deep into the young female's shocked face before she crossed her daggers over the small neck. With one smooth thrust, Nettle slit her throat, turning it into a golden ruin, and she knew the sight would stay with her for the rest of her days.

She looked for the male and caught him running toward Pool. "No!"

He jabbed with his spear, but one of the Anushi's branches whipped down and caught it. He abandoned it and leapt for Pool with his bare hands. Her unfocused eyes fixed on him, and she snarled as she rammed Shiv's small knife into his stomach. She towered over him and shouted in his ear, "This is what I think of your right as Shi!"

Nettle pulled the body away and tossed it into the swamp. The Shi's scream faded from her mind. She fell to one knee and tried to touch the wound in her back, but she could not reach it. Instead, she looked into the swamp, the chaos of the battle that stuttered under the Shi's echoing rage. Pool was still alive, but for how long? How long did any of them have?

A pounding whine carried above the cries of the drushka and the cracking sounds of the moving trees. Nettle looked to the sky. A storm? A flock of birds?

She felt Pool's horror and saw through her senses again as drushka fell and fell, the old dropping and dying as if a plague of murderous insects had come among them. Relief mixed with horror as more of them died than were able to flee. The queens' bark shredded as they fled before the terror wielded by three silver figures and one drushkan one.

"Sa." But the blood continued to pour down her back, and Nettle's sadness and hope gave way to a wall of blackness.

❖

"Pool?" Cordelia called as she climbed. She still couldn't believe the tree could move on its own, but she supposed those moving roots had to be good for something. "Pool?"

"Here."

Cordelia climbed toward the exhausted voice. She lifted her visor, scanning the branches and saw Pool and another drushka kneeling over a red-haired body.

"Nettle." She meant it to be a cry, but it came out a sob. This was too much. There were too many dead, and just like with Liam, she couldn't take another one. "Too late. We were too late."

"Be at ease, Sa," Pool said as she rose. "The shawness will save Ashki. Wait." She caught Cordelia's shoulders and shook her. "Wait."

Cordelia couldn't stop staring. Reach had already gone to help her people, and Brown and Lea were out in the trees. Cordelia didn't have anyone else to focus on but that too-still body. She wasn't even close enough to see if Nettle still breathed.

Pool slid one hand along the railgun's shiny surface. "A new gift from your god?"

"What?" She tore her gaze away from Nettle and looked at the carnage around them, the many who wouldn't rise again. "I'm sorry about your people."

Pool inclined her bloody head. "Thank you for coming to my call."

Cordelia felt tears gathering as the rest of her adrenaline left her. She had a brief thought about how she'd get home, but as the shawness helped Nettle up, the thought blew away.

"Sa." Her smile was weary, but she was alive.

Cordelia couldn't crush her in a hug, not with her armor still powered, but they managed as best they could.

As they parted, Nettle kissed her deeply. "My ever-loyal Sa."

"I couldn't let you die."

When she looked out upon the bodies, Nettle sagged again, and Cordelia kept her upright.

"I'm sorry," Cordelia said again. "We didn't enjoy this."

Nettle squeezed her arm, claws grating on the metal. "Queen, it is too much."

"Have your comrades climb into the tree," Pool said. "We must move away from this place." She bent close to Cordelia's ear. "Do not feel so sad, Sa. Even the tree that began the world had to fall. We must spread our seeds elsewhere."

Cordelia nodded and signaled Brown and Lea, but she had to wonder why Pool didn't seem as upset as her people. Maybe she thought death the price of freedom, anything to keep her people away from the old drushka. Maybe she didn't have the luxury of sadness. "We need to get back to Gale. Our fight isn't finished."

She told her story as the tree walked away from the carnage and destruction, leaving the dead to the swamp.

CHAPTER TWENTY-NINE

When Dillon first returned to his rooms in the temple, the bed beckoned. He couldn't remember the last time he'd been up for over twenty-four hours, which meant it had to be a really long time ago. Sometimes on the *Atlas*, there had been nothing to do but sleep.

But the last time he'd gone to bed filthy was also beyond memory, and he couldn't relax past the smell of soot and sweat. There were enough people awake to fetch hot water, who seemed happy to do it no matter how tired they were. That was fucking respect right there. That was how you treated a god.

It wasn't until after he dunked his head, scrubbing the grime from his hair, that he saw the bloody poleaxe in the corner. He froze, expecting to see Lessan's cold, dead fingers wrap around it any moment now.

But it just sat there, even gorier than before, and he wondered if it had followed him from Paul Ross's house, if it had continued killing people until returning to him. Who knew how many it had slaughtered in the night?

Dillon rubbed his eyes, but it stayed put. He muttered, "Dumbass." Of course it stayed there. Someone had used it as a convenient weapon; that was all. That was probably boggin blood. But how it had gotten to his rooms was a mystery.

He finished washing, dressed, and then made some inquiries. A troop of paladins had dropped it off, saying it belonged to him, and that they were returning it on Carmichael's order and that she'd meet him at the market square. Dillon's chest burned. Someone had intruded on his thoughts before, and he'd thought it was Christian and Marlowe, but maybe it had been some lapdog of Carmichael's. Unless Carmichael was as tight with the Sun-Moon worshipers as Paul Ross had been.

He rubbed his forehead as the headache that had followed him all night bloomed again. Where in the holy fuck was Lazlo? It was a mystery he *still* hadn't solved, and now he had this to deal with. Carmichael either knew what had happened to Paul Ross, or she suspected and was trying to draw him out. Maybe she was hoping he'd confess because he could discredit her telepathic spy.

His mind was whirling when he opened his door again, but everything aligned when he saw Lazlo sitting on his bed like a filthy angel come from heaven.

"Laz, I'm glad you're alive, buddy. Where the hell have you been?"

Lazlo closed his eyes and swallowed.

"Are you all right?"

"I was hiding from you."

Dillon sat beside him and gripped his shoulder. "I'm not angry with you, Laz. You don't have to worry about that."

Lazlo chuckled and rubbed his face where his glasses had once sat. "No, I'm the one that's angry."

Great. "Listen, I've got a situation. Can this wait?"

He didn't even look annoyed or pissy. Just tired. "I know about Paul Ross."

God, who didn't? Still, should he try for the lie?

Lazlo gave him a look. "Why did you come back for the poleaxe?"

"I didn't. Carmichael sent it to me. She knows, too, or at least she thinks she does."

"For fuck's sake, Dillon."

"I know."

"At least tell me it was an accident."

"Kind of."

"What the fuck is that supposed to mean?"

Dillon smiled. "You don't usually swear this much."

"Don't play with me!" Lazlo roared as he rushed to his feet. "I've had enough!"

Dillon's mouth was open, but he couldn't close it. This wasn't annoyed Lazlo. This wasn't even the angry Lazlo from the kidnapping. Dillon didn't know this enraged man, didn't quite know how to deal with him. "I don't know what you want me to say, Laz. It's done. And I have to do it again, at least once more, or I risk losing my hold here, and without it, we're fucked."

"There are other humans on this world, places we could have gone where we'd just be two more faces in the crowd."

"Oh, that's your plan, is it? Go live the life of a fucking beggar under some other fucking god? What's next, give up immortality, stop using our powers, as if we could ever go back to just being regular people?" He stood and stepped close, watching Lazlo's eyes widen, glad he could still provoke some emotion other than anger. Of course, now his own temper was burning bright. "Live together as an old married couple? You'd like that, wouldn't you?"

"I—"

Now he was trembling, and Dillon knew that with one final push, he'd ooze forgiveness for any slipup with the mayor and help kill anyone who needed it.

Before he could think too hard about it, Dillon kissed Lazlo deeply, hoping all his anger translated into passion. He kept his eyes open, waiting to see Lazlo turn into a wet rag, but when Lazlo's arms came up, they pushed, forcing Dillon to step away.

Lazlo looked a little breathless. Maybe he was so used to denying himself that he got off on it. He wiped his lips. "That tasted a lot more like desperation than I thought it would."

Dillon rocked back on his heels.

"You're not going to change except to get worse, are you?"

Well, shit. "What can I say, Laz?"

Tears gathered in Lazlo's eyes as if his fucking sockets were melting, but they didn't spill over. "You can't say anything, Dillon. I'm not going to watch you destroy yourself or this town. I'm going to help all the people I can, and then I'm leaving."

Life waned. Every second they'd spent together over the last two hundred and fifty years flitted through Dillon's mind. He'd sooner lose a kidney. "No, Laz. Look, I can fix this. Maybe Carmichael doesn't have to die."

"I'm done."

"You can't be."

"I love you," Lazlo said.

"I need you!"

"I know, and that's not enough anymore."

Dillon curled his hands into fists and felt his power gathering inside him.

Lazlo breathed deep. "Even though I love you, I will shut you down if I have to." His voice trembled a little, but those tears had vanished. And Dillon was exhausted where Lazlo's power rejuvenated him constantly. Still, they might be evenly matched.

Dillon pictured Lazlo dead on the floor and knew he couldn't do it. "You are my friend, Laz, and I know it's never been the way you wanted it to be, but—"

"I accepted that a long time ago, even though I had the occasional fantasy. I would have been happy to be your friend forever if we could have found common ground, but we just can't."

Dillon opened his mouth to repeat that he could change, but he still wanted Carmichael dead. If Lazlo agreed to stay on the condition that she remain alive, Dillon would always be looking for a way around that. It was on the tip of his tongue to order Lazlo out, to say that if he wanted to leave, there was no reason to wait, but he couldn't do that either. It was all shit.

"You'll stay for a bit?" Dillon asked.

Lazlo sagged. "To help people; then I'm gone. Don't get your hopes up."

But they were already edging up. All he needed was time. Still, he couldn't push it, not yet. "Get cleaned up. I'll talk with some people, find out where you can do the most good."

Lazlo gave him a suspicious look before he left. That was fine. He could read some of Dillon's emotions, but not his thoughts. Dillon could set up something with Carmichael and blame it on the boggins. Or he could tell Lazlo she attacked him, maybe cry a bit in Laz's lap about how hard it was being God. If he had to be a baby for Lazlo to stay, he could play that.

First things first, he had to figure out just what she was planning. He strode into the hall, half expecting everyone in the temple to be trying to catch some sleep, but quite a few people were buzzing around, maybe from too much adrenaline, maybe trying to find out what had happened to their friends and family.

When he saw several people streaming toward the exit, he sought out Caroline and found her changing into clean clothes.

"Where's everyone going?"

"Whenever anything big happens in the town, we gather in the market square," she said. "The mayor will make a speech."

Not likely, but now the townsfolk would discover that the mayor was dead. But Carmichael and her poleaxe made sense. She'd meet him in the square with everyone gathering, present her telepathic spy, and tell the Galeans all that she knew.

He tried to tell himself it didn't matter. He had a telepath standing in front of him who could dispute what she said and claim her pet telepath didn't know squat. After all, Caroline was the one who'd committed a crime on his order. She wouldn't want that to get out. But there might be some telepaths who weren't as loyal, who might corroborate Carmichael's story.

Again, so what? Would it be so bad that they knew he wouldn't be fucked with, that he'd back up his threats with good old-fashioned violence? Maybe a little fear was just what these people needed to keep them in line. He hadn't wanted it that way, but they were forcing his hand.

He couldn't help thinking on Paul Ross's words, though, about how the whispers would start, the idea that maybe God wasn't stable, that maybe he shouldn't be listened to now that he was among them. And if some underground movement started, it would be strengthened by the fact that he would have to make Carmichael answer for such blasphemy when doing so might turn her into a martyr.

She'd taken the boggin project onto her own shoulders before. What if she told the town that it had been his idea? A telepath could confirm that, too, with a little digging. There were so many dead. The people would be looking for someone to blame.

Dillon clenched a fist and tried not to punch the wall. He felt his power building and wished he had Carmichael in front of him just as he'd had Paul Ross.

His thoughts wandered to the poleaxe again. Why let him know any of her plan? Why bait him? He looked to his curled fist. She'd known it would make him angry. They didn't know each other well, but he'd been picking at her for years. She had to have figured out some of his triggers. She'd just tried to stay away from them in the past. Now she wanted him to come after her in public. She either wanted to make herself into a martyr, or she wanted to see if she could turn the crowd against him fast enough that they'd fight him. Maybe she thought she could whip them into a frenzy with the aid of her telepathic friend who just might be an agent of Christian and Marlowe. And if Lazlo wasn't beside him calming the crowd, they just might be able to do it.

Dillon headed for the temple doors, leading Caroline and whispering to her as they went.

❖

Carmichael hurried through the streets, anxious to begin Plan A. She rehearsed her speech in her mind. She'd tell everyone of Paul's death and then produce Horace to back up her story. Liam and Shiv already had him there. She'd told them she'd join them soon, but it was best that they weren't all together just in case something unforeseen happened. That was why she was taking a roundabout, back route to the square. No one would expect it.

Liam had asked what she was planning, but she'd just told him and his girlfriend to get Horace to the market and mingle with the crowd. They had agreed, still carrying the little boy, and now Shiv had added a slender sapling to their party. Carmichael had asked where it had come from, and Shiv had said she'd hidden it beyond the palisade, though why she would hide a young tree, Carmichael had no idea. It was a drushkan thing, she supposed. Maybe they randomly carried trees around. Only the ambassador could say for certain, and she was still off gallivanting through the swamp with Ross, Brown, and Lea.

Carmichael had ordered other paladins to scatter through the crowd. When the Storm Lord came, she wanted backup, even if that backup would be confused when the shit went down. If she couldn't convince the crowd fast enough, she supposed the Storm Lord might be able to kill her. She'd asked Horace to send her a telepathic message if he sensed the Storm Lord about to use his power, and Horace had agreed. She hoped she'd be fast enough to leap for cover. If not, the armor was insulated, and she hoped it would protect her from a lightning strike, provided it was a glancing blow, though the energy might overload it. In which case, she'd jettison the heavy battery and resort to Plan B. She was a good shot, a quick one.

The hearing in her left ear went out, replaced by a dull ring. Her blood pressure must be tanking. How long had it been since she'd eaten? As the ringing grew, she thought she should have made time to force something down.

She slowed, stumbling to a halt, and leaned against a partially collapsed wall. What had the place been before last night? A store, a home? It was impossible to tell anymore. As the ringing continued to build, she looked around, thought to ask someone for help, but the street was deserted. Had it been empty before? Was she late?

For what? She'd been going…somewhere.

"How fucking stupid do you think I am?"

Carmichael turned and saw him. She scratched around in her brain for his name. The Storm Lord. She had to do something about him, but what?

The woman standing beside him was staring at Carmichael intently. She looked a little worried, but her furrowed brow said she was concentrating, and she wore yafanai robes.

"Get." Carmichael licked her lips and straightened. "Get out of… mind."

"You're not the only one who knows a telepath. Made you dead easy to find." The Storm Lord sauntered closer with his shit-eating grin, and Carmichael felt a spike of something that cut through the bullshit in her head. She could stand a little straighter.

He was going to kill her, no fucking around. Time for Plan B.

The yafanai frowned, and Carmichael made herself slump again, thinking about how her life was over, how this was it, but her hand snaked down for her gun. The Storm Lord dove to the side as she aimed for him, but her first shot clipped his arm, sending a little spray of blood after him as he disappeared behind some crates.

Her mind snapped back to sharp as the telepath scrambled for cover. Carmichael ducked down an alley, but the end was blocked with debris. She leaned around the corner and squeezed off a couple more shots at their cover. Maybe she could run faster than they could follow. Whatever she did, she had to keep the telepath out of the game.

She dashed for another hiding place, shooting as she went, the sound cracking through the street. Maybe someone would hear it and come, unless everyone had already gone to the damn marketplace, and then there'd be no one to witness this. Good, if she managed to kill the Storm Lord, she could blame it on the boggins, stab him as he'd stabbed Paul. But if he managed to kill her, no one would see.

Then it would be time for Plan C.

She risked a glance back, saw no one, and started forward. The ringing started again, and she knew the telepath was reaching for her. She tried to fight, but her thoughts skewed slightly, as if the telepath was trying to convince her she was going the wrong way, and it was damn hard not to believe it. The woman was good. Maybe once the corrupting influence of the Storm Lord was gone, she could be saved.

Carmichael tripped over a piece of debris, should have been paying more attention. She couldn't afford to be sloppy while…

Blue white light filled her vision, and the ground was ripped from beneath her feet as she flew sideways. The armor absorbed the impact as she knocked into a wall, but the displays on her visor went dead.

She'd planned for this, she told herself. She had to move, to reach back and jettison her overloaded battery. Her teeth were chattering, and she bet every hair on her body was trying to stand on end.

She dropped the battery and crawled forward, flopping for cover. Without power, the visor was only useful as a sunshade. It had popped open slightly, and she slid her thumbs into the gap and forced it the rest of the way up. She'd kept hold of her gun, but she supposed she would have even if he'd electrocuted her. Her hand would have curled around it and never let go.

Even with the armor, her muscles were jumping. If they'd had the larger suits from the paladin vids and not the more formal, showy suits, she bet she wouldn't even have stumbled, but her ancestors hadn't anticipated their use on the target colony. They would have packed much differently if they'd been able to see the future as the prophets could.

Carmichael shook these thoughts away, knew they were the telepath trying to distract her, but she was rattled. She pushed up against a wall, trying to listen, waiting for footfalls. At last she heard a crunch. She stuck her sidearm out, keeping cover behind the building and risking a look.

The telepath stared, and there seemed to be two of her for a moment. Carmichael blinked, trying to clear her vision.

"Captain."

She whirled and fired, but the bullet dug into a door. He was bent low, ducking for cover. Her vision went white again, her body flying. The bastard had sneaked through the house she was taking cover behind, clever as a fucking boggin.

When she landed, the impact rattled all the way through her. She tried to bring her gun up, but her muscles wouldn't obey, and a deep ache spread through her chest, her vision going in and out. She could only breathe in coughs, as if she had the worst cold of her life, and her pulse beat in a crazy non-rhythm.

The Storm Lord stood over her, Mr. Smug incarnate. "A pain in the ass until the end."

She tried to tell him to go screw himself, tried to make the most obscene gesture she could think of, but nothing was working, damn it. She screamed in her mind, hoping the telepath was getting a head full.

"Maybe I'll tell everyone you died bravely, saving my life. No one will dig too deeply into the death of a hero."

He put a finger to her forehead, and everything in her cried out to move, but she couldn't. As the world became one giant flash inside her mind, she saw Liam again, four years old, grinning from under her helmet.

Liam bounced little Paul in his arms, making the boy laugh. Horace and Shiv stood to either side of him, both with anxious looks. He'd told them to relax, that his mother always had a plan, but some people were just natural worriers.

And Shiv had plenty of reasons to worry. Until Cordelia returned, she wouldn't know the fate of her mother or her people. She clung to the tree she'd gathered from outside the palisade, the one that entwined its small branches around her neck. They kept to the back of the crowd because of that tree, thinking it might freak people out.

When Liam had first seen it move, he'd been plenty alarmed until it clung to his finger like a baby's hand. Shiv had said it liked him because she liked him, and that had been enough for him. But everyone might not be so understanding.

"What's taking so long?" Horace muttered.

All around the square, people were growing impatient, muttering, wondering where the mayor was. Liam thought that was what his mother's announcement would be about, though why she needed Horace, he didn't know. Horace had asked him why he wasn't more curious, and he'd said he learned long ago not to pry into his mother's business.

The Storm Lord strode from an alley mouth, a woman at his side. He climbed up on top of a cart, a makeshift stage. He had a bloody bandage about one arm, but he gestured at the crowd to be calm.

Horace grabbed Liam's arm and hid behind him. "Something's wrong. She can't know I'm here."

Liam stayed put, shielding him. "A yafanai?"

"Captain Carmichael said—"

"People of Gale," the Storm Lord said, "I am overjoyed to see so many of you alive and well. We were sorely tested last night, but we survived. Your strength and perseverance are awe-inspiring, and your god stands humbled and proud before you."

He bowed, and murmurs swept the crowd before applause overtook them, many people putting their hands over their hearts and calling out their love.

The Storm Lord paused, head bowed, hand on his own chest. He took a deep breath and seemed the picture of sadness. "It is with a heavy heart that I must tell you of two deaths, two among so many, but two that will be felt by all of us." Another deep breath, and silence descended on the massive square. "Our beloved mayor, Paul Ross, has fallen."

Gasps spread through the crowd. Liam frowned. Fallen made it seem as if he died during the boggin attack, but he was murdered long before that. Unless the Storm Lord was suggesting a boggin had killed the mayor before the fighting even started.

"Damn," Horace said. "Where is she?"

The Storm Lord held up his hands. "Alas, that is not the end of our sadness. The brave Captain Carmichael, leader of the paladins…"

"No," Liam said.

"…died…"

"No."

"…defending me from the boggin threat."

All Liam could think was no, but before he could say it again, louder this time, Horace gripped his arm, and a calming wave flowed over him, driving back the buzzing in his ears.

"Be quiet, you fool. They'll hear you."

It was a mistake; that was all. Liam just had to find his mother, tell the people that she was alive, and they'd laugh about it. Easy.

"We have to get out of here," Horace said. "There are too many telepaths."

"Right."

"What is happening?" Shiv asked. "Is that not your mother he was speaking of?"

"Nope. It was someone else." Liam led them around the edge of the crowd, toward the route his mother had taken, the roundabout one.

Horace was right about one thing; there were too many people in the square watching them, too many people wondering where they might be going, and his mother needed Horace to be safe. He turned to Shiv. "Can you take Horace somewhere? Outside the palisade to watch for Cordelia and your mother?"

She sucked her teeth and searched his face. "Will you not tell me what is the matter?"

"It's a mistake." He smiled at her, but so many emotions were bubbling. He didn't know what he'd do when Horace was gone. "I just need to prove it, and then my mother and I will join you."

Horace looked back over his shoulder. "We need to move."

"As quickly as you can." Liam passed the child to Horace and kissed Shiv softly. "Please."

"Come." Shiv gestured to Horace. "Let us take the quickest way out of this place."

"Good luck," Horace said over his shoulder as he and Shiv hurried away, taking calmness with them.

Liam tried to fight the dread that twisted his stomach into knots. He walked quickly, then started running, not caring who saw him.

Even when he saw the armored body lying there, he told himself it was a mistake. The Storm Lord probably wouldn't know his mother from any other paladin.

A boggin body lay across her, a spear near its outstretched arm just as her gun was near hers. There was a bloody spot on her forehead, as if she'd opened her visor, and the boggin had stabbed her just as one had stabbed him.

There was only one problem. She'd been alive after the battle was done. Maybe the Storm Lord was going to say this one had been hiding just for her.

He shifted the boggin away. She had a snarl on her lips, her dead eyes glaring, an anger that not even death could quench. He laid a hand against her chest, but even if she'd had a pulse, he wouldn't have been able to feel it.

"Mom?" His voice broke, but he didn't want to cry. She wouldn't have wanted that. He took her shoulders and gave her a shake. "What did you do?"

Her helmeted head thumped against the ground, and he leapt back. "I'm sorry. I'm sorry. Mom?" He snarled at his own childish behavior, shaking a dead person as if she was just having a nap. "What do I do?"

Someone had closed Cordelia's uncle's eyes. Liam eased his mother's helmet off and laid one hand against her forehead before smoothing her eyes closed, but one slipped open just a bit, and his stomach turned over. He stumbled to the alley and retched, trying not to think of how ashamed she'd be. When he turned back, he spied something sticking out of the open helmet, something she'd been hiding.

He almost didn't want to touch it, hoping it was nothing personal, that it was just notes she didn't want to forget. But it was a card covered in her untidy script.

"If I'm dead," it read, "the Storm Lord killed me. He killed Paul Ross. He was responsible for the boggins. He's human, not a god. Ask my son for the right yafanai, and tell him I..." There it ended, with a ghost of a mark as if she'd drawn her pen across it while trying to think of what to say next.

Tears did fall then. He rested another hand on her chest and tried to soak up her anger, to let it fill him as if he was the corpse and had all the room in the world. He drew his sidearm and turned back toward the square.

CHAPTER THIRTY

L azlo watched from the edge of the square as Dillon lied. He sensed
the wound in Dillon's arm, but more than that, he sensed the
triumph that had replaced despair in Dillon's mind. He'd been hurt by
Lazlo's proclamation about leaving; he'd been sorry and dejected, and
a great many emotions that would have touched Lazlo before.

But now something had happened to bring the old Dillon raging
back, something other than the jot of hope Lazlo had sensed earlier that
morning. As Dillon climbed down from his makeshift stage and came
to the edge of the crowd, Lazlo moved to intercept him.

"What did you do now?"

Dillon gave him a boyish smile. "Took care of something."

Lazlo didn't want to think too hard on that. He was leaving; he just
had to remember that. A few more hours, a sweep of the town to see to
any wounded souls, and then nothing that happened here would be his
problem anymore.

Dillon had a word in one of the yafanai's ears and then started
down a side street alone. Lazlo kept on his heels even as he damned
himself for doing so. Why couldn't he let anything go? "Dillon, I'm
serious. What—"

Ahead of them, someone screamed. Dillon shoved Lazlo to the
ground as six shots cracked through the street, echoing off the buildings.
Dillon jerked with each one, staggering backward and falling after the
last. Lazlo darted up to catch him as he slumped to the ground, six
pumping holes in his chest.

An armored paladin advanced on them, tears streaming down his
cheeks. His face was familiar. He'd been at the mayor's house, might

have known what had happened there. Why else would he have opened fire?

Dillon was dying, his organs shredded like paper, but the muzzle of the paladin's gun loomed in Lazlo's vision. His power froze as he stared at that small black hole that dealt death so easily. Dillon's life bled away slowly, counting down in Lazlo's head. He tried to get a hold of himself, a hold of his power, but he couldn't heal Dillon until the paladin left, or they'd both be killed.

"Who are you?" the paladin asked. So, he didn't remember, but maybe he hadn't taken a good look.

"No one."

"Friend of his?"

"Yes." It would always be partly true.

"Sorry." He turned and walked away.

Lazlo didn't breathe again until the paladin turned a corner, and then his power flowed over Dillon, skimming through the body he knew so well. He could never let Dillon die, no matter what pain it caused. Love didn't just stop, even when it was past time for it to do so.

The tree set Cordelia down just outside the palisade. They were drawing a small crowd from Gale, curious onlookers who'd come to see the fabulous moving tree. Pool had debated about whether or not to take it out of the swamp, but in the end, she'd thought it safer for everyone to stay together.

Cordelia hadn't argued. She was too tired, even with the armor, to do anything more than ride. She told a few Galeans what had happened in the swamp and asked them to spread the word that the drushka were here to help. She was hoping everyone would know that by the day's end, that there wouldn't be any stray fights. They'd told her snatches of what had happened with the boggins, and that both the mayor and Captain Carmichael were dead.

The last pained her almost as much as the first, though she was shocked that anything could beat through her fatigue. When Liam came toward them from the gate, his face a mask of grief, she went to him, crushing their armored bodies together. She kept thinking of her uncle and seeing Carmichael in his place. She clutched Liam tighter when he said, "Mom, Mom," over and over. All the relatives they had between them were dead, and it hurt so much even though their childhoods had ended long ago. Around them, the drushka hummed some kind of dirge, and many humans wept, everyone giving over to sadness.

When murmurs started around them, Cordelia risked a look to see the Storm Lord marching their way. Wanting to join in their grief? Why not? It'd been a night to make even God weep, though he didn't look so godlike with dark circles under his eyes and the front of his robe stained with blood. Not his own, or he wouldn't be striding with such purpose. Maybe he'd killed someone else. Maybe Carmichael, if she stood in his way.

Or maybe he was coming to punish Cordelia for her lack of faith, for running to aid the drushka when Gale needed her. Well, she was guilty of that. She deserved something, though calmly going along with any punishment rankled. She thought of what Carmichael might do, what Paul would have thought. If the Storm Lord killed her in front of everyone, they would see him as the monster she suspected he was.

The Storm Lord raised his hands, and Cordelia pushed Liam out of the way. Her vision filled with a blue-white glow. She expected pain but felt lighter than air. The ground fell away, or maybe she flew. Her insides felt too big for her outside, and she thought she might pop, but as the glow in her vision intensified, something tore within her, and her body opened like a door. The pressure eased, and light and noise ceased, giving way to darkness.

No, not darkness. There were stars, thousands of them, millions maybe, the naked universe laid out before her in all its splendor. She looked down to see a green planet spinning below her or maybe above. She had no feet, no body to tell her which way she pointed. But the planet was Calamity. It had to be, but what the hell was she doing above it? She couldn't breathe but didn't need to. She didn't feel the cold, but she did feel something sharing this space with her, invisible as she was, but so much larger. The consciousness surrounded her like a giant's hand.

"And what is this?" A woman's voice split into a thousand whispers.

"I'm not sure." Cordelia wasn't even sure she spoke the words so much as thought them. "I'm very confused."

"You're a wandering bee, buzzing around my ears."

"Am I dead?"

"Hard to say. Many of the people I speak with are dead."

"Who are you?"

The power was silent a moment. "I was a copilot. Now I might be everything. I hate it sometimes, the broke, bleeding lot of it. Would you like to see?"

Pressure built around Cordelia again as if someone was trying to push her through a pinhole. She cried out and became aware of every molecule within her and the people on the planet below. All their thoughts and emotions beat inside her brain along with the noises of the stars and the planets, the sun and the moon.

"Go farther."

She heard the whispers of other people on other planets, other races. They cascaded past her vision, filling her mind with their noise, and past all of them, at the end of a long journey, spun a planet of green and blue.

"Home," the voice said. "Earth. Never to be seen with our eyes again, but always in memory."

And there were people crawling all over it, too, and over its satellite, making sound after sound, and beyond them, all this background radiation, the entire universe babbling and crying out and driving everyone mad.

"Stop," Cordelia cried. "Take it back!"

The noise vanished just as the seams of Cordelia's soul began to tear, and she would have gasped for breath if she'd needed it.

"You'll forget. I can't."

Cordelia focused on Calamity and tried to get her own thoughts in order. "Are you a god?"

"Perhaps the only one. Perhaps I'm nothing at all. Wouldn't it be interesting if I only existed in you?"

The thought chilled her to the bone. "So, is this what death is?"

"Perhaps again. I had hoped it would be quieter. Would you like to stay?"

"Um. If I'm still alive, I should be going. People to look after, you know?"

The voice laughed, its cackle echoing through the spaces of

Cordelia's mind. She heard the babble of Calamity again, and the sound drew her downward, shouting in her ears.

"What's happening?"

"Go see, little bee."

The giant hand flung her, and Cordelia shrieked as the surface of the planet roared toward her. She sped through clouds, watching vague shapes become forests and plains and then the city of Gale and the gathering of drushka. As she raced toward her body, she braced for an impact she could never survive.

❖

Lazlo had known Dillon was going to kill someone. He'd read it in every line of Dillon's body, and no amount of speaking would stop it. He kept telling himself he should knock Dillon out or at least cap his power, but part of him wanted to believe that Dillon would just forget whatever he was going to do.

But no, he'd sent lightning hurtling toward the mayor's niece, but Lazlo had gotten there first, healing her faster than Dillon could kill her, their power competing, keeping her on the cusp of living and dying. Dillon might have been aiming for the other paladin, the one who'd shot him, but once he started killing, it seemed he had a hard time stopping.

The mayor's niece hung in the air, her head thrown back, her armor throwing sparks. Somewhere in the crowd, Lazlo sensed Horace's power helping her just as his was. Lazlo tried to reach for Dillon, to shut his power off, but a long brown root whipped through the air and knocked Dillon flat.

The drushka circled the mayor's niece as she fell; their weapons were up, their teeth bared. The enormous tree Lazlo had gawked at when they'd first left the city moved up behind them.

Dillon scrambled to his feet. "What the fuck?"

"The tree hit you." Something Lazlo never thought he would say.

"Do not attack Sa Ross again!" one of the drushka shouted.

Two other paladins came forward to flank Dillon, both with railguns. "What the shit is going on?" one called. She swung her gun around as if she didn't know who to aim at.

"Is she dead?" Dillon asked.

Inside the pack of drushka, Lazlo could feel her. "No."

Dillon still seemed angry, felt angry, and Lazlo spied the paladin he'd originally been aiming at. He was trying to draw his gun, but the drushka were holding him back. This could dissolve so quickly into a complete bloodbath. It was amazing it hadn't already. Lazlo gathered his power, ready to knock Dillon out and carry him back to Gale if he had to. Dillon's eyes went wide, and his mouth worked without a sound. He wiped one hand across his face as if he couldn't believe what he was seeing.

Lazlo gripped his arm. "Let's go back."

"Get out!" Dillon cried. "Get out of my city. Take your drushka and any others you've corrupted, and get the hell out! If I see you, them, or any Sun-Moon worshipers again, I'll kill every fucking one of you." He shook Lazlo off, turned on his heel, and stalked back inside Gale.

Cordelia felt as if her skin was standing out from her body. She lay on the ground, and people were speaking, but she couldn't quite understand them, and she didn't know if they were speaking drushkan or if she'd forgotten how to speak Galean. Liam and Nettle were peering down at her, and when she focused on them, Liam sighed.

"Are you okay?" he asked.

"I understood that," she said.

Liam and Nettle exchanged a worried glance.

"Sa, how do you feel?" Nettle asked.

"Alone." Without that titanic presence, she didn't know another word for it. "Help me up?"

Another man's face appeared over Liam's shoulder. "Maybe you shouldn't."

She recognized him, but the name wouldn't come to her. She tried to get up on her own until Liam and Nettle helped her. Her armor was dead and heavy as hell with the battery pack not working. "Harold?" she asked, nodding at the man. A healer, a yafanai healer.

"Horace."

She grunted at him and swayed. Several drushka reached out to steady her. "Heavy." She started shucking her armor, and the drushka helped her, including Nettle and Shiv. As it fell away piece by piece, she was amazed by how light she felt, as if her feet could leave the ground again, but no matter how hard she willed it, she stayed put. One of Pool's limbs touched her, and she sensed the connection of root to soil, just as every molecule in the universe was connected. The drushka gasped as one, and the branch jerked away. She'd touched something sacred, but it fled as quickly as it'd come.

"Sa?" Nettle asked. "What has happened to you?"

Cordelia laughed, feeling more than a little drunk. "The Storm Lord hit me with his lightning because I abandoned Gale, and he wanted to show everyone that he's a murderer." She pointed an unsteady finger at Horace. "Then you healed me?"

"Not just me." He looked over his shoulder at another man. "Simon did, too."

Simon stepped forward. "Are you sure you're all right?"

"I took a trip, visited the universe with the copilot." She thought for a moment. Yes, that was right. "Copilot of what I don't know. Maybe of space."

Simon peered at her. "Did you say copilot?"

Everyone else watched her cautiously as if she might burst into flame.

"What does that mean?" Liam asked.

Horace shrugged. "She could be delirious."

"Perhaps you should rest," Nettle said.

Simon had a tiny smile on his face. "There's nothing wrong with her."

Liam frowned at him. "You healed the Storm Lord, didn't you?" He gripped his sidearm. "I asked who you were, and you said no one."

Horace stepped between them. "Don't."

Shiv put her arms around Liam's chest. "If he is a shawness, you cannot kill him for mending someone."

"Ahya," Nettle said, "that is what shawnessi do." Many of the drushka murmured assent.

Liam took his hand off his weapon, but he glared daggers until Simon started for Gale.

Horace shifted from foot to foot. "I'll be right back." He ran after Simon, and Liam moved to keep both of them in sight.

Cordelia tried to figure out what the hell was going on, but she was too tired. Oh well. Best to relax in the arms of the drushka and be happy that, for a few moments at least, no one was having a crisis, except…

"Did the Storm Lord tell us to get out?"

Dillon tried not to stumble as he hurried toward the Yafanai Temple. Too many goddamned things had happened too quickly, and now everything was unraveling. People tried to stay out of his way, but the happy, smiling crowds were gone. They whispered as he passed now, and their eyes were downcast. They looked sad and unhappy, and why? They were still alive. He'd fucking kept them alive, and now they were afraid of him? Because he'd defended himself?

How many of them had seen him attack Lieutenant Ross in that field? He hadn't meant to. He'd been so angry, and he'd aimed for Carmichael's rotten son, but she'd gotten in the way, and the power had just kept flooding from him. If it hadn't been for Lazlo, he'd have killed her, and then gone for the boy, too, but the drushka had been ready for a fight.

For a moment, he'd wanted that. He'd go down swinging with his anger burning in him, making him feel as if his scalp was sliding off. Then he'd seen Lessan moving through the crowd with such ease, as if she wasn't even fucking there, and she hadn't taken her dead eyes off him. Fear had turned his insides to water, and he knew that if he died while she was watching him, she would follow him to whatever afterlife might await. She would stand behind him for all eternity, vanishing whenever he looked for her, but her gaze would bore into his back forever.

So, he'd banished them, hoping they would take her, too, but now people couldn't even look at him, and he didn't know if it was fright or misery, or if they were ashamed of what a coward he was to fear a dead woman.

He swore, and several people scurried away as if he was a fucking boggin. He grabbed a passing man by the shirtfront. "Don't be scared of me!" The man blanched and dropped to his knees, but Dillon pushed him away, disgusted.

He thought he'd put an end to her. She hadn't made a peep when he'd put a few million volts through Carmichael's skull. But now here she was again. He heard her laughter echoing in his mind. "Fuck you," he muttered. "I have better things to do than fuck around with you." He'd get behind closed doors and then he'd deal with her, force her hand, and be done with her once and for all.

❖

Horace caught up to Simon just inside the palisade and wondered what to say, what he could say now that it seemed they were on opposite sides. If Simon had saved the Storm Lord, it meant they still cared for each other, didn't it? Or were the drushka right, and a healer was just a healer, no matter what?

"Simon," Horace said. "I'm glad you're all right."

Simon smiled. "I was worried for you last night."

"We all had our hands full." They stood in silence a moment before Horace asked, "Did you know? About the mayor?"

Simon ducked his head. "I found out, yeah."

"I'm going with the banished people. I can't stay and worship a murderer."

"You shouldn't worship anyone. No one deserves that."

"Come with us."

Simon's eyes lit up. "Do you mean that?" Horace grabbed his hand, thinking to tug him out of Gale, but Simon pulled up short. "I have a few things to do first, some people to heal, some to say good-bye to, but I'll catch up."

The pressure in Horace's chest eased. "I'm pretty sure I have to leave now, seeing as how the Storm Lord commanded it. Can you check on Natalya for me? I don't think she's as fit as she appeared."

"If she'll let me near her."

Horace laughed and then hugged him hard before letting go. "I don't think she'll come with us, no matter how hard I want her to, but I want to know she's okay."

Simon clung to his hands a moment longer. "I can't promise you we'll ever be anything more than friends, Horace. I mean, I don't know how long it will be before I can let go of—"

Horace nodded, so touched by the honesty that he wanted to

hold Simon again, but he told himself he could respect any boundaries Simon cared to put up. "I understand. Will you be able to find us?"

Simon grinned. "I could sense you a mile away."

"I'll try to take that as a compliment." They shared a smile as Horace backed away. "And we'll be looking for you."

CHAPTER THIRTY-ONE

Cordelia tried to listen to everyone at once, but without the power of the entity she'd spoken to, she couldn't sort one voice from another. Maybe she hadn't talked with anyone; maybe it had all been a dream.

"Just because that bastard threatened us doesn't mean we shouldn't fight," Liam said.

Cordelia swayed back and forth. She shook her head, trying to clear it, but it was like thinking through cobwebs. "We should leave."

"He murdered my mother and your uncle, Delia. We can't let him throw us out. This is our home!"

And now they knew that the Storm Lord had killed both Paul and Carmichael. That her god could betray her had knocked the wind out of her before, but now there were other gods, and the Storm Lord was a human like any other. Or maybe the copilot was human, too. That made it less of a gut punch, that it was just people killing people. Now that he was on the planet, maybe the Storm Lord would die like everyone else would.

"He'll get his," Cordelia said. "Innocent people could get dragged in if we fight."

"You'd rather leave them under the Storm Lord's thumb?"

"Anyone who wants to come with us can come."

Liam kept talking, but she stopped listening. More people had gathered at the gate, but not all of them had curious looks. Some were frightened, some hostile. And Brown and Lea had stood at the Storm Lord's side. If Cordelia fought now, she'd be fighting her own people, never mind that she wanted to free them. "Anyone who wants to come with us can come."

A hand touched her back, and she turned to find Reach holding little Paul. "Your peace soothes me, Sa. If you had run to claim vengeance, I would be by your side, but I see you are right to wait." Her gaze flicked toward the crowd, too, and Cordelia knew they were thinking the same thing.

The need for vengeance tried to rise within her, past the feelings of being one with the whole fucking universe and the peace she'd felt through Reach's song. The Storm Lord killed people, and he deserved to pay. Maybe there was some way to sneak up on him? No, not with the yafanai there, who might even now be reading her mind. So much had changed, why not the law?

"The living are more important than the dead," she said.

The drushka muttered assent, and Pool added, "There has been enough killing today."

"What the hell?" Liam shouted. "Where are we supposed to go?"

"Paul knew of other places, other peoples," Reach said. "I will collect his papers so that you might know of them, too. And I will see what became of Blake and Katey. Now that Paul is dead, I will take them into my hands." She turned to Pool. "And his body, Queen?"

"Ahya, Shawness. Bring him, and we will see him returned to the soil."

Cordelia nodded. He would have liked that.

"And your mother?" Shiv asked Liam. "Do you wish my mother to return her to the soil as well?"

Liam sagged. "I can't catch my breath. We all almost died." He shook his head, lips pressed together. "Now I have to leave my fucking home?"

Cordelia grabbed his shoulders and tried to think of the words to make him understand the vastness she'd seen. He wouldn't be so frightened, then, not if he realized how small they were, or maybe that would just frighten him more. "We'll be together." When he started to speak again, she felt the spirit of Carmichael rise within her. "Muzzle those doubts, soldier. We have to move before another fight comes our way, so get your ass in gear." He gawked, but she was already turning to Reach. "Take some people, and get it done."

Reach waved a couple of drushka over, and they raced into Gale. Cordelia turned to Nettle. "I'm going to the keep to get some things. Come with me?"

She wrinkled her nose. "Wherever you like, hunt leader."

"Liam, you coming?"

His jaw tightened, and he glanced at the city again, relaxing a little when Horace started back. "This argument isn't over."

"Understood." She looked to Pool, who spread her hands.

"Do not worry for us, Sa," Pool said. "We will mind your new tribe as it gathers."

Cordelia's mind was already racing ahead. As she walked to the keep, many people hurried over, most wanting to know if it was true that the Storm Lord had banished a group of paladins. She confirmed it and was amazed by how many people wanted to come with her. Some were afraid the boggins weren't done with them. Some had developed a new fear of the Storm Lord. There were rumors that the mayor's and captain's deaths were some kind of conspiracy, and a few people asked if both were still alive and sneaking away with her.

She tried to reassure them that everything would be all right, but she wasn't sure of that herself. When they asked about the Storm Lord, she told them what she knew and asked that they make up their own minds, as Paul had always encouraged her to do.

After packing their things, she and Liam met again at the bottom of the Paladin Keep. Brown and Lea waited there, both still armed and armored. More paladins had gathered, wanting to know what was going on. She overheard whispers that she and Liam had attacked the Storm Lord, but there were others that said he struck first, or that he'd killed her and she'd come back to life. One looked at her as if she might be a god, too.

"We've had a message from the temple," Brown said. "You can't take any armor or weapons."

Liam swore. "You going to make me take it off, Brown?"

She bristled, and Cordelia caught some of the other soldiers shuffling their feet. Some hands moved toward weapons. "We've never fought each other before," she said loudly. "We're not going to start now."

"Fucking traitors," someone mumbled.

Liam turned that way, but Cordelia caught his arm. "We're outnumbered," she whispered. "And you don't want to hurt them."

"Like hell." But he stripped out of his armor and tossed his weapon down.

"We're walking you out of town," Brown said.

"You want to stay here, Jen?" Cordelia asked. "Jon?"

"I'm a soldier," Brown said with a sigh. "Nothing will change that."

Lea shrugged. "This is where I belong." Many of the other soldiers murmured assent, but as they began to leave, she saw a handful toss their weapons or armor onto the pile and follow.

Brown gave them an incredulous look but kept at Cordelia's and Liam's backs. "I'm sorry about your mom," Brown said. "And your uncle. She was a good soldier, and he was a good mayor. Kept his speeches short."

Liam's jaw tightened as they passed under the bailey. "First you give up Gale without a fight and now your weapons?" he muttered to Cordelia. "What, you have a near-death experience and you're not you anymore?"

Was he blind that he didn't see the danger they were in, how much the people beyond the palisade needed them to keep their cool? Or was vengeance just so blinding? She remembered how she'd felt after that boggin had almost killed him and tried not to judge him too harshly. "Technology didn't protect my parents. Being in Gale didn't keep my uncle safe, and armor didn't protect your mom."

"And leaving without a fight? What's that about?"

"It's about making sure this isn't over."

He gave her a curious look and seemed to see the crowd for the first time. He seemed surprised when the soldiers who'd given up their weapons passed the gate to join the gathering of humans and drushka. Cordelia paused, turning to Brown and Lea. She offered her hand, and they took it, Brown's expression calling them foolish and Lea's not giving them anything at all.

"Watch your backs," Lea said.

Brown flashed a grin. "Fuck off, hooligans."

"Fuck off yourself, Lieutenant," Cordelia said.

A host of other people and baggage waited under Pool's branches along with two sheet-wrapped bodies. Reach had brought Paul, and someone had evidently found Carmichael. Cordelia laid a hand on both of them before Pool took everyone and everything into her branches, some of the humans letting out little squeals that turned to cries of joy as the tree moved around Gale.

Cordelia looked back to the burnt patches of the city, easy to see from the high branches of Pool's tree. Around her, everyone was staring at the place they'd called home, a place that now seemed foreign. Cordelia had lived there all her life, and she couldn't imagine staying.

Beside her, Liam dashed tears from his cheeks, and she didn't know if they were for Gale or for his mother, but she put her arm around him anyway. He leaned into her touch then stiffened, looking past Gale.

"What is it?"

He pointed, and she looked into the sky. Three bright lights stood out against the blue. All through the branches, humans and drushka were pointing, wondering what it could mean, but Cordelia remembered sitting in her uncle's house as his housekeeper told them of a bright light in the south, just before the Storm Lord's arrival. She thought of the Sun-Moon worshipers and wondered what was coming for Calamity now.

Dillon paced, stopping every so often to perch on the edge of a chair and sink his teeth into his thumb. He tried to watch every corner of the room, but Lessan was never where he looked. He sensed her, caught a flash of her every now and again from the corner of his eye.

"Enough games," he said at last, hearing the roughness in his voice. "Show yourself, motherfucker."

She ignored him, flitting at the edges of his vision. He jerked his door open, grabbed the first person he saw, and dragged him inside.

"Storm Lord?" the man asked.

Dillon gave him a hard punch to the mouth and then shook him at the room. "I'm going to kill someone. That's what gets you off, right? Come out and watch." He put his hands around the man's neck, thumbs over the windpipe, and squeezed.

The man wheezed, trying to breathe through bloody lips. He clawed at Dillon's hands.

"Don't make this worse," Dillon said and didn't quite know who he was talking to. Fear bubbled through his anger, making his face feel tighter than it should.

She appeared without warning, and he jumped. Her mouth opened wider than it had the right to, and she laughed and laughed, the noise coming from all around him as he stared down her rotting throat.

Dillon dropped the frightened man and kicked him out the door. Lessan grinned, and her right eye bulged, swelling larger and larger until it burst, filling the room with rot. Dillon covered his nose and backed away. Blood slithered down her body from the empty hole to gather in her palm like a living thing.

"What the fuck?"

Her features blurred, and Lessan's short figure and lean face became Dué's tall frame and rounded cheeks. Her hair stuck out as if she hadn't combed it in months.

Anger burned through Dillon's temples. "I should have known. I'm not crazy, no thanks to you. You've been dicking me around from orbit." She had a subtle hand. Every time she'd invaded his mind, he'd blamed any tingling on his anger, his fear. "Every single time I thought of her, was that you?"

"No. Sometimes, she was me." But her mouth didn't move. She strolled around the room, examining the furniture, but she was projecting herself in his mind. Her clothing wavered between the old flight uniform and a black evening gown sown with stars.

"Why?"

She rolled the remains of her eye into a glowing ball and smiled.

"Answer me, Dué."

She placed the glowing ball in her socket, and the light grew to fill the room like a miniature sun. "I thought you were happy to have me on your side. Don't worry, sugar. There will be plenty of time to visit now that I'm alone. We're going to be great friends."

"What do you mean alone?" He had to look away, blinking away stars. When the light dimmed, she was gone, not even a flicker in the corner of his eye.

"What the *fuck*?" he muttered again. Maybe she'd killed everyone else on the satellite. No great loss. Or maybe not. The *Atlas* had more drop pods, enough to get everyone to the surface if they were tired of waiting around for immortality.

Oh, that was all he needed.

❖

Lazlo threw some things in a bag. He hadn't acquired much since coming to Gale, but he wanted to make sure he had food and water so he could contribute to the stores. His own bubbling happiness surprised him. The biggest hurdle to leaving had always been that he'd have to be alone and that he didn't know where to go. But now he'd solved both those problems and made peace with leaving Dillon. Even after all the carnage of the night before, he had so many reasons to be happy.

When Samira knocked on his open door, he beamed at her.

"Did you hear that a group of people left Gale?" she asked. "What did I miss?" He pulled her inside and gave her the short version. She listened with wide, exhaustion-bruised eyes. "And you're going now?"

"I wanted to say good-bye to you first. I've already said good-bye to Dillon, the Storm Lord, don't want to do that again."

"And Horace went, too?" She smiled a little.

"I'm going for more reasons than that."

"The romantic in me will never lose hope."

"There's one more thing I have to do." He hurried down the hall, making for Natalya's room, but she wasn't there, wasn't in the temple, according to anyone he asked.

"I haven't seen her," Samira said. "Several people said she was out last night with the Storm Lord's group."

Lazlo scrubbed his hand down his face. "I hope she didn't die."

"We could search the city."

Lazlo shook his head. "I'll just have to tell Horace and hope he understands. Maybe someone less conspicuous can come back to check for her."

"Like me."

"If you'd like to look for her, I'd appreciate it. Maybe you could get word to us somehow."

"Shouldn't be too hard since I'm coming with you."

Lazlo gawked. "You're not!"

"Oh yes, I am."

"Samira…"

"Simon." She stepped close and whispered, "I don't want to stay here with a murderer any more than you do. Unless you don't want me to come?"

"No, no! I'd be delighted. It's just, well, I thought you were saying you wanted to go just because I was going."

"Maybe they should call you Dr. Ego." She winked, and he laughed. "Just let me grab some things."

Before they got far, a small woman stepped from a hallway, a packed bag hanging from one shoulder. "Lydia?" Samira asked. "What are you doing here?"

"You're leaving, and I'm coming with you."

Lazlo looked back and forth between them.

"Did you foresee something?" Samira asked.

"Yes, I saw you leaving, and me coming with you."

"But why?"

Lazlo nodded slowly. "You're a prophet."

"I can't stay here, Samira. This is where Freddie died." She looked as if she might weep but couldn't quite manage it. Lazlo soothed her with his power as Samira hugged her tightly.

"Lydia, I'm so sorry. Please, come with us."

Lydia laughed, but it had no humor in it. "I already know I will. I'll meet you at the gates."

"Weird," Lazlo said after she'd walked away. But the only other prophet he'd ever known was the queen of weird. "Come on." He could sense Dillon in the temple, and he wanted to be gone before Dillon came looking, cowardly as he knew that was. He couldn't get their awkward kiss out of his mind and wouldn't repeat it for anything in the world.

Dillon tracked Lazlo to a woman's room, of all places. He burst in on them, the better to see what they were up to. When he saw their bags, he knew it was worse than he thought.

"So. This is it." Dillon tried to keep the emotion out of his voice, but too much had happened, and he knew he sounded angry and bitter.

"Samira, give us a minute," Lazlo said.

Dillon watched her walk out, the sway of her dark hair, legs that went on and on.

"Stop ogling her," Lazlo said as the door shut behind her.

"I never thought you'd leave me for a woman."

"You're hilarious."

"I'm not here to fight. I wanted to warn you. I think the others from the *Atlas* are on their way down. I had my suspicions, and then I got a message from the keep. They've spotted what they call a godsend, and since no one up there would be sending us anything good…"

"It must be them." Lazlo sank onto the bed, staring at nothing.

"You have to stay here now, Laz."

"No."

"If they get hold of you, they'll make you a slave, force you to regenerate them. As much as you hate me right now, I never made you do anything, did I?"

Lazlo rolled his eyes. "I don't hate you."

Dillon knelt by his side, sensing his weakness. He searched his memory, came up empty, and took a stab in the dark. "Look, Stephen, I know we haven't always seen eye-to-eye—"

Lazlo laughed, the sound a bit crazed. "What?"

He was staring so hard, Dillon looked over his shoulder, certain Dué had reappeared, but there was nothing. "Why are you looking at me like that?"

"Did you call me Stephen?"

"I know I've been saying Laz for a long time, but if you'd quit interrupting—"

"Simon!" It was a hysterical-sounding whisper, like someone naming a murderer.

"What?"

Lazlo stood, nearly bowling Dillon over. "My name is Simon! Hundreds of fucking years together, and you don't even know my name?" A vein stood out in his temple, outracing even his ability to calm himself.

Dillon stood slowly. Spittle flecked Lazlo's lips, and he was red as blood. "Holy shit, Laz. I'm sorry. Really." He could barely speak beyond real shame, too much to blame on someone else.

Lazlo took in a large, shuddering breath that he let out after a count of ten. He nodded, acknowledging the apology but not accepting it. "Get out of the way."

Dillon held up a hand and knew this was the end, that he'd done this. If he didn't let Lazlo go now, they might be saying good-bye forever and not just until Lazlo recovered his senses. "Let me go first and tell them to leave you alone. Then you can sneak out while they're occupied."

Lazlo eyed him warily. "You're going to kill them."

If he could. "I want you to be safe, Laz." And he did, truly. He owed him that after calling him the wrong fucking name.

"All right." But his gaze shifted away as if he was thinking of a different plan. Dillon wished he was a telepath. Lazlo hadn't hatched many plans in the past, but he'd come up with some doozies lately. Fine. Whatever kept him away from Christian and Marlowe.

CHAPTER THIRTY-TWO

As he strode through the fields south of Gale, Dillon hoped the Sun-Moon and their cronies were ready for a fight. He'd had a lot of death and destruction the night before, but too much had gone wrong since, and he wanted to fry someone, Lessan-Dué be damned. He'd borrowed a suit of powered armor from the Paladin Keep, just in case. The Sun-Moon would get their hands on Lazlo over his dead body. He bet none of them knew Laz's first name either.

They were staggering around in a rocky meadow when he arrived, trying to breathe. When Marie Martin spotted him, she shrieked, and tingles rippled over his scalp just before pain stabbed him in the eye: a telepathic attack.

Anger burned through him, and he launched a bolt, throwing her across the meadow; a red emergency blanket fell from her smoldering carcass, and Lessan-Dué laughed in Dillon's mind. He resisted the urge to whoop.

Marlowe threw a boulder in Dillon's direction, and he ducked behind a larger rock, working his way over a rise, out of sight. His scalp prickled as they searched for him, and he tried to stay on the move, harder to find. He tried to think of himself in the third person, confusing them more. All the minds present had to be fucking with their mojo, but the rock where he'd been hiding blew to pieces, a few of the shards bouncing off his armor.

He caught a glimpse of someone trying to follow him, drew his sidearm, and fired, winging them. After the night before, Gale couldn't afford to lose many bullets, but he promised to make every one count. The grass behind him burst into flame. They were trying to smoke him out.

He grinned. "Just giving me cover, baby."

Another boulder exploded off to his left. He moved from hiding place to hiding place, trying to circle them. He'd managed to pull last night's storm back around, and now he could poach the lightning from it. In the field, they'd be fish in a barrel.

❖

Cordelia watched the horizon, Nettle, Pool, and Liam beside her. They'd seen the lightning, heard the boom of combat and the crack of a gun. With so many humans aboard the tree, Pool had been moving slowly, and when the lightning started, everyone had gone to the ground, the tree lying down with them.

"Is the Storm Lord following us?" Liam asked. His frown said he wanted that to happen more than anything. "Does this have something to do with the lights?"

Cordelia nudged Nettle. "Up for a look?"

"Take shawness Horace," Pool said. "In case of injury."

"And me," Liam said.

"The fewer targets, the better." Cordelia gave him a warning look. She just wanted to see what the Storm Lord was up to and then move out. She didn't need anyone going off half-cocked.

He rolled his eyes. "Just be safe, okay? Your oneness with the universe, or whatever the hell, won't save you from a gunshot."

After they collected Horace, they hurried on their way, staying low. When they came to the edge of a hill, they crawled through the grass on their bellies. The Storm Lord hid along the slope of a hill and fought with a group of people scattered through a bowl-shaped meadow. The ground exploded in several places, making everyone duck.

Horace whistled softly. "That's a lot of power down there. Lots of psychic tendrils."

The Storm Lord laughed as he fired at one of the others, making them jump for cover.

"They can't get to him on that side of the hill," Cordelia said.

"He seems happy."

"Let's sneak back, let them fight it out."

Horace grabbed her arm. "Simon!"

The man who'd healed her was walking up the hill behind the Storm Lord. Behind him, two women waited by a clump of rocks.

"He said he was going to follow us," Horace said. "He must not realize what's going on."

"Shit," Cordelia muttered. "Can't he feel it? What the hell is he doing?"

"Perhaps if I run—" Nettle started.

Horace grabbed her, too. "Wait, he's shut off their powers."

The explosions stopped, and all the people in the bowl were staring around, calling to each other. The Storm Lord turned to Simon and gestured wildly.

"Let's get a little closer, hear what they're saying," Cordelia said.

They slithered through the grass, and Cordelia knew they should get away while they could, but having a healer who was strong enough to shut off the Storm Lord's power was too good to pass up. After he was done saying his piece, they'd grab him and be on their way.

As she watched him, a hazy memory tugged at her. He looked familiar, and not just from her experience outside Gale. Her uncle's house? He was the man who'd said her uncle had been killed by the poleaxe. She narrowed her eyes as they stopped, close enough to listen as the group of newcomers joined the Storm Lord, all of them speaking to Simon in rapid voices, their strange accents hard to parse.

"—I help you here," Simon was saying, "you won't need me anymore."

"You've developed something new?" a pair of people said, speaking in sync. The robes of the Sun-Moons, the way the pairs moved together, flashed through her mind, and her mouth went dry.

"And after I do it, no more fighting? Agreed? We all go our separate ways?" Simon asked.

The newcomers conferred. "Agreed," the pair said. But their wary stances said they had doubts.

The Storm Lord hesitated, nodding after a long look from Simon.

Simon's gaze shifted to the side, looking straight at Cordelia's hiding place. No doubt he could feel her, or maybe it was Horace he was feeling.

"Good, this saves me some trouble." Simon closed his eyes, and everyone around him sighed with looks of contented bliss.

"He's strengthening them in some way," Horace whispered.

For what purpose? One of the many things she'd ask him after she found out what he knew about her uncle. The living might be more important than the dead, but honesty was plenty important, too.

Horace coughed and tried to muffle the sound with his hand. Cordelia looked to the crowd, but no one seemed to notice. Horace moaned, grabbing his head as shudders overtook him. Cordelia put an arm around him, covering his mouth. In the field, Simon sank to his knees, hands to his head.

"What is happening?" Nettle whispered.

Horace was sobbing, his head buried in Cordelia's chest. "Horace, what is it?"

"My…power." He shuddered again, and blood dribbled from his nose. "He burnt out my power."

Lazlo tried not to weep. He couldn't feel those around him, couldn't sense them in any way except with his ears, his eyes. He'd regenerated them one last time, and then he'd gotten rid of them the only way he knew how. Without his powers, they wouldn't pursue him, wouldn't bother. And now Horace would never be a slave to them, either.

"Samira!" he cried, and she was at his side in an instant.

"He burnt out his power," she said to Christian and Marlowe, to Dillon.

The others babbled, and Lazlo knew that Horace had to be suffering, but he couldn't sense it, couldn't help. On the long walk from Gale, the idea to do this had been pounding in his head. It was Dillon's face in the temple, even after the bastard had called him Stephen. Dillon had been sorry, sorrier than he'd ever been, maybe, but there had still been that damned *hope*. Lazlo couldn't fool himself into thinking the hope was that they could still be friends. The hope was that Lazlo would stay, sure, but it was also the hope that Lazlo could keep him alive and healthy. Dillon had said he couldn't live without Lazlo, but with Lazlo around, he wouldn't even try.

And the idea that the rest of the *Atlas* crew was coming, everyone but Dué, just strengthened his resolve. There had been one sure way to make certain they left him alone, that they just got on with their lives.

And Horace? Well, Lazlo *wanted* to be alone, right? The thought hurt more than he expected.

"Why?" Christian and Marlowe asked. "This wasn't our agreement."

"You don't need me anymore," Lazlo said as he stood with Samira's help. "Now, you've got a long way to travel if you want to reach your own domain, and this is the only life you have. You can't waste it fighting each other."

They stared for a long moment, and he knew they could do as they pleased. He couldn't leash their powers anymore.

"We'll keep our word." They started away, the breachies trailing in their wake, all of them carrying supplies they'd no doubt brought from the satellite. "Good-bye, Dr. Lazlo. I doubt we'll see one another again."

Dillon paced up and down, looking toward them as if he'd start another fight.

Lazlo stepped in the path of his rage. "Dillon, don't."

"Why in the fuck did you do that, Laz?"

"Now I'm nothing to fight over."

"For fuck's sake! You could have bunked anywhere you wanted. I wouldn't have bothered you!"

"Not true, and you know it."

"What are you going to do now? You can't go out in the world like this." He gestured as if Lazlo had picked the wrong outfit.

"We'll be okay." But he didn't know that. Horace wouldn't have him now. Who would?

Dillon gawped. "Look, just stay, all right? I'm sorry if I made you feel trapped, but—"

"You can't make someone feel."

Dillon lifted his hands, dropped them, and Lazlo wished he could get a peek in that mind. Was he weighing his options, wondering if Lazlo was speaking the truth? Did he want to run after Christian and Marlowe and kill them? Lazlo would just have to watch him go.

Dillon shook his head. "I guess I'll see you around if you don't get yourself killed. Which you will. Have a nice life." He stalked toward Gale, muttering to himself. Lazlo supposed that was fitting. They'd already had the other kinds of farewells. Their final one being angry was par for the course.

As Dillon crested the hill, Lydia came out of hiding. She raised a hand, eyes wide. Lazlo turned in time to catch a punch in the face from a wild-eyed woman, the same one he'd healed outside of Gale. Cordelia. It came to him just as his teeth rattled, and the sky whipped around him as he fell.

Samira took a step forward, but a drushka rose from the grass and put a knife to her neck. "Stand easy, mind thrower."

Lazlo reached to his bleeding mouth. He fumbled for his power, but there was nothing. He couldn't fix this. Cordelia was snarling down at him, and Horace stood behind her, staring at nothing.

"Horace," Lazlo said.

Cordelia grabbed Lazlo by the shirtfront. "What the fuck did you do to him?"

"Burnt out his power and mine, for his own good. If they'd found him, they would have turned him into me."

"What does that mean?"

"They're used to living forever. They'd never stop chasing it, and with his new abilities, he could heal them over and over like I did."

She shook him. "So you cripple my only healer?"

"His telepathic abilities remain. I was careful."

She shook him harder and stabbed a finger in Horace's direction. "You call that careful? What is telepathy going to do if one of us gets hurt?"

"Let him go!" Samira cried, but the drushka didn't budge.

Cordelia pulled him closer. "When you told me my uncle had been stabbed, were you lying? Did you know the Storm Lord killed him?"

"Yes." She had every right to her rage. Dillon and the others had been playing with these people for too long, and he'd helped them.

Cordelia let him drop as she paced up and down. "Motherfucker."

"Please," Lazlo said to the drushka. "Let her go. Samira, don't attack these people."

"Simon—"

"There's been too much death."

Her lips were thin and angry. "Fine."

The drushka stepped away and gestured toward where Lydia waited on the hill. "And that one?"

"She's no threat to you."

"You could have asked me," Horace said as if just realizing they were talking. "You didn't. You just—"

"I'm sorry," Lazlo said. "Truly. I saw my chance and took it."

"There seems to be lots of taking where you come from," Cordelia said.

"The Storm Lord knew about Horace. The others would have found out. Please, please, understand. They would have made you their slave, done whatever they could until you guaranteed their immortality."

"Immortality?" Horace asked. "I could have given them—"

"It's a curse."

Horace looked as if he might cry, and Lazlo stood, wanted to go to him, but Cordelia glared at him again, and he knew he'd be knocked flat if he tried.

"You're not coming with us," she said.

"I'm sorry I lied to you. I needed time. We'd been together so long, you see, and—"

"Save it." She gathered Horace under one arm and led him away. "You're lucky I saw the universe today, or you'd be a fucking smear on the ground." The drushka gave him and Samira a final look before following her.

"I'm supposed to go with you," Lydia called. Everyone turned to her. "I'm not a friend of his," she said, gesturing to Lazlo. "I just met him today as he was leaving the city."

"Come if you're coming," Cordelia said.

Lydia hurried to join them, not even waving good-bye. Lazlo couldn't even call to Horace, not after his betrayal.

"Well," Samira said, "that went about as well as you thought." When he'd told her what he was planning, she'd tried to talk him out of it but had relented in the end. Now he wondered if he should have listened. His mouth was aching, his head pounding, and there was so much he couldn't fix.

"Where should we go?" Samira asked. "Or do you want me to pick off that woman and the drushka from here, and you and Horace can ride off together?"

"I know you're joking, but..." He shook his head.

She smiled sheepishly. "You're stuck with me, Simon. I'll try to be better company."

"I don't know." And he didn't know much, couldn't feel much except the wind in his hair, on his body. For a moment, he just stood and let himself feel it, the things he couldn't change, the pain, the sensations. For the first time in a long time, he'd be at the mercy of whatever the world wanted to throw at him.

"Onward?" she asked. "Maybe we should have kept Lydia, seen what the future holds."

He thought of Dué and shuddered. "I don't know that it makes anything better."

She threaded her arm through his, and they picked up their supplies and headed into the plains to the east. Lazlo thought of how Christian, Marlowe, and the breachies had gone so easily, and knew he hadn't heard the last of them, no matter what they said. He looked back over his shoulder at Gale, Dillon's domain, and wondered what would happen there, too.

He tried to put it out of his mind, telling himself it didn't concern him anymore. All that was left for him was to put one foot in front of the other and walk into the future with no troubles but those he caused from here on out. He smiled at Samira. Without his powers, how much trouble could he possibly cause?

EPILOGUE

Natalya lay in an alley, listening to the dull sound of her own head banging against the stone. The strikes never hurt her. No matter what she did, nothing hurt her. She'd used her powers more than she ever had before, so her whole body should be aching, but the only thing that bothered her was the buzzing of her mind.

"Get out, get out, get out," she said. But nothing would banish these feelings, these powers. She began to wonder if she'd have to open her skull and pour out her brain.

The last few days were hazy. It was light now, but it had been night a moment before. Hadn't it? She'd been helping the Storm Lord, being his strong right hand, and she never could have done it without the calming force that came over her at times, the one that compelled her to do certain, awful things, but anything was better than the buzzing, than this constant need to just lash out.

She stared at her own hand. Maybe these newfound powers would be enough to destroy her if she timed them just right.

"You don't want that." Calmness washed over her, and she sighed. Her powers dampened, guided by an expert hand, by the voice that spoke in her mind.

"Where have you been?" she wailed. The buzzing muted, and her legs could hold her up again.

"Having a little fun here and there."

"With the Storm Lord?" Oh, how she'd wanted him to notice her, to see how powerful she was, how she could be his most trusted servant, but the way he'd looked at her the night before, it chilled her to the core.

"He's afraid of you," the voice said.

"He should be afraid of me." Natalya walked up and down the alley. Several people had glanced in at her, but she'd brushed them away with her power, tweaking their fear so they couldn't help but flee. "Even my imaginary friend has better things to do than spend time with me!"

The voice laughed, the sound echoing through her mind into hundreds of voices, thousands. "You want me to leave again?"

The blanket of sanity pulled away slightly, and Natalya felt the rhythm of the molecules around her, the gravity of the people and the buildings, the planet. Her chest tightened, and she staggered. It was too much. She had to destroy it all just so it would leave her be!

"I am as real as real can be," the voice said, a sultry whisper. "And I'm not afraid of you. I'll appreciate you, unlike some. I have need of a strong right hand."

The comfort wrapped her again, and Natalya breathed into it. "I'm going mad."

"None of that without my permission. Now, you've got all this power, and it's driving you crazy, so…"

Natalya waited. "So?"

"Well, shouldn't someone pay?"

Yes, she hadn't been given any warning about what might happen when she volunteered to be augmented. She'd been happy enough before the process. She could have earned the Storm Lord's trust instead of scaring him with her madness. The desire for revenge burned so hot within her, she tasted bile. "Simon Lazlo."

The voice tittered. "Among others. It's time to play, darling. The world is my chess board, and you my queen." She began to sing, a tune Natalya had never heard, but it comforted her, strengthened her shields so the world wasn't beating down her brain.

"Are you a god?"

"Oh, unequivocally yes. The only one, you might say. Or could say. Or should?"

"What is your name, Goddess?"

"That is a tough one. Naos. I think. Yes, I like it best. Although sometimes…" She trailed into muttering.

Natalya waited, sensing her future included a lot of waiting.

"Focus!" the voice barked. "The first thing we have to do is leave."

Natalya stared at the wall before her. Her power flowed over it, and it crumbled like stale bread. She stepped over the broken bricks and then looked back and reassembled them with a thought, no seams or cracks to show where she'd taken it apart. It made her giddy.

"A straight line, lovey, just like that."

She went through the city, making her holes, repairing them, scaring people or sending them scattering from her path. When she knocked a hole in the palisade, she caught the pieces with her mind before they even touched ground and mended them effortlessly behind her.

With a satisfied smile, Natalya walked east into the plains bordering Gale, not bothering to look back.

About the Author

Barbara Ann Wright writes fantasy and science fiction novels and short stories when not ranting on her blog. *The Pyramid Waltz* was one of Tor.com's Reviewer's Choice books of 2012, was a *Foreword Review* Book of the Year Award Finalist and a Goldie finalist, and won the 2013 Rainbow Award for Best Lesbian Fantasy. *A Kingdom Lost* was a Goldie finalist and won the 2014 Rainbow Award for Best Lesbian Fantasy Romance.

Barbara Ann can be contacted at zendragreatandterrible@gmail.com, or visit her website: http://www.barbaraannwright.com.

Books Available From Bold Strokes Books

A Touch of Temptation by Julie Blair. Recent law school graduate Kate Dawson's ordained path to the perfect life gets thrown off course when handsome butch top Chris Brent initiates her to sexual pleasure. (978-1-62639-488-9)

Beneath the Waves by Ali Vali. Kai Merlin and Vivien Palmer love the water and the secrets trapped in the depths, but if Kai gives in to her feelings, it might come at a cost to her entire realm. (978-1-62639-609-8)

Girls on Campus, edited by Sandy Lowe and Stacia Seaman. College: four years when rules are made to be broken. This collection is required reading for anyone looking to earn an A in sex ed. (978-1-62639-733-0)

Heart of the Pack by Jenny Frame. Human Selena Miller falls for the domineering Caden Wolfgang, but will their love survive Selena learning the Wolfgangs are werewolves? (978-1-62639-566-4)

Miss Match by Fiona Riley. Matchmaker Samantha Monteiro makes the impossible possible for everyone but herself. Is mysterious dancer Lucinda Moss her perfect match? (978-1-62639-574-9)

Paladins of the Storm Lord by Barbara Ann Wright. Lieutenant Cordelia Ross must choose between duty and honor when a man with godlike powers forces her soldiers to provoke an alien threat. (978-1-62639-604-3)

Taking a Gamble by P.J. Trebelhorn. Storage auction buyer Cassidy Holmes and postal worker Erica Jacobs want different things out of life, but taking a gamble on love might prove lucky for them both. (978-1-62639-542-8)

The Copper Egg by Catherine Friend. Archeologist Claire Adams wants to find the buried treasure in Peru. Her ex, Sochi Castillo, wants to steal it. The last thing either of them wants is to still be in love. (978-1-62639-613-5)

Capsized by Julie Cannon. What happens when a woman turns your life completely upside down? (978-1-62639-479-7)

A Reunion to Remember by TJ Thomas. Reunited after a decade, Jo Adams and Rhonda Black must navigate a significant age difference, family dynamics, and their own desires and fears to explore an opportunity for love. (978-1-62639-534-3)

Built to Last by Aurora Rey. When Professor Olivia Bennett hires contractor Joss Bauer to restore her dilapidated farmhouse, she learns her heart, as much as her house, is in need of a renovation. (978-1-62639-552-7)

Girls With Guns by Ali Vali, Carsen Taite, and Michelle Grubb. Three stories by three talented crime writers—Carsen Taite, Ali Vali, and Michelle Grubb—each packing her own special brand of heat. (978-1-62639-585-5)

Heartscapes by MJ Williamz. Will Odette ever recover her memory, or is Jesse condemned to remember their love alone? (978-1-62639-532-9)

Murder on the Rocks by Clara Nipper. Detective Jill Rogers lives with two things on her mind: sex and murder. While an ice storm cripples Tulsa, two things stand in Jill's way: her lover and the DA. (978-1-62639-600-5)

Necromantia by Sheri Lewis Wohl. When seeing dead people is more than a movie tagline. (978-1-62639-611-1)

Salvation by I. Beacham. Claire's long-term partner now hates her, for all the wrong reasons, and she sees no future until she meets Regan, who challenges her to face the truth and find love. (978-1-62639-548-0)

Trigger by Jessica Webb. Dr. Kate Morrison races to discover how to defuse human bombs while learning to trust her increasingly strong feelings for the lead investigator, Sergeant Andy Wyles. (978-1-62639-669-2)

Wild Shores by Radclyffe. Can two women on opposite sides of an oil spill find a way to save both a wildlife sanctuary and their hearts? (978-1-62639-645-6)

Soul to Keep by Rebekah Weatherspoon. What won't a vampire do for love… (978-1-62639-616-6)

Lightning Source UK Ltd.
Milton Keynes UK
UKOW03f0106070417

298557UK00001B/38/P